THE COMPLETE WORKS OF
F. MARION CRAWFORD

In Thirty-two Volumes ✺ *Authorized Edition*

Whosoever Shall Offend

BY

F. MARION CRAWFORD

WITH FRONTISPIECE

"Whosoever shall offend one of these little ones which believe in Me, it were better for him that a mill-stone were hanged about his neck, and that he were drowned in the depth of the sea."

P. F. COLLIER & SON
NEW YORK

THE COMPLETE WORKS OF F. MARION CRAWFORD

I. Mr. Isaacs
II. Doctor Claudius
III. To Leeward
IV. A Roman Singer
V. An American Politician
VI. Marzio's Crucifix
    Zoroaster
VII. A Tale of a Lonely Parish
VIII. Paul Patoff
IX. Love in Idleness: A Tale of Bar Harbor
    Marion Darche
X. Saracinesca
XI. Sant' Ilario
XII. Don Orsino
XIII. Corleone: A Sicilian Story
XIV. With the Immortals
XV. Greifenstein
XVI. A Cigarette-Maker's Romance
    Khaled
XVII. The Witch of Prague
XVIII. The Three Fates
XIX. Taquisara
XX. The Children of the King
XXI. Pietro Ghisleri
XXII. Katharine Lauderdale
XXIII. The Ralstons
XXIV. Casa Braccio (Part I)
XXV. Casa Braccio (Part II)
XXVI. Adam Johnstone's Son
    A Rose of Yesterday
XXVII. Via Crucis
XXVIII. In the Palace of the King
XXIX. Marietta: A Maid of Venice
XXX. Cecilia: A Story of Modern Rome
XXXI. The Heart of Rome
XXXII. Whosoever Shall Offend

Copyright 1904
By THE MACMILLAN COMPANY

All Rights Reserved

"SUDDENLY HE HEARD AN ITALIAN VOICE VERY NEAR TO HIM, CALLING HIM BY NAME, IN A TONE OF SURPRISE."
—*Whosoever Shall Offend.*

WHOSOEVER SHALL OFFEND

WHOSOEVER SHALL OFFEND

CHAPTER I

When the widow of Martino Consalvi married young Corbario, people shook their heads and said that she was making a great mistake. Consalvi had been dead a good many years, but as yet no one had thought it was time to say that his widow was no longer young and beautiful, as she had always been. Many rich widows remain young and beautiful as much as a quarter of a century, or even longer, and the Signora Consalvi was very rich indeed. As soon as she was married to Folco Corbario every one knew that she was thirty-five years old and he was barely twenty-six, and that such a difference of ages on the wrong side was ridiculous if it was not positively immoral. No well-regulated young man had a right to marry a rich widow nine years older than himself, and who had a son only eleven years younger than he.

A few philosophers who said that if the widow was satisfied the matter was nobody's business were treated with the contempt they deserved. Those who, on the contrary, observed that young Corbario had married for money and nothing else were heard with favour, until the man who knew everything pointed out that as the greater part of the fortune would be handed over to Marcello when he came of age, six years hence, Corbario had not made a good bargain and might have done better. It was true that Marcello Consalvi had inherited a delicate constitution of body; it had even been hinted that he was consumptive. Corbario would have done better to wait another year or two to see what happened, said a cynic, for young people often died of consumption between fifteen and twenty. The cynic was answered by a practical woman of the world, who said that Corbario had six years of luxury and extravagance before him, and that many men would have sold themselves to the devil for less. After the six years the deluge might come if it must; it was much pleasanter to drown in the end than never to have had the chance of swimming in the big stream at all, and bumping sides with the really big fish, and feeling oneself as good as any of them. Besides, Marcello was pale and thin, and had been heard to cough; he might die before he came of age. The only objection to this theory was that it was based on a fiction; for the whole fortune had been left to the Signora by a childless relation.

These amiable and interesting views were expressed with variations by people who knew the three persons concerned, and with such a keen sense of appropriate time and place as made it quite sure that none of the three should ever know what was said of them. The caution of an old fox is rash temerity compared with the circumspection of a first-rate gossip; and when the gossips were tired of discussing Folco Corbario and his wife and her son, they talked about other matters, but they had a vague suspicion that they had been cheated out of something. A cat that has clawed all the feathers off a stuffed canary might feel just what they did.

For nothing happened. Corbario did not launch into wild extravagance after all, but behaved himself with the faultless dulness of a model middle-aged husband. His wife loved him and was perfectly happy, and happiness finally stole her superfluous years away, and they evaporated in the sunshine, and she forgot all about them. Marcello Consalvi, who had lost his father when he was a mere child, found a friend in his mother's husband, and became very fond of him, and thought him a good man to imitate; and in return Corbario made a companion of the fair-haired boy, and taught him to ride and shoot in his holidays, and all went well.

Moreover, Marcello's mother, who was a good woman, told him that the world was very wicked; and with the blind desire for her son's lasting innocence, which is the most touching instinct of loving motherhood, she entreated him to lead a spotless life. When Marcello, in the excusable curiosity of budding youth, asked his stepfather what that awful wickedness was against which he was so often warned, Corbario told him true stories of men who had betrayed their country and their friends, and of all sorts of treachery and meanness, to which misdeeds the boy did not feel himself at all inclined; so that he wondered why his mother seemed so very anxious lest he should go astray. Then he repeated to her what Corbario had told him, and she smiled sweetly and said nothing, and trusted her husband all the more. She felt that he understood her, and was doing his best to help her in making Marcello what she wished him to be.

The boy was brought up at home; in Rome in the winter, and in summer on the great estate in the south, which his father had bought and which was to be a part of his inheritance.

He was taught by masters who came to the house to give their lessons and went away as soon as the task was over. He had no tutor, for his mother had not found a layman whom she could trust in that capacity, and yet she understood that it was not good for a boy to be followed everywhere by a priest. Besides, Corbario gave so much of his time to his stepson that a tutor was hardly needed; he walked with him and rode with him, or spent hours with him at home when the weather was bad. There had never been a cross word between the two since they had met. It was an ideal existence. Even the gossips stopped talking at last, and there was not one, not even the most ingeniously evil-tongued of all, that prophesied evil.

They raised their eyebrows, and the more primitive among them shrugged their shoulders a little, and smiled. If Providence really insisted upon making people so perfect, what was to be done? It was distressing, but there was nothing to be said; they must just lead their lives, and the gossips must bear it. No doubt Corbario had married for money, since he had nothing in particular and his wife had millions, but if ever a man had married for money and then behaved like an angel, that man was Folco Corbario and no other. He was everything to his wife, and all things to his stepson — husband, father, man of business, tutor, companion, and nurse; for when either his wife or Marcello was ill, he rarely left the sick-room, and no one could smooth a pillow as he could, or hold a glass so coaxingly to the feverish lips, or read aloud so untiringly in such a gentle and soothing voice.

No ascendency of one human being over another is more complete than that of a full-grown man over a boy of sixteen, who venerates his elder as an ideal. To find a model, to believe it perfection, and to copy it energetically, is either a great piece of good fortune, or a misfortune even greater; in whatever follows in life, there is the same difference between such development and the normally slow growth of a boy's mind as that which lies between enthusiasm and indifference. It is true that where there has been no enthusiastic belief there can be no despairing disillusionment when the light goes out; but it is truer still that hope and happiness are the children of faith by the ideal.

A boy's admiration for his hero is not always well founded; sometimes it is little short of ridiculous, and it is by no means always harmless. But no one found fault with Marcello for admiring his stepfather, and the attachment was a source of constant satisfaction to his mother. In her opinion Corbario was the handsomest, bravest, cleverest, and best of men, and after watching him for some time even the disappointed gossips were obliged to admit, though without superlatives, that he was a good-looking fellow, a good sportsman, sufficiently well gifted, and of excellent behaviour. There was the more merit in the admission, they maintained, because they had been inclined to doubt the man, and had accused him of marrying out of pure love of money. A keen judge of men might have thought that his handsome features were almost too still and too much like a mask, that his manner was so quiet as to be almost expressionless, and that the soft intonation of his speech was almost too monotonous to be natural. But all this was just what his wife admired, and she encouraged her son to imitate it. His father had been a man of quick impulses, weak to-day, strong to-morrow, restless, of uncertain temper, easily enthusiastic and easily cast down, capable of sudden emotions, and never able to conceal what he felt if he had cared to do so. Marcello had inherited his father's character and his mother's face, as often happens; but his unquiet disposition was tempered as yet by a certain almost girlish docility, which had clung to him from childhood as the result of being brought up almost entirely by the mother he worshipped. And now, for the first time, comparing him with her second husband, she realised the boy's girlishness, and wished him to outgrow it. Her own ideal of what even a young man should be was as unpractical as that of many thoroughly good and thoroughly unworldly mothers. She wished her son to be a man at all points, and yet she dreamed that he might remain a sort of glorified young girl; she desired him to be well prepared to face the world when he grew up, and yet it was her dearest wish that he might never know anything of the world's wickedness. Corbario seemed to understand her better in this than she understood herself, and devoted his excellent gifts and his almost superhuman patience to the task of forming a modern Galahad. Her confidence in her husband increased month by month, and year by year.

"I wish to make a new will," she said to her lawyer in the third year of her marriage. "I shall leave my husband a life-interest in a part of my fortune, and the reversion of the whole in case anything should happen to my son."

The lawyer was a middle-aged man, with hard black eyes. While he was listening to a client, he had a habit of folding his arms tightly across his chest and crossing one leg over the other. When the Signora Corbario had finished speaking he sat quite still for a moment, and then noiselessly reversed the crossing of his legs and the folding of his arms, and looked into her face. It was very gentle, fair, and thoughtful.

"I presume," answered the lawyer, "that the clause

providing for a reversion is only intended as an expression of your confidence in your husband?"

"Affection," answered the Signora, "includes confidence."

The lawyer raised one eyebrow almost imperceptibly, and changed his position a little.

"Heaven forbid," he said, "that any accident should befall your son!"

"Heaven forbid it!" replied the Signora. "He is very strong," she continued, in the tone people use who are anxious to convince themselves of something doubtful. "Yet I wish my husband to know that, after my son, he should have the first right."

"Shall you inform him of the nature of your will, Signora?" inquired the lawyer.

"I have already informed him of what I mean to do," replied Signora Corbario.

Again the lawyer's eyebrow moved a little nervously, but he said nothing. It was not his place to express any doubt as to the wisdom of the disposition. He was not an old family adviser, who might have taken such a liberty. There had been such a man, indeed, but he was dead. It was the duty of the rich woman's legal adviser to hinder her from committing any positive legal mistake, but it was not his place to criticise her judgment of the man she had chosen to marry. The lawyer made a few notes without offering any comment, and on the following day he brought the will for the Signora to sign. By it, at her death, Marcello, her son, was to inherit her great fortune. Her husband, Folco Corbario, was constituted Marcello's sole guardian, and was to enjoy a life-interest in one-third of the inheritance. If Marcello died, the whole fortune was to go to Corbario, without any condition or reservation whatsoever.

When the will was executed, the Signora told her husband that she had done what she intended.

"My dear," said Corbario, gently, "I thank you for the true meaning of it. But as for the will itself, shall we talk of it thirty years hence, when Marcello's children's children are at your knee?"

He kissed her hand tenderly.

CHAPTER II

MARCELLO stood at an open window listening to the musical spring rain and watching the changing lights on the city below him, as the dove-coloured cloud that floated over Rome like thin gauze was drawn up into the sunshine. Then there were sudden reflections from distant windows and wet domes, that blazed like white fires for a little while, till the raindrops dried and the waves of changing hues that had surged up under the rain, rising, breaking, falling, and spreading, subsided into a restful sea of harmonious colour.

After that, the sweet smell of the wet earth came up to Marcello's nostrils. A light breeze stirred the dripping emerald leaves, and the little birds fluttered down and hopped along the garden walks and over the leaves, picking up the small unwary worms that had been enjoying a bath while their enemies tried to keep dry under the ilex boughs.

Marcello half closed his eyes and drank the fragrant air with parted lips, his slim white hands resting on the marble sill. The sunshine made his pale face luminous, and gilded his short fair hair, casting the shadow of the brown lashes upon his delicate cheeks. There was something angel-like in his expression — the look of the frescoed angels of Melozzo da Forlì in the Sacristy of

St. Peter's. They are all that is left of something very beautiful, brought thither broken from the Church of the Holy Apostles; and so, too, one might have fancied that Marcello, standing at the window in the morning sunshine, belonged to a world that had long passed away — fit for a life that was, fit for a life to come hereafter, perhaps, but not fit for the life that is. There are rare and beautiful beings in the world who belong to it so little that it seems cruelty and injustice to require of them what is demanded of us all. They are born ages too late, or ages too soon; they should not have been born now. Their very existence calls forth our tenderest sympathy, as we should pity a fawn facing its death among wolves.

But Marcello Consalvi had no idea that he could deserve pity, and life looked very bright to him, very easy, and very peaceful. He could hardly have thought of anything at all likely to happen which could darken the future, or even give him reasonable cause for anxiety. There was no imaginative sadness in his nature, no morbid dread of undefined evil, no melancholy to dye the days black; for melancholy is more often an affliction of the very strong in body or mind than of the weak, or of average men and women. Marcello was delicate, but not degenerate; he seemed gentle, cheerful, and ready to believe the world a very good place, as indeed it is for people who are not too unlike their neighbours to enjoy it, or too unlucky to get some of its good things, or too weak to work, fight, and love, or too clever to be as satisfied with themselves as most men are. For plain, common, everyday happiness and contentment belong to plain, average people, who do what others do and have a cheerfully good opinion of themselves. Can a man make a good fight of it if he does not believe himself to be about as good as his adversary?

It had never occurred to Marcello that he might have to fight for anything, and if some one had told him on that spring morning that he was on the very verge of a desperate struggle for existence against overwhelming odds, he would have turned his bright eyes wonderingly to the prophet of evil, asking whence danger could come, and trying to think what it might be like.

At the first appearance of it he would have been startled into fear, too, as many a grown man has been before now, when suddenly brought face to face with an unknown peril, being quite untried: and small shame to him. He who has been waked from a peaceful sleep and pleasant dreams to find death at his throat, for the first time in his life, knows the meaning of that. Samson was a tried warrior when Delilah first roused him with her cry, "The Philistines are upon thee!"

Marcello was no youthful Samson, yet he was not an unmanly boy, for all his bringing up. So far as his strength would allow he had been accustomed to the exercises and sports of men: he could ride fearlessly, if not untiringly; he was a fair shot; he had hunted wild boar with his stepfather in the marshy lands by the sea; he had been taught to fence and was not clumsy with weapons, though he had not yet any great skill. He had always been told that he was delicate and must be careful, and he knew that he was not strong; but there was one good sign in that his weakness irritated him and bred at least the desire for strength, instead of the poor-spirited indolence that bears bodily infirmity as something inevitable, and is ready to accept pity if not to ask for it.

The smell of the damp earth was gone, and as the sun shone out the air was filled with the scent of warm roses and the faintly sweet odour of wistaria. Marcello heard a light footstep close to him, and met his mother's eyes as he turned.

Even to him, she looked very young just then, as she stood in the light, smiling at him. A piece of lace was drawn half over her fair hair, and the ends went round her throat like a scarf and fell behind her. Its creamy tints heightened the rare transparency of her complexion by faint contrast. She was a slight woman and very graceful.

"I have looked for you everywhere," she said, and she still smiled, as if with real pleasure at having found him.

"I have been watching the shower," Marcello answered, drawing her to the window. "And then the earth and the roses smelt so sweet that I stayed here. Did you want me, mother?"

"I always like to know where you are."

She passed her arm through his with a loving pressure, and looked out of the window with him. The villa stood on the slope of the Janiculum, close to the Corsini gardens.

"Do I run after you too much?" the mother asked presently, as if she knew the answer. "Now that you are growing up, do I make you feel as if you were still a little boy? You are nearly nineteen, you know! I suppose I ought to treat you like a man."

Marcello laughed, and his hand slipped into hers with an almost childish and nestling movement.

"You have made a man of me," he answered.

Had she? A shadow of doubt crossed her thoughtful face as she glanced at his. He was so different from other young men of his age, so delicately nurtured, so very gentle; there was the radiance of maidenly innocence in his look, and she was afraid that he might be more like a girl than a man almost grown.

"I have done my best," she said. "I hope I have done right."

He scarcely understood what she meant, and his expression did not change.

"You could not do anything that was not right," he answered.

Perhaps such a being as Marcello would be an impossibility anywhere but in Italy. Modern life tears privacy to tatters, and privacy is the veil of the temple of home, within which every extreme of human development is possible, good and bad. Take privacy away and all the strangely compound fractions of humanity are soon reduced to a common denominator. In Italy life has more privacy than anywhere else west of Asia. The Englishman is fond of calling his home his castle, but it is a thoroughfare, a market-place, a club, a hotel, a glass house, compared with that of an average Italian. An Englishman goes home to escape restraint : an Italian goes out. But the northern man, who lives much in public, learns as a child to conceal what he feels, to be silent, to wear an indifferent look ; whereas the man of the south, who hides nothing when the doors of his house are shut, can hide but little when he meets his enemy in the way. He laughs when he is pleased, and scowls when he is not, threatens when he is angry, and sheds tears when he is hurt, with a simplicity that too often excites the contempt of men accustomed to suffer or enjoy without moving a muscle.

Privacy favours the growth of individual types, differing widely from each other ; the destruction of it makes people very much alike. Marcello's mother asked herself whether she had done well in rearing him as a being apart from those amongst whom he must spend his life.

And yet, as she looked at him, he seemed to be so nearly the ideal of which she had dreamt throughout long years of loving care that she was comforted, and the shadow passed away from her sweet face. He had answered that she could do nothing that was not right ; she prayed that his words might be near the truth, and in her heart she was willing to believe that they were almost true. Had she not followed every good impulse of her own good heart ? Had she not tried to realize literally for him the most beautiful possibilities of the Christian faith? That, at least, was true, and she could tell herself so without any mistaken pride. How, then, had she made any mistake? The boy had the face of a young saint.

"Are you ready, my dear?" she asked suddenly, as a far-off clock struck.

"Yes, mother, quite ready."

"I am not," she answered with a little laugh. "And Folco is waiting, and I hear the carriage driving up."

She slipped from Marcello's side and left the room quickly, for they were going to drive down to the sea, to a little shooting-lodge that belonged to them near Nettuno, a mere cottage among the trees by the Roman shore, habitable only in April and May, and useful only then, when the quail migrate along the coast and the malarious fever is not yet to be feared. It was there that Marcello had first learned to handle a gun, spending a week at a time there with his stepfather; and his mother used to come down now and then for a day or two on a visit, sometimes bringing her friend the Contessa dell' Armi. The latter had been very unhappy in her youth, and had been left a widow with one beautiful girl and a rather exiguous fortune. Some people thought that it was odd that the Signora Corbario, who was a saint if ever there was one, should have grown so fond of the Contessa, for the latter had seen stormy days in years gone by; and of course the ill-disposed gossips made up their minds that the

Contessa was trying to catch Marcello for her daughter Aurora, though the child was barely seventeen.

This was mere gossip, for she was quite incapable of any such scheme. What the gossips did not know was something which would have interested them much more, namely, that the Contessa was the only person in Rome who distrusted Folco Corbario, and that she was in constant fear lest she should turn out to be right, and lest her friend's paradise should be suddenly changed into a purgatory. But she held her tongue, and her quiet face never betrayed her thoughts. She only watched, and noted from month to month certain small signs which seemed to prove her right; and she should be ready, whenever the time should come, by day or night, to help her friend, or comfort her, or fight for her.

If Corbario guessed that the Contessa did not trust him, he never showed it. He had found her installed as his wife's friend, and had accepted her, treating her with much courtesy and a sort of vicarious affection; but though he tried his best he could not succeed in reaching anything like intimacy with her, and while she seemed to conceal nothing, he felt that she was hiding her real self from him. Whether she did so out of pride, or distrust, or jealousy, he could never be sure. He was secretly irritated and humiliated by her power to oppose him and keep him at a distance without ever seeming to do so; but, on the other hand, he was very patient, very tenacious of his purpose, and very skilful. He knew something of the Contessa's past, but he recognised in her the nature that has known the world's worst side and has done with it for ever, and is lifted above it, and he knew the immense influence which the spectacle of a blameless life exercises upon the opinion of a good woman who has not always been blameless herself. Whatever he had been before he met his wife, whatever strange plans had been maturing in his brain since he had married her, his life had seemed as spotless from that day as the existence of the best man living. His wife believed in him, and the Contessa did not; but even she must in time accept the evidence of her senses. Then she, too, would trust him. Why it was essential that she should, he alone knew, unless he was merely piqued by her quiet reserve, as a child is when it cannot fix the attention of a grown-up person.

The Contessa and her daughter were to be of the party that day, and the carriage stopped where they lived, near the Forum of Trajan. They appeared almost directly, the Contessa in grey with a grey veil and Aurora dressed in a lighter shade, the thick plaits of her auburn hair tied up short below her round straw hat, on the theory that she was still a school-girl, whose skirt must not quite touch the ground, who ought not to wear a veil, and whose mind was supposed to be a sensitive blank, particularly apt to receive bad impressions rather than good ones. In less than a year she would be dancing all night with men she had scarcely heard of before, listening to compliments of which she had never dreamt — of course not — and to declarations which no right-minded girl one day under eighteen could under any circumstances be thought to expect. Such miracles as these are wrought by the eighteenth birthday.

Corbario's eyes looked from the mother to the daughter, as he and Marcello stood on the pavement to let them get in. The Contessa touched his outstretched hand without restraint but without cordiality, smiling just as much as was civil, and less readily than would have been friendly. Aurora glanced at him and laughed prettily without any apparent reason, which is the privilege of very young girls, because their minds are supposed to be a blank. Also because her skirt must not quite touch the ground, one very perfect black silk ankle was distinctly visible for a moment as she stepped into the carriage. Note that from the eve of her eighteenth birthday till she is old enough to be really wicked no well-regulated young woman shows her ankles. This also is one of the miracles of time.

Marcello blushed faintly as he sat down beside Aurora. There were now five in the big carriage, so that she was between the two men; and though there was enough room Marcello felt the slight pressure of her arm against his. His mother saw his colour change, and looked away and smiled. The idea of marrying the two in a few years had often crossed her mind, and she was pleased whenever she saw that Marcello felt a little thrill of emotion in the girl's presence. As for Aurora, she looked straight before her, between the heads of the two elder women, and for a long time after they had started she seemed absorbed in watching the receding walls of the city and the long straight road that led back to it. The Contessa and her friend talked quietly, happy to be together for a whole day. Corbario now and then looked from one to the other, as if to assure himself that they were quite comfortable, and his still face wore an unchanging look of contented calm as his eyes turned again to the sunlit sweep of the low Campagna. Marcello looked steadily away from Aurora, happily and yet almost painfully aware that her arm could not help pressing against his. The horses' hoofs beat rhythmically on the hard high road, with the steady, cheerful energy which would tell a blind man that a team is well fed, fresh from rest, and altogether fit for a long day's work. The grey-haired coachman sat on his box like an old dragoon in the saddle; the young groom sat bolt upright beside him with folded arms, as if he could never tire of sitting straight. The whole party looked prosperous, harmonious, healthy, and perfectly happy, as if nothing in the least unpleasant could possibly happen to them, still less anything terrible, that could suddenly change all their lives.

One of fate's favourite tricks is to make life look particularly gay and enjoyable, and full of sunshine and flowers, at the very moment when terror wakes from sleep and steps out of the shadow to stalk abroad.

The cottage where the party were going to spend the next few days together was built like an Indian bungalow, consisting of a single story surrounded by a broad, covered verandah, and having a bit of lawn in front.

It was sheltered by trees, and between it and the beach a bank of sand from ten to fifteen feet high ran along the shore, the work of the southwest gales during many ages. In many places this bank was covered with scrub and brushwood on the landward side.

A little stream meandered down to the sea on the north side of the cottage, ending in a pool full of tall reeds, amongst which one could get about in a punt. The seashore itself is very shelving at that place, and there is a bar about a cable's length out, over which the sea breaks with a tremendous roar during westerly storms. Two hundred yards from the cottage, a large hut had been built for the men-servants and for the kitchen; near by it there was a rough coach-house and a stable with room for a dozen horses. The carriage usually went back to Rome on the day after every one had arrived, and was sent for when wanted; but there were a number of rough Campagna horses in the stable, such as are ridden by the cattle herders about Rome, tough little beasts of fairly good temper and up to a much heavier weight than might be guessed by a stranger in the country. In the morning the men of the party usually went shooting, if the wind was fair, for where quail are concerned much depends on that. Dinner was in the middle of the day, and every one was supposed to go to sleep after it. In the late afternoon the horses were saddled, and the whole party went for a gallop on the sands, or up to classic Ardea, or across the half-cultivated country, coming back to supper when it was dark. A particularly fat and quiet pony was kept for Marcello's mother, who was no great rider, but the Contessa and Aurora rode anything that was brought them, as the men did. To tell the truth, the Campagna horse is rarely vicious, and, even when only half broken, can be ridden by a lady if she be an average horsewoman.

Everything happened as usual. The party reached the cottage in time for a late luncheon, rested afterwards, and then rode out. But the Signora Corbario would not go.

"Your pony looks fatter and quieter than ever," said Maddalena dell' Armi with a smile. "If you do not ride him, he will turn into a fixture."

"He is already a very solid piece of furniture," observed Folco, looking at the sleek animal.

"He is very like the square piano I practise on," said Aurora. "He has such a flat back and such straight thick legs."

"More like an organ," put in Marcello, gravely. "He has a curious, half-musical wheeze when he tries to move, like the organ in the church at San Domenico, when the bellows begin to work."

"It is a shame to make fun of my horse," answered the Signora, smiling. "But really I am not afraid of him. I have a little headache from the drive, that is all."

"Take some phenacetine," said Corbario with concern. "Let me make you quite comfortable before we start."

He arranged a long straw chair for her in a sheltered

corner of the verandah, with cushions and a rug and a small table beside it, on which Marcello placed a couple of new books that had been brought down. Then Folco went in and got a little glass bottle of tablets from his wife's travelling-bag and gave her one. She was subject to headaches and always had the medicine with her. It was the only remedy she ever carried or needed, and she had such confidence in it that she felt better almost as soon as she had swallowed the tablet her husband gave her.

"Let me stay and read to you," he said. "Perhaps you would go to sleep."

"You are not vain of your reading, my dear," she answered with a smile. "No, please go with the others."

Then the Contessa offered to stay, and the good Signora had to use a good deal of persuasion to make them all understand that she would much rather be left alone. They mounted and rode away through the trees towards the beach, whence the sound of the small waves, breaking gently under the afternoon breeze, came echoing softly up to the cottage.

The two young people rode in front, in silence; Corbario and the Contessa followed at a little distance.

"How good you are to my wife!" Folco exclaimed presently, as they emerged upon the sand. "You are like a sister to her!"

Maddalena glanced at him through her veil. She had small and classic features, rather hard and proud, and her eyes were of a dark violet colour, which is very unusual, especially in Italy. But she came from the north. Corbario could not see her expression, and she knew it.

"You are good to her, too," she said presently, being anxious to be just. "You are very thoughtful and kind."

Corbario thought it wiser to say nothing, and merely bent his head a little in acknowledgment of what he instinctively felt to be an admission on the part of a secret adversary. Maddalena had never said so much before.

"If you were not, I should never forgive you," she added, thinking aloud.

"I don't think you have quite forgiven me as it is," Folco answered more lightly.

"For what?"

"For marrying your best friend."

The little speech was well spoken, so utterly without complaint, or rancour, or suggestion of earnestness, that the Contessa could only smile.

"And yet you admit that I am not a bad husband," continued Folco. "Should you accept me, or, say, my exact counterpart, for Aurora, in a year or two?"

"I doubt whether you have any exact counterpart," Maddalena answered, checking the sharp denial that rose to her lips.

"Myself, then, just for the sake of argument?"

"What an absurd question! Do you mind tightening the girth for me a little? My saddle is slipping."

She drew rein, and he was obliged to submit to the

check. As he dismounted he glanced at Aurora's graceful figure, a hundred yards ahead, and for one instant he drew his eyelids together with a very strange expression. He knew that the Contessa could not see his face.

Marcello and Aurora had been companions since they were children, and just now they were talking familiarly of the place, which they had not seen since the previous year. All sorts of details struck them. Here, there was more sand than usual; there, a large piece of timber had been washed ashore in the winter gales; at another place there was a new sand-drift that had quite buried the scrub on the top of the bank; the keeper of the San Lorenzo tower had painted his shutters brown, though they had always been green; here was the spot where Aurora had tumbled off her pony when she was only twelve years old — so long ago! And here — they looked at each other and then quickly at the sea, for it was here that Marcello, in a fit of boyish admiration, had once suddenly kissed her cheek, telling her that she was perfectly beautiful. Even now, he blushed when he thought of it, and yet he longed to do it again, and wondered inwardly what would happen if he did.

As for Aurora, though she looked at the sea for a moment, she seemed quite self-possessed. It is a strange thing that if a boy and a girl are brought up in just the same way, by women, and without many companions, the boy should generally be by far the more shy of the two when childhood is just past.

"You are very fond of your stepfather, are you not?" asked Aurora, so suddenly that Marcello started a little and hesitated slightly before he answered.

"Yes," he said, almost directly, "of course I am! Don't you like him, too?"

"I used to," answered Aurora in a low voice, "but now his eyes frighten me — sometimes. For instance, though he is a good way behind, I am sure he is looking at me now, just in that way."

Marcello turned his head instinctively, and saw that Folco had just dismounted to tighten the girth of the Contessa's saddle. It was exactly while Aurora was speaking that he had drawn his eyelids together with such a strange expression — a mere coincidence, no doubt, but one that would have startled the girl if she could have suddenly seen his face.

They rode on without waiting for the others, at an even canter over the sand.

"I never saw anything in Folco's eyes that could frighten anybody," Marcello said presently.

"No," answered Aurora. "Very likely not."

Marcello had always called Corbario by his first name, and as he grew up it seemed more and more natural to do so. Folco was so young, and he looked even younger than he was.

"It must be your imagination," Marcello said.

"Women," said Aurora, as if she were as near thirty as any young woman would acknowledge herself, "women have no imagination. That is why we have so much sense," she added thoughtfully.

Marcello was so completely puzzled by this extraordinary statement that he could find nothing to say for a few moments. Then he felt that she had attacked his idol, and that Folco must be defended.

"If you could find a single thing, however small, to bring against him, it would not be so silly to say that his eyes frighten you."

"There!" laughed Aurora. "You might as well say that because at this moment there is only that one little cloud near the sun, there is no cloud at all!"

"How ridiculous!" Marcello expressed his contempt of such girlish reasoning by putting his rough little horse to a gallop.

"Men always say that," retorted Aurora, with exasperating calm. "I'll race you to the tower for the first choice of oranges at dessert. They are not very good this year, you know, and you like them."

"Don't be silly!" Marcello immediately reined his horse back to a walk, and looked very dignified.

"It is impossible to please you," observed Aurora, slackening her pace at once.

"It is impossible, if you abuse Folco."

"I am sure I did not mean to abuse him," Aurora answered meekly. "I never abuse anybody."

"Women never do, I suppose," retorted Marcello, with a little snort of dissatisfaction.

They were little more than children yet, and for pretty nearly five minutes neither spoke a word, as their horses walked side by side.

"The keeper of the tower has more chickens this

year," observed Aurora. "I can see them running about."

This remark was evidently intended as an overture of reconciliation. It acted like magic upon Marcello, who hated quarrelling, and was moreover much more in love with the girl than he knew. Instinctively he put out his left hand to take her right. They always made peace by taking hands.

But Aurora's did not move, and she did not even turn her head towards him.

"Take care!" she said quickly, in a low tone. "They are watching us."

Marcello looked round and saw that the others were nearer than he had supposed, and he blushed foolishly.

"Well, what harm would there be if you gave me your hand?" he asked. "I only meant—"

"Yes, I understand," Aurora answered, in the same tone as before. "And I am glad you like me, Marcello — if you really do."

"If I do!" His tone was full of youthful and righteous indignation.

"I did not mean to doubt it," she said quickly. "But it is getting to be different now, you know. We are older, and somehow everything means more, even the little things."

"Oh!" ejaculated Marcello. "I begin to see. I suppose," he added, with what seemed to him reckless brutality, "that if I kissed you now you would be furious."

He glanced uneasily at Aurora's face to note the

effect of this terrible speech. The result was not exactly what he had expected. A faint colour rose in her cheeks, and then she laughed.

"When you do," she said, "I would rather it should not be before people."

"I shall try to remember that," answered Marcello, considerably emboldened.

"Yes, do! It would be so humiliating if I boxed your ears in the presence of witnesses."

"You would not dare," laughed Marcello.

From a distance, as Aurora had guessed, Folco was watching them while he quietly talked to the Contessa; and as he watched, he understood what a change had taken place since last year, when he had seen Marcello and Aurora riding over the same stretch of sand on the same little horses. He ventured a reflection, to see what his companion would answer.

"I daresay many people would say that those two young people were made for each other."

Maddalena looked at him inquiringly and then glanced at her daughter.

"And what do you say?" she asked, with some curiosity.

"I say 'no.' And you?"

"I agree with you. Aurora is like me — like what I was. Marcello would bore her to death in six months, and Aurora would drive him quite mad."

Corbario smiled.

"I had hoped," he said, "that women with marriageable daughters would think Marcello a model husband.

But of course I am prejudiced. I have had a good deal to do with his bringing up during the last four years."

"No one can say that you have not done your duty by him," Maddalena answered. "I wish I could feel that I had done as well by Aurora — indeed I do!"

"You have, but you had quite a different nature to deal with."

"I should think so! It is my own."

Corbario heard the little sigh as she turned her head away, and being a wise man he said nothing in answer. He was not a Roman, if indeed he were really an Italian at all, but he had vaguely heard the Contessa's story. She had been married very young to a parliamentary high-light, who had made much noise in his day, had spent more than half of her fortune after getting rid of his own, and had been forgotten on the morrow of his premature death. It was said that she had loved another man with all her heart, but Corbario had never known who it was.

The sun was almost setting when they turned homeward, and it was dark when they reached the cottage. They found an unexpected arrival installed beside the Signora in the doorway of the sitting-room.

"Professor Kalmon is here," said the Signora's voice out of the gloom. "I have asked him to stay till tomorrow."

The Professor rose up in the shadow and came forward, just as a servant brought a lamp. He was celebrated as a traveller, and occupied the chair of comparative physiology in the University of Milan. He belonged to the modern type of scientific man, which has replaced the one of fifty years ago, who lived in a dressing-gown and slippers, smoked a long pipe, and was always losing his belongings through absence of mind. The modern professor is very like other human beings in dress and appearance, and has even been known to pride himself on the fit of his coat, just like the common people.

There were mutual greetings, for the Professor knew all the party, and everybody liked him. He was a big man, with a well-kept brown beard, a very clear complexion, and bright brown eyes that looked as if they would never need spectacles.

"And where have you been since we last saw you?" asked Corbario.

"Are your pockets full of snakes this time?" asked Aurora.

The Professor looked at her and smiled, realising that she was no longer the child she had been when he had seen her last, and that she was very good to look at. His brown eyes beamed upon her benevolently.

"Ah, my dear young lady, I see it is all over," he said. "You will never pull my beard again and turn my pockets inside out for specimens when I come back from my walks on the beach."

"Do you think I am afraid of you or your specimens?" laughed Aurora.

"I have got a terrible thing in my waistcoat pocket," the Professor answered. "Something you might very well be afraid of."

"What is it? It must be very small to be in your waistcoat pocket."

"It is a new form of death."

He beamed on everybody with increasing benevolence; but somehow nobody smiled, and the Signora Corbario shivered and drew her light cloak more closely round her, as the first gust of the night breeze came up from the rustling reeds that grew in the pool below.

"It is time to get ready for supper," said Folco. "I hope you are not hungry, Kalmon, for you will not get anything very elaborate to eat!"

"Bread and cheese will do, my dear fellow."

When Italians go to the country they take nothing of the city with them. They like the contrast to be complete; they love the total absence of restraint; they think it delightful to dine in their shooting-coats and to eat coarse fare. If they had to dress for dinner it would not be the country at all, nor if dinner had to begin with soup and end with sweets just as it does in town. They eat extraordinary messes that would make a Frenchman turn pale and a German look grave. They make portentous pasties, rich with everything under the sun; they eat fat boiled beef, and raw fennel, and green almonds, and vast quantities of cream cheese, and they drink sour wine like water; and it all agrees with them perfectly, so that they come back to the city refreshed and rested after a gastronomic treatment which would bring any other European to death's door.

The table was set out on the verandah that evening, as usual in spring, and little by little the Professor absorbed the conversation, for they all asked him questions, few of which could be answered shortly. He was one of those profoundly cultivated Italians who are often to be met nowadays, but whose gifts it is not easy to appreciate except in a certain degree of intimacy. They are singularly modest men as a rule, and are by no means those about whom there is the most talk in the world.

The party sat in their places when supper was over, with cloaks and coats thrown over them against the night air, while Kalmon talked of all sorts of things that seemed to have the least possible connection with each other, but which somehow came up quite naturally. He went from the last book on Dante to a new discovery in chemistry, thence to Japanese monks and their beliefs, and came back smiling to the latest development of politics, which led him quite naturally to the newest play, labour and capital, the German Emperor, and the immortality of the soul.

"I believe you know everything!" exclaimed Marcello, with an admiring look. "Or else I know nothing, which is really more probable!" The boy laughed.

"You have not told us about the new form of death yet," said Aurora, leaning on her elbows and burying her young hands in her auburn hair as she looked across the table at Kalmon.

"You will never sleep again if I tell you about it,"

answered the Professor, opening his brown eyes very wide and trying to look terrible, which was quite impossible, because he had such a kindly face. "You do not look frightened at all," he added, pretending to be disappointed.

"Let me see the thing," Aurora said. "Perhaps we shall all be frightened."

"It looks very innocent," Kalmon answered. "Here it is."

He took a small leather case from his pocket, opened it, and drew out a short blue glass tube, with a screw top. It contained half a dozen white tablets, apparently just like those in common use for five-grain doses of quinine.

A little murmur of disappointment went around the table. The new form of death looked very commonplace. Corbario was the only one who showed any interest.

"May I see?" he asked, holding out his hand to take the tube.

Kalmon would not give it to him, but held the tube before his eyes under the bright light of the lamp.

"Excuse me," he said, "but I make it a rule never to let it go out of my hands. You understand, don't you? If it were passed round, some one might lay it down, it might be forgotten, somebody might take it for something else."

"Of course," said Folco, looking intently at the tube, as though he could understand something about the contents by mere inspection. "You are quite right. You should take no risks with such things — especially as they look so innocent!"

He leaned back in his chair again, as if satisfied, and his eyes met the Contessa's at the same moment. There was no reason why she should not have looked at him just then, but he rested one elbow on the table and shaded his eyes from the light.

"It is strange to reflect," said Kalmon, looking at the tube thoughtfully, "that one of those little things would be enough to put a Hercules out of misery, without leaving the slightest trace which science could discover."

Corbario was still shading his eyes from the light.

"How would one die if one took it?" asked Aurora. "Very suddenly?"

"I call it the sleeping death," answered the Professor. "The poisoned person sinks into a sweet sleep in a few minutes, smiling as if enjoying the most delightful dreams."

"And one never wakes up?" inquired Marcello.

"Never. It is impossible, I believe. I have made experiments on animals, and have not succeeded in waking them by any known means."

"I suppose it congests the brain, like opium," observed Corbario, quietly.

"Not at all, not at all!" answered Kalmon, looking benevolently at the little tube which contained his discovery. "I tell you it leaves no trace whatever, not even as much as is left by death from an electric current. And it has no taste, no smell,—it seems the most innocent stuff in the world."

Corbario's hand again lay on the table and he was gazing out into the night, as if he were curious about the weather. The moon was just rising, being past the full.

"Is that all you have of the poison?" he asked in an idle tone.

"Oh, no! This is only a small supply which I carry with me for experiments. I have made enough to send all our thirty-three millions of Italians to sleep for ever!"

Kalmon laughed pleasantly.

"If this could be properly used, civilisation would make a gigantic stride," he added. "In war, for instance, how infinitely pleasanter and more æsthetic it would be to send the enemy to sleep, with the most delightful dreams, never to wake again, than to tear people to pieces with artillery and rifle bullets, and to blow up ships with hundreds of poor devils on board, who are torn limb from limb by the explosion."

"The difficulty," observed the Contessa, "would be to induce the enemy to take your poison quietly. What if the enemy objected?"

"I should put it into their water supply," said Kalmon.

"Poison the water!" cried the Signora Corbario. "How barbarous!"

"Much less barbarous than shedding oceans of blood.

Only think — they would all go to sleep. That would be all."

"I thought," said Corbario, almost carelessly, "that there was no longer any such thing as a poison that left no traces or signs. Can you not generally detect vegetable poisons by the mode of death?"

"Yes," answered the Professor, returning the glass tube to its case and the latter to his pocket. "But please to remember that although we can prove to our own satisfaction that some things really exist, we cannot prove that any imaginable thing outside our experience cannot possibly exist. Imagine the wildest impossibility you can think of; you will not induce a modern man of science to admit the impossibility of it as absolute. Impossibility is now a merely relative term, my dear Corbario, and only means great improbability. Now, to illustrate what I mean, it is altogether improbable that a devil with horns and hoofs and a fiery tail should suddenly appear, pick me up out of this delightful circle, and fly away with me. But you cannot induce me to deny the possibility of such a thing."

"I am so glad to hear you say that," said the Signora, who was a religious woman.

Kalmon looked at her a moment and then broke into a peal of laughter that was taken up by the rest, and in which the good lady joined.

"You brought it on yourself," she said at last.

"Yes," Kalmon answered. "I did. From your point of view it is better to admit the possibility of a mediæval devil with horns than to have no religion at all. Half a loaf is better than no bread."

"Is that stuff of yours animal, vegetable, or mineral?" asked Corbario as the laughter subsided.

"I don't know," replied the Professor. "Animal, vegetable, mineral? Those are antiquated distinctions, like the four elements of the alchemists."

"Well — but what is the thing, then?" asked Corbario, almost impatiently. "What should you call it in scientific language?"

Kalmon closed his eyes for a moment, as if to collect his thoughts.

"In scientific language," he began, "it is probably H three C seven, parenthesis, H two C plus C four O five, close parenthesis, HC three O."

Corbario laughed carelessly.

"I am no wiser than before," he said.

"Nor I," answered the Professor. "Not a bit."

"It is much simpler to call it 'the sleeping death,' is it not?" suggested the Contessa.

"Much simpler, for that is precisely what it is."

It was growing late, according to country ideas, and the party rose from the table and began to move about a little before going to bed. The moon had risen high by this time.

Marcello and Aurora, unheeded by the rest, went round the verandah to the other side of the house and stood still a moment, looking out at the trees and listening to the sounds of the night. Down by the pool a frog croaked now and then; from a distance came the plaintive, often repeated cry of a solitary owlet; the night breeze sighed through the long grass and the low shrubbery.

The boy and girl turned to each other, put out their hands and then their arms, and clasped each other silently, and kissed. Then they walked demurely back to their elders, without exchanging a word.

"We have had to give you the little room at the end of the cottage," Corbario was saying to Kalmon. "It is the only one left while the Contessa is here."

"I should sleep soundly on bare boards to-night," Kalmon answered. "I have been walking all day."

Corbario went with him, carrying a candle, and shielding the flame from the breeze with his hand. The room was furnished with the barest necessities, like most country rooms in Italy. There were wooden pegs on which to hang clothes instead of a wardrobe, an iron bedstead, a deal wash-stand, a small deal table, a rush-bottomed chair. The room had only one window, which was also the only door, opening to the floor upon the verandah.

"You can bolt the window, if you like," said Corbario when he had bidden the Professor good-night, "but there are no thieves about."

"I always sleep with my windows open," Kalmon answered, "and I have no valuables."

"No? Good-night again."

"Good-night."

Corbario went out, leaving him the candle, and turned the corner of the verandah. Then he stood still a long time, leaning against one of the wooden pillars and looking out. Perhaps the moonlight falling through the stiff little trees upon the long grass and shrubbery reminded him of some scene familiar long ago. He smiled quietly to himself as he stood there.

Three hours later he was there again, in almost exactly the same attitude. He must have been cold, for the night breeze was stronger, and he wore only his light sleeping clothes and his feet were bare. He shivered a little from time to time, and his face looked very white, for the moon was now high in the heavens and the light fell full upon him. His right hand was tightly closed, as if it held some small object fast, and he was listening intently, first to the right, whence he had come, then to the left, and then he turned his ear towards the trees, through which the path led away towards the hut where the men slept. But there was no sound except the sighing of the wind. The frog by the pool had stopped croaking, and the melancholy cry of the owlet had ceased.

Corbario went softly on, trying the floor of the verandah with his bare feet at each step, lest the boards should creak a little under his weight. He reached the window door of his own room, and slipped into the darkness without noise.

Kalmon cared little for quail-shooting, and as the carriage was going back to Rome he took advantage of it to reach the city, and took his departure about nine o'clock in the morning.

"By the way, how did you sleep?" asked Corbario as he shook hands at parting. "I forgot to ask you."

"Soundly, thank you," answered the Professor.

And he drove away, waving his felt hat to his hosts.

CHAPTER III

MARCELLO coughed a little as he and Corbario trudged home through the sand under the hot May sun. It was sultry, though there were few clouds, and everything that grew looked suddenly languid; each flower and shrub gave out its own peculiar scent abundantly, the smell of last year's rotting leaves and twigs all at once returned and mingled with the odours of green things and of the earth itself, and the heavy air was over-rich with it all, and hard to breathe. By and by the clouds would pile themselves up into vast grey and black fortresses, far away beyond Rome, between the Alban and the Samnite hills, and the lightning would dart at them and tear them to pieces in spite, while the thunder roared out at each home-thrust that it was well done; and then the spring rain would sweep the Campagna, by its length and breadth, from the mountains to the sea, and the world would be refreshed. But now it was near noon and a heavy weariness lay upon the earth.

"You are tired," said Corbario, as they reached the shade of some trees, less than half a mile from the cottage. "Let us sit down for a while."

They sat down, where they could see the sea. It was dull and glassy under the high sun; here and there, far out, the sluggish currents made dark, irregular streaks.

Corbario produced cigarettes and offered one to Marcello, but the boy would not smoke; he said that it made him cough.

"I should smoke all the time, if I were quite well," he said, with a smile.

"And do many other things that young men do, I daresay," laughed Corbario. "Ride steeplechases, play cards all night, and drink champagne at breakfast."

"Perhaps." Marcello was amused at the picture. "I wonder whether I ever shall," he added.

Corbario glanced at him curiously. There was the faintest accent of longing in the tone, which was quite new.

"Why not?" Folco asked, still smiling. "It is merely a question of health, my dear boy. There is no harm in steeplechases if you do not break your neck, nor in playing cards if you do not play high, nor in drinking a glass of champagne now and then — no harm at all, that I can see. But, of course, so long as your lungs are delicate, you must be careful."

"Confound my lungs!" exclaimed Marcello with unusual energy. "I believe that I am much stronger than any of you think."

"I am sometimes inclined to believe it too," Corbario answered encouragingly.

"And I am quite sure that it would do me good to forget all about them and live as if there were nothing the matter with me. Don't you think so yourself?"

Corbario made a gesture of doubt, as if it were possible after all.

"Of course I don't mean dissipation," Marcello went on to say, suddenly assuming the manner of an elderly censor of morals, simply because he did not know what he was talking about. "I don't mean reckless dissipation."

"Of course not," Folco answered gravely. "You see, there are two sorts of dissipation. You must not forget that. The one kind means dissipating your fortune and your health; the other merely means dissipating melancholy, getting rid of care now and then, and of everything that bores one. That is the harmless sort."

"What they call 'harmless excitement'—yes, that is what I should like sometimes. There are days when I feel that I must have it. It is as if the blood went to my head, and my nerves are all on edge, and I wish something would happen, I don't know what, but something, something!"

"I know exactly what you mean, my dear boy," said Corbario in a tone of sympathy. "You see I am not very old myself, after all—barely thirty—not quite, in fact. I could call myself twenty-nine if it were not so much more respectable to be older."

"Yes. But do you mean to say that you feel just what I do now and then?" Marcello asked the question in considerable surprise. "Do you really know that sensation? That burning restlessness—that something like what the earth must feel before a thunderstorm—like the air at this moment?"

Not a muscle of Folco's still face moved.

"Yes," he answered quietly. "I know it very well. It is nothing but the sudden wish for a little harmless excitement, nothing else in the world, my dear boy, and it is certainly nothing to be ashamed of. It does not follow that it is at all convenient to yield to it, but we feel it because we lead such a very quiet life."

"But surely, we are perfectly happy," observed Marcello.

"Perfectly, absolutely happy. I do not believe that there are any happier people in the world than we three, your mother, you, and I. We have not a wish unfulfilled."

"No, except that one, when it comes."

"And that does not count in my case," answered Folco. "You see I have had a good deal of — 'harmless excitement' in my life, and I know just what it is like, and that it is quite possible to be perfectly happy without it. In fact, I am. But you have never had any at all, and it is as absurd to suppose that young birds will not try to fly as that young men will not want amusement, now and then."

"I suppose that women cannot always understand that," said Marcello, after a moment.

"Women," replied Folco, unmoved, "do not always distinguish quite closely between excitement that is harmless for a man and excitement which is not. To tell the truth," he added, with a laugh, "they hardly ever distinguish at all, and it is quite useless to talk to them about it."

"But surely, there are exceptions?"

"Not many. That is the reason why there is a sort of freemasonry among men of the world, a kind of tacit agreement that women need not be told what goes on at the clubs, and at men's dinners, and late at night when old friends have spent an evening together. Not that there is any harm in it all; but women would not understand. They have their innocent little mysteries which they keep from us, and we have harmless little secrets which we do not let them know."

Folco laughed softly at his own way of putting it, and perhaps because Marcello so easily accepted his point of view.

"I see," said the boy. "I wonder whether my mother would not understand that. It seems so simple!"

"She will, when the time comes, no doubt," answered Corbario. "Your mother is a great exception, my dear boy. On the other hand, she is so anxious about your health just now, that, if I were you, I would not say anything about feeling the want of a little excitement. Of course your life is monotonous. I know it. But there is nothing more monotonous than getting well, is there? The best part of it is the looking forward to what one will do when one is quite strong. You and I can talk of that, sometimes, and build castles in the air; but it is of no use to give your mother the idea that you are beating your wings against the bars of your cage, is it?"

Folco was quite lyric that day, but the words made exactly the impression he wished.

"You are right," Marcello said. "You always are. There is nobody like you, Folco. You are an elder brother to me, and yet you don't preach. I often tell my mother so."

This was true, and what Marcello told her added to her happiness, if anything could do that, and she encouraged the two to go off together as much as possible. She even suggested that they should go down to San Domenico for a fortnight, to look after the great Calabrian estate.

They rose and began to walk toward the cottage. The shooting had been good that morning, as quail-shooting goes, and the man who acted as keeper, loader, gardener, and general factotum, and who went out with any one who wanted to shoot, had gone on to the cottage with the bag, the two guns, and the animal which he called his dog. The man's name was Ercole, that is to say, Hercules; and though he was not a giant, he certainly bore a closer resemblance to the hero than his dog did to dogs in general.

"He was born in my house," Ercole said, when any one asked questions. "Find a better one if you can. His name? I call him Nino, short for John, because he barks so well at night. You don't understand? It is the 'voice of one crying in the wilderness.' Did you never go to Sunday school? Or do you call this place a garden, a park, a public promenade? I call it a desert. There are not even cats."

When an Italian countryman says of a place that even cats will not stay in it, he considers that he has evoked a picture of ultimate desolation that cannot be surpassed. It had always been Ercole's dream to live in the city, though he did not look like a man naturally intended for town life. He was short and skinny, though he was as wiry as a monkey; his face was slightly pitted with the smallpox, and the malaria of many summers had left him with a complexion of the colour of cheap leather; he had eyes like a hawk, matted black hair, and jagged white teeth. He and his fustian clothes smelt of earth, burnt gunpowder, goat's cheese, garlic, and bad tobacco. He was no great talker, but his language was picturesque and to the point; and he feared neither man nor beast, neither tramp nor horned cattle, nor yet wild boar. He was no respecter of persons at all. The land where the cottage was had belonged to a great Roman family, now ruined, and when the land had been sold, he had apparently been part of the bargain, and had come into the possession of the Signora Corbario with it. In his lonely conversations with Nino, he had expressed his opinion of each member of the family with frankness.

"You are a good dog, Nino," he would say. "You are the consolation of my soul. But you do not understand these things. Corbario is an assassin. Money, money, money! That is all he thinks of from morning till night. I know it, because he never speaks of it, and yet he never gives away anything. It is all for himself, the Signora's millions, the boy's millions, everything. When I look at his face, a chill seizes me, and I tremble as when I have the fever. You never had the malaria fever, Nino. Dogs don't have it, do they?"

At the question Nino turned his monstrous head to one side and looked along his muzzle at his master. If he had possessed a tail he would have wagged it, or thumped the hard ground with it a few times; but he had none. He had probably lost it in some wild battle of his stormy youth, fought almost to death against the huge Campagna sheep-dogs; or perhaps a wolf had got it, or perhaps he had never had a tail at all. Ercole had probably forgotten, and it did not really matter much.

"Corbario is an assassin," he said. "Remember that, Nino. As for his poor lady, she is a little lacking, or she would never have married him. But she is a saint, and what do saints want with cleverness? They go to paradise. Does that need much sense? We should all go if we could. Why do you cock your head on one side and look at me like a Christian? Are you trying to make me think you have a soul? You are made of nothing but corn meal and water, and a little wool, poor beast! But you have more sense than the Signora, and you are not an assassin, like her husband."

At this, Nino threw himself upon his back with his four legs in the air and squirmed with sheer delight, showing his jagged teeth and the roof of a very terrible mouth, and emitting a series of wolfish snorts; after which he suddenly rolled over upon his feet again, shook himself till his shaggy coat bristled all over his body, walked sedately to the open door of the hut, and sat down to look at the weather.

"He is almost a Christian," Ercole remarked under his breath, as if he were afraid the dog might hear the compliment and grow too vain.

For Ercole was a reticent man, and though he told Nino what he thought about people, he never told any one else. Marcello was the only person to whom he ever showed any inclination to attach himself. He regarded even the Contessa with suspicion, perhaps merely because she was a woman; and as for Aurora, girls did not count at all in his cosmogony.

"God made all the other animals before making women," he observed contemptuously one day, when he had gone out alone with Marcello.

"I like them," laughed the boy.

"So did Adam," retorted Ercole, "and you see what came of it."

No answer to this argument occurred to Marcello just then, so he said nothing; and he thought of Aurora, and his mother, and the sad-eyed Contessa, and wondered vaguely whether they were very unlike other women, as Ercole implied.

"When you know women," the man vouchsafed to add presently, "you will wish you were dead. The Lord sent them into the world for an affliction and for the punishment of our sins."

"You were never married, were you?" asked Marcello, still smiling.

Ercole stopped short in the sand, amongst the sea-thistles that grew there, and Nino trotted up and looked at him, to be ready if anything happened. Marcello knew the man's queer ways, and waited for him to speak.

"Married?" he snorted. "Married? You have said it!"

This seemed enigmatical, but Marcello understood the words to convey an affirmation.

"Well?" he asked, expecting more.

"Well? Well, what?" growled Ercole. "This is a bad world. A man falls in love with a pretty little caterpillar; he wakes up and finds himself married to a butterfly. Oh, this is a very bad world!"

Marcello was struck by the simile, but he reflected that Aurora looked much more like a butterfly than a caterpillar, a fact which, if it meant anything, should signify that he knew the worst beforehand. Ercole declined to enter into any account of his conjugal experiences, and merely shrugged his shoulders and went on through the sand.

With such fitting and warning as this to keep him out of trouble, Marcello was to face life: with his saintly mother's timid allusions to its wickedness, with Corbario's tempting suggestions of harmless dissipation, with an unlettered peasant's sour reflections on the world in general and women in particular.

In the other scale of the balance fate set his delicate and high-strung nature, his burning desire for the great unknown something, the stinging impatience of bodily weakness, and the large element of recklessness he inherited from his father, besides a fine admixture of latent boyish vanity for women to play upon, and all the ordinary weaknesses of human nature in about the same proportion as every one has them.

Given a large fortune and ordinary liberty, it might be foreseen that the boy would not reach the haven of maturity without meeting a storm, even if the outward circumstances of chance were all in his favour, even if no one had an interest in ruining him, even if Folco Corbario did not want all for himself, as poor Ercole told his dog that he did in the solitude of his hut.

Marcello had a bad chance at the start, and Maddalena dell' Armi, who knew the world well in all its moods, and had suffered by it and sinned for it, and had shed many tears in secret before becoming what she was now, foresaw danger, and hoped that her daughter's fate might not be bound up with that of her friend's son, much as she herself liked the gentle-hearted boy. She wondered how long any one would call him gentle after he got his first taste of pleasure and pain.

CHAPTER IV

IT was very early morning, and there was no shooting, for a southwesterly gale had been blowing all night, and the birds passed far inland. All along the beach, for twenty-five miles in an unbroken line, the surf thundered in, with a double roar, breaking on the bar, then gathering strength again, rising grey and curling green and crashing down upon the sand. Then the water opened out in vast sheets of crawling foam that ran up to the very foot of the bank where the scrub began to grow, and ran regretfully back again, tracing myriads of tiny channels where the sand was loose; but just as it had almost subsided, another wave curled and uncurled itself, and trembled a moment, and flung its whole volume forwards through a cloud of unresisting spray.

It had rained a little, too, and it would rain again. The sky was of an even leaden grey, and as the sun rose unseen, a wicked glare came into it, as if the lead were melting; and the wind howled unceasingly, the soft, wet, southwest wind of the great spring storms.

Less than a mile from the shore a small brigantine, stripped to a lower topsail, storm-jib, and balance-reefed mainsail, was trying to claw off shore. She had small chance, unless the gale shifted or moderated, for she evidently could not carry enough sail to make any way against the huge sea, and to heave to would be sure destruction within two hours.

The scrub and brushwood were dripping with raindrops, and the salt spray was blown up the bank with the loose sand. Everything was wet, grey, and dreary, as only the Roman shore can be at such times, with that unnatural dreariness of the south which comes down on nature suddenly like a bad dream, and is a thousand times more oppressive than the stern desolation of any northern sea-coast.

Marcello and Aurora watched the storm from a break in the bank which made a little lee. The girl was wrapped in a grey military cloak, of which she had drawn the hood over her loose hair. Her delicate nostrils dilated with pleasure to breathe the salt wind, and her eyelids drooped as she watched the poor little vessel in the distance.

"You like it, don't you?" asked Marcello, as he looked at her.

"I love it!" she answered enthusiastically. "And I may never see it all again," she added after a little pause.

"Never?" Marcello started a little. "Are you going away?"

"We are going to Rome to-day. But that is not what I mean. We have always come down every year for ever so long. How long is it, Marcello? We were quite small the first time."

"It must be five years. Four or five — ever since my mother bought the land here."

"We were mere children," said Aurora, with the dignity of a grown person. "That is all over."

"I wish it were not!" Marcello sighed.

"How silly you are!" observed Aurora, throwing back her beautiful head. "But then, I am sure I am much more grown up than you are, though you are nineteen, and I am not quite eighteen."

"You are seventeen," said Marcello firmly.

"I shall be eighteen on my next birthday!" retorted Aurora with warmth. "Then we shall see who is the more grown up. I shall be in society, and you — why, you will not even be out of the University."

She said this with the contempt which Marcello's extreme youth deserved.

"I am not going to the University."

"Then you will be a boy all your life. I always tell you so. Unless you do what other people do, you will never grow up at all. You ought to be among men by this time, instead of everlastingly at home, clinging to your mother's skirts!"

A bright flush rose in Marcello's cheeks. He felt that he wanted to box her ears, and for an instant he wished himself small again that he might do it, though he remembered what a terrible fighter Aurora had been when she was a little girl, and had preserved a vivid recollection of her well-aimed slaps.

"Don't talk about my mother in that way," he said, angrily.

"I'm not talking of her at all. She is a saint, and I love her very much. But that is no reason why you should always be with her, as if you were a girl! I don't suppose you mean to begin life as a saint yourself, do you? You are rather young for that, you know."

"No," Marcello answered, feeling that he was not saying just the right thing, but not knowing what to say. "And I am sure my mother does not expect it of me, either," he added. "But that is no reason why you should be so disagreeable."

He felt that he had been weak, and that he ought to say something sharp. He knew very well that his mother believed it quite possible for a boy to develop into saintship without passing through the intermediate state of sinning manhood; and though his nature told him that he was not of the temper that attains sanctity all at once, he felt that he owed to his mother's hopes for him a sort of loyalty in which Aurora had made him fail. The reasonings of innocent sentiment are more tortuous than the wiles of the devil himself, and have amazing power to torment the unfledged conscience of a boy brought up like Marcello.

Aurora's way of thinking was much more direct.

"If you think I am disagreeable, you can go away," she said, with a scornful laugh.

"Thank you. You are very kind." He tried to speak sarcastically, but it was a decided failure.

To his surprise, Aurora turned and looked at him very quietly.

"I wonder whether I shall like you, when you are a man," she said in a tone of profound reflection. "I am rather ashamed of liking you now, because you are such a baby."

He flushed again, very angry this time, and he moved away to leave her, without another word.

She turned her face to the storm and took no notice of him. She thought that he would come back, but there was just the least doubt about it, which introduced an element of chance and was perfectly delightful while it lasted. Was there ever a woman, since the world began, who did not know that sensation, either by experience or by wishing she might try it? What pleasure would there be in angling if the fish did not try to get off the hook, but stupidly swallowed it, fly and all? It might as well crawl out of the stream at once and lay itself meekly down in the basket.

And Marcello came back, before he had taken four steps.

"Is that what you meant when you said that you might never come here again?" he asked, and there was something rough in his tone that pleased her.

"No," she answered, as if nothing had happened. "Mamma talked to me a long time last night."

"What did she say?"

"Do you want to know?"

"Yes."

"There is no reason why I should not tell you. She says that we must not come here after I go into society, because people will think that she is trying to marry me to you."

She looked at him boldly for a moment, and then turned her eyes to the sea.

"Why should she care what people think?" he asked.

"Because it would prevent me from marrying any one else," answered Aurora, with the awful cynicism of youth. "If every one thought I was engaged to you, or going to be, no other man could ask for me. It's simple enough, I'm sure!"

"And you wish other men to ask you to marry them, I suppose?"

Marcello was a little pale, but he tried to throw all the contempt he could command into his tone. Aurora smiled sweetly.

"Naturally," she said. "I'm only a woman."

"Which means that I'm a fool to care for you!"

"You are, if you think I'm not worth caring for." The girl laughed.

This was so very hard to understand that Marcello knit his smooth young brow and looked very angry, but could find nothing to say on the spur of the moment. All women are born with the power to put a man into such a position that he must either contradict himself, hold his tongue, or fly into a senseless rage. They do this so easily, that even after the experience of a life-time we never suspect the trap until they pull the string and we are caught. Then, if we contradict ourselves, woman utters an inhuman cry of triumph and jeers at our unstable purpose; if we lose our tempers instead, she bursts into tears and calls us brutes; and finally, if we say nothing, she declares, with a show of reason, that we have nothing to say.

Marcello lost his temper.

"You are quite right," he said angrily. "You are not worth caring for. You are a mere child, and you are a miserable little flirt already, and you will be a detestable woman when you grow up! You will lead men on, and play with them, and then laugh at them. But you shall not laugh at me again. You shall not have that satisfaction! You shall wish me back, but I will not come, not if you break your silly little heart!"

With this terrific threat the boy strode away, leaving her to watch the storm alone in the lee of the sandbank. Aurora knew that he really meant to go this time, and at first she was rather glad of it, since he was in such a very bad temper. She felt that he had insulted her, and if he had stayed any longer she would doubtless have called him a brute, that being the woman's retort under the circumstances. She had not the slightest doubt of being quite reconciled with him before luncheon, of course, but in her heart she wished that she had not made him angry. It had been very pleasant to watch the storm together, and when they had come to the place, she had felt a strong presentiment that he would kiss her, and that the contrast between the kiss and the howling gale would be very delightful.

The presentiment had certainly not come true, and now that Marcello was gone it was not very amusing to feel the spray and the sand on her face, or to watch the tumbling breakers and listen to the wind. Besides, she had been there some time, and she had not even had her little breakfast of coffee and rolls before coming down to the shore. She suddenly felt hungry and cold and absurdly inclined to cry, and she became aware that the sand had got into her russet shoes, and that it would be very uncomfortable to sit down in such a place to take them off and shake it out; and that, altogether, misfortunes never come singly.

After standing still three or four minutes longer, she turned away with a discontented look in her face, all rosy with the wind and spray. She started as she saw Corbario standing before her, for she had not heard his footsteps in the gale. He wore his shooting-coat and heavy leathern gaiters, but he had no gun. She thought he looked pale, and that there was a shade of anxiety in his usually expressionless face.

"We wondered where you were," he said. "There is coffee in the verandah, and your mother is out already."

"I came down to look at the storm," Aurora answered. "I forgot all about breakfast."

They made a few steps in the direction of the cottage. Aurora felt that Corbario was looking sideways at her as they walked.

"Have you seen Marcello?" he asked presently.

"Did you not meet him?" Aurora was surprised. "It is not five minutes since he left me."

"No. I did not meet him."

"That is strange."

They went on in silence for a few moments.

"I cannot understand why you did not meet Marcello," Aurora said suddenly, as if she had thought it over. "Did you come this way?"

"Yes."

"Perhaps he got back before you started. He walks very fast."

"Perhaps," Corbario said, "but I did not see him. I came to look for you both."

"Expecting to find us together, of course!" Aurora threw up her head a little disdainfully, for Marcello had offended her.

"He is generally somewhere near you, poor boy," answered Corbario in a tone of pity.

"Why do you say 'poor boy' in that tone? Do you think he is so much to be pitied?"

"A little, certainly." Corbario smiled.

"I don't see why."

"Women never do, when a man is in love!"

"Women"—the flattery was subtle and Aurora's face cleared. Corbario was a man of the world, without doubt, and he had called her a woman, in a most natural way, as if she had been at least twenty years old. It did not occur to her to ask herself whether Folco had any object in wishing to please her just then, but she knew well enough that he did wish to do so. Even a girl's instinct is unerring in that; and Corbario further pleased her by not pursuing the subject, for what he had said seemed all the more spontaneous because it led to nothing.

"If Marcello is not in the cottage," he observed, as they came near, "he must have gone off for a walk after he left you. Did you not see which way he turned?"

"How could I from the place where I stood?" asked Aurora in reply. "As soon as he had turned behind the bank it was impossible to say which way he had gone."

"Of course," assented Folco. "I understand that."

Marcello had not come home, and Aurora was sorry that she had teased him into a temper and had then allowed him to go away. It was not good for him, delicate as he was, to go for a long walk in such weather without any breakfast, and she felt distinctly contrite as she ate her roll in silence and drank her coffee, on the sheltered side of the cottage, under the verandah. The Signora Corbario had not appeared yet, but the Contessa was already out. As a rule the Signora preferred to have her coffee in her room, as if she were in town. For some time no one spoke.

"Had we not better send Ercole to find Marcello?" the Contessa asked at last.

"I had to send Ercole to Porto d'Anzio this morning," Corbario answered. "I took the opportunity, because I knew there would be no quail with this wind."

"Marcello will come in when he is hungry," said Aurora, rather sharply, because she really felt sorry.

But Marcello did not come in.

Soon after eight o'clock his mother appeared on the

verandah. Folco dropped his newspaper and hastened to make her comfortable in her favourite chair. Though she was not strong, she was not an invalid, but she was one of those women whom it seems natural to help, to whom men bring cushions, and with whom other women are always ready to sympathise. If one of Fra Angelico's saints should walk into a modern drawing-room all the men would fall over each other in the scramble to make her comfortable, and all the women would offer her tea and ask her if she felt the draught.

The Signora looked about, expecting to see her son.

"Marcello has not come in," said Folco, understanding. "He seems to have gone for a long walk."

"I hope he has put on his thick boots," answered the Signora, in a thoughtful tone. "It is very wet."

She asked why Folco was not with him shooting, and was told that there were no birds in such weather. She had never understood the winds, nor the points of the compass, nor why one should see the new moon in the west instead of in the east. Very few women do, but those who live much with men generally end by picking up a few useful expressions, a little phrase-book of jargon terms with which men are quite satisfied. They find out that a fox has no tail, a wild boar no teeth, a boat no prow, and a yacht no staircase; and this knowledge is better than none.

The Signora accepted the fact that there were no birds that morning, and began to talk to Maddalena. Aurora got a book and pretended to read, but she was really listening for Marcello's footsteps, and wondering whether he would smile at her, or would still be cross when he came in. Corbario finished his paper and went off to look at the weather from the other side of the house, and the two women talked in broken sentences as old friends do, with long intervals of silence.

The wind had moderated a good deal, but as the sun rose higher the glare in the sky grew more yellow, the air was much warmer, and the trees and shrubs and long grass began to steam as if they had been half boiled. All manner of tiny flies and gnats chased each other in the lurid light.

"It feels as if there were going to be an earthquake," said Maddalena, throwing back the lace from her grey hair as if even its light weight oppressed her.

"Yes."

The women sat in silence, uneasy, their lips a little parted. Not that an earthquake would have disturbed them much, for slight ones are common enough in Italy, and could do no harm at all to a wooden cottage; it was a mere physical breathlessness that they felt, as the gale suddenly dropped and the heavy air became quite still on the sheltered side of the cottage.

Aurora threw aside her book impatiently and rose from her chair.

"I am going to look for Marcello," she said, and she went off without turning her head.

On the other side of the cottage, as she went round, she found Folco sitting on the steps of the verandah, his elbows on his knees and his chin resting on his folded hands, apparently in deep thought. He had a cigar between his teeth, but it had gone out.

"I am going to look for Marcello," said Aurora, as she passed close beside him.

He said nothing, and hardly moved his head. Aurora turned and looked at him as she stepped upon the path.

"What is the matter?" she asked, as she saw his face. "Is anything wrong?"

Corbario looked up quickly, as if he had been in a reverie.

"Anything the matter? No. Where did you say you were going?"

"To find Marcello. He has not come in yet."

"He has gone for a walk, I suppose. He often walks alone on off days. He will be back before luncheon, and you are not going to town till the afternoon."

"Will you come with me?" Aurora asked, for she was in a good humour with Folco.

He rose at once.

"I'll go with you for a stroll," he said, "but I don't think it is of any use to look for Marcello near the house."

"It can do no harm."

"And it will do us good to walk a bit."

They went down the path and through the trees towards the break in the bank.

"The sand was very wet this morning, even inside

the bank," Aurora said. "I daresay we shall find his footsteps and be able to guess which way he went."

"Very likely," Folco answered.

He pushed back his tweed cap a little and passed his handkerchief across his smooth brow. Aurora noticed the action, because he did not usually get warm so easily.

"Are you hot?" she asked carelessly.

"A little," he answered. "The air is so heavy this morning."

"Perhaps you are not quite well," said Aurora. "You are a little pale."

Apparently something in her youthfully patronising tone came as near irritating him as anything ever could.

"What does it matter, whether I am hot or not?" he asked, almost impatiently, and again he passed his handkerchief over his forehead.

"I did not mean to annoy you," Aurora answered with uncommon meekness.

They came near the break in the bank, and she looked at the sand on each side of her. She thought it seemed smoother than usual, and that there were not so many little depressions in it, where there had been footsteps on previous days, half obliterated by wind and rain.

"I cannot see where you and I passed an hour ago," she said, in some surprise.

"The wind draws through the gap with tremendous strength," Folco explained. "Just before the gale moderated there was a heavy squall with rain."

"Was there? I did not notice that — but I was on the lee side of the house. The wind must have smoothed the sand, just like a flat-iron!"

"Yes." Corbario answered indifferently and gazed out to sea.

Aurora left his side and looked about, going to a little distance from the gap, first on one side and then on the other.

"It is as if the wind had done it on purpose!" she cried impatiently. "It is as smooth as if it had all been swept with a gardener's broom."

Corbario turned, lighted his extinguished cigar, and watched her, as she moved about, stooping now and then to examine the sand.

"I don't believe it is of any use to look here," he said. "Besides, he will be back in time for luncheon."

"I suppose so," answered Aurora. "Why do you look at me in that way?" she asked, standing upright and meeting his eyes suddenly.

He laughed softly and took his cigar from his mouth.

"I was watching you. You are very graceful when you move."

She did not like his expression.

"I wish you would think less about me and more about finding Marcello," she said rather sharply.

"You talk as if he were lost. I tell you he will surely come back before long."

"I hope so."

But Marcello did not come back, and after Aurora had returned to the cottage and was seated in her chair again, with her book, she grew restless, and went over in her memory what had passed in the morning. It was not possible that Marcello should really mean to carry out his threat, to go away without a word, to leave her, to leave his mother; and yet, he was gone. A settled conviction came over her that he was really gone, just as he was, most probably back to Rome. She had teased him, and he had been very angry, absurdly angry; and yet she was perhaps responsible, in a way, for his disappearance. Presently his mother would grow anxious and would ask questions, and then it would all come out. It would be better to be brave and to say at once that he had been angry with her; she could confess the truth to her mother, to the Signora, if necessary, or even to both together, for they were women and would understand. But she could not tell the story before Corbario. That would be out of the question; and yet, anything would be better than to let them all think that something dreadful had happened to Marcello. He had gone to Rome, of course; or perhaps only to Porto d'Anzio, in which case he would meet Ercole coming back.

The hours wore on to midday, and Signora Corbario's uneasiness grew into real anxiety. The Contessa did her best to soothe her, but was anxious herself, and still Aurora said nothing. Folco was grave, but assured every one that the boy would soon return, though the Signora would not believe it.

"He will never come back! Something dreadful has happened to him!" And therewith she broke down completely and burst into tears.

"You must go and look for him," said Maddalena quietly to Corbario.

"I think you are right," he answered. "I am going to find him," he said softly, bending down to his wife as she lay in her chair, trying to control her sobs. "I will send some of the men towards Porto d'Anzio and will go towards Nettuno myself."

She loved him and believed in him, and she was comforted when she saw him go away and heard him calling the men from their hut.

Aurora was left alone with the two women.

"I am afraid Marcello is gone to Rome," she said, with an effort.

The Signora raised herself in her long chair and stared hard at the girl. The Contessa looked at her in surprise.

"What do you know about it?" cried the Signora. "Why have you not spoken, if you know anything? Don't you see that I am half mad with anxiety?"

Aurora had never seen the good lady in such a state, and was almost frightened; but there was nothing to be done now, except to go on. She told her little story timidly, but truthfully, looking from her mother to the Signora while she spoke, and wondering what would happen when she had finished.

"He said, 'You shall wish me back, but I will not come.' I think those were his last words."

"You have broken my boy's heart!" cried the Signora Corbario, turning her face away.

Maddalena, whose heart had really been broken long ago, could not help smiling.

"I am sure I did not mean to," cried Aurora, contritely. "And after all, though I daresay it was my fault, he called me a miserable little flirt, and I only called him a baby."

Maddalena would have laughed if her friend had not been in such real distress. As for Aurora, she did not know whether she would have laughed or cried if she had not felt that her girl's dignity was at stake. As it was, she grew preternaturally calm.

"You have driven him away," moaned the Signora piteously. "You have driven away my boy! Was he not good enough for you?"

She asked the question suddenly and vehemently, turning upon poor Aurora with something like fury. She was quite beside herself, and the Contessa motioned the girl away. Aurora rose and disappeared round the corner of the house.

Alone with her friend, Maddalena did her best to comfort her. There were arguments enough: it was barely noon, and Marcello had not been gone four hours; he was used to taking long walks, he had probably gone as far as the tower, and had rested there before coming back; or he had gone to meet Ercole on the road to Porto d'Anzio; or he had gone off towards the Nettuno woods to get over his anger in solitude; it was natural enough; and after all, if he had gone to Rome as Aurora thought, no harm could come to him, for he would go home, and would surely send a telegram before evening. It was unlike him, yes; but just at his age boys often did foolish things.

"Marcello is not foolish!" objected the Signora indignantly.

She could by no means listen to reason, and was angry because her friend tried to argue with her. She rose with an energy she seldom displayed, and began to walk up and down the verandah. Her face was very pale, her lip quivered when she spoke, and there was an unnatural light in her eyes. There was room for much moderate affection in her gentle nature; she had loved her first husband; she loved Corbario dearly; but the passion of her life was her son, and at the first presentiment of real danger to him the dominant preoccupation of her heart took violent possession of everything else in her, regardless of reason, friendship, consideration for others, or common sense.

Maddalena walked up and down beside her, putting one arm affectionately round her waist, and doing the best she could to allay the tempest.

It subsided suddenly, and was followed by a stony silence that frightened the Contessa. It was time for luncheon, and Aurora came back, hoping to find that she had been forgiven during her absence, but the Signora only looked at her coldly once or twice and would not speak. None of the three even pretended to have an appetite.

"I shall not go back to Rome to-day," said the Contessa. "I cannot leave you in such anxiety."

"Folco will take care of me," answered the Signora in a dull tone. "Do not change your plans on my account. The carriage is ordered at three o'clock."

She spoke so coldly that Maddalena felt a little pardonable resentment, though she knew that her friend was not at all herself.

"Very well," she answered quietly. "If you had rather that I should not stay with you we will go back this afternoon."

"It will be much better."

When the carriage appeared neither Folco nor any of the men had returned. The Signora made an evident attempt to show a little of her habitual cordiality at parting, and she even kissed Aurora coldly on the forehead, and embraced Maddalena with something like her usual affection. The two looked back as they drove away, calling out a last good-bye, but they saw that the Signora was not even looking after them; she was leaning against one of the wooden supports of the verandah, gazing towards the trees, and pressing one hand to her forehead.

"Do you think it was my fault, mamma?" asked Aurora, when they were out of sight of the cottage.

"No, dear," answered Maddalena. "Something has happened, I wish I knew what!"

"I only told him he was a baby," said Aurora, settling herself in the corner of the carriage, and arranging her parasol behind her so that it rested on the open hood; for the weather had cleared and the sun was shining brightly after the storm.

So she and her mother went back to Rome that afternoon. But when the Signora was alone, she was sorry that her friend was gone, and was all at once aware that her head was aching terribly. Every movement she made sent an agonizing thrill through her brain, and her hand trembled from the pain, as she pressed her palm to her forehead.

She meant to go down to the beach alone, for she was sure that she could find Marcello, and at least she would meet the men who were searching for him, and have news sooner than if she stayed in the cottage. But she could not have walked fifty steps without fainting while her headache lasted. She would take five grains of phenacetine, and in a little while she would be better.

She found the glass tube with the screw cap, and swallowed one of the tablets with a little water. Then she sat down on the edge of her long chair in the verandah to wait for the pain to pass. She was very tired, and presently, she scarcely knew how it was, she was lying at full length in her chair, her head resting comfortably against the cushion.

The sunlight fell slanting across her feet. Amongst the trees two or three birds were twittering softly; it was warm, it was dreamy, she was forgetting Marcello. She tried to rouse herself as the thought of him crossed her mind, and she fancied that she almost rose from the chair; but she had hardly lifted one hand. Then she saw his face close before her, her lips relaxed, the pain was gone, she smiled happily, and she was asleep.

Half an hour later her maid came quietly out to ask whether she needed anything, and seeing that she was sleeping peacefully spread a light shawl over her feet, placed the silver handbell within easy reach on the table, and went away again.

Towards evening Folco came back and then the men, straggling in on their tired little horses, for they had ridden far and fast. Marcello was not with them.

Corbario came in alone, and saw his wife lying in her chair in the evening light. He stood still a moment, and then came over and bent near her, looking earnestly into her quiet face.

"Already," he said aloud, but in a very low voice.

His hand shook as he laid it on her heart, bending low. Then he started violently and stood bolt upright, as an unearthly howl rent the air.

Nino, Ercole's queer dog, was close beside him, his forepaws planted on the upper step of the verandah, his head thrown up, his half-open jaws showing his jagged teeth, his rough coat bristling like spikes of bearded barley.

And Ercole, still a hundred yards away amongst the trees, shook his head and hurried forward as he heard the long-drawn note of brute terror.

"Somebody is dead," he said to himself.

CHAPTER V

FOR a few weeks all Italy was profoundly interested in the story of Marcello Corbario's disappearance and of his mother's almost unaccountable death. It was spoken of as the "double tragedy of the Campagna," and the newspapers were full of it.

The gates of the beautiful villa on the Janiculum were constantly assailed by reporters; the servants who came out from time to time were bribed, flattered, and tempted away to eat sumptuous meals and drink the oldest wine in quiet gardens behind old inns in Trastevere, in the hope that they might have some information to sell. But no one gained admittance to the villa except the agents of the police, who came daily to report the fruitless search; and the servants had nothing to tell beyond the bare truth. The young gentleman had gone for a walk near the sea, down at the cottage by the Roman shore, and he had never been heard of again. His mother had been suffering from a bad headache, had lain down to rest in a cane chair on the verandah, and had been found dead, with a smile on her face, by her husband, when he came back from his first attempt to find Marcello. The groom who always went down with the carriage could describe with greatest accuracy the spot where the Signorina Aurora had last seen him; the house servants gave the most minute details about the cane chair, the verandah, and the position in which the poor lady had been found; but that was all, and it was not at all what the reporters wanted. They had all been down to the cottage, each with his camera and note-book, and had photographed everything in sight, including Nino, Ercole's dog. What they wanted was a clue, a story, a scandal if possible, and they found nothing of the sort.

Folco Corbario's mourning was unostentatious and quiet, but none of the few persons who saw him, whether detectives or servants, could doubt that he was profoundly affected. He grew paler and thinner every day, until his own man even began to fear that his health was failing. He had done, and continued to do, everything that was humanly possible. He had brought his wife's body to Rome, and had summoned the very highest authorities in the medical profession to discover, if possible, the cause of her death. They had come, old men of science, full of the experience of years, young men of the future, brimming with theories, experts in chemistry, experts in snake poisons; for Folco had even suggested that she might have been bitten by a viper or stung by a venomous spider, or accidentally poisoned by some medicine or something she had eaten.

But the scientific gentlemen were soon agreed that no such thing had happened. Considerably disappointed, and with an unanimity which is so unusual in the confraternity as to be thought absolutely conclusive when it is observed, they decided that the Signora

Corbario had died of collapse after intense excitement caused by the disappearance of her son. Thereafter she was buried out at San Lorenzo, with the secret, if there were any ; masses were said, the verdict of the doctors was published, with the signatures of the most eminent practitioners and specialists in Italy ; and the interest of the public concentrated itself upon the problem of Marcello's mysterious removal, or abduction, or subduction, or recession, or flight, from the very bosom of his family.

This problem had the merit of defying solution. In a comparatively open country, within a space of time which could certainly be limited to five minutes, at a place whence he should have been clearly seen by Folco Corbario as soon as Aurora dell' Armi could no longer see him, the boy had been spirited away, leaving not even the trace of his footsteps in the sand. It was one of the most unaccountable disappearances on record, as Folco insisted in his conversations with the Chief of Police, who went down with him to the cottage and examined the spot most carefully, with several expert detectives. Folco showed him exactly where Aurora had stood, and precisely the direction he himself had followed in approaching the gap, and he declared it to be almost a physical impossibility that Marcello should have become suddenly invisible just then.

The official thought so too, and shook his head. He looked at the detectives, and they shook their heads also. And then they all looked at Corbario and expressed the opinion that there was some mistake about the length of time supposed by Aurora to have elapsed between the moment when Marcello left her and the instant of Folco's appearance before her. She had not looked at her watch; in fact, she had not carried a watch. The whole story therefore depended upon her more or less accurate judgment of time. It might have been a quarter of an hour instead of five minutes, in which case Corbario had not yet left the cottage, and Marcello would have had ample leisure to disappear in any direction he pleased. Ercole had been away at Porto d'Anzio, the men had been all at the hut; if Folco had not been on the path precisely at the time guessed by Aurora, everything could be accounted for.

"Very well," Corbario answered. "Let us suppose that my stepson had time to get away. In that case he can be found, alive or dead. Italy is not China, nor Siberia, and I can place unlimited funds at your disposal. Find him for me; that is all I ask."

"We shall find him, never fear!" answered the Chief of Police with a confidence he did not feel.

"We shall find him!" echoed the three detectives in chorus.

Ercole watched the proceedings and listened to what was said, for he considered it his duty to attend on such an occasion, his dog at his heels, his gun slung over his shoulder. He listened and looked from one to the other with his deep eyes and inscrutable parchment face, shrivelled by the malarious fever. But he said nothing. The Chief of Police turned to him at last.

"Now what do you think about it?" asked the official. "You know the country. Had there been any suspicious characters about, fellows who could have carried off the boy?"

"Such people would ask a ransom," answered Ercole. "You would soon hear from them. But I saw no one. There have been no brigands about Rome for more than twenty years. Do you dream that you are in Sicily? Praise be to Heaven, this is the Roman Campagna; we are Christians and we live under King Victor! Where are the brigands? They have melted. Or else they are making straw hats in the galleys. Do I know where they are? They are not here. That is enough."

"Quite right, my friend," answered the Chief of Police. "There are no brigands. But I am sorry to say that there are thieves in the Campagna, as there are near every great city."

Ercole shrugged his angular shoulders contemptuously.

"Thieves would not carry a man away," he answered. "You know that, you who are of the profession, as they say. Such ruffians would have knocked the young gentleman on the head to keep him quiet, and would have made off. And besides, we should have found their tracks in the sand, and Nino would have smelt them."

Nino pricked up one ragged ear at the sound of his name.

"He does not look very intelligent," observed the

official. "A clever dog might have been used to track the boy."

"How?" inquired Ercole with scorn. "The footsteps of the young gentleman were everywhere, with those of all the family, who were always coming and going about here. How could he track them, or any of us? But he would have smelt a stranger, even if it had rained. I know this dog. He is the head dog on the Roman shore. There is no other dog like him."

"I daresay not," assented the Chief of Police, looking at Nino. "In fact, he is not like any animal I ever saw."

The detectives laughed at this.

"There is no other," said Ercole without a smile. "He is the only son of a widowed mother. I am his family, and he is my family, and we live in good understanding in this desert. If there were no fever we should be like the saints in paradise — eating our corn meal together. And I will tell you another thing. If the young gentleman had been wounded anywhere near here, Nino would have found the blood even after three days. As for a dead man, he would make a point for him and howl half a mile off, unless the wind was the wrong way."

"Would he really?" asked Corbario with a little interest.

Ercole looked at him and nodded, but said no more, and presently the whole party of men went back to Rome, leaving him to the loneliness of the sand-banks and the sea.

Then Ercole came back to the gap and stood still a little while, and his dog sat bolt upright beside him.

"Nino," he said at last, in a rather regretful tone, "I gave you a good character. What could I say before those gentlemen? But I tell you this, you are growing old. And don't answer that I am getting old too, for that is my business. If your nose were what it was once, we should know the truth by this time. Smell that!"

Ercole produced a small green morocco pocket-book, of the sort made to hold a few visiting cards and a little paper money, and held it to Nino's muzzle.

Nino smelt it, looked up to his master's face inquiringly, smelt it again, and then, as if to explain that it did not interest him, lay down in the sand with his head on his forepaws.

"You see!" growled Ercole. "You cannot even tell whether it belonged to the boy or to Corbario. An apoplexy on you! You understand nothing! Ill befall the souls of your dead, you ignorant beast!"

Nino growled, but did not lift his head.

"You understand that," said Ercole, discontentedly. "If you were a Christian you would stick a knife into me for insulting your dead! Yet you cannot tell whose pocket-book this is! And if I knew, I should know something worth knowing."

The pocket-book disappeared in the interior recesses of Ercole's waistcoat. It was empty and bore no initial, and he could not remember to have seen it in Corbario's or Marcello's hands, but he was quite sure that it belonged to one of them. He was equally sure that if he showed it to Corbario the latter would at once say that it was Marcello's, and would take it away from him, so he said nothing about it. He had found it in the sand, a little way up the bank, during his first search after Marcello's disappearance.

Ercole's confidence in the good intentions of his fellow-men was not great; he was quite lacking in the sort of charity which believeth all things, and had a large capacity for suspicion of everybody and everything; he held all men to be liars and most women to be something worse.

"Men are at least Christians," he would say to Nino, "but a female is always a female."

If he took a liking for any one, as for Marcello, he excused himself for the weakness on the ground that he was only human after all, and in his heart he respected his dog for snarling at everybody without discrimination. There was no doubt, however, that he felt a sort of attachment for the boy, and he admitted the failing while he deplored it. Besides, he detested Corbario, and had felt that his own common sense was insulted by the fact that Folco seemed devoted to Marcello. The suspicion that Folco had got rid of his stepson in order to get his fortune was therefore positively delightful, accompanied as it was by the conviction that he should one day prove his enemy a murderer. Perhaps if he could have known what Folco Corbario was suffering, he might have been almost satisfied, but he had no means of guessing that.

In his opinion the man knew what had become of Marcello, and could be made to tell if proper means were used. At night Ercole put himself to sleep by devising the most horrible tortures for his master, such as no fortitude could resist, and by trying to guess what the wretched man would say when his agony forced him to confess the truth.

He was almost sure by this time that Marcello was dead, though how Folco could have killed him, carried off his body to a great distance and buried him, without ever absenting himself from the cottage, was more than Ercole could imagine. He paid Corbario's skill the compliment of believing that he had not employed any accomplice, but had done the deed alone.

How? That was the question. Ercole knew his dog well enough, and was perfectly sure that if the body had been concealed anywhere within a mile of the cottage Nino would have found it out, for the dog and his master had quartered every foot of the ground within three days after Marcello had been lost. It was utterly, entirely impossible that Folco, without help, could have dragged the dead boy farther. When he had gone on his pretended search he had not been alone; one of the men had ridden with him, and had never lost sight of him, as Ercole easily ascertained without seeming to ask questions. Ercole had obtained a pretty fair knowledge of Corbario's movements on that day, and it appeared that he had not been absent from the cottage more than half an hour at any time before he went to look for Marcello.

"If Corbario himself had disappeared in that way," said Ercole to himself and Nino, "it would be easy to understand. We should know that the devil had carried him off."

But no such supernatural intervention of the infernal powers could be supposed in Marcello's case, and Ercole racked his brains to no purpose, and pondered mad schemes for carrying Corbario off out of Rome to a quiet place where he would extract the truth from him, and he growled at the impossibility of such a thing, and fell to guessing again.

In the magnificent library of the villa on the Janiculum, Folco was guessing, too, and with no better result. But because he could not guess right, and could get no news of Marcello, his eyes were growing hollow and his cheeks wan.

The lawyers came and talked about the will, and explained to him that all the great property was his, unless Marcello came back, and that in any case he was to administer it. They said that if no news of the boy were obtained within a limited time, the law must take it for granted that he had perished in some unaccountable way. Folco shook his head.

"He must be found," he said. "I have good nerves, but if I do not find out what has become of him I shall go mad."

The lawyers spoke of courage and patience, but a sickly smile twisted Folco's lips.

"Put yourself in my place, if you can," he answered.

The lawyers, who knew the value of the property to

a farthing, wished they could, though if they had known also what was passing in his mind they might have hesitated to exchange their lot for his.

"He was like your own son," they said sympathetically. "A wife and a son gone on the same day! It is a tragedy. It is more than a man can bear."

"It is indeed!" answered Corbario in a low voice and looking away.

Almost the same phrases were exchanged each time that the two men came to the villa about the business, and when they left they never failed to look at each other gravely and to remark that Folco was a person of the deepest feeling, to whom such an awful trial was almost worse than death; and the elder lawyer, who was of a religious turn of mind, said that if such a calamity befell him he would retire from the world, but the younger answered that, for his part, he would travel and see the world and try to divert his thoughts. In their different ways they were hard-headed, experienced men; yet neither of them suspected for a moment that there was anything wrong. Both were honestly convinced that Folco had been a model husband to his dead wife, and a model father to her lost son. What they could not understand was that he should not find consolation in possessing their millions, and they could only account for the fact by calling him a person of the deepest feeling — a feeling, indeed, quite past their comprehension.

Even the Contessa dell' Armi was impressed by the

unmistakable signs of suffering in his face. She went twice to see him within three weeks after her friend's death, and she came away convinced that she had misjudged him. Aurora did not go with her, and Corbario barely asked after her. He led Maddalena to his dead wife's room and begged her to take some object that had belonged to the Signora, in memory of their long friendship. He pressed her to accept a necklace, or a bracelet, or some other valuable ornament, but Maddalena would only take a simple little gold chain which she herself had given long ago.

Her own sorrow for her friend was profound but undemonstrative, as her nature had grown to be. Aurora saw it, and never referred to it, speaking only now and then of Marcello, to ask if there were any news of him.

"He is not dead," the girl said one day. "I know he will come back. He went away because I called him a baby."

Her mother smiled sadly and shook her head.

"Did you love him, dear?" she asked softly.

"We were children then," Aurora answered. "How do I know? I shall know when he comes back."

It was true that the girl had changed within a few weeks, and her mother saw it. Her smile was not the same, and her eyes were deeper. She had begun to gather her hair in a knot, closer to her head, and that altered her expression a little and made her look much older; but there was more than that, there was something very hard to describe, something one might call conviction — the conviction that the world is real, which comes upon girlhood as suddenly as waking on sleep, or sleep on waking. She had crossed the narrow borderland between play and earnest, and she had crossed it very soon.

"He will come back," she said. "He went away on that little ship that was tossing in the storm. I know it, though I cannot tell how he got out to it through the breaking waves."

"That is perfectly impossible, child," said Maddalena with certainty.

"Never mind. If we knew what ship that was, and where she is now, we could find Marcello. I am as sure of it as I am sure of seeing you at this moment. You know you often say that my presentiments come true. As soon as we knew he was gone I thought of the little ship."

It was natural, perhaps. The picture of the small brigantine, fighting for existence, had graved itself in her memory. With its crew so near death, it had been the only thing within sight that suggested human life after Marcello was gone. The utter impossibility of a man's swimming out through the raging sea that broke upon the bar was nothing compared with Aurora's inward conviction that the little vessel had borne away the secret of his disappearance. And she had not been wrecked: Aurora knew that, for a wreck anywhere on the Roman shore would have been spoken of at once. They are unfortunately common enough, and since her childhood Aurora had more than once seen a schooner's masts sticking up out of the treacherous water a cable's length from the shore. The brigantine had got away, for the gale had moderated very suddenly, as spring gales do in the Mediterranean, just when the captain was making up his mind to let go both anchors and make a desperate attempt to save his vessel by riding out the storm — a forlorn hope with such ground tackle as he had in his chain lockers. And then he had stood out, and had sailed away, one danger more behind him in his hard life, and one less ahead. He had sailed away — whither? No one could tell. Those little vessels, built in the south of Italy, often enough take salt to South America, and are sold there, cargo and all; and some of the crew stay there, and some get other ships, but almost all are dispersed. The keeper of the San Lorenzo tower, who had been a deep-water man, had told Aurora about it. He himself had once gone out in a Sicilian brigantine from Trapani, and had stayed away three years, knocking about the world in all sorts of craft.

Yet this one might have been on a coastwise trip to Genoa and Marseilles. That was quite possible. If one could only find out her name. And yet, if she had put into a near port Marcello would have come back; for Aurora was quite sure that he had got on board her somehow. It was all a mystery, all but the certainty she felt that he was still alive, and which nothing could shake, even when every one else had given him up. Aurora begged her mother to speak to Corbario about it. With his experience and knowledge of things he would know what to do; he could find some way of tracing the vessel, wherever she might be.

The Contessa was convinced that the girl's theory was utterly untenable, and it was only to please her that she promised to speak of it if she saw Corbario again. Soon afterward she decided to leave Rome for the summer, and before going away she went once more to the villa. It was now late in June, and she found Folco in the garden late in the afternoon.

He looked ill and tired, but she thought him a little less thin than when she had seen him last. He said that he, too, meant to leave Rome within a few days, that he intended to go northward first to see an old friend of his who had recently returned from South America, and that he should afterwards go down to Calabria, to San Domenico, and spend the autumn there. He had no news of Marcello. He looked thoughtfully down at his hands as he said this in a tone of profound sorrow.

"Aurora has a fixed idea," said Maddalena. "While she was talking with Marcello at the gap in the bank there was a small ship tossing about not far from the shore."

"Well?" asked Corbario. "What of it?"

As he looked up from the contemplation of his hands Maddalena was struck by his extreme pallor and the terrible hollowness of his eyes.

"How ill you look!" she exclaimed, almost involuntarily. "The sooner you go away the better."

"What did Aurora say about the brigantine?" he asked earnestly, by way of answer.

Maddalena knew too little about the sea to understand that he must have noticed the vessel's rig to name it correctly, as he did, and without hesitation.

"She is convinced that Marcello got on board of her," she answered.

Corbario's face relaxed a little, and he laughed harshly.

"That is utterly absurd!" he answered. "No swimmer that ever lived could have got to her, nor any boat either! There was a terrific surf on the bar."

"Of course not," assented Maddalena. "But you saw the ship, too?"

"Yes. Aurora was looking at her when I reached the gap. That is why I noticed the vessel," Corbario added, as if by an afterthought. "She was a Sicilian brigantine, and was carrying hardly any sail. If the gale had lasted she would probably have been driven ashore. Her only chance would have been to drop anchor."

"You know all about ships and the sea, don't you?" asked Maddalena, with a very little curiosity, but without any particular intention.

"Oh, no!" cried Corbario, as if he were protesting against something. "I have made several long voyages, and I have a knack of remembering the names of things, nothing more."

"I did not mean to suggest that you had been a sailor," Maddalena answered.

"What an idea! I, a sailor!"

He seemed vaguely amused at the idea. The Contessa took leave of him, after giving him her address in the north of Italy, and begging him to write if he found any clue to Marcello's disappearance. He promised this, and they parted, not expecting to meet again until the autumn.

In a few days they had left Rome for different destinations. The little apartment near the Forum of Trajan where the Contessa and her daughter lived was shut up, and at the great villa on the Janiculum the solemn porter put off his mourning livery and dressed himself in brown linen, and smoked endless pipes within the closed gates when it was not too hot to be out of doors. The horses were turned out to grass, and the coachman and grooms departed to the country. The servants opened the windows in the early morning, shut them at ten o'clock against the heat, and dozed the rest of the time, or went down into the city to gossip with their friends in the afternoon. It was high summer, and Rome went to sleep.

CHAPTER VI

"WHAT do we eat to-day?" asked Paoluccio, the innkeeper on the Frascati road, as he came in from the glare and the dust and sat down in his own black kitchen.

"Beans and oil," answered his wife.

"An apoplexy take you!" observed the man, by way of mild comment.

"It is Friday," said the woman, unmoved, though she was of a distinctly apoplectic habit.

The kitchen was also the eating-room where meals were served to the wine-carters on their way to Rome and back. The beams and walls were black with the smoke of thirty years, for no whitewash had come near them since the innkeeper had married Nanna. It was a rich, crusty black, lightened here and there to chocolate brown, and shaded off again to the tint of strong coffee. High overhead three hams and half a dozen huge sausages hung slowly curing in the acrid wood smoke. There was an open hearth, waist high, for roasting, and having three square holes sunk in it for cooking with charcoal. An enormous bunch of green ferns had been hung by a long string from the highest beam to attract the flies, which swarmed on it like bees on a branch. The floor was of beaten cement, well swept and watered. Along three of the walls there were heavy tables of rough-hewn oak, with benches, polished by long and constant use. A trap-door covered the steps that led down to the deep cellar, which was nothing but a branch of those unexplored catacombs that undermine the Campagna in all directions. The place was dim, smoky, and old, but it was not really dirty, for in his primitive way the Roman wine-carter is fastidious. It is not long since he used to bring his own solid silver spoon and fork with him, and he will generally rinse a glass out two or three times before he will drink out of it.

The kitchen of the inn was cool compared with the road outside, and though it smelt chiefly of the stale smoke of green wood, this was pervaded and tempered by odours of fern, fresh cabbages, goats'-milk cheese, and sour red wine. The brown earthen pot simmered over one of the holes in the hearth, emitting little clouds of steam ; but boiling beans have no particular smell, as everybody knows.

Paoluccio had pushed his weather-beaten soft hat back on his head, and sat drumming on the oak table with his knotty fingers. He was a strong man, thickset and healthy, with grizzled hair and an intensely black beard. His wife was fat, and purple about the jaws and under the ears. She stood with her back to the hearth, looking at him, with a wooden spoon in her hand.

"Beans," she said slowly, and she looked up at the rafters and down again at her husband.

"You have told me so," he growled, "and may the devil fly away with you!"

"Beans are not good for people who have the fever," observed Nanna.

"Beans are rather heavy food," assented the innkeeper, apparently understanding. "Bread and water are better. Pour a little oil on the bread."

"A man who has the fever may die of eating beans," said Nanna thoughtfully. "This is also to be considered."

"It is true." Paoluccio looked at his wife in silence for a moment. "But a person who is dead must be buried," he continued, as if he had discovered something. "When a person is dead, he is dead, whether he dies of eating beans or —"

He broke off significantly, and his right hand, as it lay before him, straightened itself and made a very slight vibrating motion, with the fingers all close together. It is the gesture that means the knife among the southern people. Nanna instantly looked round, to be sure that no one else was in the room.

"When you have given that medicine, you cannot send for the doctor," she observed, lowering her voice. "But if he eats, and dies, what can any one say? We have fed him for charity; it is Friday and we have given him beans. What can we know? Are not beans good food? We have nothing else, and it is for charity, and we give what we have. I don't think they could expect us to give him chickens and French wine, could they?"

Paoluccio growled approval.

"It is forty-seven days," continued Nanna. "You can make the account. Chickens and milk and fresh meat for forty-seven days! Even the bread comes to something in that time, at least two soldi a day — two forties eighty, two sevens fourteen, ninety-four — nearly five francs. Who will give us the five francs? Are we princes?"

"There is the cow," observed Paoluccio with a grin.

"Imbecile," retorted his wife. "It has been a good year; we bought the wine cheap, we sell it dear, without counting what we get for nothing from the carters; we buy a cow with our earnings, and where is the miracle?"

The innkeeper looked towards the door and the small window suspiciously before he answered in a low voice.

"If I had not been sure that he would die, I would not have sold the watch and chain," he said. "In the house of my father we have always been honest people."

"He will die," answered Nanna, confidently and with emphasis. "The girl says he is hungry to-day. He shall eat beans. They are white beans, too, and the white are much heavier than the brown."

She lifted the tin cover off the earthen pot and stirred the contents.

"White beans!" grumbled Paoluccio. "And the weather is hot. Do you wish to kill me?"

"No," answered Nanna quietly. "Not you."

"Do you know what I say?" Paoluccio planted a

huge finger on the oaken board. "That sick butterfly upstairs is tougher than I am. Forty-seven days of fever, and nothing but bread and water! Think of that, my Nanna! Think of it! You or I would be consumed, one would not even see our shadows on the floor! But he lives."

"If he eats the white beans he has finished living," remarked Nanna.

A short silence followed, during which Paoluccio seemed to be meditating, and Nanna began to ladle the beans out into four deep earthenware bowls, roughly glazed and decorated with green and brown stripes.

"You are a jewel; you are the joy of my heart," he observed thoughtfully, as Nanna placed his portion before him, covered it with oil, and scattered some chopped basil on the surface.

"Eat, my love," she said, and she cut a huge piece from a coarse loaf and placed it beside him on a folded napkin that looked remarkably clean in such surroundings, and emitted a pleasant odour of dried lavender blossoms.

"Where is the girl?" asked Paoluccio, stirring the mess and blowing upon it.

As he spoke, the door was darkened, and the girl stood there with a large copper "conca," the water-jar of the Roman province, balanced on her head — one of the most magnificent human beings on whom the sun of the Campagna ever shone. She was tall, and she bent her knees without moving her neck, in order to enter the door without first setting down the heavy vessel.

Her thick dark hair grew low on her forehead, almost black, save for the reddish chestnut lights where a few tiny ringlets curled themselves about her small and classic ears. Straight black eyebrows outlined the snow-white forehead, and long brown lashes shaded the fearless eyes, that looked black too. She smiled a little, quite unconsciously, as she lowered herself with the weight and gracefully rose to her height again after she had entered. One shapely brown hand steadied the conca above, the other gathered her coarse skirt; then she stood still, lifted the load from her head with both hands and without any apparent effort, and set it down in its place on a stone slab near the hearth. Most women need a little help to do that.

She laid aside the twisted cloth on which the conca had rested while she carried it, and she smoothed her hair carelessly.

"There are beans," said Nanna, giving the girl one of the bowls. "There is the bread. While they are cooling take the other portion upstairs."

The girl looked at the bowl, and at Nanna, and then at Paoluccio, and stood stock still.

"Hey, there!" the man cried, with a rough laugh. "Hey! Reginella! Are you going to sleep, or are you turning into a statue?"

"Am I to give him the beans to eat?" asked Regina, looking hard at the innkeeper.

"You said he was hungry. That is what there is for dinner. We give him what we have."

Regina's dark eyes lightened; her upper lip rose in a

curve and showed her closed teeth, strong and white as those of a young animal.

"Do as you are told," added Paoluccio. "This is charity. When you examine your conscience at Easter you can say, 'I have fed the hungry and cared for the sick.' The beans are mine, of course, but that makes no difference. I make you a present of them."

"Thank you!"

"Welcome," answered Paoluccio, with his mouth full.

Regina took the fourth bowl and a piece of bread and went out. The steps to the upper part of the house were on the outside, as is common in the houses of the Campagna.

"How old is she?" Paoluccio asked when she was gone.

"She must be twenty," answered Nanna. "It must be ten years since her mother died, and her mother said she was ten years old. She has eaten many loaves in this house."

"She has worked for her food," said the innkeeper. "And she is an honest girl."

"What did you expect? That I should let her be idle, or make eyes at the carters? But you always defend her, because she is pretty, you ugly scamp!"

Nanna uttered her taunt in a good-natured tone, but she glanced furtively at her husband to see the effect of her words, for it was not always safe to joke with Paoluccio.

"If I did not defend her," he answered, "you would beat the life out of her."

"I daresay," replied Nanna, and filled her mouth with beans.

"But now," said Paoluccio, swallowing, "if you are not careful she will break all your bones. She has the health of a horse."

So the couple discussed matters amiably, while Regina was out of the way.

In a garret that had a small unglazed window looking to the north, the girl was bending over a wretched trestle-bed, which was literally the only piece of furniture in the room; and on the coarse mattress, stuffed with the husks and leaves of maize, lay all that the fever had left of Marcello Consalvi, shivering under a tattered brown blanket. There was little more than the shadow of the boy, and his blue eyes stared dully up at the girl's face. But there was life in him still, thanks to her, and though there was no expression in his gaze, his lips smiled faintly, and faint words came from them.

"Thank you," he said, "I am better to-day. Yes, I could eat something."

Regina bent lower, smiling happily, and she kissed the boy's face three times; she kissed his eyes and dry lips. And he, too, smiled again.

Then she left the bedside and went to a dark corner, where she cautiously moved aside a loose board. From the recess she took a common tumbler and a bottle of old wine and a battered iron spoon. She crouched upon the floor, because there was no table; she took two fresh eggs out of the folds of the big red and yellow cotton handkerchief that covered her shoulders and was crossed over her bosom, and she broke them into the glass, and hid the empty shells carefully in the folds again, so that they should not be found in the room. For she had stolen these for Marcello, as usual, as well as the old wine. She poured a little of the latter into the glass and stirred the eggs quickly and softly, making hardly any noise. From the recess in the wall she got a little sugar, which was wrapped up in a bit of newspaper brown with age and smoke, and she sweetened the eggs and wine and stirred again; and at last she came and fed Marcello with the battered spoon. She had put off her coarse slippers and walked about in her thick brown woollen stockings, lest she should be heard below. She was very quiet and skilful, and she had strangely small and gentle hands for a peasant girl. Marcello's head was propped up by her left arm while she fed him.

She had kept him alive six weeks, and she had saved his life. She had found him lying against the door of the inn at dawn, convulsed with ague and almost unconscious, and had carried him into the house like a child, though he had been much heavier then. Of course the innkeeper had taken his watch and chain, and his jacket and sleeve-links and studs, to keep them safe, he said. Regina knew what that meant, but Paoluccio had ordered her to take care of him, and she had done her best. Paoluccio felt that if the boy died it would be the will of heaven, and that he probably would not live long with such care and such nourishment as he would get up there in the attic. When he was dead, it would be time enough to tell the carabineers who passed the house twice every twenty-four hours on their beat; they would see that a sick boy had been taken in, and that he had died of the fever, and as they need never know how long he had been in the inn, the whole affair would redound to Paoluccio's credit with them and with customers. But as long as he was alive it was quite unnecessary that any one should know of his existence, especially as the watch and chain had been converted into money, and the money into a fine young cow. That Marcello could get well on bread and water never entered Paoluccio's head.

But he had counted without Regina; that is to say that he had overlooked the love and devotion of an intensely vital creature, younger, quicker, and far cleverer that he, who would watch the sick boy day and night, steal food and wine for him, lose sleep for him, risk blows for him, and breathe her strong life into his weak body; to whom the joy of saving him from death would be so much greater than all fatigue, that there would be no shadow under her eyes, no pallor in her cheek, no weariness in her elastic gait to tell of sleepless nights spent by his bedside in soothing his ravings, or in listening for the beat of his heart when he lay still and exhausted, his tired head resting on her strong white arm. And when he seemed better and at ease she often fell asleep beside him, half sitting, half lying, on the pallet bed, her cheek on the straw pillow, her breath mingling with his in the dark.

He was better now, and she felt the returning life in him, almost before he was sure of it himself; and while her heart was almost bursting with happiness, so that she smiled to herself throughout her rough work all day long, she knew that he could not stay where he was. Paoluccio expected him to die, and was beginning to be tired of waiting, and so was Nanna. If he recovered, he would ask for his watch and other things; he was evidently a fine young gentleman to whom some strange accident had happened, and he must have friends somewhere. Half delirious, he had spoken of them and of his mother, and of some one called Aurora, whom Regina already hated with all her heart and soul. The innkeeper and his wife had never come near him since the former had helped the girl to carry him upstairs, but if they suspected that he was recovering she would not be able to prevent them from seeing him; and if they did, she knew what would happen. They would send her on an errand, and when she came back Marcello would be dead. She might refuse to go, but they were strong people and would be two to one. Brave as Regina was, she did not dare to wait for the carabineers when they came by on their beat and to tell them the truth, for she had the Italian peasant's horror and dread of the law and its visible authority; and moreover she was quite sure that Paoluccio would murder her if she told the secret.

"If I could only take you to Rome!" she whispered,

bending over him when he had swallowed the contents of the glass. "You could tell me where your friends are."

"Rome?" he repeated, with a vacant questioning.

She nodded and smiled, and then sighed. She had long been sure that the fever had affected his memory, and she had tried many times to awaken it.

She loved him because he had the face of an angel, and was fair-haired, and seemed so gentle and patient, and smiled so sweetly when she kissed him. That was all. He could thank her; he could tell her that he was better or worse; he could speak of what he saw; he could even tell her that she was beautiful, and that was much. He was Marcello, he had told her that, but when she asked what other name he had, he looked at her blankly at first, and then an expression of painful effort came over his face, and she would not disturb him any more. He could not remember. He did not know how he had come to the inn door; he had been walking in the Campagna alone and had felt tired. He knew no more.

If only she could get him to Rome. It was not more than seven or eight miles to the city, and Regina had often been there with Nanna. She had been to Saint John Lateran's at midsummer for the great festival, and she knew where the hospital was, in which famous professors cured every ill under the sun. If she could bring Marcello to them, he would get well; if he stayed much longer at the inn, Paoluccio would kill him; being a woman, and a loving one, Regina only regarded as possible what she wished, where the man she loved was concerned.

She made up her mind that if it could not be done by any other means she would carry Marcello all the way. During his illness she had often lifted him from his bed like a little child, for he was slightly built by nature and was worn to a shadow by the fever. Even Aurora could have raised him, and he was a feather-weight in the arms of such a creature as Regina. But it would be another matter to carry such an awkward burden for miles along the highroad; and besides, she would meet the carabineers, and as she would have to go at night, they would probably arrest her and put her in prison, and Marcello would die. She must find some other way.

She laid his head tenderly on the pillow and left him, promising to come back as soon as she could. For safety she had brought the dish of beans with her, lest Nanna should follow her, and she took it with her, just as it was; but at the foot of the outer stairs she ran along the back of the house to the pig-sty, and emptied the mess into the trough, carefully scraping the bowl with the spoon so that it looked as if some one had eaten the contents. Then she went back to the kitchen.

"Has he eaten?" inquired Nanna, and Paoluccio looked up, too.

"You see," answered Regina, showing the empty bowl.

"Health to him!" answered Paoluccio. "He has a good appetite."

"Eat your own," said Nanna to the girl.

She suspected that Regina might have eaten the beans meant for Marcello, but her doubt vanished as she saw how the hungry young thing devoured her own portion.

"Are there any more left?" Regina asked when she had finished, for she understood perfectly what was going on in the minds of the other two.

She looked into the earthen cooking-pot which now stood on the corner of the hearth.

"Not even the smell of any more," answered Nanna. "There is bread."

Regina's white teeth crushed the hard brown crust as if she had not eaten for a week. There could be no doubt but that the sick boy had eaten the beans; and beans, especially white ones, are not good for people who have the fever, as Nanna had justly observed.

"On Sunday he shall have a dish of liver and cabbage," she said, in a cheerful tone. "There is much strength in liver, and cabbage is good for the blood. I shall take it to him myself, for it will be a pleasure to see him eat."

"The beans were soon finished," said Regina, with perfect truth.

"I told you how it would be," Paoluccio answered.

But Regina knew that the time had come to get Marcello away from the inn if he ever was to leave it alive, and in the afternoon, when Nanna was dozing in her chair in the kitchen and Paoluccio was snoring upstairs, and when she had smoothed Marcello's pillow, she went out and sat down in front of the house, where there was shade at that hour, though the glare from the dusty road would have blinded weaker eyes than hers. She sat on the stone seat that ran along the house, and leaned against the rough wall, thinking and scheming, and quite sure that she should find a way.

At first she looked about, while she thought, from the well-known mountains that bounded her world to the familiar arches of the distant aqueduct, from the dry ditch opposite to the burning sky above and the greyish green hillocks below Tivoli. But by and by she looked straight before her, with a steady, concentrated stare, as if she saw something happening and was watching to see how it would end.

She had found what she wanted, and was quite sure of it; only a few details remained to be settled, such as what was to become of her after she left the inn where she had grown up. But that did not trouble her much.

She was not delicately nurtured that she should dread the great world of which she knew nothing, nor had Nanna's conversation during ten years done much to strengthen her in the paths of virtue. Her pride had done much more and might save her wherever she went, but she was very well aware of life's evil truths. And what would her pride be compared with Marcello, the first and only being she had ever loved? To begin with, she knew that the handsome people from the country earned money by serving as models for painters and sculptors, and she had not the slightest illusion about her own looks. Since she had been a child people who came to the inn had told her that she was beautiful; and not the rough wine-carters only, for the fox-hunters sometimes came that way, riding slowly homeward after a long run, and many a fine gentleman in pink had said things to her which she had answered sharply, but which she remembered well. She had not the slightest doubt but that she was one of the handsomest girls in Italy, and the absolute certainty of the conviction saved her from having any small vanity about her looks. She knew that she had only to show herself and that every one would stand and look at her, only to beckon and she would be followed. She did not crave admiration; a great beauty rarely does. She simply defied competition, and was ready to laugh at it in a rather good-natured way, for she knew what she had, and was satisfied.

As for the rest, she was merely clever and fearless, and her moral inheritance was not all that might be desired; for her father had left her mother in a fit of pardonable jealousy, after nearly killing her and quite killing his rival, and her mother had not redeemed her character after his abrupt departure. On the contrary, if an accident had not carried her off suddenly, Regina's virtuous parent would probably have sold the girl into slavery. Poor people are not all honest, any more than other kinds of people are. Regina did not mourn her mother, and hardly remembered her father at all, and she never thought of either.

She owed Paoluccio and Nanna nothing, in her opinion. They had fed her sufficiently, and clothed her decently for the good of the house; she had done the work of two women in return, because she was strong, and she had been honest, because she was proud. Even the innkeeper and his wife would not have pretended that she owed them much gratitude; they were much too natural for that, and besides, the girl was too handsome, and there might be some scandal about her any day which would injure the credit of the inn. Nanna thought Paoluccio much too fond of watching her, as it was, and reflected that if she went to the city she would be well out of the way, and might go to the devil if she pleased.

Regina's plan for taking Marcello was simple, like most plans which succeed, and only depended for its success on being carried out fearlessly.

The wine-carters usually came to the inn from the hills between nine and eleven o'clock at night, and the carts, heavy-laden with wine casks, stood in a line along the road, while the men went into the kitchen to eat and drink. They generally paid for what they consumed by giving a measure or two of wine from the casks they were bringing, and which they filled up with water, a very simple plan which seems to have been in use for ages. It has several advantages; the owner of the wine does not suffer by it, since he gets his full price in town; the man who buys the wine in Rome does not suffer, because he adds so much water to the wine before selling it that a little more or less makes no difference; the public does not suffer, as it is well known that wine is much better for the health when drunk with plenty of water; and the carters do not suffer, because nobody would think of interfering with them. Moreover, they get food and drink for nothing.

While the men were having supper in the inn, their carts were guarded by their little woolly dogs, black, white, or brown, and always terribly wide-awake and uncommonly fierce in spite of their small size.

Now, just at this time, there was one carter who had none, and Regina knew it, for he was one of her chief admirers. He was the hardest-drinking ruffian of all the men who came and went on the Frascati road, and he had been quite willing to sell his dog in the street to a gentleman who admired it and offered him fifty francs for it, though that is a small price for a handsome "lupetto." But Mommo happened to be deeper in debt than usual, took the money, and cast about to steal another dog that might serve him. So far he had not seen one to his liking.

It is the custom of the wine-carters, when they have had plenty to eat and drink, to climb to their seats under the fan-like goat-skin hoods of their carts, and to go to sleep, wrapped in their huge cloaks. Their mules plod along and keep out of the way of other vehicles without any guidance, and their dogs protect them from thieves, who might steal their money; for they always carry the sum necessary to pay the octroi duty at the city gates, where every cart is stopped. As they are on the road most of their lives, winter and summer, they would not get much sleep if they tried to keep awake all night; and they drink a good deal, partly because wine is really a protection against the dangerous fever, and partly because their drink costs them nothing. Some of them drank their employers' wine at supper, others exchanged what they brought for Paoluccio's, which they liked better.

They usually got away about midnight, and Mommo was often the last to go. It was a part of Regina's work to go down to the cellar and draw the wine that was wanted from the hogsheads when the host was too lazy to go down himself, and being quite unwatched she could draw a measure from the oldest and strongest if she chose. Mommo could easily be made a little sleepier than usual, after being tempted to outstay the others.

And so it turned out that night. After the necessary operation of tapping one of his casks and filling it up with water, he lingered on before a measure of the best, while Nanna and Paoluccio dozed in their chairs; and at last all three were asleep.

Then Regina went out softly into the dark summer night, and climbed the stairs to the attic.

"I am going to take you to Rome to-night," she whispered in Marcello's ear.

"Rome?" he repeated vaguely, half asleep.

She wrapped him in the tattered blanket as he was, and lifted him lightly in her arms. Down the stairs she bore him, and then lifted him upon the tail of the cart, propping him up as best she could, and passing round him the end of one of the ropes that held the casks in place. He breathed more freely in the open air, and she had fed him again before the carters came to supper.

"And you?" he asked faintly.

"I shall walk," she whispered. "Now wait, and make no noise, or they will kill you. Are you comfortable?"

She could see that he nodded his head.

"We shall start presently," she said.

She went into the kitchen, waked Mommo, and made him swallow the rest of his wine. He was easily persuaded that he had slept too long, and must be on the road. The innkeeper and Nanna grumbled a good-night as he went out rather unsteadily, followed by Regina. A moment later the mules' bells jingled, the cart creaked, and Mommo was off.

Paoluccio and his wife made their way to the outer stairs and to bed, leaving Regina to put out the lights and lock up the kitchen. She lost no time in doing this, ran up the steps in the dark, hung the key on its nail in the entry, and went to her attic, making a loud noise with her loose slippers, so that the couple might hear her. She came down again in her stockings almost at once, carrying the slippers and a small bundle containing her belongings. She made no noise now, though it was almost quite dark, and in another instant she was out on the road to Rome. It had all been done so quickly that she could still hear the jingling of Mommo's mule bells in the distance. She had only a few hundred yards to run, and she was walking at the tail of the cart with one hand resting on Marcello's knee as he lay there wrapped up in the ragged blanket.

CHAPTER VII

IT was clear dawn, and there was confusion at the Porta San Giovanni. Mommo had wakened, red-eyed and cross as usual, a little while before reaching the gate, and had uttered several strange noises to quicken the pace of his mules. After that, everything had happened as usual, for a little while; he had stopped inside the walls before the guard-house of the city customs, had nodded to the octroi inspectors, and had got his money ready while the printed receipt was being filled out. Then the excitement had begun.

"You have a passenger," said one, and Mommo stared at him, not understanding.

"You have a dead man on behind!" yelled a small boy, standing at safe distance.

Mommo began to swear, but one of the inspectors stopped him.

"Get down," said the man. "The carabineers are coming."

Mommo finished his swearing internally, but with increased fervour. The small boy was joined by others, and they began to jeer in chorus, and perform war-dances.

"There is a tax on dead men!" they screamed. "You must pay!"

"May you all be butchered!" shouted Mommo, in a voice of thunder. "May your insides be fried!"

"Brute beast, without education!" hooted the biggest boy, contemptuously.

"I'll give you the education, and the instruction too," retorted the carter, making at them with his long whip.

They scattered in all directions, like a flock of cawing jackdaws that fly a little way in tremendous haste, and then settle again at a distance and caw louder than before.

"Animal!" they yelled. "Animal! Animal and beast!"

By this time a crowd had collected round the cart, and two carabineers had come up to see what was the matter, quiet, sensible men in extraordinary cocked hats and well-fitting swallow-tailed uniforms of the fashion of 1810. The carabineers are quite the finest corps in the Italian service, and there are a good many valid reasons why their antiquated dress should not be changed. Their presence means law and order without unnecessary violence.

Mommo was surly, but respectful enough. Yes, it was his cart, and he was a regular carter on the Frascati road. Yes, this was undoubtedly a sick man, who had climbed upon the cart while Mommo was asleep. Of course he had slept on the road, all carters did, and he had no dog, else no one would have dared to take liberties with his cart. No, he had never seen the sick man. The carabineers might send him to penal servitude for life, tear out his tongue, cut off his ears and nose, load him with chains, and otherwise annoy him, but he had never seen the sick man. If he had seen him, he would have pulled him off, and kicked him all the way to the hospital, where he ought to be. What right had such brigands as sick men to tamper with the carts of honest people? If the fellow had legs to jump upon the cart, he had legs to walk. Had Mommo ever done anything wrong in his life, that this should be done to him? Had he stolen, or killed anybody, or tried to evade the octroi duty? No. Then why should an ugly thief of a sick man climb upon his cart? The wretch had hardly clothes enough to cover him decently — a torn shirt and a pair of old trousers that he must have stolen, for they were much too short for him! And so on, and so forth, to the crowd, for the carabineers paid no more attention to him after he had answered their first questions; but the crowd listened with interest, the small boys drew near again, the octroi inspectors looked on, and Mommo had a sympathetic audience. It was the general opinion that he had been outrageously put upon, and that some one had murdered the sick man, and had tied the body to the cart in order that Mommo should be accused of the crime, it being highly likely that a murderer should take so much unnecessary trouble to carry his victim and the evidence of his crime about with him in such a very public manner.

"If he were dead, now," observed an old peasant, who had trudged in with a bundle on his back, "you would immediately be sent to the galleys."

This was so evident that the crowd felt very sorry for Mommo.

"Of course I should," he answered. "By this time to-morrow I should have chains on my legs, and be breaking stones! What is the law for, I should like to know?"

Meanwhile, the carabineers had lifted Marcello very gently from the cart and had carried him into the octroi guard-house, where they set him in a chair, wrapped the ragged blanket round his knees and waist, and poured a little wine down his throat. Seeing that he was very weak, and having ascertained that he had nothing whatever about him by which he could be identified, they sent for the municipal doctor of that quarter of the city.

While they were busy within, one of the inspectors chanced to look at the closed window, and saw the face of a handsome girl pressed against the pane outside, and a pair of dark eyes anxiously watching what was going on. The girl was so very uncommonly handsome that the inspector went out to look at her, but she saw him coming and moved away, drawing her cotton kerchief half across her face. Regina's only fear was that Mommo might recognise her, in which case she would inevitably be questioned by the carabineers. It was characteristic of the class in which she had been brought up, that while she entertained a holy dread of being cross-questioned by them, she felt the most complete conviction that Marcello was safe in their hands. She had meant that he should somehow be taken off the cart at the gate, probably by the inspectors, and conveyed at once to the great hospital near by. She knew nothing about hospitals, and supposed that when he was once there, she might be allowed to come and take care of him. It would be easy, she thought, to invent some story to account for her interest in him. But she could do nothing until Mommo was gone, and he might recognise her figure even if he could not see her face.

Finding that nothing more was wanted of him, and that he was in no immediate danger of penal servitude for having been found with a sick man on his cart, Mommo started his mules up the paved hill towards the church, walking beside them, as the carters mostly do within the city. The crowd dispersed, the small boys went off in search of fresh matter for contemptuous comment, and Regina went boldly to the door of the guard-house.

"Can I be of any use with the sick man?" she asked of the inspector who had seen her through the window.

The inspector prided himself on his gallantry and good education.

"Signorina," he said, lifting his round hat with a magnificent gesture, "if you were to look only once at a dying man, he would revive and live a thousand years."

He made eyes at her in a manner he considered irresistible, and replaced his hat on his head, a little on one side. Regina had never been called "Signorina" before, and she was well aware that no woman who wears a kerchief out of doors, instead of a hat, is entitled to be addressed as a lady in Rome; but she was not at all offended by the rank flattery of the speech, and she saw that the inspector was a good-natured young coxcomb.

"You are too kind," she answered politely. "Do you think I can be of any use?"

"There are the carabineers," objected the inspector, as if that were a sufficient answer. "But you may look in through the door and see the sick man."

"I have seen him through the window. He looks very ill."

"Ah, Signorina," sighed the youth, "if I were ill, I should pray the saints to send you —"

He was interrupted by the arrival of the doctor, who asked him what was the matter, and was at once led in by him. Regina withdrew to a little distance in the direction of the church and waited. The doctor had come in a cab, and in a few moments she saw Marcello carried out and placed in it. Then she walked as fast as she could towards the church, quite sure that the cab would stop at the door of the hospital, and anxious to be within sight of it. Everything had turned out well, even beyond her expectations. The cab passed her at a brisk pace before she reached the top of the hill, and though she walked as fast as she could, it was no longer there when she had gone far enough to see the door. The doctor, who was a busy man, had handed Marcello over to the men on duty at the entrance, with an order he had pencilled on his card while driving up, and had gone on at once. But Regina was convinced that Marcello was there, as she hurried forward.

A man in blue linen clothes and a laced cap stopped her on the steps and asked what she wanted.

"A young man has just been brought here, very ill," she explained, "and I want to see him."

"A very young man? Fair? Thin? From the Campagna? In rags?"

"Yes. I want to see him."

"You can see him to-morrow, if he is alive," answered the orderly in a business-like tone.

"To-morrow?" repeated Regina, in a tone of profound disappointment.

"To-morrow is Sunday. Friends and relatives can visit patients on Sundays between nine and four."

"But he has no other friends," pleaded Regina. "Please, please let me go to him!"

"To-morrow between nine and four."

"No, no — to-day — now — he knows me — my name is Regina."

"Not if you were the Queen of the world," answered the orderly, jesting with perfect calm. "You must have a written order from the Superintendent."

"Yes, yes! Let me see him!"

"You can see him on Mondays between ten and twelve."

"The day after to-morrow?" cried Regina in despair.

"Yes, between ten and twelve, the day after to-morrow."

"But I may come to-morrow without an order?"

"Yes. Friends and relatives can visit patients on Sundays between nine and four."

The man's imperturbability was exasperating, and Regina, who was not patient, felt that if she stayed any longer she should try to take him by the collar, shake him, and force her way in. But she was much too sensible to do anything so rash. There was no choice but to go away.

"Thank you," she said, as she turned to go down the steps.

"You are welcome," the man answered very civilly, for he was watching her and was reflecting that he had never seen such a face and figure before.

Some hours later, when the police communicated with the Superintendent, and when he found that a woman had come to the door who said that she knew the waif, and had been sent away, he called the orderly who had been on duty several hard names in his heart for having followed the rule of the hospital so scrupulously. He was an antediluvian, he was a case of arrested mental development, he was an ichthyosaurus, he was a new kind of idiot, he was a monumental fool, he was the mammoth ass reported to have been seen by a mediæval traveller in the desert, that was forty cubits high, and whose braying was like the blast of ten thousand trumpets. The Superintendent wished he had time to select more choice epithets for that excellent orderly, but the police seemed so particularly curious about the new patient that he had no leisure for thinking out what he wanted.

Nevertheless, the man had done his duty and nothing more nor less according to the rules, and Regina was forced to go away discomfited.

She walked a hundred yards or more down the hill, towards San Clemente, and then stood still to think. The sun had risen, and Marcello was safe, though she could not see him. That was something. She stood there, young, strong, beautiful, and absolutely penniless; and Rome was before her.

For the first time since the previous evening she asked herself what was to become of her, and how she was to find bread for that day and for the next, and for all the days afterwards. She would have robbed a church to feed Marcello, but she would sooner have lost her right hand than steal so much as a crust for herself. As for begging, she was too proud, and besides, no one would have given her anything, for she was the picture of health, her rough clothes were whole and clean, she had tiny gold earrings in her ears, and the red and yellow cotton kerchief on her head was as good as new. Nobody would believe that she was hungry.

Meanwhile Marcello was made comfortable in one of the narrow white beds of an airy ward in the San Giovanni hospital. The institution is intended for women only, but there is now a ward for male patients, who are admitted when too ill to be taken farther. The doctor on duty had written him down as much reduced by malarious fever and wandering in his mind, but added that he might live and get well. It was wonderful, the doctor reflected for the thousandth time in his short experience, that humanity should bear so much as it daily did.

The visiting physician, who was a man of learning and reputation, came three hours later and examined Marcello with interest. The boy had not suffered much by sleeping on the tail of the cart in the warm summer's night, and was now greatly refreshed by the cleanliness and comparative luxury of his new surroundings. He had no fever now and had slept quietly for two hours, but when he tried to remember what had happened to him, where he had been, and how he had come to the place where he was, it all grew vague and intricate by turns, and his memories faded away like the dreams we try to recall when we can only just recollect that we have had a dream of some sort. He knew that he was called Marcello, but the rest was gone; he knew that a beautiful creature had taken care of him, and that her name was Regina. How long? How many days and nights had he lain in the attic, hot by day and cold at night? He could not guess, and it tired him to try.

The doctor asked two or three questions while he examined him, and then stood quite still for a few seconds, watching him intently. The two young house surgeons who accompanied the great man kept a respectful silence, waiting for his opinion. When he found an interesting case he sometimes delivered a little lecture on it, in a quiet monotonous tone that did not disturb the other patients. But to-day he did not seem inclined to talk.

"Convalescent," he said, "at least of the fever. He needs good food more than anything else. In two days he will be walking about."

He passed on, but in his own mind he was wondering what was the matter with the young man, why he had lost his memory, and what accident had brought him alone and friendless to one of the city hospitals. For the present it would be better to let him alone rather than tire him by a thorough examination of his head. There was probably a small fracture somewhere at the back of the skull, the doctor thought, and it would be easy enough to find it when the patient was strong enough to sit up.

The doctor had not been long gone when an elderly man with a grizzled moustache and thoughtful eyes was led to Marcello's bedside by the Superintendent himself. The appearance of the latter at an unusual hour was always an event in the ward, and the nurses watched him with curiosity. They would have been still more curious had they known that the elderly gentleman was the Chief of the Police himself. The Superintendent raised his hand to motion them away.

"What is your name, sir?" asked the Chief, bending down and speaking in a low voice.

"Marcello."

"Yes," replied the other, almost in a whisper, "you are Marcello. But what else? What is your family name? It is very important. Will you tell me?"

The vague look came into Marcello's eyes, and then the look of pain, and he shook his head rather feebly.

"I cannot remember," he answered at last. "It hurts me to remember."

"Is it Consalvi?" asked the officer, smiling encouragement.

"Consalvi?" Marcello's eyes wandered, as he tried to think. "I cannot remember," he said again after an interval.

The Chief of Police was not discouraged yet.

"You were knocked down and robbed by thieves, just after you had been talking with Aurora," he said, inventing what he believed to have happened.

A faint light came into Marcello's eyes.

"Aurora?" He repeated the name almost eagerly.

"Yes. You had been talking to Signorina Aurora dell' Armi. You remember that?"

The light faded suddenly.

"I thought I remembered something," answered Marcello. "Aurora? Aurora? No, it is gone. I was dreaming again. I want to sleep now."

The Chief stood upright and looked at the Superintendent, who looked at him, and both shook their heads. Then they asked what the visiting doctor had said, and what directions he had given about Marcello's treatment.

"I am sure it is he," said the Chief of Police when they were closeted in the Superintendent's office, five minutes later. "I have studied his photograph every day for nearly three months. Look at it."

He produced a good-sized photograph of Marcello which had been taken about a year earlier, but was the most recent. The Superintendent looked at it critically, and said it was not much like the patient. The official objected that a man who was half dead of fever and had lain starving for weeks, heaven only knew where, could hardly be quite himself in appearance. The Superintendent pointed out that this was precisely the difficulty; the photograph was not like the sick man. But the Chief politely insisted that it was. They differed altogether on this point, but quarrelled over it in the most urbane manner possible.

The Superintendent suggested that it would be easy to identify Marcello Consalvi, by bringing people who knew him to his bedside, servants and others. The official answered that he should prefer to be sure of everything before calling in any one else. The patient had evidently lost his memory by some accident, and if he could not recall his own name it was not likely that he could recognise a face. Servants would swear that it was he, or not he, just as their interest suggested. Most of the people of his own class who knew him were out of town at the present season; and besides, the upper classes were not, in the Chief's opinion, a whit more intelligent or trustworthy than those that served them. The world, said the Chief, was an exceedingly bad place. That this was true, the Superintendent could not doubt, and he admitted the fact; but he was not sure how the Chief was applying the statement of it in his own reasoning. Perhaps he thought that some persons might have an interest in recognising Marcello.

"In the meantime," said the Chief, rising to go away, "we will put him in a private room, where we shall not be watched by everybody when we come to see him. I have funds from Corbario to pay any possible expenses in the case."

"Who is that man?" asked the Superintendent. "There has been a great deal of talk about him in the papers since his stepson was lost. What was he before he married the rich widow?"

The Chief of Police did not reply at once, but lit a cigarette preparatory to going away, smoothed his hat on his arm, and flicked a tiny speck of dust from the lapel of his well-made coat. Then he smiled pleasantly and gave his answer.

"I suppose that before he married Consalvi's widow he was a gentleman of small means, like many others. Why should you think that he was ever anything else?"

To this direct question the Superintendent had no answer ready, nor, in fact, had the man who asked it, though he had looked so very wise. Then they glanced at each other and both laughed a little, and they parted.

Half an hour later, Marcello was carried to an airy room with green blinds, and was made even more comfortable than he had been before. He slept, and awoke, and ate and slept again. Twice during the afternoon people were brought to see him. They were servants from the villa on the Janiculum, but he looked at them dully and said that he could not remember them.

"We do not think it is he," they said, when questioned. "Why does he not know us, if it is he? We are old servants in the house. We carried the young gentleman in our arms when he was small. But this youth does not know us, nor our names. It is not he."

They were dismissed, and afterwards they met and talked up at the villa.

"The master has been sent for by telegraph," they said one to another. "We shall do what he says. If he tells us that it is the young gentleman we will also say that it is; but if he says it is not he, we will also deny it. This is the only way."

Having decided upon this diplomatic course as the one most likely to prove advantageous to them, they went back to their several occupations and amusements. But at the very first they said what they really thought; none of them really believed the sick youth at the hospital to be Marcello. An illness of nearly seven weeks and a long course of privation can make a terrible difference in the looks of a very young person, and when the memory is gone, too, the chances of his being recognised are slight.

But the Chief of Police was not disturbed in his belief, and after he had smoked several cigarettes very thoughtfully in his private office, he wrote a telegram to Corbario, advising him to come back to Rome at once. He was surprised to receive an answer from Folco late that night, inquiring why he was wanted. To this he replied in a second telegram of more length, which explained matters clearly. The next morning Corbario telegraphed that he was starting.

The visiting physician came early and examined Marcello's head with the greatest minuteness. After much trouble he found what he was looking for — a very slight depression in the skull. There was no sign of a wound that had healed, and it was clear that the injury must have been either the result of a fall, in which case the scalp had been protected by a stiff hat, or else of a blow dealt with something like a sandbag, which had fractured the bone without leaving any mark beyond a bruise, now no longer visible.

"It is my opinion," said the doctor, "that as soon as the pressure is removed the man's memory will come back exactly as it was before. We will operate next week, when he has gained a little more strength. Feed him and give him plenty of air, for he is very weak."

So he went away for the day. But presently Regina came and demanded admittance according to the promise she had received, and she was immediately brought to the Superintendent's office, for he had given very clear instructions to this effect in case the girl came again. He had not told the Chief of Police about her, for he thought it would be amusing to do a little detective work on his own account, and he anticipated the triumph of finding out Marcello's story alone, and of then laying the facts before the authorities, just to show what ordinary common sense could do without the intervention of the law.

Regina was ushered into the high cool room where the Superintendent sat alone, and the heavy door closed behind her. He was a large man with close-cropped hair and a short brown beard, and he had kind brown eyes. Regina came forward a few steps and then stood still, looking at him, and waiting for him to speak. He was astonished at her beauty, and at once decided that she had a romantic attachment for Marcello, and probably knew all about him. He leaned back in his chair, and pointed to a seat near him.

"Pray sit down," he said. "I wish to have a little talk with you before you go upstairs to see Marcello."

"How is he?" asked Regina, eagerly. "Is he worse?"

"He is much better. But sit down, if you please. You shall stay with him as long as you like, or as long as it is good for him. You may come every day if you wish it."

"Every day?" cried Regina in delight. "They told me that I could only come on Sunday."

"Yes. That is the rule, my dear child. But I can give you permission to come every day, and as the poor young man seems to have no friends, it is very fortunate for him that you can be with him. You will cheer him and help him to get well."

"Thank you, thank you!" answered the girl fervently, as she sat down.

A great lady of Rome had been to see the Superintendent about a patient on the previous afternoon; he did not remember that she moved with more dignity than this peasant girl, or with nearly as much grace. Regina swept the folds of her short coarse skirt forward and sideways a little, so that they hid her brown woollen ankles as she took her seat, and with the other hand she threw back the end of the kerchief from her face.

"You do not mind telling me your name?" said the Superintendent in a questioning tone.

"Spalletta Regina," answered the girl promptly, putting her family name first, according to Italian custom. "I am of Rocca di Papa."

"Thank you. I shall remember that. And you say that you know this poor young man. Now, what is his name, if you please? He does not seem able to remember anything about himself."

"I have always called him Marcello," answered Regina.

"Indeed? You call him Marcello? Yes, yes. Thank you. But, you know, we like to write down the full name of each patient in our books. Marcello, and then? What else?"

By this time Regina felt quite at her ease with the pleasant-spoken gentleman, but in a flash it occurred to her that he would think it very strange if she could not answer such a simple question about a young man she professed to know very well.

"His name is Botti," she said, with no apparent hesitation, and giving the first name that occurred to her.

"Thank you. I shall enter him in the books as 'Botti Marcello.'"

"Yes. That is the name." She watched the Superintendent's pen, though she could not read writing very well.

"Thank you," he said, as he stuck the pen into a little pot of small-shot before him, and then looked at his watch. "The nurse is probably just making him comfortable after the doctor's morning visit, so you had better wait five minutes, if you do not mind. Besides, it will help us a good deal if you will tell me something about his illness. I suppose you have taken care of him."

"As well as I could," Regina answered.

"Where? At Rocca di Papa? The air is good there."

"No, it was not in the village." The girl hesitated a moment, quickly making up her mind how much of the truth to tell. "You see," she continued presently, "I was only the servant girl there, and I saw that the people meant to let him die, because he was a burden on them. So I wrapped him in a blanket and carried him downstairs in the night."

"You carried him down?" The Superintendent look at her in admiration.

"Oh, yes," answered Regina quietly. "I could carry you up and down stairs easily. Do you wish to see?"

The Superintendent laughed, for she actually made a movement as if she were going to leave her seat and pick him up.

"Thank you," he said. "I quite believe you. What a nurse you would make! You say that you carried him down in the night — and then? What did you do?"

"I laid him on the tail of a cart. The carter was asleep. I walked behind to the gate, for I was sure that when he was found he would be brought here, and that he would have care, and would get well."

"Was it far to walk?" inquired the Superintendent, delighted with the result of his efforts as a detective. "You must have been very tired!"

"What is it to walk all night, if one carries no load on one's head?" asked Regina with some scorn. "I walk as I breathe."

"You walked all night, then? That was Friday night. I do not wish to keep you, my dear child, but if you would tell me how long Botti has been ill —" he waited.

"This is the forty-ninth day," Regina answered at once.

"Dear me! Poor boy! That is a long time!"

"I stole eggs and wine to keep him alive," the girl explained. "They tried to make me give him white beans and oil. They wanted him to die, because he was an expense to them."

"Who were those people?" asked the Superintendent, putting the question suddenly.

But Regina had gained time to prepare her story.

"Why should I tell you who they are?" she asked. "They did no harm, after all, and they let him lie in their house. At first they hoped he would get well, but you know how it is in the country. When sick people linger on, every one wishes them to die, because they are in the way, and cost money. That is how it is."

"But you wished him to live," said the Superintendent in an encouraging tone.

Regina shrugged her shoulders and smiled, without the slightest affectation or shyness.

"What could I do?" she asked. "A passion for him had taken me, the first time that I saw him. So I stole for him, and sat up with him, and did what was possible. He lay in an attic with only one blanket, and my heart spoke. What could I do? If he had died I should have thrown myself into the water below the mill."

Now there had been no mill within many miles of the inn on the Frascati road, in which there could be water in summer. Regina was perfectly sincere in describing her love for Marcello, but as she was a clever woman she knew that it was precisely when she was speaking with the greatest sincerity about one thing, that she could most easily throw a man off the scent with regard to another. The Superintendent mentally noted the allusion to the mill for future use; it had created an image in his mind; it meant that the place where Marcello had lain ill had been in the hills and probably near Tivoli, where there is much water and mills are plentiful.

"I suppose he was a poor relation of the people," said the Superintendent thoughtfully, after a little pause. "That is why they wished to get rid of him."

Regina made a gesture of indifferent assent, and told something like the truth.

"He had not been there since I had been servant to them," she answered. "It must have been a long time since they had seen him. We found him early in the morning, lying unconscious against the door of the house, and we took him in. That is the whole story. Why should I tell you who the people are? I have eaten their bread, I have left them, I wish them no harm. They knew their business."

"Certainly, my dear, certainly. I suppose I may say that Marcello Botti comes from Rocca di Papa?"

"Oh, yes," answered Regina readily. "You may say that, if you like."

As a matter of fact she did not care what he wrote in his big book, and he might as well write one name as another, so far as she was concerned.

"But I never saw him there," she added by an afterthought. "There are many people of that name in our village, but I never saw him. Perhaps you had better say that he came from Albano."

"Why from Albano?" asked the Superintendent, surprised.

"It is a bigger place," explained Regina quite naturally.

"Then I might as well write 'Rome' at once?"

"Yes. Why not? If you must put down the name of a town in the book, you had better write a big one. You will be less likely to be found out if you have made a mistake."

"I see," said the Superintendent, smiling. " I am much obliged for your advice. And now, if you will come with me, you shall see Botti. He has a room by himself and is very well cared for."

The orderlies and nurses who came and went about the hospital glanced with a little discreet surprise at the handsome peasant girl who followed the Superintendent, but she paid no attention to them and looked straight before her, at the back of his head; for her heart was beating faster than if she had run a mile uphill.

Marcello put out his arms when he saw her enter, and returning life sent a faint colour to his emaciated cheeks.

"Regina — at last!" he cried in a stronger and clearer tone than she had ever heard him use.

A splendid blush of pleasure glowed in her own face as she ran forward and leaned over him, smoothing the smooth pillow unconsciously, and looking down into his eyes.

The Superintendent observed that Marcello certainly had no difficulty in recalling the girl's name, whatever might have become of his own during his illness. What Regina answered was not audible, but she kissed Marcello's eyes, and then stood upright beside the bed, and laughed a little.

"What can I do?" she asked. "It is a passion! When I see him, I see nothing else. And then, I saved his life. Are you glad that Regina saved your life?" She bent down again, and her gentle hand played with Marcello's waving fair hair. "What should you have done without Regina?"

"I should have died," Marcello answered happily.

With much more strength than she had been used to find in him, he threw his arms round her neck and drew her face down to his.

The Superintendent spoke to the nurse in a low tone, by the door, and both went out, leaving the two together. He was a sensible man, and a kind-hearted one; and though he was no doctor, he guessed that the peasant girl's glorious vitality would do as much for the sick man as any medicine.

CHAPTER VIII

CORBARIO reached Rome in the afternoon, and the footman who stood waiting for him on the platform was struck by the change in his appearance. His eyes were hollow and bright, his cheeks were sunken, his lips looked dry; moreover, he moved a little nervously and his foot slipped as he got out of the carriage, so that he nearly fell. In the crowd, the footman asked his valet questions. Was he ill? What had happened to him? Was he consuming himself with grief? No, the valet thought not. He had been much better in Paris and had seen some old friends there. What harm was there in that? A bereaved man needed diversion. The change had come suddenly, when he had decided to return to Rome, and he had eaten nothing for thirty-six hours. The valet asked if the youth at the hospital, of whom Corbario had told him, were really Marcello. The footman answered that none of the servants thought so, after they had all been taken to see him.

Having exchanged these confidences in the half-dumb language which servants command, they reached the gate. The footman rushed out to call the carriage, the valet delivered the tickets and followed the footman more slowly, carrying Corbario's bag and coat, and Corbario lighted a cigar and followed his man at a leisurely pace, absorbed in thought.

Until the moment of passing the gate he had meant to drive directly to the hospital, which is at some distance from the station in a direction almost opposite to that of the Janiculum. He could have driven there in ten minutes, whereas he must lose more than an hour by going home first and then coming back. But his courage failed him, he felt faint and sick, and quite unable to bear any great emotion until he had rested and refreshed himself a little. A long railway journey stupefies some men, but makes others nervous and inclined to exaggerate danger or trouble. During the last twelve hours Corbario had been forcing himself to decide that he would go to the hospital and know the worst at once, but now that the moment was come he could not do it.

He was walking slowly through the outer hall of the station when a large man came up with him and greeted him quietly. It was Professor Kalmon. Corbario started at the sound of his voice. They had not met since Kalmon had been at the cottage.

"I wish I had known that you were in the train," the Professor said.

"So do I," answered Corbario without enthusiasm. "Not that I am very good company," he added, looking sideways at the other's face and meeting a scrutinising glance.

"You look ill," Kalmon replied. "I don't wonder."

"I sometimes wish I had one of those tablets of

yours that send people to sleep for ever," said Corbario, making a great effort to speak steadily.

But his voice shook, and a sudden terror seized him, the abject fright that takes hold of a man who has been accustomed to do something very dangerous and who suddenly finds that his nerve is gone at the very moment of doing it again.

The cold sweat stood on Folco's forehead under his hat; he stopped where he was and tried to draw a long breath, but something choked him. Kalmon's voice seemed to reach him from a great distance. Then he felt the Professor's strong arm under his own, supporting him and making him move forward.

"The weather is hot," Kalmon said, "and you are ill and tired. Come outside."

"It is nothing," Corbario tried to say. "I was dizzy for a moment."

Kalmon and the footman helped him into his low carriage, and raised the hood, for the afternoon sun was still very hot.

"Shall I go home with you?" Kalmon asked.

"No, no!" cried Corbario nervously. "You are very kind. I am quite well now. Good-bye. Home!" he added to the footman, as he settled himself back under the hood, quite out of sight.

The Professor stood still in the glaring heat, looking after the carriage, his travelling-bag in his hand, while the crowd poured out of the station, making for the cabs and omnibuses that were drawn up in rows, or crossing the burning pavement on foot to take the tram.

When the carriage was out of sight, Kalmon looked up at the hot sky and down at the flagstones, and then made up his mind what to do.

"To the hospital of San Giovanni," he said, as he got into a cab.

He seemed to be well informed, for he inquired at the door about a certain Marcello Botti, who was in a private room; and when he gave his name he was admitted without even asking permission of the Superintendent, and was at once led upstairs.

"Are you a friend of his, sir?" asked Regina, when he had looked a long time at the patient, who did not recognise him in the least.

"Are you?" Kalmon looked at her quietly across the bed.

"You see," she answered. "If I were not, why should I be here?"

"She has saved my life," said Marcello suddenly, and he caught her hand in his and held it fast. "As soon as I am quite well we shall be married."

"Certainly, my dear boy, certainly," replied Kalmon, as if it were quite a matter of course. "You must make haste and get well as soon as possible."

He glanced at Regina's face, and as her eyes met his she shook her head almost imperceptibly, and smiled. Kalmon was not quite sure what she meant. He made a sign to her to go with him to the window, which was at some distance from the bed.

"It may be long before he is well," he whispered. "There must be an operation."

She nodded, for she knew that.

"And do you expect to marry him when he is recovered?"

She shook her head and laughed, glancing at Marcello.

"He is a gentleman," she whispered, close to Kalmon's ear. "How could he marry me?"

"You love him," Kalmon answered.

Again she nodded, and laughed too.

"What would you do for him?" asked Kalmon, looking at her keenly.

"Die for him!"

She meant it, and he saw that she did. Her eyes shone as she spoke, and then the lids drooped a little and she looked at him almost fiercely. He turned from her and his fingers softly tapped the marble window-sill. He was asking himself whether he could swear to Marcello's identity, in case he should be called upon to give evidence. On what could he base his certainty? Was he himself certain, or was he merely moved by the strong resemblance he saw, in spite of long illness and consequent emaciation? Was the visiting surgeon right in believing that the little depression in the skull had caused a suspension of memory? Such things happened, no doubt, but it also happened that doctors were mistaken and that nothing came of such operations. Who could prove the truth? The boy and girl might have a secret to keep; she might have arranged to get him into the hospital because it was his only chance, but the rest of the story, such as it was, might be a pure invention; and when Marcello was discharged cured, they would disappear together. There was the coincidence of the baptismal name, but men of science know how deceptive coincidences can be. Besides, the girl was very intelligent. She might easily have heard about the real Marcello's disappearance, and she was clever enough to have given her lover the name in the hope that he might be taken for the lost boy at least long enough to ensure him a great deal more comfort and consideration in the hospital than he otherwise would have got; she was clever enough to have seen that it would be a mistake to say outright that he was Marcello Consalvi, if she was practising a deception. Kalmon did not know what to think, and he wished the operation could be performed before Corbario came; but that was impossible.

Regina stood beside him, waiting for him to speak again.

"Do you need money?" he asked abruptly, with a sharp look at her face.

"No, thank you, sir," she answered. "He has everything here."

"But for yourself?" He kept his eyes on her.

"I thank you, sir, I want nothing." Her look met his almost coldly as she spoke.

"But when he is well again, how shall you live?"

"I shall work for him, if it turns out that he has no friends. We shall soon know, for his memory will come back after the operation. The doctors say so. They know."

"And if he has friends after all? If he is really the man I think he is, what then? What will become of you?"

"I do not know. I am his. He can do what he likes with me."

The Professor did not remember to have met any one who took quite such an elementary view of life, but he could not help feeling a sort of sympathy for the girl's total indifference to consequences.

"I shall come to see him again," he said presently, turning back towards the bed and approaching Marcello. "Are you quite sure that you never saw me before?" he asked, taking the young man's hand.

"I don't remember," answered Marcello, wearily. "They all want me to remember," he added almost peevishly. "I would if I could, if it were only to please them!"

Kalmon went away, for he saw that his presence tired the patient. When he was gone Regina sat down beside the bed and stroked Marcello's hand, and talked soothingly to him, promising that no one should tease him to remember things. By and by, as she sat, she laid her head on the pillow beside him, and her sweet breath fanned his face, while a strange light played in her half-closed eyes.

"Heart of my heart," she sighed happily. "Love of my soul! Do you know that I am all yours, soul and body, and earrings too?" And she laughed low.

"You are the most beautiful woman in the world," Marcello answered. "I love you!"

She laughed again, and kissed him.

"You love me better than Aurora," she said suddenly.

"Aurora?"

"Yes, for you have forgotten her. But you will not forget Regina now, not even when you are very, very old, and your golden hair is all grey. You will never forget Regina, now!"

"Never!" echoed Marcello, like a child. "Never, never, never!"

"Not even when your friends try to take me away from you, love, not even if they try to kill me, because they want you to marry Aurora, who is a rich girl, all dressed with silk and covered with jewels, like the image of the Madonna at Genazzano. I am sure Aurora has yellow hair and blue eyes!"

"I don't want any one but you," answered Marcello, drawing her face nearer.

So the time passed, and it was to them as if there were no time. Then the door opened again, and a very pale man in deep mourning was brought in by the Superintendent himself. Regina rose and drew back a little, so that the shadow should not fall across Marcello's face, and she fixed her eyes on the gentleman in black.

"This is the patient," said the Superintendent in a low voice.

Corbario laid his hand nervously on his companion's arm, and stood still for a moment, holding his breath and leaning forward a little, his gaze riveted on Marcello's face. Regina had never before seen a man transfixed with fear.

He moved a step towards the bed, and then another, forcing himself to go on. Then Marcello turned his head and looked at him vacantly. Regina heard the long breath Corbario drew, and saw his body straighten, as if relieved from a great burden. He stood beside the bed, and put out his hand to take Marcello's.

"Do you know me?" he asked; but even then his voice was unsteady.

Instead of answering, Marcello turned away to Regina.

"You promised that they should not tease me any more," he said querulously. "Make them go away! I want to sleep."

Regina came to his side at once, and faced the two men across the bed.

"What is all this for?" she asked, with a little indignation. "You know that he cannot remember you, even if he ever saw you before. Cannot you leave him in peace? Come back after the operation. Then he will remember you, if you really know him."

"Who is this girl?" asked Corbario of the Superintendent.

"She took care of him when he had the fever, and she managed to get him here. She has undoubtedly saved his life."

At the words a beautiful blush coloured Regina's cheeks, and her eyes were full of triumphant light; but at the same words Corbario's still face darkened, and as if it had been a mask that suddenly became transparent, the girl saw another face through it, drawn into an expression of malignant and devilish hatred.

The vision only lasted a moment, and the impenetrable pale features were there once more, showing neither hate nor fear, nor any feeling or emotion whatever. Corbario was himself again, and turned quietly to the Superintendent.

"She is quite right," he said. "His memory is gone, and we shall only disturb him. You tell me that the doctors have found a very slight depression in his head, as if from a blow. Do you think — but it will annoy him — I had better not."

"What do you mean?" asked the other, as he hesitated.

"It is such a strange case that I should like to see just where it is, out of pure curiosity."

"It is here," said Regina, answering, and setting the tip of one straight finger against her own head to point out the place.

"Oh, at the back, on the right side? I see — yes — thank you. A little on one side, you say?"

"Here," repeated Regina, turning so that Corbario could see exactly where the end of her finger touched her hair.

"To think that so slight an injury may have permanently affected the young man's memory!" Corbario appeared much impressed. "Well," he continued, speaking to Regina, "if we ever find out who he is, his relations owe you a debt of gratitude quite beyond all payment."

"Do you think I want to be paid?" asked Regina, and in her indignation she turned away and walked to the window.

But Marcello called her back.

"Please, Regina — please tell them to go away!" he pleaded.

Corbario nodded to the Superintendent, and they left the room.

"There is certainly a strong resemblance," said Folco, when they were outside, "but it really cannot be my poor Marcello. I was almost too much affected by the thought of seeing him again to control myself when we first entered, but when I came near I felt nothing. It is not he, I am sure. I loved him as if he were my own son; I brought him up; we were always together. It is not possible that I should be mistaken."

"No," replied the Superintendent, "I should hardly think it possible. Besides, from what the girl has told me, I am quite sure that he lay ill near Tivoli. How is it possible that he should have got there, all the way from the Roman shore?"

"And with a fractured skull! It is absurd!" Corbario was glad to find that the Superintendent held such a strong opinion. "It is not Marcello. The nose is not the same, and the expression of the mouth is quite different."

He said these things with conviction, but he was not deceived. He knew that Marcello Consalvi was living and that he had seen him, risen from the dead, and apparently likely to remain among the living for some time. The first awful moment of anxiety was past, it was true, and Folco was able to think more connectedly than he had since he had received the telegram recalling him from Paris; but there was to be another. The doctors said that his memory would return — what would he remember? It would come back, beginning, most probably, at the very moment in which it had been interrupted. For one instant he would fancy that he saw again what he had seen then. What had he seen? That was the question. Had he seen anything but the sand, the scrubby bushes, and the trees round the cottage in the distance? Had he heard anything but the howling of the southwest gale and the thundering of the big surf over the bar and up the beach? The injury was at the back of his head, but it was a little on one side. Had he been in the act of turning? Had he turned far enough to see before the blow had extinguished memory? How far was the sudden going out of thought really instantaneous? What fraction of a second intervened between full life and what was so like death? How long did it take a man to look round quickly? Much less than a second, surely! Without effort or hurry a man could turn his head all the way from left to right, so as to look over each shoulder alternately, while a second pendulum swung once. A second was a much longer time than most people realised. Instruments made for scientific photography could be made to expose the plate not more than one-thousandth of a second. Corbario knew that, and wondered whether a man's eye could receive any impression in so short a time. He shuddered when he thought that it might be possible.

The question was to be answered sooner than he expected. The doctors had reported that a week must pass before Marcello would be strong enough to undergo the operation, but he improved so quickly after he reached the hospital that it seemed useless to wait. It was not considered to be a very dangerous operation, nor one which weakened the patient much.

Regina was not allowed to be present, and when Marcello had been wheeled out of his room, already under ether, she went and stood before the window, pressing down her clasped hands upon the marble sill with all her might, and resting her forehead against the green slats of the blind. She did not move from this position while the nurse made Marcello's bed ready to receive him on his return. It was long to wait. The great clock in the square struck eleven some time after he had been taken away, then the quarter, then half-past.

Regina felt the blood slowly sinking to her heart. She would have given anything to move now, but she could not stir hand or foot; she was cold, yet somehow she could not even shiver; that would have been a relief; any motion, any shock, any violent pain would have been a thousand times better than the marble stillness that was like a spell.

Far away on the Janiculum Folco Corbario sat in his splendid library alone, with strained eyes, waiting for the call of the telephone that stood on the polished table at his elbow. He, too, was motionless, and longed for release as he had never thought he could long for anything. A still unlighted cigar was almost bitten through by his sharp front teeth; every faculty was tense; and yet it was as if his brain had stopped thinking at the point where expectation had begun. He could not think now, he could only suffer. If the operation were successful there would be more suffering, doubt still more torturing, suspense more agonising still.

The great clock over the stables struck eleven, then the quarter, then half-past. The familiar chimes floated in through the open windows.

A wild hope came with the sound. Marcello, weak as he was, had died under ether, and that was the end. Corbario trembled from head to foot. The clock struck the third quarter, but no other sound broke the stillness of the near noon-tide. Yes, Marcello must be dead.

Suddenly, in the silence, came the sharp buzz of the instrument. He leapt in his seat as if something had struck him unawares, and then, instantly controlling himself, he grasped the receiver and held it to his ear.

"Signor Corbario?" came the question.

"Yes, himself."

"The hospital. The operation has been successful. Do you hear?"

"Yes. Go on."

"The patient has come to himself. He remembers everything."

"Everything!" Corbario's voice shook.

"He is Marcello Consalvi. He asks for his mother, and for you."

"How — in what way does he ask for me? Will my presence do him good — or excite him?"

The moment had come, and Folco's nerve was restored with the sense of danger. His face grew cold and expressionless as he waited for the answer.

"He speaks most affectionately of you. But you had better not come until this afternoon, and then you must not stay long. The doctors say he must rest quietly."

"I will come at four o'clock. Thank you. Good-bye."

"Good-bye."

The click of the instrument, as Folco hung the receiver on the hook, and it was over. He shut his eyes and leaned back in his chair, his arms hanging by his sides as if there were no strength in them, and his head falling forward till his chin rested on his chest. He remained so for a long time without moving.

But in the room at the hospital Marcello lay in bed with his head bound up, his cheek on the pillow, and his eyes fixed on Regina's face, as she knelt beside him and fanned him slowly, for it was hot.

"Sleep, heart of my heart," she said softly. "Sleep and rest!"

There was a sort of peaceful wonder in his look now. Nothing vacant, nothing that lacked meaning or understanding. But he did not answer her, he only gazed into her face, and gazed and gazed till his eyelids drooped and he fell asleep with a smile on his lips.

CHAPTER IX

Two years had passed since Marcello had been brought home from the hospital, very feeble still, but himself again and master of his memory and thoughts.

In his recollection, however, there was a blank. He had left Aurora standing in the gap, where the storm swept inland from the sea; then the light had gone out suddenly, in something violent which he could not understand, and after that he could remember nothing except that he had wandered in lonely places, trying to find out which way he was going, and terrified by the certainty that he had lost all sense of direction; so he had wandered on by day and night, as in a dark dream, and had at last fallen asleep, to wake in the wretched garret of the inn on the Frascati road, with Regina kneeling beside him and moistening his lips from a glass of water.

He remembered that and other things, which came back to him uncertainly, like the little incidents of his early childhood, like the first words he could remember hearing and answering, like the sensation of being on his mother's knee and resting his head upon her shoulder, like the smell of the roses and the bitter-orange blossoms in the villa, like the first sensation of being set upon a pony's back in San Domenico, while Corbario held him up in the saddle, and tried to make his little hands hold the bridle. The inn was quite as far away as all that, and but for Regina he might have forgotten it altogether.

She was "Consalvi's Regina" now; half Rome called her that, and she was famous. Naples and Florence and Milan had heard of her; she had been seen at Monte Carlo, and even in Paris and London her name was not unknown in places where young men congregate to discuss the wicked world, and where young women meet to compare husbands, over the secret and sacrificial teapot which represents virtue, or the less sacred bridge-table which represents vice. Smart young dandies who had never exchanged a word with her spoke of her familiarly as "Regina"; smarter and older men, who knew her a little, talked of her as "the Spalletta," not without a certain respect; their mothers branded her as "that creature," and their wives, who envied her, called her "Consalvi's Regina."

When people remonstrated with Folco Corbario for allowing his stepson too much liberty, he shook his head gravely and answered that he did what he could to keep Marcello in the right way, but that the boy's intellect had been shaken by the terrible accident, and that he had undoubtedly developed vicious tendencies — probably atavistic, Folco added. Why did Folco allow him to have so much money? The answer was that he was of age and the fortune was his. But why had Folco let him have it before he was twenty-one, ever since he was found and brought home? He had not had much, was the reply; at least it had not been much compared with the whole income he now enjoyed; one could not bring up the heir of a great estate like a pauper, could one? So the questioners desisted from questioning, but they said among themselves that, although Folco had been an admirable husband and stepfather while his wife had lived, he had not shown as much good sense after her death as they had been led to expect. Meanwhile, no one had any right to interfere, and Marcello did as he pleased.

Children instinctively attach themselves to whichever of their parents gives them the most liberty. It is sheer nonsense to deny it. Marcello had loved his mother dearly, but she had always been the one to hinder him from doing what he wished to do, because she had been excessively anxious about his bodily health, and over-desirous of bringing him up to manhood in a state of ideal moral perfection. Folco, on the other hand, had been associated with all the boy's sports and pleasures, and had always encouraged him to amuse himself, giving as a reason that there was no medicine like healthy happiness for a boy of delicate constitution. Corbario, like Satan, knew the uses of truth, which are numerous and not all good. Though Marcello would not have acknowledged it to himself, his stepfather had been nearer to him, and more necessary to him, than his mother, during several years; and besides, it was less hard to bear the loss of which he learned when he recovered, because it had befallen him during that dark and uncertain period of his illness that now seemed as if it had lasted for years, and whereby everything that had been before it belonged to a remote past.

Moreover, there was Regina, and there was youth, and there was liberty; and Corbario was at hand, always ready to encourage and satisfy his slightest whim, on the plea that a convalescent must be humoured at any cost, and that there would be time enough to consider what should be done with Regina after Marcello was completely recovered. After all, Corbario told him, the girl had saved his life, and it was only right to be grateful, and she should be amply rewarded for all the trouble she had taken. It would have been sheer cruelty to have sent her away to the country; and what was the cost of a quiet lodging for her in Trastevere, and of a few decent clothes, and of a respectable middle-aged woman-servant to take care of her? Nothing at all; only a few francs, and Marcello was so rich! Regina, also, was so very unusually well-behaved, and so perfectly docile, so long as she was allowed to see Marcello every day! She did not care for dress at all, and was quite contented to wear black, with just a touch of some tender colour. Corbario made it all very easy, and saw to everything, and he seemed to know just how such things were arranged. He was so fortunate as to find a little house that had a quiet garden with an entrance on another street, all in very good condition because it had lately been used by a famous foreign painter who preferred to live in Trastevere, away from the interruptions and distractions of the growing city; and by a very simple transaction the house became the property of the minor, Marcello Consalvi, to do with as he thought fit. This was much more convenient than paying rent to a tiresome landlord who might at any time turn his tenant out. Corbario thought of everything. Twice a week a gardener came, early in the morning, and soon the garden was really pretty; and the respectable woman-servant watered the flowers every evening just before sunset. There was a comfortable Calcutta chair for Marcello in a shady corner, the very first time he came there, and Regina had learned how to make tea for him; for the respectable woman-servant knew how to do all sorts of things belonging to civilised life. She was so intensely respectable and quiet that Marcello was almost afraid of her, until it occurred to him that as she took so much trouble, he ought to give her a present of money; and when he had done this twice, he somehow became aware that she was his devoted slave — middle-aged and excessively respectable. Folco was really a very good judge of character, Marcello thought, since he could at once pick out such a person from the great horde of the unemployed.

Her name was Settimia, and it was wonderful to see how she quietly transformed Regina into a civilised creature, who must attract attention by her beauty and carriage, but who might have belonged to a middle-class Roman family so far as manners and dress were concerned. It is true that the girl possessed by nature the innate dignity of the Roman peasant, with such a figure and such grace as any aristocrat might have envied, and that she spoke with the Roman accent which almost all other Italians admire; but though her manners had a certain repose, they were often of an extremely unexpected nature, and she had an astonishingly simple way of calling things by their names which sometimes disconcerted Marcello and sometimes amused him. Settimia civilised her, almost without letting her know it, for she was quick to learn, like all naturally clever people who have had no education, and she was imitative, as all womanly women are when they are obliged to adapt themselves quickly to new surroundings. She was stimulated, too, by the wish to appear well before Marcello, lest he should ever be ashamed of her. That was all. She never had the least illusion about herself, nor any hope of raising herself to his social level. She was far too much the real peasant girl for that, the descendant of thirty or more generations of serfs, the offspring of men and women who had felt that they belonged body and soul to the feudal lord of the land on which they were born, and had never been disturbed by tempting dreams of liberty, equality, fraternity, and the violent destruction of ladies and gentlemen.

So she lived, and so she learned many things of Settimia, and looked upon herself as the absolute property of the man she loved and had saved; and she was perfectly happy, if not perfectly good.

"When I am of age," Marcello used to say, "I shall buy a beautiful little palace near the Tiber, and you shall live in it."

"Why?" she always asked. "Are we not happy here? Is it not cool in summer, and sunny in winter? Have we not all we want? When you marry, your wife will live in the splendid villa on the Janiculum, and when you are tired of her, you will come and see Regina here. I hope you will always be tired of her. Then I shall be happy."

Marcello would laugh a little, and then he would look grave and thoughtful, for he had not forgotten Aurora, and sometimes wondered what she was doing, as a young man does who is losing his hold upon himself, and on the things in which he has always believed. He who has never lived through such times and outlived them, knows neither the world nor himself.

Marcello wondered whether Aurora would ever meet Regina face to face, and what would happen if he were called upon to choose between the two. He would choose Regina, he said to himself, when he was going down the steep way from the villa to the little house, eager for her touch, her voice, her breath, and feeling in his pocket the key that opened the garden gate. But when the hours had passed, and he slowly walked up the road under the great plane-trees, in the cool of the late evening, glancing at the distant lights of Rome beyond the Tiber, and dimly conscious that something was still unsatisfied, then he hesitated and he remembered his boyish love, and fancied that if he met Aurora in the way they would stand still, each finding the other in the other's eyes, and silently kiss, as they had kissed long ago. Yet, with the thought, he felt shame, and he blushed, alone there under the plane-trees.

But Aurora had never come back to Rome, and the small apartment that overlooked the Forum of Trajan had other tenants. It was strange that the Contessa and her daughter should not have returned, and sometimes Marcello felt a great longing to see them. He said "them" to himself at such times, but he knew what he meant.

So time went on. Corbario said that he himself must really go to San Domenico, to look after the Calabrian property, but added that it would be quite useless for Marcello to go with him. Marcello could stay in Rome and amuse himself as he pleased, or he might make a little journey to the north, to Switzerland, to the Tyrol — there were so many places. Settimia would take care of Regina, and perhaps Regina herself had better make a little trip for a change. Yes, Settimia had travelled a good deal; she even knew enough French to travel in a foreign country, if necessary. Corbario said that he did not know where she had learned French, but he was quite sure she knew it tolerably well. Regina would be safe under her care, in some quiet place where the air would do her good.

Thereupon Corbario went off to the south, leaving Marcello plentifully supplied with money and promising to write to him. They parted affectionately.

"If you wish to go away," Corbario said, as he was leaving, "it might be as well to leave your next address, so that you may get letters. But please don't fancy that I want to know everything you do, my dear boy. You are quite old enough to take care of yourself, and quite sensible enough, too. The only thing you had better avoid for a few years is marriage!"

Folco laughed softly as he delivered this piece of advice, and lit a cigar. Then he looked critically at Marcello.

"You are still very pale," he observed thoughtfully. "You have not got back all your strength yet. Drink plenty of champagne at luncheon and dinner. There is nothing like it when a man is run down. And don't sit up all night smoking cigarettes more than three times a week!"

He laughed again as he shook hands and got into the carriage, and Marcello was glad when he was gone, though he was so fond of him. It was a bore to be told that he was not strong, because it certainly was true, and, besides, even Folco was sometimes a little in the way.

In a week Marcello and Regina were in Venice; a month later they were in Paris. The invaluable Settimia knew her way about, and spoke French with a fluency that amazed Marcello; she even taught Regina a few of those phrases which are particularly useful at a dressmaker's and quite incomprehensible anywhere else. Marcello told her to see that Regina was perfectly dressed, and Settimia carried out his instructions with taste and wisdom. Regina had arrived in Paris with one box of modest dimensions; she left with four more, of a size that made the railway porters stagger.

One day Marcello brought home a string of pearls in his pocket, and tried to fasten it round her throat; but she would not let him do it. She was angry.

"Keep those things for your wife!" she said, with flashing eyes and standing back from him. "I will wear the clothes you buy for me, because you like me to be pretty and I don't want you to be ashamed of me. But I will not take jewels, for jewels are money, just as gold is! You can buy a wife with that stuff, not a woman who loves you!"

Her brows were level and stern, her face grew whiter as she spoke, and Marcello was suddenly aware, for the first time in his life, that he did not understand women. That knowledge comes sooner or later to almost every man, but many are spared it until they are much older than he was.

"I did not mean to offend you," he said, in a rather injured tone, as he slipped the pearls into his pocket.

"Of course not," she answered. "But you do not understand. If I thought you did, I would go back to the inn and never see you again. I should die, but it would not matter, for I should still respect myself!"

"I only wished to please you," said Marcello apologetically.

"You wish to please me? Love me! That is what I want. Love me as much as you can, it will always be less than I love you, and as long as you can, it will always be less long than I shall love you, for that will be always. And when you are tired of me, tell me so, heart of my heart, and I will go away, for that is better than to hang like a chain on a young man's neck. I will go away, and God will forgive me, for to love you is all I know."

His kisses closed her flashing eyes, and her lips parted in a faint, expectant smile, that was not disappointed.

So time passed, and Marcello heard occasionally from Corbario, and wrote to him once or twice, when he needed money. Folco never alluded to Regina, and Marcello wondered whether he guessed that she had left Rome. He was never quite sure how much Folco knew of his life, and Folco was careful never to ask questions.

But the existence Marcello was leading was not calculated to restore his strength, which had never been great, even before his illness. Though Regina did not understand the language, she grew very fond of the theatre, for Marcello translated and explained everything; and it was such a pleasure to give her pleasure, that he forgot the stifling air and the late hours. Moreover, he met in Paris a couple of acquaintances a little older than himself, who were only too glad to see something of the beautiful Regina, so that there were often supper-parties after the play, and trips in motor-cars in the morning, horse races in the afternoon, and all manner of amusements, with a general tendency to look upon sleep as a disease to be avoided and the wish to rest as a foolish weakness. It was true that Marcello never coughed, but he was very thin, and his delicate face had grown perfectly colourless, though he followed Corbario's advice and drank a good deal of champagne, not to mention other less harmless things, because the quick stimulant was as pleasant as a nap and did not involve such a waste of time.

As for Regina, the life suited her, at least for a while, and her beauty was refined rather than marred by a little bodily weariness. The splendid blush of pleasure rarely rose in her cheeks now, but the clear pallor of her matchless complexion was quite as lovely. The constitution of a healthy Roman peasant girl does not break down easily under a course of pleasure and amusement, and it might never have occurred to Regina that Marcello was almost exhausted already, if her eyes had not been opened to his condition by some one else.

They were leaving the Théâtre Français one evening, intending to go home on foot as the night was fine and warm. They had seen *Hernani*, and Regina had naturally found it hard to understand the story, even with Marcello's explanations; the more so as he himself had never seen the play before, and had come to the theatre quite sure that it must be easily comprehensible from the opera founded on it, which he had heard. Regina's arm was passed through his, and as they made their way through the crowd, under the not very brilliant lights in the portico, Marcello was doing his best to make the plot of the piece clear, and Regina was looking earnestly into his face, trying to follow what he said. Suddenly he heard an Italian voice very near to him, calling him by name, in a tone of surprise.

"Marcello!"

He started, straightened himself, turned his head, and faced the Contessa dell' Armi. Close beside her was Aurora, leaning forward a little, with an expression of cold curiosity; she had already seen Regina, who did not withdraw her hand from Marcello's arm.

"You here?" he cried, recovering himself quickly.

As he spoke, the Contessa realised the situation, and at the same moment Marcello met Aurora's eyes. Regina felt his arm drop by his side, as if he were disowning her in the presence of these two smart women who were friends of his. She forgave him, for she was strangely humble in some ways, but she hated them forthwith.

The Contessa, who was a woman of the world, nodded quietly and smiled as if she had seen nothing, but she at once began to steer her daughter in a divergent direction.

"You are looking very ill," she said, turning her head back as she moved away. "Come and see us."

"Where?" asked Marcello, making half a step to follow, and looking at the back of Aurora's head and at the pretty hat she wore.

The Contessa named a quiet hotel in the Rue Saint Honoré, and was gone in the crowd. Marcello stood quite still for a moment, staring after the two. Then he felt Regina's hand slipping through his arm.

"Come," she said softly, and she led him away to the left.

He did not speak for a long time. They turned

under the arches into the Palais Royal, and followed the long portico in silence, out to the Rue Vivienne and the narrow Rue des Petits Champs. Still Marcello did not speak, and without a word they reached the Avenue de l'Opéra. The light was very bright there, and Regina looked long at Marcello's face, and saw how white it was.

"She said you were looking very ill," said she, in a voice that shook a little.

"Nonsense!" cried Marcello, rousing himself. "Shall we have supper at Henry's or at the Café de Paris? We are near both."

"We will go home," Regina answered. "I do not want any supper to-night."

They reached their hotel. Regina tossed her hat upon a chair in the sitting-room and drew Marcello to the light, holding him before her, and scrutinising his face with extraordinary intensity. Suddenly her hands dropped from his shoulders.

"She was right; you are ill. Who is this lady that knows your face better than I?"

She asked the question in a tone of bitterness and self-reproach.

"The Contessa dell' Armi," Marcello answered, with a shade of reluctance.

"And the girl?" asked Regina, in a flash of intuition.

"Her daughter Aurora." He turned away, lit a cigarette, and rang the bell.

Regina bit her lip until it hurt her, for she remembered how often he had pronounced that name in his delirium, many months ago. She could not speak for a moment. A waiter came in answer to the bell, and Marcello ordered something, and then sat down. Regina went to her room and did not return until the servant had come back and was gone again, leaving a tray on the table.

"What is the matter?" asked Marcello in surprise, as he caught sight of her face.

She sat down at a little distance, her eyes fixed on him.

"I am a very wicked woman," she said, in a dull voice.

"You?" Marcello laughed and filled the glasses.

"I am letting you kill yourself to amuse me," Regina said. "I am a very, very wicked woman. But you shall not do it any more. We will go away at once."

"I am perfectly well," Marcello answered, holding out a glass to her; but she would not take it.

"I do not want wine to-night," she said. "It is good when one has a light heart, but my heart is as heavy as a stone. What am I good for? Kill me. It will be better. Then you will live."

"I should have died without you long ago. You saved my life."

"To take it again! To let you consume yourself, so that I may see the world! What do I care for the world, if you are not well? Let us go away quickly."

"Next week, if you like."

"No! To-morrow!"

"Without waiting to hear Melba?"

"Yes — to-morrow!"

"Or Sarah Bernhardt in Sardou's new play?"

"To-morrow! To-morrow morning, early! What is anything compared with your getting well?"

"And your new summer costume that Doucet has not finished? How about that?"

Marcello laughed gaily and emptied his glass. But Regina rose and knelt down beside him, laying her hands on his.

"We must go to-morrow," she said. "You shall say where, for you know what countries are near Paris, and where there are hills, and trees, and waterfalls, and birds that sing, where the earth smells sweet when it rains, and it is quiet when the sun is high. We will go there, but you know where it is, and how far."

"I have no doubt Settimia knows," laughed Marcello. "She knows everything."

But Regina's face was grave, and she shook her head slowly.

"What is the use of laughing?" she asked. "You cannot deceive me, you know you cannot! I deceived myself and was blind, but my eyes are open now, and I can only see the truth. Do you love me, Marcello?"

His eyes looked tired a moment ago, even when he laughed, but the light came into them now. He breathed a little faster and bent forward to kiss her. She could feel the rising pulse in his thin hands. But she leaned back as she knelt, and pressed her lips together tightly.

"Not that," she said, after they had both been motionless ten seconds. "I don't mean that! Love is not all kisses. There is more. There are tears, but there is more too. There is pain, there is doubting, there is jealousy, and more than that! There is avarice also, for a woman who loves is a miser, counting her treasure when others sleep. And she would kill any one who robbed her, and that is murder. Yet there is more, there are all the mortal sins in love, and even then there is worse. For there is this. She will not count her own soul for him she loves, no, not if the saints in Paradise came down weeping and begging her to think of her salvation. And that is a great sin, I suppose."

Marcello looked at her, thinking that she was beautiful, and he said nothing.

"But perhaps a man cannot love like that," she added presently. "So what is the use of my asking you whether you love me? You love Aurora too, I daresay! Such as your man's love is, and of its kind, you have enough for two!"

Marcello smiled.

"I do not love Aurora now," he said.

"But you have, for you talked to her in your fever, and perhaps you will again, or perhaps you wish to marry her. How can I tell what you think? She is prettier than I, for she has fair hair. I knew she had. I hate fair women, but they are prettier than we dark things ever are. All men think so. What does it matter? It was I that saved your life when you were dying, and the people meant you to die. I shall always have that satisfaction, even when you are tired of me."

"Say never, then!"

"Never? Yes, if I let you stay here, you will not have time to be tired of me, for you will grow thinner and whiter, and one day you will be breathing, and not breathing, and breathing a little again, and then not breathing at all, and you will be lying dead with your head on my arm. I can see how it will be, for I thought more than once that you were dead, just like that, when you had the fever. No! If I let that happen you will never be tired of me while you are alive, and when you are dead Aurora cannot have you. Perhaps that would be better. I would almost rather have it so."

"Then why should we go away?" asked Marcello, smiling a little.

"Because to let you die would be a great sin, much worse than losing my soul for you, or killing some one to keep you. Don't you see that?"

"Why would it be worse?"

"I do not know, but I am sure it would. Perhaps because it would be losing your soul instead of mine. Who knows? It is not in the catechism. The catechism has nothing about love, and I never learned anything else. But I know things that I never learned. Every woman does. How? The heart says them, and they are true. Where shall we go to-morrow?"

"Do you really want to leave Paris?"

To impress upon him that she was in earnest Regina squeezed his hands together in hers with such energy that she really hurt him.

"What else have I been saying for half an hour?" she asked impatiently. "Do you think I am playing a comedy?" She laughed. "Remember that I have carried you up and down stairs in my arms," she added, "and I could do it again!"

"If you insist on going away, I will walk," Marcello answered with a laugh.

She laughed too, as she rose to her feet. He put out his hand to fill his glass again, but she stopped him.

"No," she said, "the wine keeps you awake, and makes you think you are stronger than you are. You shall sleep to-night, and to-morrow we will go. I am so glad it is settled!"

She could do what she would with him, and so it turned out that Marcello left Paris without going to see the Contessa and Aurora; and when he was fairly away he felt that it was a relief not to be able to see them, since it would have been his duty to do so if he had stayed another day. Maddalena dell' Armi had not believed that he would come, but she stopped at home that afternoon on the bare possibility. Aurora made up her mind that if he came she would shut herself up in her own room. She expected that he would certainly call before the evening, and was strangely disappointed because he did not.

"Who was that lady with him last night?" she asked of her mother.

"I do not know that — lady," answered the Contessa, with a very slight hesitation before pronouncing the last word.

But they had both heard of Regina already.

CHAPTER X

THE Contessa wrote to Corbario two days later, addressing her letter to Rome, as she did not know where he was. It was not like her to meddle in the affairs of other people, or to give advice, but this was a special case, and she felt that something must be done to save Marcello; for she was a woman of the world, with much experience and few illusions, and she understood at a glance what was happening to her dead friend's son. She wrote to Folco, telling him of the accidental meeting in the portico of the Théâtre Français, describing Marcello's looks, and saying pretty clearly what she thought of the extremely handsome young woman who was with him.

Now Paris is a big city, and it chanced that Corbario himself was there at that very time. Possibly he had kept out of Marcello's way for some reason of his own, but he had really not known that the Contessa was there. Her letter was forwarded from Rome and reached him four days after it was written. He read it carefully, tore it into several dozen little bits, looked at his watch, and went at once to the quiet hotel in the Rue Saint Honoré. The Contessa was alone, Aurora having gone out with her mother's maid.

Maddalena was glad to see him, not because she liked him, for she did not, but because it would be so much easier to talk of what was on her mind than to write about it.

"I suppose you are surprised to see me," said Folco, after the first conventional greeting.

"No, for one may meet any one in Paris, at any time of the year. When I wrote, I thought Marcello must be alone here — I mean, without you," she added.

"I did not know he had been here, until I heard that he was gone. He left three or four days ago. I fancy that when you wrote your letter he was already gone."

"Do you let him wander about Europe as he pleases?" asked the Contessa.

"He is old enough to take care of himself," answered Corbario. "There is nothing worse for young men than running after them and prying into their affairs. I say, give a young fellow his independence as soon as possible. If he has been brought up in a manly way, with a feeling of self-respect, it can only do him good to travel alone. That is the English way, you know, and always succeeds."

"Not always, and besides, we are not English. It is not 'succeeding,' as you call it, in Marcello's case. He will not live long, if you let him lead such a life."

"Oh, he is stronger than he looks! He is no more threatened with consumption than I am, and a boy who can live through what happened to him two years ago can live through anything."

Not a muscle of his face quivered as he looked quietly into the Contessa's eyes. He was quite sure that she did not suspect him of having been in any way concerned in Marcello's temporary disappearance.

"Suppose him to be as strong as the strongest," Maddalena answered. " Put aside the question of his health. There is something else that seems to me quite as important."

" The moral side? " Corbario smiled gravely. " My dear lady, you and I know the world, don't we? We do not expect young men to be saints! "

Maddalena, who had not always been a saint, returned his look coldly.

" Let us leave the saints out of the discussion," she said, "unless we speak of Marcello's mother. She was one, if any one ever was. I believe you loved her, and I know that I did, and I do still, for she is very real to me, even now. Don't you owe something to her memory? Don't you know how she would have felt if she could have met her son the other night, as I met him, looking as he looked? Don't you know that it would have hurt her as nothing else could? Think a moment! "

She paused, waiting for his answer and watching his impenetrable face, that did not change even when he laughed, that could not change, she thought; but she had not seen him by Marcello's bedside at the hospital, when the mask had been gone for a few seconds. It was there now, in all its calm stillness.

"You may be right," he answered, almost meekly,

after a little pause. "I had not looked at it in that light. You see, I am not a very sensitive man, and I was brought up rather roughly. My dear wife went to the other extreme, of course. No one could really be what she wished to make Marcello. He felt that himself, though I honestly did all I could to make him act according to his mother's wishes. But now that she is gone — " he broke off, and was silent a moment. "You may be right," he repeated, shaking his head thoughtfully. "You are a very good woman, and you ought to know."

She leaned back in her chair, and looked at him in silence, wondering whether she was not perhaps doing him a great injustice; yet his voice rang false to her ear, and the old conviction that he had never loved his wife came back with increased force and with the certainty that he had been playing a part for years without once breaking down.

"I will join Marcello, and see what I can do," he said.

"Do you know where he is?"

"Oh, yes! He keeps me informed of his movements; he is very good about writing. You know how fond of each other we are, too, and I am sure he will be glad to see me. He is back in Italy by this time. He was going to Siena. We were to have met in Rome in about a month, to go down to San Domenico together, but I will join him at once."

"If you find that — that young person with him, what shall you do?"

"Send her about her business, of course," answered Folco promptly.

"Suppose that she will not go, what then?"

"It can only be a question of money, my dear lady. Leave that to me. Marcello is not the first young fellow who has been in a scrape!"

Still Maddalena did not trust him, and she merely nodded with an air of doubt.

"Shall I not see Aurora?" he asked suddenly.

"She is out," answered the Contessa. "I will tell her that you asked after her."

"Is she as beautiful as ever?" inquired Folco.

"She is a very pretty girl."

"She is beautiful," Folco said, with conviction. "I have never seen such a beautiful girl as she was, even when she was not quite grown up. No one ever had such hair and such eyes, and such a complexion!"

"Dear me!" exclaimed Maddalena with a little surprise. "I had no idea that you thought her so good-looking!"

"I always did. As for Marcello, we used to think he would never have eyes for any one else."

"Young people who have known each other well as children rarely fall in love when they grow up," answered Maddalena.

"So much the better," Folco said. "Aurora and Marcello are not at all suited to one another."

"That is true," answered the Contessa.

"And besides, he is much too young for her. They are nearly of the same age."

"I never thought of their marrying," replied Maddalena, with a little emphasis, "and I should certainly not choose this time to think of it!"

"I fancy few men can look at your daughter without wishing that they might marry her, my dear lady," said Corbario, rising to go away. "Pray present my homage to her, and tell her how very sorry I am not to have seen her."

He smiled as if he were only half in earnest, and he took his leave. He was scarcely gone when Aurora entered the sitting-room by another door.

"Was it Marcello?" she asked quietly enough, though her voice sounded a little dull.

"No, dear," answered her mother. "It was Folco Corbario. I wrote to him some days ago and he came to see me. Marcello has left Paris. I did not know you had come home."

Aurora sat down rather wearily, pulled out her hatpins, and laid her hat on her knee. Then she slowly turned it round and round, examining every inch of it with profound attention, as women do. They see things in hats which we do not.

"Mamma —" Aurora got no further, and went on turning the hat round.

"Yes? What were you going to say?"

"Nothing — I have forgotten." The hat revolved steadily. "Are we going to stay here long?"

"No. Paris is too expensive. When we have got the few things we want we will go back to Italy — next week, I should think."

"I wish we were rich," observed Aurora.

"I never heard you say that before," answered her mother. "But after all, wishing does no harm, and I am silly enough to wish we were rich too."

"If I married Marcello, I should be very rich," said Aurora, ceasing to turn the hat, but still contemplating it critically.

Maddalena looked at her daughter in some surprise. The girl's face was quite grave.

"You had better think of getting rich in some other way, my dear," said the Contessa presently, with an asperity that did not escape Aurora, but produced no impression on her.

"I was only supposing," she said. "But if it comes to that, it would be much better for him to marry me than that good-looking peasant girl he has picked up."

The Contessa sat up straight and stared at her in astonishment. There was a coolness in the speech that positively horrified her.

"My dear child!" she cried. "What in the world are you talking about?"

"Regina," answered Aurora, looking up, and throwing the hat upon the table. "I am talking about Marcello's Regina. Did you suppose I had never heard of her, and that I did not guess that it was she, the other night? I had a good look at her. I hate her, but she is handsome. You cannot deny that."

"I do not deny it, I'm sure!" The Contessa hardly knew what to say.

"Very well. Would it not be much better for

Marcello if he married me than if he let Regina marry him, as she will!"

"I — possibly — you put it so strangely! But I am sure Marcello will never think of marrying her."

"Then why does he go about with her, and what is it all for?" Aurora gazed innocently at her mother, waiting for an answer which did not come. "Besides," she added, "the girl will marry him, of course."

"Perhaps. I daresay you are right, and after all, she may be in love with him. Why should you care, child?"

"Because he used to be my best friend," Aurora answered demurely. "Is it wrong to take an interest in one's friends? And I still think of him as my friend, though I have never had a chance to speak to him since that day by the Roman shore, when he went off in a rage because I laughed at him. I wonder whether he has forgotten that! They say he lost his memory during his illness."

"What a strange girl you are! You have hardly ever spoken of him in all this time, and now" — the Contessa laughed as if she thought the idea absurd — "and now you talk of marrying him!"

"I have seen Regina," Aurora replied, as if that explained everything.

The Contessa returned no answer, and she was rather unusually silent and preoccupied during the rest of that day. She was reflecting that if Aurora had not chanced to meet Marcello just when Regina was with him the girl might never have thought of him again, except with a half-amused recollection of the little romantic tenderness she had once felt for the friend and playfellow of her childhood. Maddalena was a wise woman now, and did not underestimate the influence of little things when great ones were not far off. That is a very important part of worldly wisdom, which is the science of estimating chances in a game of which love, hate, marriage, fortune, and social life and death may be the stakes.

Her impulse was to prevent Aurora from seeing Marcello for a long time, for the thought of a possible marriage had never attracted her, and since the appearance of Regina on the scene every instinct of her nature was against it. Her pride revolted at the idea that her daughter might be the rival of a peasant girl, quite as much as at the possibility of its being said that she had captured her old friend's son for the sake of his money. But she remembered her own younger years and she judged Aurora by herself. There had been more in that little romantic tenderness for Marcello than any one had guessed, much of it had remained, it had perhaps grown instead of dying out, and the sight of Regina had awakened it to something much stronger than a girlish fancy.

Maddalena remembered little incidents now, of which the importance had escaped her the more easily because the loss of her dearest friend had made her dull and listless at the time. Aurora had scarcely asked about Marcello during the weeks that followed his disappearance, but she had often looked pale and almost ill just then. She had been better after the news had come that he had been found, though she had barely said that she was glad to hear of him. Then she had grown more restless than she used to be, and there had sometimes been a dash of hardness in the things she said; and her mother was now quite sure that Aurora had intentionally avoided all mention of Marcello. To-day, she had suddenly made that rather startling remark about marrying him. All this proved clearly enough that he had been continually in her thoughts. When very young people take unusual pains to ignore a certain subject, and then unexpectedly blurt out some very rough observation about it, the chances are that they have been thinking of nothing else for a long time.

A good deal had happened on that afternoon, for what Corbario had said about Aurora, half playfully and half in earnest, had left Maddalena under the impression that he had been trying a little experiment on his own account, to feel his way. Aurora had more than once said in the preceding years that she did not like his eyes and a certain way he had of looking at her. He had admired her, even then, and now that he was a widower it was not at all unlikely that he should think of marrying her. He was not much more than thirty years old, and he had a singularly youthful face. There was no objection on the score of his age. He was rich, at least for his life-time. He had always been called a model husband while his wife had been alive, and was said to have behaved with propriety since. Maddalena tried to look at the matter coolly and dispassionately, as if she did not instinctively dislike him. Why should he not wish to marry Aurora? No one of the Contessa's acquaintances would be at all surprised if he did, and most people would say that it was a very good match, and that Aurora was fortunate to get such a husband.

This was precisely what Folco thought; and as it was his nature to think slowly and act quickly, it is not impossible that he may have revolved the plan in his mind for a year or two while Aurora was growing up. The final decision had perhaps been reached on that evening down by the Roman shore, when Professor Kalmon had held up to his eyes the sure means of taking the first step towards its accomplishment; and it had been before him late on the same night when he had stood still in the verandah holding the precious and terrible little tablet in the hollow of his hand; and the next morning when he had suddenly seen Marcello close before him, unconscious of his presence and defenceless. He had run a great risk in vain that day, since Marcello was still alive, a risk more awful than he cared to remember now; but it had been safely passed, and he must never do anything so dangerous again. There was a far safer and surer way of gaining his end than clumsy murder, and from what the Contessa had told him of the impression she had received the accomplishment was not far off. She had said that Marcello had looked half dead; his delicate constitution could not bear such a life much longer, and he would soon be dead in earnest.

Marcello did not write as regularly as Folco pretended, but the latter had trustworthy and regular news of him from some one else. Twice a week, wherever he might be, a square envelope came by the post addressed in a rather cramped feminine hand, the almost unmistakable writing of a woman who had seen better days and had been put to many shifts in order to keep up some sort of outward respectability. The information conveyed was tolerably well expressed, in grammatical Italian; the only names contained in the letters were those of towns, and hotels, and the like, and Marcello was invariably spoken of as "our dear patient," and Regina as "that admirable woman" or "that ideal companion." The writer usually said that the dear patient seemed less strong than a month ago, or a week ago, and expressed a fear that he was slowly losing ground. Sometimes he was better, and the news was accompanied by a conventional word or two of satisfaction. Again, there would be a detailed account of his doings, showing that he had slept uncommonly little and had no appetite, and mentioning with a show of regret the sad fact that he lived principally on cigarettes, black coffee, and dry champagne. The ideal companion seemed to be always perfectly well, showed no tendency to be extravagant, and gave proof of the most constant devotion. The writer always concluded by promising that Corbario's instructions with regard to the dear patient should be faithfully carried out in future as they had been in the past.

This was very reassuring, and Folco often congratulated himself on the wisdom he had shown in the selection of Settimia as a maid for Regina. The woman not only did what was required of her with the utmost exactitude; she took an evident pleasure in her work, and looked forward to the fatal result at no very distant time with all the satisfaction which Corbario could desire. So far everything had gone smoothly.

CHAPTER XI

It was high summer again, and the Roman shore was feverish. In the hot afternoon Ercole had tramped along the shore with his dog at his heels as far as Torre San Lorenzo to have a chat with the watchman. They sat in the shade of the tower, smoking little red clay pipes with long wooden stems. The chickens walked about slowly, evidently oppressed by the heat and by a general lack of interest in life, since not a single grain of maize from the morning feed remained to be discovered on the disused brick threshing-floor or in the sand that surrounded it. From some dark recess came the occasional grunt of the pig, attending in solitude to the business of getting fat before October. Now and then the watchman's wife moved a chair in the lower room of the tower, or made a little clatter with some kitchen utensils, and the sounds came out to the solitude sharply and distinctly.

There had been a flat calm for several days. Forty yards below the tower the sea lay along the sandy beach like a strip of glistening white glass, beyond which was a broader band of greenish blue that did not glitter; and beyond that, the oily water stretched out to westward in an unending expanse of neutral tints, arabesqued with current streaks and struck right across by the dazzling dirty-white blaze of the August sun.

Swarms of flies chased each other where the two men sat, settled on their backs and dusty black hats, tried to settle on their faces and were brushed away, crawled on the ground, on the walls, even on the chickens, and on the rough coat of Nino, the dog. He followed the motions of those he saw before him with one bloodshot eye; the other seemed to be fast asleep.

From time to time the men exchanged a few words. Ercole had apparently come over to enjoy the novelty of seeing a human being, and Padre Francesco, the watchman, was glad to talk with some one besides his wife. He enjoyed the title of "Padre," because he had once been master of a small martingane that traded between Città Vecchia and the south. In still earlier days he had been in deep water and had been boatswain of a square-rigger, yet there was nothing about his appearance now to show that he had been a sailor man. It was ten years since he had left the sea, and he had turned into a peasant.

Ercole had told Padre Francesco that the second hay crop had been half spoilt by thunderstorms; also that the price of wine in Ardea had gone up, while the price of polenta had remained the same; also that a wild boar had broken out of the king's preserves near Nettuno and was supposed to be wandering in the brush not far away; also that if

Ercole and Nino found him they would kill him, and that there would be a feast. Padre Francesco observed that his wife understood the cooking of wild boar with vinegar, sugar, pine-nuts, and sweet herbs, and that he himself knew how to salt the hams; he had also salted the flesh of porpoises at sea, more than once, and had eaten pickled dog-fish, which he considered to be nothing but young sharks, in the West Indies. This did not interest Ercole much, as he had heard it before, and he smoked in silence for a while. So did Padre Francesco; and both brushed away the flies. Nino rolled one blood-shot eye at his master, every time the latter moved; and it grew excessively hot, and the air smelt of chickens, rotten seaweed, and the pig. Yet both men were enjoying themselves after a fashion, though Ercole distrusted Padre Francesco, as he distrusted all human beings, and Padre Francesco looked upon Ercole as a person having no knowledge of the world, because he had never eaten pickled dog-fish in the West Indies.

After a time, Padre Francesco remembered a piece of news which he had not yet told, cleared his throat, stirred the contents of his pipe with the point of a dangerous-looking knife, and looked at his companion for a full minute.

"Speak," said Ercole, who understood these premonitory signs.

"There has been one here who asked after you," Padre Francesco began.

"What species of Christian?" inquired Ercole.

"He was at the cottage when the blessed soul of the Signora departed, or just before that. It is a big gentleman with a brown beard and bright eyes. He looks for things in the sand and in the bushes and amongst the seaweed. Who knows what he looks for? Perhaps he looks for gold."

"Or the souls of his dead," suggested Ercole with fine irony. "But I know this Signore who was at the cottage, with the brown beard and the bright eyes. He sometimes came to shoot quail. He also killed some. He is a professor of wisdom."

"He asked if I knew you, but of course I said I did not. Why should he ask? How could I know what he wanted of you. I said that I had never heard of you."

"You did well. Those who have business with me know where to find me. What else did he say?"

"He asked if I had seen the young gentleman this year, and he told me that he had not seen him since the night before he was lost. So then I knew that he was a gentleman of some kind, since he had been at the cottage. I also asked if your masters were never coming to the Roman shore again."

"What did he answer?" inquired Ercole, with an air of utter indifference.

"He said an evil thing. He said that your young gentleman had gone off to foreign countries with a pretty peasant from Frascati, whose name was Regina; that it was she who had nursed him when he was ill, in some inn, and that out of gratitude, and because she was very pretty, he had given her much money, and silk dresses and earrings. That is what he said."

Ercole gazed down at Nino's bloodshot eye, which was turned to him just then.

"A girl called Regina," Ercole grumbled, in a tone even harsher than usual.

"That is what he said. Why should he tell me one thing for another? He said that your young gentleman would perhaps come back when he was tired of Regina. And he laughed. That is all."

A low growl from Nino interrupted the conversation. It was very low and long and then rose quickly and ended in a short bark, as the dog gathered his powerful hindquarters suddenly and raised himself, bristling all over and thrusting his sinewy forepaws out before him. Then the growl began again, but Ercole touched him lightly with the toe of his hobnailed boot, and the dog was instantly silent. Both men looked about, but no one was to be seen.

"There is a boat on the beach," said Padre Francesco, who had caught the faint soft sound of the keel running upon the sand.

They both rose, Ercole picking up his gun as he did so; Nino, seeing that his master was on the alert, slunk to his heels without growling any more. A moment later a man's voice was heard calling on the other side of the tower.

"Hi! Watchman of the tower! A favour! Watchman of the tower! Hi!"

Padre Francesco turned the corner, followed by Ercole. A sailor in scanty ragged clothes and the remains of a rush hat was standing barefoot in the burning sand, with an earthen jug in his hand. A battered boat, from which all traces of paint had long since disappeared, was lying with her nose buried in the sand, not moving in the oily water. Another man was in her, very much like the first in looks.

On seeing Nino at Ercole's heels, the man who was ashore drew back with an exclamation, as if he were going to run away, but Ercole spoke in a reassuring tone.

"Be not afraid," he said. "This dog does not eat Christians. He gets enough to eat at home. He is not a dog, he is a lamb, and most affectionate."

"It is an evil beast," observed the sailor, looking at Nino. "I am afraid."

"What do you desire?" inquired Padre Francesco politely. "Is it water that you wish?"

"As a favour," answered the man, seeing that the dog did not fly at him. "A little water to drink. We have been pulling all day; it is hot, and we have drunk what we had."

"Come with me," said Padre Francesco. "Where is your vessel?"

"At Fiumicino. The master sent us on an errand to Porto d'Anzio last night and we are going back."

"It is a long pull," observed the watchman. "Tell the other man to come ashore and rest in the shade.

I also have been to sea. The water is not very good here, but what there is you shall have."

"Thank you," said the man gratefully, and giving Nino a very wide berth as he followed Padre Francesco. "We could have got some water at the Incastro creek, but it would have been the same as drinking the fever."

"May the Madonna never will that you drink of it," said Padre Francesco, as they reached the shady side of the tower. "I see that you know the Roman shore."

"It is our business," replied the man, taking off his ragged rush hat, and rubbing his still more ragged blue cotton sleeve over his wet forehead. "We are people of the sea, bringing wine and lemons to Cività Vecchia and taking charcoal back. Evil befall this calm weather."

"And when it blows from the west-southwest we say, evil befall this time of storm," said Padre Francesco, nodding wisely. "Be seated in the shade. I will fetch water."

"And also let us drink here, so that we may take the jug away full."

"You shall also drink here." The old watchman went into the tower.

"The last time I passed this way, it was in a west-southwest gale," said the man, addressing Ercole, who had sat down in his old place with his dog at his feet.

"It is an evil shore," Ercole answered. "Many vessels have been lost here."

"We were saved by a miracle that time," said the sailor, who seemed inclined to talk. "I was with a brigantine with wine for Marseilles. That vessel was like a rock in the sea, she would not move with less than seven points of the wind in fair weather. We afterwards went to Rio Janeiro, and it was two years before we got back."

"So it was two years ago that you passed?" inquired Ercole.

"Two years ago May or the beginning of June. She was so low in the water that she would have swamped if we had tried to carry on sail, and with the sail she could carry she could make no headway; so there we were, hove to under lower topsail and balance-reefed mainsail and storm-jib, with a lee shore less than a mile away. We recommended ourselves to the saints and the souls of purgatory, and our captain said to us, 'My fine sons, unless the wind shifts in half an hour we must run her ashore and save the cargo!' That is what he said. But I said that I knew this Roman shore from a boy, and that sometimes there was no bar at the mouth of the Incastro, so that a vessel might just slip into the pool where the reeds grow. You certainly know the place."

"I know it well," said Ercole.

"Yes. So I pointed out the spot to our captain, standing beside him, and he took his glasses and looked to see whether the sea was breaking on the bar."

"The bar has not been open since I came here," said

Padre Francesco, returning with water. "And that is ten years."

The men drank eagerly, one after the other, and there was silence. The one who had been speaking wiped his mouth with the back of his hand and drew a long breath of satisfaction.

"No, I daresay not," he said at last. "The captain looked all along the shore for a better place. Then he saw a bad thing with his glasses; for they were fine glasses, and though he was old, he had good sight. And I stood beside him, and he told me what he saw while he was looking."

"What did he see?" asked Ercole, watching the man.

"What did he see? I tell you it was a bad sight! Health to us all, as many as are here, he saw one man kill another and drag his body into some bushes."

"Apoplexy!" observed Ercole, glancing at Padre Francesco. "Are there brigands here?"

"I tell you what the captain said. 'There are two men,' said he, 'and they are like gentlemen by their dress.' 'They shoot quail,' said I, knowing the shore. 'They have no guns,' said he. Then he cried out, keeping his glasses to his eyes and steadying himself by the weather vang. 'God be blessed,' he cried — for he never said an evil word, that captain, — 'one of those gentlemen has struck the other on the back of the head and killed him! And now he drags his body away towards the bushes.' And he saw nothing more, but he showed me the place, where there is a gap in the high bank. Afterwards he said he thought he had seen a woman too, and that it must have been an affair of jealousy."

Ercole and Padre Francesco looked at each other in silence for a moment.

"Did you hear of no murder at that time?" asked the sailor, taking up the earthen jar full of water.

"We heard nothing," said Ercole promptly.

"Nothing," echoed Padre Francesco. "The captain was dreaming. He saw trees moving in the wind."

"Don Antonino had good eyes," answered the sailor incredulously.

"What was the name of your vessel?" asked Padre Francesco.

"The *Papa*," replied the sailor without a smile. "She was called *Papa*."

Ercole stared at him a moment and then laughed; and he laughed so rarely that it distorted the yellow parchment of his face as if it must crack it. The sound of his laughter was something like the creaking of a cart imitated by a ventriloquist. But Padre Francesco knit his bushy brows, for he thought the sailor was making game of him, who had been boatswain on a square-rigger.

"I went to sea for thirty years," he said, "but I never heard of a vessel called the *Papa*. You have said a silly thing. I have given you water to drink, and filled your jar. It is not courtesy to jest at men older than you."

"Excuse me," answered the man politely. "May

it never be that I should jest at such a respectable man as you seem to be; and, moreover, you have filled the jar with your own hands. The brigantine was called as I say. And if you wish to know why, I will tell you. She was built by two rich brothers of Torre Annunziata, who wished much good to their papa when he was old and no longer went to sea. Therefore, to honour him, they called the vessel the *Papa*. This is the truth."

Lest this should seem extravagantly unlikely to the readers of this tale, I shall interrupt the conversation to say that I knew the *Papa* well, that "she" was built and christened as the sailor said, and that her name still stood on the register of Italian shipping a few years ago. She was not a brigantine, however, but a larger vessel, and she was bark-rigged; and she was ultimately lost in port, during a hurricane.

"We have learned something to-day," observed Ercole, when the man had finished speaking.

"It is true," the man said. "And the name of the captain was Don Antonino Maresca. He was of Vico."

"Where is Vico?" inquired Ercole, idly scratching his dog's back with the stock of his gun.

"Near Castellamare," answered Padre Francesco, willing to show his knowledge.

"One sees that you are a man of the sea," said the sailor, meaning to please him. "And so we thank you, and we go."

Ercole and the old watchman saw the two ragged sailors put off in the battered boat and pull away over the bar; then they went back to the shade of the tower and sat down again and refilled their pipes, and were silent for a long time. Padre Francesco's old wife, who had not shown herself yet, came and stood in the doorway, nodded to Ercole, fanned herself with her apron, counted the chickens in sight, and observed that the weather was hot. Then she went in again.

"It is easy to remember the name of that ship," said Ercole at last, without glancing at his companion.

"And the master was Antonino Maresca of Vico," said Padre Francesco.

"But the truth is that it is none of our business," said Ercole.

"The captain was mistaken," said Padre Francesco.

"He saw trees moving in the wind," said Ercole.

Then they looked at each other and nodded.

"Perhaps the Professor was mistaken about the girl, and the silk dress and the gold earrings," suggested Padre Francesco, turning his eyes away.

"He was certainly mistaken," asserted Ercole, watching him closely. "And moreover it is none of our business."

"None whatever."

They talked of other things, making remarks at longer and longer intervals, till the sun sank near the oily sea, and Ercole took his departure, much wiser in regard to Marcello's disappearance than when he had come. He followed the long beach for an hour till he came to the gap in the bank. There he stopped, and proceeded to examine the place carefully, going well inside it, and then turning to ascertain exactly where Marcello must have been when he was struck, since at that moment he must have been distinctly visible from the brigantine. The gap was so narrow that it was not hard to fix upon the spot where the deed had been done, especially as the captain had seen Marcello dragged quickly away towards the bushes. Every word of the sailor's story was stamped with truth; and so it came about that when Corbario believed himself at last quite safe, a man in his own pay suddenly discovered the whole truth about the attempted crime, even to the name of the principal witness.

It was only in the quail season, when there were poachers about, during April, May, and early June, that Ercole lived in his straw hut, a little way from the cottage. He spent the rest of the year in a small stone house that stood on a knoll in sight of Ardea, high enough to be tolerably safe from the deadly Campagna fever. Every other day an old woman from the village brought him a copper conca full of water; once a month she came and washed for him. When he needed supplies he went to Ardea for them himself. His dwelling was of elementary simplicity, consisting of two rooms, one above the other, with grated windows and heavy shutters. In the lower one he cooked and ate, in the upper chamber he slept and kept his few belongings, which included a plentiful supply of ammunition, his Sunday clothes, his linen, and his papers. The latter consisted of a copy of his certificate of birth, his old military pass-book, showing that he had served his time in an infantry regiment, had been called in for six weeks' drill in the reserve, had been a number of years in the second reserve, and had finally been discharged from all military service. This booklet serves an Italian throughout life as a certificate of identity, and is necessary in order to obtain a passport to leave the country. Ercole kept his, with two or three other yellow papers, tied up in an old red cotton handkerchief in the bottom of the chest that held his clothes.

When he got home after his visit to Padre Francesco he took the package out, untied the handkerchief, and looked through all the papers, one by one, sitting by the grated window in the twilight. He could read, and had once been able to write more or less intelligibly, and he knew by heart the contents of the paper he wanted, though he had not unfolded it for years. He now read it carefully, and held it some time open in his hand before he put it back with the rest. He held it so long, while he looked out of his grated window, that at last he could see the little lights twinkling here and there in the windows of Ardea, and it was almost dark in the room. Nino grew restless, and laid his grim head on Ercole's knee, and his bloodshot eyes began to glow in the dark like coals. Then Ercole moved at last.

"Ugly animal, do you wish me well?" he asked, rubbing the dog's head with his knotty hand. "If you are good, you shall go on a journey with me."

Nino's body moved in a way which showed that he

would have wagged his tail if he had possessed one, and he uttered a strange gurgling growl of satisfaction.

The next morning, the old woman came before sunrise with water.

"You need not bring any more, till I let you know," Ercole said. "I am going away on business for a few days, and I shall shut up the house."

"For anything that is in it, you might leave the door open," grumbled the hag, who was of a sour temper. "Give me my pay before you go."

"You fear that I am going to America," retorted Ercole, producing an old sheepskin purse from the inside of his waistcoat. "Here is your money. Four trips, four pennies. Count them and go in peace."

He gave her the coppers, and she carefully tied them up in a corner of her ragged kerchief.

"And the bread?" she asked anxiously.

Ercole went to the blackened cupboard, took out the remains of a stale loaf, drew a big clasp-knife from his pocket, and cut off a moderate slice.

"Eat," he said, as he gave it to her.

She went away grumbling, and Nino growled after her, standing on the door-step. When she was a hundred yards from the house, he lay down with his jaw on his forepaws and continued to watch her till she was out of sight; then he gave a snort of satisfaction and immediately went to sleep.

Ercole left his home after sunset that evening. He locked both the upper and lower doors and immediately dropped the huge key into a crevice in the stone steps, from which one might have supposed that it would not be easy to recover it; but he doubtless knew what he was about. He might have had one of the little horses from the farm if he had wanted one, for he was a privileged person, but he preferred to walk. To a man of his wiry frame thirty or forty miles on foot were nothing, and he could easily have covered the distance in a night; but he was not going so far, by any means, and a horse would only have been in the way. He carried his gun, from force of habit, and he had his gun-licence in his pocket, with his other papers, tied up in the old red handkerchief. There was all that was left of the stale loaf, with the remains of some cheese, in a canvas bag, he had slung over his shoulder, and he had plenty of money; for his wages were good, and he never spent more than half of what he received, merely because he had no wants, and no friends.

Under the starlight he walked at a steady pace by familiar paths and byways, so as to avoid the village and strike the highroad at some distance beyond it. Nino followed close at his heels and perfectly silent, and the pair might have been dangerous to any one inclined to quarrel with them.

When Ercole was in sight of Porta San Sebastiano it was past midnight, and he stood still to fill and light his little clay pipe. Then he went on; but instead of entering the gate he took the road to the right again, along the Via Appia Nuova. Any one might have supposed that he would have struck across to that highroad some time before reaching the city, but it was very long since Ercole had gone in that direction; many new roads had been opened and some old ones had been closed, and he was simply afraid of losing his way in a part of the Campagna no longer familiar to him.

A short distance from the gate, where the inn stands that goes by the name of Baldinotti, he took the turning to the left, which is the Frascati road; and after that he walked more slowly, often stopping and peering into the gloom to right and left, as if he were trying to recognise objects in the Campagna.

CHAPTER XII

CORBARIO was not pleased with the account given by Settimia in the letter she wrote him after reaching Pontresina with Regina and Marcello, who had chosen the Engadine as the coolest place he could think of in which to spend the hot months, and had preferred Pontresina to Saint Moritz as being quieter and less fashionable. Settimia wrote that the dear patient had looked better the very day after arriving; that the admirable companion was making him drink milk and go to bed at ten o'clock; that the two spent most of the day in the pine-woods, and that Marcello already talked of an excursion up the glacier and of climbing some of the smaller peaks. If the improvement continued, Settimia wrote, it was extremely likely that the dear patient would soon be better than he had ever been in his life.

Folco destroyed the letter, lit a cigarette, and thought the matter over. He had deemed it wise to pretend assent when the Contessa had urged him to join Marcello at once, but he had not had the least intention of doing so, and had come back to Paris as soon as he was sure that the Contessa was gone. But he had made a mistake in his calculations. He had counted on Regina for the love of excitement, display, and inane dissipation which women in her position very often develop when they find that a man will give them anything they like ; and he had counted very little on her love for Marcello. Folco was still young enough to fall into one of the most common errors of youth, which is to believe most people worse than they are. Villains, as they grow older, learn that unselfish devotion is more common than they had thought, and that many persons habitually speak the truth for conscience' sake ; finding this out, villains have been known to turn into good men in their riper years, and have sometimes been almost saints in their old age. Corbario smoked his cigarette and mentally registered his mistake, and it is to be feared that the humiliation he felt at having made it was much more painful than the recollection of having dropped one deadly tablet into a little bottle that contained many harmless ones. He compared it in his mind to the keen disappointment he had felt when he had gone down to hide Marcello's body, and had discovered that he had failed to kill him. It is true that what he had felt then had been accompanied by the most awful terror he could imagine, but he distinguished clearly between the one sensation and the other. There was nothing to fear now ; he had simply lost time, but that was bad enough, since it was due to his own stupidity.

He thought over the situation carefully and considered how much it would be wise to risk. Another year of the life Marcello had been leading in Paris would have killed him to a certainty; perhaps six months would have done it. But a summer spent at Pontresina, living as it was clear that Regina meant him to live, would give the boy strength enough to last much longer, and might perhaps bring him out of all danger.

Corbario considered what might be done, went over many plans in his mind, compared many schemes, for the execution of some of which he might have paid dearly; and in the end he was dissatisfied with all, and began over again. Still he reached no conclusion, and he attributed the fault to his own dulness, and his dulness to the life he had been leading of late, which was very much that which he wished Marcello to lead. But he had always trusted his nerves, his ingenuity, and his constitution; if one of the three were to fail him, now that he was rich, it was better that it should be his ingenuity.

He made up his mind to go to the Engadine and see for himself how matters looked. He could stay at Saint Moritz, or even Samaden, so as not to disturb Marcello's idyl, and Marcello could come down alone to see him. He should probably meet acquaintances, and would give them to understand that he had come in order to get rid of Regina and save his stepson from certain destruction. Society was very lenient to young men as rich as Marcello, he reflected, but was inclined to lay all the blame of their doings on their natural guardians. There was no reason why Corbario should expose himself to such criticism, and he was sure that the Contessa had only said what many people clearly thought, namely, that he was allowing Marcello far too much liberty. The world should see that he was doing his duty by the boy.

He left Paris with regret, as he always did, after writing to Marcello twenty-four hours beforehand. He wrote at the same time to Settimia.

"Folco will be here to-morrow," Marcello said, as he and Regina sat under the pine-trees beyond the stream, a little way above the town.

Regina sat leaning against the trunk of a tree, and Marcello lay on his side, resting on his elbow and looking up to her. He saw her face change.

"Why should he come here?" she asked. "We are so happy!"

"He will not disturb us," Marcello answered. "He will stop at Saint Moritz. I shall go down to see him there. I am very fond of him, you know, and we have not seen each other for at least two months. I shall be very glad to see him."

The colour was sinking in Regina's face, and her eyelids were almost closed.

"You are the master," she said quietly enough. "You will do as you will."

He was surprised, and he felt a little resentment at her tone. He liked her better when she dominated him, as on that night in Paris when she had made him promise to come away, and had refused to let him drink more wine, and had sent him to bed like a child. Now she spoke as her forefathers, serfs born to the plough and bound to the soil, must have spoken to their lords and owners. There was no ancient aristocratic blood in his own veins; he was simply a middle-class Italian gentleman who chanced to be counted with the higher class because he had been born very rich, had been brought up by a lady, and had been more or less well educated. That was all. It did not seem natural to him that she should call him "the master" in that tone. He knew that she was not his equal, but somehow it was a little humiliating to have to own it, and he often wished that she were. Often, not always; for he had never been sure that he should have cared to make her his wife, had she been ever so well born. He scarcely knew what he really wanted now, for he had lost his hold on himself, and was content with mere enjoyment from day to day. He could no longer imagine living without her, and while he was conscious that the present state of things could not last very long, he could not face the problem of the future.

He did not answer at once, and she sat quite still, almost closing her eyes.

"Why should you be displeased because I am going to see Folco?" he asked after a while.

"He comes to take you away from me," she answered, without moving.

"That is absurd!" cried Marcello, annoyed by her tone.

"No. It is true. I know it."

"You are unreasonable. He is the best friend I have in the world. Do you expect me to promise that I will never see him again?"

"You are the master."

She repeated the words in the same dull tone, and her expression did not change in the least. Marcello moved and sat up opposite to her, clasping his hands round his knees. He was very thin, but the colour was already coming back to his face, and his eyes did not look tired.

"Listen to me," he said. "You must put this idea out of your head. It was Folco who found the little house in Trastevere for you. He arranged everything. It was he who got you Settimia. He did everything to make you comfortable, and he has never disturbed us once when we have been together. He never so much as asked where I was going when I used to go down to see you every afternoon. No friend could have done more."

"I know it," Regina answered; but still there was something in her tone which he could not understand.

"Then why do you say that he means to separate us?"

Regina did not reply, but she opened her eyes and looked into Marcello's long and lovingly. She knew something that he did not know, and which had haunted her long. When Folco had come to the bedside in the hospital, she had seen the abject terror in his face, the paralysing fear in his attitude, the trembling limbs and the cramped fingers. It had only lasted a moment, but she could never forget it. A child would have remembered how Folco looked then, and Regina knew that there was a mystery there which she could not understand, but which frightened her when she thought of it. Folco had not looked as men do who see one they love called back from almost certain death.

"What are you thinking?" Marcello asked, for her deep look stirred his blood, and he forgot Folco and everything in the world except the beautiful creature that sat there, within his reach, in the lonely pine-woods.

She understood, and turned her eyes to the distance; and she saw the quiet room in the hospital, the iron bedstead painted white, the smooth pillow, Marcello's emaciated head, and Corbario's face.

"I was thinking how you looked when you were ill," she answered simply.

The words and the tone broke the soft little spell that had been weaving itself out of her dark eyes. Marcello drew a short, impatient breath and threw himself on his side again, supporting his head on his hand and looking down at the brown pine-needles.

"You do not know Folco," he said discontentedly. "I don't know why you should dislike him."

"I will tell you something," Regina answered. "When you are tired of me, you shall send me away. You shall throw me away like an old coat."

"You are always saying that!" returned Marcello, displeased. "You know very well that I shall never be tired of you. Why do you say it?"

"Because I shall not complain. I shall not cry, and throw myself on my knees, and say, 'For the love of heaven, take me back!' I am not made like that.

I shall go, without any noise, and what must be will be. That is all. Because I want nothing of you but love, I shall go when you have no more love. Why should I ask you for what you have not? That would be like asking charity of the poor. It would be foolish. But I shall tell you something else."

"What?" asked Marcello, looking up to her face again, when she had finished her long speech.

"If any one tries to make me go before you are tired of me, it shall be an evil day for him. He shall wish that he had not been born into this world."

"You need not fear," Marcello said. "No one shall come between us."

"Well, I have spoken. It does not matter whether I fear Signor Corbario or not, but if you like I will tell him what I have told you, when he comes. In that way he will know."

She spoke quietly, and there was no murderous light in her eyes, nor any dramatic gesture with the words; but she was a little paler than before, and there was an odd fixedness in her expression, and Marcello knew that she was deeply moved, by the way she fell back into her primitive peasant's speech, not ungrammatical, but oddly rough and forcible compared with the language of educated society which she had now learned tolerably well from him.

After that she was silent for a while, and then they talked as usual, and the day went by as other days had gone.

On the next afternoon Folco Corbario reached Saint

Moritz and sent a note up to Marcello asking him to come down on the following morning.

Regina was left alone for a few hours, and she went out with the idea of taking a long walk by herself. It would be a relief and almost a pleasure to walk ten miles in the clear air, breathing the perfume of the pines and listening to the roar of the torrent. Marcello could not walk far without being tired, and she never thought of herself when he was with her; but when she was alone a great longing sometimes came over her to feel the weight of a conca full of water on her head, to roll up her sleeves and scrub the floors, to carry burdens and work with her hands all day long, as she had done ever since she was a child, with the certainty of being tired and hungry and sleepy afterwards. Her hands had grown smooth and white in a year, and her feet were tender, and she had almost forgotten what bodily weariness meant.

But she was alone this morning, and she was full of gloomy presentiments. To stay indoors, or even to go and sit in the accustomed place under the pine-trees, would be unbearable. She felt quite sure that when Marcello came back he would be changed, that his expression would be less frank and natural, that he would avoid her eyes, and that by and by he would tell her something that would hurt her very much. Folco had come to take him away, she was quite sure, and it would be intolerable to sit still and think of it.

She walked fast along the road that leads to the Rosegg glacier, not even glancing at the few people she met, though most of them stared at her, for almost every one in Pontresina knew who she was. The reputation of a great beauty is soon made, and Regina had been seen often enough in Paris alone with Marcello in a box at the theatre, or dining with him and two or three other young men at Ritz's or the Café Anglais, to be an object of interest to the clever Parisian "chroniclers." The papers had duly announced the fact that the beauty had arrived at Pontresina, and the dwellers in the hotel were delighted to catch a glimpse of her, while those at Saint Moritz wished that she and Marcello had taken up their quarters there instead of in the higher village. Old maids with shawls and camp-stools glared at her round the edge of their parasols. English girls looked at her in frank admiration, till they were reproved by their mothers, who looked at her with furtive interest. Young Englishmen pretended not to see her at all, as they strode along with their pipes in their mouths; but they had an odd habit of being about when she passed. An occasional party of German students, who are the only real Bohemians left to the world in these days of progress, went sentimentally mad about her for twenty-four hours, and planned serenades in her honour which did not come off. A fashionable Italian composer dedicated a song to her, and Marcello asked him to dinner, for which he was more envied by the summer colony than for his undeniable talent. The Anglican clergyman declared that he would preach a sermon against her wickedness, but the hotel-keepers heard of his intention and unanimously requested him to let her alone, which he did, reluctantly yielding to arguments which shall remain a secret. A certain Archduchess who was at Saint Moritz and was curious to see her adopted the simple plan of asking her to tea without knowing her, at which Marcello was furious; a semi-imperial Russian personage unblushingly scraped acquaintance with Marcello and was extremely bland for a few days, in the hope of being introduced to Regina. When he found that this was impossible, he went away, not in the least disconcerted, and he was heard to say that the girl " would go far."

Regina would have been blind if she had not been aware that she attracted all this attention, and as she was probably not intended by nature for a saint, she would have been pleased by it if there had been room in her thoughts for any one but Marcello — even for herself.

She walked far up the road, and after the first mile or two she met no one. At that hour the people who made excursions were already far away, and those who meant to do nothing stayed nearer to Pontresina. She grew tired of the road after a time. It led straight to the foot of the glacier, and she was not attracted by snow and ice as northern people are; there was something repellent to her in the thought of the bleakness and cold, and the sunshine itself looked as hard as the distant peaks on which it fell. But on the right there were rocky spurs of the mountains, half covered with short trees and brilliant with wild flowers that grew in little natural gardens here and there, not far below the level of perpetual snow. She left the road, and began to climb where there was no path. The air was delicious with the scent of flowers and shrubs; there were alp-roses everywhere, and purple gentian, and the little iva blossom that has an aromatic smell, and on tiny moss ledges the cold white stars of the edelweiss seemed to be keeping themselves as far above reach as they could. But she climbed as lightly as a savage woman, and picked them and sat down to look at them in the sunshine. Just beyond where she rested, the rock narrowed suddenly to a steep pass, within which were dark shadows. People who do not attempt anything in the way of ascending peaks often wander in that direction in search of edelweiss, but Regina fancied that she was sure to be alone as long as she pleased to stay.

If she had not been sure of that she would not have taken off her left shoe to shake out some tiny thing that had got into it and that annoyed her. It turned out to be a bit of pine-needle. It was pleasant to feel her foot freed from the hot leather and resting on the thick moss, and so the other shoe came off too, and was turned upside down and shaken, as an excuse, for there was nothing in it, and both feet rested in the moss, side by side. She wished she could take off her stockings, and if there had been a stream she would have done it, so sure was she that no one would disturb her, up there amongst the rocks and ever so far from Pontresina. It would have been delightful to paddle in the cold running water, for it was much hotter than she had ever supposed that it could be in such a place.

She took off her straw hat, and fanned herself gently with it, letting the sunshine fall full upon her thick black hair. She had never owned a hat in her life till she had been installed in the little house in Trastevere, and she hated the inconvenient things. What was her hair for, if it could not protect her head? But a straw hat made a very good fan. The air was hot and still, and there were none of those thousand little sounds which she would have heard in the chestnut woods above Frascati.

A little cry broke the silence, and she turned her head in the direction whence it came. Then she dropped her hat, sprang to her feet, and ran forwards, forgetting that she had no shoes on. She saw a figure clinging to the rocks, where they suddenly narrowed, and she heard the cry again, desperate with fear and weak with effort. A young girl had evidently been trying to climb down, when she had lost her footing, and had only been saved from a bad fall because her grey woollen frock had caught her upon a projecting point of granite, giving her time to snatch at the strong twigs of some alp-roses, and to find a very slight projection on which she could rest the toe of one shoe. She was hanging there with her face to the rock, eight or ten feet from the ground, which was strewn with big stones, and she was in such a position that she seemed unable to turn her head in order to look down.

In ten seconds Regina was standing directly below

the terrified girl, raising herself on tiptoe, and trying to reach her feet with her hands, to guide them to a hold; but she could not.

"Don't be frightened," Regina said in Italian, which was the only language she knew.

"I cannot hold on!" answered the girl, trying to look down, but feeling that her foot would slip if she turned her head far enough.

"Yes, you can," Regina replied, too much roused to be surprised that the answer had come in her own language. "Your dress will hold you, even if you let go with your hands. It is new and it is strong, and it is fairly caught on the rock. I can see that."

"But I can't hang here until you go and get help," cried the girl, not much reassured.

"I am going to climb to the top by an easier way and pull you up again," Regina answered. "Then we can get down together."

While Regina was speaking she had already begun the ascent, which was easy enough for her, at the point she had chosen, though many an Alpine climber might have envied the quickness and sureness of her hold with feet and hands. She realised that she had forgotten her shoes now, and was glad that she had taken them off.

"One minute more!" she cried in an encouraging tone, when she had almost reached the top.

"Quick!" came the imploring answer.

Then Regina was lying flat on the ledge above the girl, stretching both hands down and catching the slender white wrists with a hold like steel. And then, feeling herself held and safe to move, the girl looked up, and Regina was looking into Aurora's face below her. For one instant the two did not recognise each other, for they had only seen each other once, by night, under the portico of the Théâtre Français. But an instant later a flush of anger rose to Aurora's forehead, and the dark woman turned pale, and her brows were suddenly level and stern. They hated each other, as the one hung there held by the other's hands, and the black eyes gazed savagely into the angry blue ones. Aurora was not frightened any longer; she was angry because she was in Regina's power. The strong woman could save her if she would, and Aurora would despise herself ever afterwards for having been saved by her. Or the strong woman could let her fall, and she would probably be maimed for life if she were not killed outright. That seemed almost better. She had never understood before what it could mean to be altogether in the power of an enemy.

Regina meant to save her; that was clear. With quick, commanding words she told her what to do.

"Set your knees against the rock and pull yourself up a little by my hands. So! I can pull you higher now. Get one knee well on that ledge. Now I will hold your left hand with both mine while you disentangle your frock from the point. Now put your right hand round my neck while I raise myself a little. Yes, that way. Now, hold on tight!"

Regina made a steady effort, lifting fully half

Aurora's weight with her, as she got first upon one knee and then upon both.

"There! Take breath and then scramble over the edge," she said.

A few seconds, another effort, and Aurora sank exhausted beside Regina, half sitting, half lying, and resting on one hand.

She looked up sideways at the dark woman's face; for Regina stood upright, gazing down into the valley. Aurora turned her eyes away, and then looked up again; she had recovered her breath now.

"Thank you," she said, with an effort.

"It is nothing," Regina answered in an indifferent tone, and without so much as moving her head; she was no more out of breath than if she had been sitting still.

The fair girl hated her at that moment as she had never hated any one in her short life, nor had ever dreamed of hating. The flush of anger rose again and again to her forehead, to the very roots of her auburn hair, and lingered a second and sank again. Regina stood perfectly motionless, her face as unchanging as marble.

Aurora rose to her feet, and leaned against the rock. She had suddenly felt herself at a disadvantage in remaining seated on the ground while her adversary was standing. It was the instinct of the animal that expects to be attacked. When two people who hate each other or love each other very much meet without warning in a very lonely place, the fierce old passions of the stone age may take hold of them and sway them, even nowadays.

For a time that seemed long, there was silence; without words each knew that the other had recognised her. The peasant woman spoke first, though with an evident effort, and without turning her eyes.

"When you are rested, we will go down," she said.

Aurora moved a step towards the side on which Regina had climbed up.

"I think I can get down alone," she answered coldly.

Regina looked at her and laughed with a little contempt.

"You will break your neck if you try," she said. "You cannot climb at all!"

"I think I can get down," Aurora repeated.

She went to the edge and was going to begin the attempt when Regina seized her by the wrist and dragged her back in spite of her resistance.

"I have something to tell you first," Regina said. "Afterwards I will take you down, and you shall not fall. You shall reach the bottom safely and go home alone, or I will show you the way, as you please."

"Let go of my wrist!" Aurora spoke angrily, for the strong grasp hurt her and humiliated her.

"Listen to me," continued Regina, loosing her hold at once. "I am Regina. You are Aurora. We have heard of each other, and we have met. Let us talk.

This is a good place and we are alone, and the day is long, and we may not meet again soon. We will say what we have to say now, and then we will part."

"What is there to be said?" Aurora asked coldly and drawing back a little.

"We two love the same man," Regina said. "Is that nothing? You know it is true. If we were not Christians we should try to kill each other here, where it is quiet. I could easily have killed you just now, and I wished to."

"I wonder why you did not!" exclaimed Aurora, rather scornfully.

"I thought with myself thus: 'If I kill her, I shall always have the satisfaction of it as long as I live. This is the truth. But I shall go to prison for many years and shall not see him again, therefore I will not do it. Besides, it will not please him. If it would make him happy I would kill her, even if I were to go to the galleys for it. But it would not. He would be very angry.' This is what I thought; and I pulled you up. And now, I will not let you hurt yourself in getting down, because he would be angry with me if he knew that it was my fault."

Aurora listened to this extraordinary argument in silent surprise. She was not in the least frightened, but she saw at a glance that Regina was quite in earnest, and she knew her own people, and that the Roman peasants are not the gentlest of the Italians.

"He would be very angry," Regina repeated. "I am sure he would!"

"Why should he be angry?" Aurora asked, in a tone half contemptuous and yet half sad.

"I know he would, because when he raved in his fever he used to call for you."

Aurora started and fixed her eyes on Regina's.

"Yes," Regina said, answering the look. "He often called you by name. He loved you once."

She pronounced the words with an accent of pity, drawing herself up to her full height; and there was triumph in the light of her eyes. It is not every woman that has a chance of saying so much to her rival.

"We were children then," Aurora said, in the very words she had used to her mother more than two years earlier.

She was almost as pale as Regina now, for the thrust had been straight and sure, and right at her heart. But she was prouder than the peasant woman who had wounded her.

"I have heard that you saved his life," she said presently. "And he loves you. You are happy!"

"I should always be happy if he and I were alone in the world," Regina answered, for she was a little softened by the girl's tone. "But even now they are trying to part us."

"To part you?" Again Aurora looked up suddenly. "Who is trying to do that? A woman?"

Regina laughed a little.

"You are jealous," she said. "That shows that you love him still. No. It is not a woman."

"Corbario?" The name rose instinctively to Aurora's lips.

"Yes," Regina answered. "That is why I am left alone this morning. Signor Corbario is at Saint Moritz and Marcello is gone down to see him. I know he is trying to separate us. You did not know that he was so near?"

"We only came yesterday afternoon," Aurora answered. "We did not know that — that Signor Consalvi was here, or we should not have come at all."

It had stung her to hear Regina speak of him quite naturally by his first name. Regina felt the rebuke.

"I am truly sorry that I should have accidentally found myself in your path," she said, emphasising the rather grand phrase, and holding her handsome head very high.

Aurora almost smiled at this sudden manifestation of the peasant's nature, and wondered whether Regina ever said such things to Marcello, and whether, if she did, they jarred on him very much. The speech had the very curious effect of restoring Aurora's sense of superiority, and she answered more kindly.

"You need not be sorry," she said. "If you had not chanced to be here I should probably be lying amongst the rocks down there with several broken bones."

"If it were not by my fault I should not care," Regina retorted, with elementary frankness.

"But I should!" Aurora laughed, in spite of herself, and liking this phase of Regina's character better than any she had yet seen. "Come," she said, with a sudden generous impulse, and holding out her hand, "let us stop quarrelling. You saved me from a bad accident, and I was too ungenerous to be grateful. I thank you now, with all my heart."

Regina was surprised and stared hard at her for a moment, and then glanced at her outstretched hand.

"You would not take my hand if there were any one here to see."

"Why not?"

"Because they have told you that I am a wicked woman," Regina answered, a slight blush rising in her cheeks. "And perhaps it is true. But it was for him."

"I would take your hand anywhere, because you saved his life," said Aurora, and her voice shook a little as she said the last words. "And besides, no one has told me that you are wicked. Come, what is the use of hating each other?"

Regina took her hand reluctantly, but not suspiciously, and held it a moment.

"It does not mean that I shall not hate you if he ever loves you again," she said. "If I made you think that it would be treachery, and that is the worst sin."

"It only means that I thank you now, quite honestly," Aurora answered, and their hands parted.

"Very well." Regina seemed satisfied. "And I thank you for taking my hand," she added, with something oddly like real gratitude, "and because you said you would do it anywhere, even before other women. I know what I am, and what people call me.

But it was for him. Let us not talk of it any more. I will help you down, and you shall go home alone."

"My mother is waiting for me far down, towards the village," Aurora said.

"All the better. A young lady like you should not go about without any one. It is not proper."

Aurora suppressed a smile at the thought of being reproved concerning the proprieties by "Marcello's Regina," and she began the descent. Regina went down first, facing the rock, and planting the young girl's feet in the best stepping places, one after the other, with constant warnings and instructions as to holding on with her hands. They reached the bottom in safety, and came to the place where Regina had left her hat and shoes. She sat down where she had been sitting when she had first heard the cry, and began to put them on.

"I had taken them off for coolness as I sat here," she explained. "You see, until I was fourteen I only wore them on Sundays."

"And yet you have such beautiful feet," Aurora said.

"Have I?" Regina asked indifferently. "I thought all feet were alike. But I have torn my stocking — it is hard to get the shoe on."

"Let me help you." Aurora knelt down quickly, and began to loosen the lacing further, but Regina protested, flushing deeply and trying to draw her foot back.

"No, no!" she cried. "You are a lady!"

"What difference does that make?" asked Aurora, laughing and insisting.

"This is not right!" Regina still protested, and the blush had not left her cheeks.

But Aurora smoothed the torn stocking under the sole of each foot, and slipped on the shoes, which were by no means tight, and tied the lacing fast.

"Thank you, Signorina," Regina said, much confused. "You are too good!"

She picked up her hat and put it on, but she was not clever with the pin, for she was used to having Settimia do everything for her which she had not learned to do for herself before she had come to Rome.

"I can never manage it without Settimia," she said, as if excusing herself for her awkwardness, as she again submitted to Aurora's help.

"Settimia?" repeated the young girl, as she put the hat on and thrust a long pin through it. "Who is Settimia?"

"Our — I mean my maid," Regina explained. "Thank you. You are too good!"

"It is an uncommon name," Aurora said, looking critically at the hat. "But I think I have heard it before."

"She is a wonderful woman. She knows French. She knows everything!"

Aurora said nothing to this, but seemed to be trying to recall something she had long forgotten. Regina was very busy in her turn, pulling down the girl's frock all round, and brushing it with her hand as well as she could, and picking off bits of dry grass and thistles that clung to the grey woollen. Aurora thanked her.

"The way down is very easy now," Regina said. "A few steps farther on we can see the road."

"After all, why should you not come with me till we find my mother?" Aurora asked.

"No," Regina answered with quiet decision. "I am what I am. You must not be seen with Regina. Do not tell your mother that you have been with me, and I shall not tell Marcello — I mean, Signor Consalvi."

"Why not?"

"Neither of them would be pleased. Trust me. I know the world. Good-bye, and the Madonna accompany you; and remember what I said when I took your hand."

So they parted, and Regina stood up a long time, and watched the slender grey figure descending to the road in the valley.

CHAPTER XIII

"Variety, my dear Marcello, variety! There is nothing like it. If I were you, I would make some change, for your life must be growing monotonous, and besides, though I have not the least intention of reading you a lecture, you have really made your doings unnecessarily conspicuous of late. The Paris chroniclers have talked about you enough for the present. Don't you think so? Yes, finish the bottle. I always told you that champagne was good for you."

Marcello filled his glass and sipped the wine before he answered. It had not gone to his head, but there was colour in his lean cheeks, his eyes were brighter than usual, and he felt the familiar exhilaration which he had missed of late.

"I have been drinking milk for ten days," he said with a smile, as he set down the glass.

"Good in its way, no doubt," Corbario answered genially, "but a little tiresome. One should often change from simple things to complicated ones. It is the science of enjoyment. Besides, it is bad for the digestion to live always on bread and milk."

"I don't live on that altogether," laughed Marcello.

"I mean it metaphorically, my dear boy. There is such a thing as simplifying one's existence too much.

That sometimes ends in getting stuck. Now you cannot possibly allow yourself to get stuck in your present position. You know what I mean. Oh, I don't blame you! If I were your age I should probably do the same thing, especially if I had your luck. Blame you? No! Not in the least. The cigarettes are there. You've not given up smoking too? No, that's right. A man without a small vice is as uninteresting as a woman without a past or a landscape without shadows. Cigarettes never hurt anybody. Look at me! I used to smoke fifty a day when I was your age."

Marcello blew a cloud of smoke, stirred his coffee, and leaned back. He had scarcely heard what Corbario said, but the elder man's careless chatter had put him at his ease.

"Folco," he said quietly, "I want to ask you a question, and I want you to answer me seriously. Will you?"

"As well as I can," answered Corbario, instantly changing his tone and growing earnest.

"Don't be surprised," Marcello said, half apologetically, as if he were already weakening. "I shall never do anything without your advice. Of course you know how I feel about all this, that I am leading a disorderly life, and — well, you understand!"

"Perfectly, my dear boy. I only wish to help you out of it as soon as possible, if you want to be helped. I'm quite sure that you will pull through in time. I have always believed in you."

"Thank you. I know you have. Well, I'll ask you my question. You know well enough that I shall never care for society much, don't you?"

"Society will care for you," answered Folco. "What is the question?"

"I'm coming to it, but I want to explain, or it will not be quite clear. You see, it is not as if I were a personage in the world."

"What sort of personage? Please explain."

"I mean, if I were the head of a great house, with a great title and hereditary estate."

"What has that to do with it?" Folco was mystified.

"If I were, it would make a difference, I suppose. But I'm not. I'm plain Marcello Consalvi, no better than any one else."

"But vastly richer," Folco suggested.

"I wish I were not. I wish I were a poor clerk, working for my living."

"The air of this place is not good for you, my boy." Folco laughed gaily.

"No, don't laugh! I'm in earnest. If I were a poor man, nobody would think it at all strange if—" Marcello hesitated.

"If what?"

"If I married Regina," said Marcello rather desperately.

Folco's expression changed instantly.

"Was that the question you were going to ask me?" he inquired.

"Yes."

Marcello grew very red and smoked so fast that he choked himself.

"Is there any earthly reason why you should marry her?" asked Folco very quietly.

"It would be right," Marcello answered, gaining courage.

"Yes, yes, undoubtedly," Folco hastened to admit. "In principle it would undoubtedly be right. But it is a very serious matter, my dear boy. It means your whole life and future. Have you"—he hesitated, with an affectation of delicacy—"have you said anything to her about it?"

"I used to, at first, but she would not hear of it. You have no idea how simple she is, and how little she expects anything of the sort. She always tells me that I am to send her away when I am tired of her, to throw her away like an old coat, as she says herself. But I could never do that, you know. Could I?"

Marcello blushed again, hardly knowing why. Corbario seemed deeply interested.

"She must be a very unusual sort of girl," he observed thoughtfully. "There are not many like her, I fancy."

"There is nobody like her," Marcello answered with conviction. "That is why I want to marry her. I owe it to her. You must admit that. I owe her my life, for I certainly should have died if she had not taken care of me. And then, there is the rest. She has given me all she has, and that is herself, and she asks nothing in return. She is very proud, too. I tried to make her accept a string of pearls in Paris, just because I thought they would be becoming to her, but she absolutely refused."

"Really? I suppose you gave the pearls back to the jeweller?"

"No, I kept them. Perhaps I shall get her to wear them some day."

Folco smiled.

"You may just as well encourage her simple tastes," he said. "Women always end by learning how to spend money, unless it is their own."

Having delivered himself of this piece of wisdom Folco chose a cigar, nipped off the end of it neatly with a gold cutter, lit it and snuffed the rich smoke up his nose in a deliberate manner.

"Regina is a very remarkable woman," he said at last. "If she had been well educated, she would make an admirable wife; and she loves you devotedly, Marcello. Now, the real question is — at least, it seems to me so — you don't mind my talking to you just as I would to myself, do you? Very well. If I were in your position, I should ask myself, as a man of honour, whether I really loved her as much as she loved me, or whether I had only been taken off my feet by her beauty. Don't misunderstand me, my boy! I should feel that if I were not quite sure of that, I ought not to marry her, because it would be much worse for her in the end than if we parted. Have you ever asked yourself that question, Marcello?"

"Yes, I have."

Marcello spoke in a low voice, and bent his head, as if he were not sure of the answer. Corbario, satisfied with the immediate effect of his satanic speech, waited a moment, sighed, looked down at his cigar, and then went on in gentle tones.

"That is so often the way," he said. "A man marries a woman out of a sense of duty, and then makes her miserably unhappy, quite in spite of himself. Of course, in such a case as yours, you feel that you owe a woman amends — you cannot call it compensation, as if it were a matter of law! She has given everything, and you have given nothing. You owe her happiness, if you can bestow it upon her, don't you?"

"Indeed I do!" assented Marcello.

"Yes. The question is, whether the way to make her happy is to marry her, when you have a reasonable doubt as to whether you can be a good husband to her. That is the real problem, it seems to me. Do you love her enough to give up the life to which you were born, and for which you were educated? You would have to do that, you know. Our friends — your dear mother's friends, my boy — would never receive her, least of all after what has happened."

"I know it."

"You would have to wander about Europe, or live in San Domenico, for you could not bear to live in Rome, meeting women who would not bow to your wife. I know you. You could not possibly bear it."

"I should think not!"

"No. Therefore, since you have the doubt, since you

are not absolutely sure of yourself, I think the only thing to do is to find out what you really feel, before taking an irreparable step."

"Yes," said Marcello, who had fallen into the trap laid for him. "I know that. But how am I to make sure of myself?"

"There is only one way," Folco answered. "I know it is not easy, and if I were not sure that you are perfectly sincere I should be afraid to propose it to you."

"What is it? Tell me. You are the only friend I have in the world, Folco, and I want to do what is right. God knows, I am in earnest! There are moments when I cannot imagine living without Regina — it seemed hard to leave her this morning, even for these few hours, and I long to be back at Pontresina already! Yet you know how fond I am of you, and how I like to be with you, for we have always been more like brothers than anything else."

"Indeed we have!" Folco assented fervently. "You were saying that there were moments — yes?"

"Sometimes she jars upon me dreadfully," Marcello said in a low voice, as if he were ashamed of owning it. "Then I want to get away."

"Exactly. You want to get away, not to leave her, but to be alone for a few hours, or a few days. That would be the very best thing you could do — to separate for a little while. You would very soon find out whether you could live without her or not; and believe me, if you feel that you can live without her, that means that you could not live with her for your whole life."

"I should go back to her in twenty-four hours. I am sure I should."

"Perhaps you would, if you went, say, from here to Paris alone, with nothing to distract your attention. But suppose that you and I should go together, to some place where we should meet our friends, all amusing themselves, where you could talk to other women, and meet men of your own age, and lead the life people expect you to lead, just for a few weeks. You know that society will be only too glad to see something of you, whenever you choose to go near it. You are what is called a good match, and all the mothers with marriageable daughters would run after you."

"Disgusting!" exclaimed Marcello, with contempt.

"No doubt, but it would be a wholesome change and a good test. When a young girl is determined to be a nun, she is generally made to spend a year in society, in order to make acquaintance with what she intends to give up. I don't see much difference between that and your case. Before you say good-bye for ever to your own world, find out what it is like. At the same time, you will settle for ever any doubts you have about really loving Regina."

"Perhaps you are right. It would only be for a few days."

"And besides," Folco continued, "if you have not yet found it dull at Pontresina, you certainly will before long. There is no reason why you should lead the life of an invalid, for you are quite strong now."

"Oh, quite. I always tell Regina so, but she insists that I am too thin, and it amuses her to take care of me."

"Naturally. That is how you first made acquaintance. A woman who has once taken care of a man she loves wants him to be ever afterwards an invalid, for ever getting better! A man gets tired of that in time. It was a great pity you left Paris just when I came, for there are many things we could have enjoyed together there."

"I daresay," Marcello answered, not paying much attention to the other's words.

"Take my advice, my dear boy," said Folco. "Come away with me for a few days. I will wait here till you are quite ready, for of course you cannot be sure of getting off at once. You will have to prepare Regina for this."

"Of course. I am not sure that it is possible at all."

Folco laughed gaily.

"Anything is possible that you really wish to do," he said.

"Regina may insist upon coming with me."

"Nonsense. Women always submit in the end, and they never die of it. Assert yourself, Marcello! Be a man! You cannot be ordered about like a child by any woman, not even if she has saved your life, not even if she loves you to distraction. You have a right to a will of your own."

"I know. And yet — oh, I wish I knew what I ought to do!"

"Think over all I have said, and you will see that I am right," said Folco, rising from the table. "And if you take my advice, you will be doing what is fair and honest by Regina as well as by yourself. Your own conscience must tell you that."

Poor Marcello was not very sure what had become of his own conscience during the past year, and Folco's arguments swayed him as he groped for something definite to follow, and found nothing but what Corbario chose to thrust into his hand.

As they stood by the table, a servant brought a note on a little salver, holding it out to them as if he were not sure which of them was to receive it. Both glanced at the address; it was for Corbario, who took it quickly and put it into his pocket; but Marcello had recognised the handwriting — that rather cramped feminine hand of a woman who has seen better days, in which Settimia kept accounts for Regina. The latter insisted that an account should be kept of the money which Marcello gave her, and that he should see it from time to time. At the first moment, being absorbed with other matters, and inwardly much engaged in the pursuit of his own conscience, which eluded him at every turn like a figure in a dream, he paid no attention to what he had seen; but the writing had impressed itself on his memory.

They had been lunching in Folco's sitting-room, and Corbario made an excuse to go into his bedroom for a moment, saying that he wanted certain cigars that his man had put away. Marcello stood at the window gazing down the broad valley. Scarcely a minute elapsed before Folco came back with a handful of Havanas which he dropped on a writing-table.

"By the bye," he said carelessly, "there is another reason why you may not care to stay long in Pontresina. The Contessa and Aurora are there."

"Are they?" Marcello turned sharply as he asked the question.

He was surprised, and at the same instant it flashed upon him that Folco had just received the information from Settimia in the note that had been brought.

"Yes," Folco answered with a smile. "And Pontresina is such a small place that you can hardly help meeting them. I thought I might as well tell you."

"Thank you. Yes, it would be awkward, and unpleasant for them."

"Precisely. The Contessa wrote me that she and Aurora had come upon you two unexpectedly in leaving a theatre, and that she had felt very uncomfortable."

"Oh! I suppose she suggested that I should mend my ways?"

"As a matter of fact, she did." Corbario smiled. "You know what a very proper person she is!"

"She is quite right," answered Marcello gravely.

"It certainly cannot have been pleasant for her, on account of Aurora."

Folco looked at him thoughtfully, for his tone had suddenly changed.

"If you don't mind," Folco said, "I think I will drive up with you and call on them this afternoon. You can drop me at their hotel, and I shall find my way back alone."

"Certainly."

"Are you sure you don't mind?" Folco affected to speak anxiously.

"Why should I?"

"You see," Folco said, without heeding the question, "they let me know that they were there, and as we are such old friends it would be strange if I did not go to see them."

"Of course it would," answered Marcello in an absent tone.

He already connected Folco's knowledge of the Contessa's arrival in Pontresina so closely with Settimia's note that Folco's last statement had taken him by surprise, and a multitude of confused questions presented themselves to his mind. If Settimia had not written about the Contessa, why had she written at all? How did she know where Corbario was stopping in Saint Moritz? Was she in the habit of writing to him? Corbario had found her for Regina; was Settimia helping Corbario to exercise a sort of paternal vigilance over him? Somehow Marcello did not like that idea at all. So far as he knew, Folco had always been singularly frank with him, and had never deceived him in the smallest thing, even "for his own good." Marcello could only attribute good motives to him, but the mere idea of being watched was excessively disagreeable. He wondered whether Settimia had influenced Regina to get him away from Paris, acting under directions from Corbario. Was Regina deceiving him too, "for his own good"? If there is anything a man cannot bear from those he loves best, it is that they should take counsel together secretly to direct him "for his own good."

Marcello tried to put the thought out of his mind; but it had dawned upon him for the first time that Folco could tell even a pious falsehood. Yet he had no proof whatever that he had guessed right; it was a sudden impression and nothing more. He was much more silent during the rest of the afternoon as he drove up to Pontresina with Folco, and it seemed to him that he had at last touched something definite; which was strange enough, considering that it was all a matter of guess-work and doubt.

And now fate awoke again and did one of those little things that decide men's lives. If Folco and Marcello had stopped at the door of the Contessa's hotel two minutes earlier, or thirty seconds later, than they did, they would not have chanced upon the Contessa and Aurora just coming in from a walk. But fate brought the four together precisely at that moment. As the carriage stopped, the two ladies had come from the opposite direction and were on the door-step.

"What a surprise!" exclaimed the Contessa, giving her hand graciously to Folco and then to Marcello.

The latter had got hold of a thread. Since the Contessa was surprised to see Folco, she could not possibly have already let him know that she was in Pontresina.

"I came as soon as I knew that you were here," said Corbario quickly.

Marcello heard the words, though he was at that moment shaking hands with Aurora, and their eyes had met. She was perfectly calm and collected, none the worse for her adventure in the morning, and considerably the wiser.

"Will you come in?" asked the Contessa, leading the way, as if expecting both men to follow.

Corbario went at once. Marcello hesitated, and flushed a little, and Aurora seemed to be waiting for him.

"Shall I come, too?" he asked.

"Just as you please," she answered. "My mother will think it strange if you don't."

Marcello bent his head, and the two followed the others towards the stairs at a little distance.

"Did your mother send word to Folco that you were here?" asked Marcello quickly, in a low tone.

"Not that I know. Why?"

"It is no matter. I wanted to be sure. Thank you."

They went upstairs side by side, not even glancing at each other, much more anxious to seem perfectly indifferent than to realise what they felt now that they had met at last.

Marcello stayed ten minutes in the small sitting-room, talking as well as he could. He had no wish to be alone with Aurora or her mother, and since the visit had been pressed upon him he was glad that Folco was present. But he got away as soon as he could, leaving Corbario to his own devices. The Contessa gave him her hand quietly, as if she had not expected him to stay, and she did not ask him to come again. Aurora merely nodded to him, and he saw that just as he went out she left the room by another door, after glancing at him once more with apparent coldness.

He walked quickly through the village until he came near to his own hotel, and then his pace slackened by degrees. He knew that he had felt a strong emotion in seeing Aurora again, and he was already wishing that he had not come away so soon. The room had been small, and it had been uncomfortable to be there, feeling himself judged and condemned by the Contessa and distrusted by Aurora; but he had been in an atmosphere that recalled all his youth, with people whose mere presence together brought back the memory of his dead mother as nothing else had done since his illness. He was just in that state of mind in which he would have broken away and freed himself within the hour, at any cost, if he had been involved in a common intrigue.

At the same time he had become convinced that Folco had deceived him, for some reason or other which he could not guess, and the knowledge was the first serious disillusionment of his life. The deception had been small, and perhaps intended in some mysterious way to be "for his own good"; but it had been a distinct deception and no better than a lie. He was sure of that.

He went upstairs slowly and Regina met him at the door of their rooms, and took his hat and stick without a word, for she saw that something had happened, and she felt suddenly cold. He was quite unlike himself. The careless look was gone from his face, his young lips were tightly closed, and he looked straight before him, quite unconscious that his manner was hurting her desperately.

"Has Settimia been out to-day?" he asked, looking at her quickly.

"I don't know," she answered, surprised. "I went for a long walk this morning. She probably went out into the village. I cannot tell. Why do you ask?"

"I wish to know whether she sent a note to Saint Moritz by a messenger. Can you find out, without asking her a direct question? I am very anxious to know."

"I will try, but it will not be easy," said Regina, watching him.

She had made up her mind that the blow was coming, and that Marcello was only putting off the moment when she must be told that he meant to leave her. She was very quiet, and waited for him to speak again, for she was too proud to ask him questions. His inquiry about Settimia was in some way connected with what was to come. He sat down by the table, and drummed upon it absently with his fingers for a moment. Then he looked up suddenly and met her eyes; his look of troubled preoccupation faded all at once, and he smiled and held out one hand to draw her nearer.

"Forgive me," he said. "All sorts of things have happened to-day. I have been annoyed."

She came and bent over him, turning his face up to hers with her hands, very gently. His eyes lightened slowly, and his lips parted a little.

"You are not tired of Regina yet," she said.

"No!" he laughed. "But you were right," he added, almost immediately.

"I knew I was," she answered, but not as she had expected to say the words when she had seen him come in.

She dared not hope to keep him always, but she had not lost him yet, and that was enough for the moment. The weight had fallen from her heart, and the pain was gone.

"Was it what I thought?" she asked softly. "Does your stepfather wish to separate us?"

"For a little while," Marcello answered. "He says we ought to part for a few weeks, so that I may find out whether I love you enough to marry you!"

"And he almost persuaded you that he was right," said Regina. "Is that what happened?"

"That — and something else."

"Will you tell me, heart of my heart?"

In the falling twilight he told her all that had passed

through his mind, from the moment when he had seen Settimia's handwriting on the note. Then Regina's lips moved.

"He shall pay!" she was saying under her breath. "He shall pay!"

"What are you saying?" Marcello asked.

"An Ave Maria," she answered. "It is almost dark."

CHAPTER XIV

THE little house in Trastevere was shut up, but the gardener had the keys, and came twice a week to air the rooms and sweep the paths and water the shrubs. He was to be informed by Settimia of Regina's return in time to have everything ready, but he did not expect any news before the end of September; and if he came regularly, on Tuesday and Saturday, and did his work, it was because he was a conscientious person in his way, elderly, neat, and systematic, a good sort of Roman of the old breed. But if he came on other days, as he often did, not to air the rooms, but to water and tend certain plants, and to do the many incomprehensible things which gardeners do with flower-pots, earth, and seeds, that was his own affair, and would bring a little money in the autumn when the small florists opened their shops and stands again, and the tide of foreigners set once more towards Rome. Also, if he had made friends with the gardeners at the beautiful villa on the Janiculum, that was not Corbario's business; and they gave him cuttings, and odds and ends, such as can be spared from a great garden where money is spent generously, but which mean a great deal to a poor man who is anxious to turn an honest penny by hard work.

The immediate result of this little traffic was that the gardeners at the villa knew all about the little house in Trastevere; and what the gardeners knew was known also by the porter, and by the other servants, and through them by the servants of other people, and the confidential valet told his master, and the maid told her mistress; and so everybody had learned where "Consalvi's Regina" lived, and it was likely that everybody would know when she came back to Rome, and whether Marcello came with her or not.

He had not taken Folco's advice, much to the latter's disappointment and annoyance. On the contrary, he and Regina had left the Engadine very suddenly, without so much as letting Corbario guess that they were going away; and Regina had managed to keep Settimia so very busy and so constantly under her eye that the maid had not been able to send Folco a word, warning him of the anticipated move. Almost for the first time Marcello had made up his mind for himself, and had acted upon his decision; and it seemed as if the exercise of his will had made a change in his character.

They wandered from place to place; they went to Venice in the hottest season, when no one was there, and they came down to Florence and drove up to Vallombrosa, where they stumbled upon society, and were stared at accordingly. They went down to Siena, they stopped in Orvieto, and drove across to Assisi and Perugia; but they were perpetually drawn towards Rome, and knew that they longed to be there again.

Marcello had plenty of time to think, and there was little to disturb his meditations on the past and future; for Regina was not talkative, and was content to be silent for hours, provided that she could see his face. He never knew whether she felt her ignorance about all they saw, and his own knowledge was by no means great. He told her what he knew and read about places they visited, and she remembered what he said, and sometimes asked simple questions which he could answer easily enough. For instance, she wished to know whether America were a city or an island, and who the Jews were, and if the sun rose in the west on the other side of the world, since Marcello assured her that the world was round.

He was neither shocked nor amused; Ercole had asked him similar questions when he had been a boy; so had the peasants in Calabria, and there was no reason why Regina should know more than they did. Besides, she possessed wonderful tact, and now spoke her own language so well that she could pass for a person of average education, so long as she avoided speaking of anything that is learned from books. She was very quick to understand everything connected with the people she heard of, and she never forgot anything that Marcello told her. She was grateful to him for never laughing at her, but in reality he was indifferent. If she had known everything within bounds of knowledge, she would not have been a whit more beautiful, or more loving, or more womanly.

But he himself was beginning to think, now that his faith in Folco had been shaken, and he began to realise that he had been strangely torpid and morally listless during the past years. The shock his whole system had received, the long interval during which his memory had been quite gone, the physical languor that had lasted some time after his recovery from the fever, had all combined to make the near past seem infinitely remote, to cloud his judgment of reality, and to destroy the healthy tension of his natural will. A good deal of what Corbario had called "harmless dissipation" had made matters worse, and when Regina had persuaded him to leave Paris he had really been in that dangerous moral, intellectual, and physical condition in which it takes very little to send a man to the bad altogether, and not much more to kill him outright, if he be of a delicate constitution and still very young. Corbario had almost succeeded in his work of destruction.

He would not succeed now, for the worst danger was past, and Marcello had found his feet after being almost lost in the quicksand through which he had been led.

He had not at first accused Folco of anything worse than that one little deception about the arrival of the Contessa, and of having caused him to be too closely watched by Settimia. Little by little, however, other possibilities had shaped themselves and had grown into certainties at an alarming rate. He understood all at once how Folco himself had been spending his time, while society had supposed him to be a broken-hearted widower. A few hints which he had let fall about the things he would have shown Marcello in Paris suggested a great deal; his looks and manner told the rest, now that Marcello had guessed the main truth. He had not waited three months after his wife's death to profit by his liberty and the wealth she had left him. Marcello remembered the addresses he had given from time to time — Monte Carlo, Hombourg, Pau, and Paris very often. He had spoken of business in his letters, as an excuse for moving about so much, but "business" did not always take a man to places of amusement, and Folco seemed to have visited no others. Men whom Marcello had met had seen Corbario, and what they said about him was by no means indefinite. He had been amusing himself, and not alone, and the young men had laughed at his attempts to cloak his doings under an appearance of sorrowing respectability.

As all this became clear to Marcello he suffered acutely at times, and he reproached himself bitterly for having been so long blind and indifferent. It was bad enough that he should have been leading a wild life with Regina in Paris within a few months of his mother's death, but even in the depths of his self-reproach he saw how much worse it was that Folco should have forgotten her so soon. It was worse than a slight upon his mother's memory, it was an insult. The good woman who was gone would have shed hot tears if she could have come to life and seen how her son was living; but she would have died again, could she have seen the husband she adored in the places where many had seen him since her death. It was no wonder that Marcello's anger rose at the mere thought.

Moreover, as Marcello's understanding awoke, he realised that Folco had encouraged him in all he had done, and had not seemed pleased when he had begun to live more quietly. Folco would have made him his companion in pleasure, if he could, and the idea was horrible to Marcello as soon as it presented itself.

It was the discovery that he had been mistaken in Corbario that most directly helped him to regain his foothold in life and his free will. There was more in the Spartan method than we are always ready to admit, for it is easier to disgust most men by the sight of human degradation than to strengthen them against temptation by preaching, or by the lessons of example which are so very peculiarly disagreeable to the normal man.

"I am virtuous, I am sober, I resist temptation, imitate me!" cries the preacher. You say that you are virtuous, and you are apparently sober, my friend; and perhaps you are a very good man, though you need not scream out the statement at the top of your voice. But how are we to know that you have any temptations to resist? Or that your temptations are the same as ours, even supposing that you have any? Or that you are speaking the truth about yourself, since what you say is so extremely flattering to your vanity? Wherever there is preaching, those who are preached at are expected to accept a good deal on the mere word of the preacher, quite aside from anything they have been brought to believe elsewhere.

"Temptation?" said a certain great lady who was not strong in theology. "That is what one yields to, isn't it?"

She probably knew what she was talking about, for she had lived in the world a good while, as we have. But the preacher is not very often one of us, and he knows little of our ways and next to nothing of our real feelings; yet he exhorts us to be like him. It would be very odd if we succeeded. The world would probably stand still if we did, and most of us are so well aware of the fact that we do not even try; and the sermon simply has no effect at all, which need not prevent the preacher from being richly remunerated for delivering it.

"Vice is very attractive, of course," he says, "but you must avoid it because it is sinful."

And every time vice is mentioned we think how attractive it must be, since it is necessary to preach against it so much; and the more attractive it seems, the greater the temptation.

"Should you like to try a vice or two?" said the Spartan. "Very well. Come with me, my boy, and you shall see what vice is; and after that, if you care to try it, please yourself, for I shall have nothing more to say!"

And forthwith he played upon the string of disgust, which is the most sensitive of all the strings that vibrate in the great human instrument; and the boy's stomach rose, and he sickened and turned away, and remembered for ever, though he might try ever so hard to forget.

Marcello at last saw Folco as he was, though still without understanding the worst, and with no suspicion that Folco wished him out of the world, and had deliberately set to work to kill him by dissipation; and the disgust he felt was the most horrible sensation that he could remember. At the same time he saw himself and his whole life, and the perplexity of his position frightened him.

It seemed impossible to go back and live under the same roof with Corbario now. He flushed with shame when he remembered the luncheon at Saint Moritz, and how he had been almost persuaded to leave poor Regina suddenly, and to go back to Paris with his stepfather. He saw through the devilish cleverness of the man's arguments, and when he remembered that his dead mother's name had been spoken, a thrill of real pain ran through his body and he clenched his teeth and his hands.

He asked himself how he could meet Folco after that, and the only answer was that if they met they must quarrel and part, not to meet again.

He told Regina that he would not go back to the villa after they reached Rome, but would live in the little house in Trastevere. To his surprise, she looked grave and shook her head. She had never asked him what was making him so silent and thoughtful, but she had guessed much of the truth from little things; she herself had never trusted Corbario since she had first seen his face at the hospital, and she had long foreseen the coming struggle.

"Why do you shake your head?" he asked. "Do you not want me at the little house?"

"The villa is yours, not his," she said. "He will be glad if you will leave him there, for he will be the master. Then he will marry again, and live there, and it will be hard to turn him out."

"What makes you think he wishes to marry again?"

"He would be married already, if the girl would have him," answered Regina.

"How do you know?"

"You told me to watch, to find out. I have obeyed you. I know everything."

Marcello was surprised, and did not quite understand. He only remembered that he had asked her to ascertain whether Settimia had sent a note to Folco at Saint Moritz. After a day or two she told him that she was quite sure of it. That was all, and Regina had scarcely ever spoken of Folco since then. Marcello reminded her of this, and asked her what she had done.

"I can read," she said. "I can read writing, and that is very hard, you know. I made Settimia teach me. I said with myself, if he should be away and should write to me, what should I do? I could not let Settimia read his letters, and I am too well dressed to go to a public letter-writer in the street, as the peasants do. He would think me an ignorant person, and the people in the street would laugh. That would not help me. I should have to go to the priest, to my confessor."

"Your confessor? Do you go to confession?"

"Do you take me for a Turk?" Regina asked, laughing. "I go to confession at Christmas and Easter. I tell the priest that I am very bad, and am sorry, but that it is for you and that I cannot help it. Then he asks me if I will promise to leave you and be good. And I say no, that I will not promise that. And he tells me to go away and come back when I am ready to promise, and that he will give me absolution then. It is always the same. He shakes his head and frowns when he sees me coming, and I smile. We know each other quite well now. I have told him that when you are tired of me, then I will be good. Is not that enough? What can I do? I should like to be good, of course, but I like still better to be with you. So it is."

"You are better than the priest knows," said Marcello thoughtfully, "and I am worse."

"It is not true. But if I had a letter from you, I would not take it to the priest to read for me. He would be angry, and tear it up, and send me away. I understood this at the beginning, so I made Settimia teach me how to read the writing, and I also learned to write myself, not very well, but one can understand it."

"I know. I have seen you writing copies. But how has that helped you to find out what Folco is doing?"

"I read all Settimia's letters," Regina answered, with perfect simplicity.

"Eh?" Marcello thought he had misunderstood her.

"I read all the letters she gets," Regina replied, unmoved. "When she was teaching me to read I saw where she kept all her letters. It is always the same place. There is a pocket inside a little black bag she has, which opens easily, though she locks it. She puts the letters there, and when she has read them over she burns them. You see, she has no idea that I read them. But I always do, ever since you asked me about that note. When I know that she has had a letter, I send her out on an errand. Then I read. It is so easy!"

Regina laughed, but Marcello looked displeased.

"It is not honest to do such things," he said.

"Not honest?" Regina stared at him in amazement. "How does honesty enter into the question? Is Settimia honest? Then honest people should all be in the galleys! And if you knew how he writes to her! Oh, yes! You are the 'dear patient,' and I am the 'admirable companion.' They have known each other long, those two. They have a language between them, but I have learned it. They have no more secrets that I do not know. Everything the admirable companion does that makes the dear patient better is wrong, and everything that used to make him worse was right. They were killing you in Paris, they wanted you to stay there until you were dead. Do you know who saved your life? It was the

Contessa, when I heard her say that you were looking ill! If you ever see her again, thank her, for I was blind and she opened my eyes. The devil had blinded me, and the pleasure, and I could not see. I see now, thanks to heaven, and I know all, and they shall not hurt you. But they shall pay!"

She was not laughing now, as she said the last words under her breath, and her beautiful lips just showed her white teeth, set savagely tight as though they had bitten through something that could be killed. Folco Corbario was not timid, but if he had seen her then, and known that the imaginary bite was meant for his life, he would have taken special care of his bodily safety whenever she was in his neighbourhood.

Marcello had listened in profound surprise, for what she said threw new light on all he had thought out for himself of late.

"And you say that Folco is thinking of marrying again," he said, almost ashamed to profit by information obtained as Regina had got it.

"Yes, he is in love with a young girl, and wishes to marry her."

Marcello said nothing.

"Should you like to know her name?" asked Regina.

Still Marcello was silent, as if refusing to answer, and yet wishing that she should go on.

"I will tell you," Regina said. "Her name is Aurora dell' Armi."

Marcello started, and looked into her face, doubting her word for the first time. He changed colour, too, flushing and then turning pale.

"It is not true!" he cried, rather hoarsely. "It cannot be true!"

"It is true," Regina answered, "but she will not have him. She would not marry him, even if her mother would allow it."

"Thank God!" exclaimed Marcello fervently.

Regina sighed, and turned away.

CHAPTER XV

ERCOLE sat on the stone seat that ran along the wall of the inn, facing the dusty road. He was waiting in the cool dawn until it should please the innkeeper to open the door, and Nino crouched beside him, his head resting on his forepaws.

A great many years had passed since Ercole had sat there the last time, but nothing had changed, so far as he could see. He had been young, and the women had called him handsome; his face had not been shrivelled to parchment by the fever, and there had been no grey threads in his thick black hair. Nino had not been born then, and now Nino seemed to be a part of himself. Nino's grandam had lain in almost the same spot then, wolfish and hungry as her descendant was now, and only a trifle less uncannily hideous. It was all very much the same, but between that time and this there lay all Ercole's life by the Roman shore.

When he had heard, as every one had, how Marcello had been brought to Rome on the tail of a wine-cart, he had been sure that the boy had been laid upon it while the cart was standing before Paoluccio's inn in the night. He knew the road well, and the ways of the carters, and that they rarely stopped anywhere else between Frascati and Rome. Again and again he had been on the point of tramping up from the seashore to the place, to see whether he could not find some clue to Marcello's accident there, but something had prevented him, some old dislike of returning to the neighbourhood after such a long absence. He knew why he had not gone, but he had not confided the reason even to Nino, who was told most things. He had, moreover, been tolerably sure that nothing short of thumb-screws would extract any information from Paoluccio or his wife, for he knew his own people. The only thing that surprised him was that the boy should ever have left the inn alive after being robbed of everything he had about him that was worth taking.

Moreover, since Marcello had been found, and was alive and well, it was of very little use to try and discover exactly what had happened to him after he had been last seen by the shore. But the aspect of things had changed since Ercole had heard the sailor's story, and his wish to see the place where the boy had been hidden so long overcame any repugnance he felt to visiting a neighbourhood which had unpleasant associations with his younger years.

He sat and waited at the door, and before the sun rose a young woman came round the house with the big key and opened the place, just as Regina had done in old days. She looked at Ercole, and he looked at her, and neither said anything as she went about her work, sprinkling the floor with water and then sweeping it, and noisily pulling the heavy benches about. When this operation was finished, Ercole rose and went in, and sat down at the end of a table. He took some bread and cheese from his canvas bag and began to eat, using his clasp-knife.

"If you wish wine," said the woman, "you will have to wait till the master comes down."

Ercole only answered by raising his head and throwing out his chin, which means " no " in gesture language. He threw pieces of the bread and the rind of the cheese to his dog. Nino caught each fragment in the air with a snap that would have lamed a horse for a month. The woman glanced nervously at the animal, each time she heard his jagged teeth close.

Paoluccio appeared in due time, without coat or waistcoat, and with his sleeves rolled up above the elbows, as if he had been washing. If he had, the operation had succeeded very imperfectly. He glanced at Ercole as he passed in.

"Good-morning," he said, for he made it a point to be polite to customers, even when they brought their own food.

"Good-morning," answered Ercole, looking at him curiously.

Possibly there was something unusual in the tone of Ercole's voice, for Nino suddenly sat up beside his master's knee, forgetting all about the bread, and watched Paoluccio too, as if he expected something. But nothing happened. Paoluccio opened a cupboard in the wall with a key he carried, took out a bottle of the coarse aniseed spirits which the Roman peasants drink, and filled himself a small glass of the stuff, which he tossed off with evident pleasure. Then he filled his pipe, lit it carefully, and went to the door again. By this time, though he had apparently not bestowed the least attention on Ercole, he had made up his mind about him, and was not mistaken. Ercole belonged to the better class of customers.

"You come from the Roman shore?" he said, with an interrogation.

"To serve you," Ercole assented, with evident willingness to enter into conversation. "I am a keeper and watchman on the lands of Signor Corbario."

Paoluccio took his pipe from his mouth and nodded twice.

"That is a very rich gentleman, I have heard," he observed. "He owns much land."

"It all belongs to his stepson, now that the young gentleman is of age," Ercole answered. "But as it was his mother's, and she married Signor Corbario, we have the habit of the name."

"What is the name of the stepson?" asked Paoluccio.

"Consalvi," Ercole replied.

Paoluccio said nothing to this, but lit his pipe again with a sulphur match.

"Evil befall the soul of our government!" he grumbled presently, with insufficient logic, but meaning that the government sold bad tobacco.

"You must have heard of the young gentleman," Ercole said. "His name is Marcello Consalvi. They say that he lay ill for a long time at an inn on this road —"

"For the love of heaven, don't talk to me about Marcello Consalvi!" cried Paoluccio, suddenly in a fury. "Blood of a dog! If you had not the face of an honest man I should think you were another of those newspaper men in disguise, pigs and animals that they are and sons of evil mothers, and ill befall their wicked dead, and their little dead ones, and those that shall be born to them!"

Paoluccio's eyes were bloodshot and he spat furiously, half across the road. Nino watched him and hitched the side of his upper lip on one of his lower fangs, which produced the effect of a terrific smile. Ercole was unmoved.

"I suppose," he observed, "that they said it happened in your inn."

"And why should it happen in my inn, rather than in any other inn?" inquired Paoluccio angrily.

"Indeed," said Ercole, "I cannot imagine why they should say that it did! Some one must have put the story about. A servant, perhaps, whom you sent away."

"We did not send Regina away," answered Paoluccio, still furious. "She ran away in the night, about that time. But, as you say, she may have invented the story and sent the newspaper men here to worry our lives with their questions, out of mere spite."

"Who was this Regina?" Ercole asked. "What has she to do with it?"

"Regina? She was the servant girl we had before this one. We took her out of charity."

"The daughter of some relation, no doubt," Ercole suggested.

"May that never be, if it please the Madonna!" cried Paoluccio. "A relation? Thank God we have always been honest people in my father's house! No, it was not a relation. She came of a crooked race. Her mother took a lover, and her father killed him, here on the Frascati road, and almost killed her too; but the law gave him the right and he went free."

"And then, what did he do?" asked Ercole, slowly putting the remains of his bread into his canvas bag.

"What did he do? He went away and never came back. What should he do?"

"Quite right. And the woman, what became of her?"

"She took other men, for she had no shame. And at last one of them was jealous, and struck her on the head with a paving stone, not meaning to kill her; but she died."

"Oh, she died, did she?"

"She died. For she was always spiteful. And so that poor man went to the galleys, merely for hitting her on the head, and not meaning to kill her."

"And you took the girl for your servant?"

"Yes. She was old enough to work, and very strong, so we took her for charity. But for my part, I was glad when she ran away, for she grew up handsome, and with that blood there surely would have been a scandal some day."

"One sees that you are a very charitable person,"

Ercole observed thoughtfully. "The girl must have been very ungrateful if she told untrue stories about your inn, after all you had done for her. You had nourished a viper in your house."

"That is what my wife says," Paoluccio answered, now quite calm. "Those are my wife's very words. As for believing that the young man was ever in this house, I tell you that the story is a wicked lie. Where should we have put him? In the cellar with the hogsheads, or in the attic with the maid? or in our own room? Tell me where we could have put him! Or perhaps they will say that he slept on the ceiling, like the flies? They will say anything, chattering, chattering, and coming here with their questions and their photographing machines, and their bicycles, and the souls of their dead! If you do not believe me, you can see the place where they say that he lay! I tell you there is not room for a cat in this house. Believe me if you like!"

"How can I not believe such a respectable person as you seem to be?" inquired Ercole gravely.

"I thank you. And since it happens that you are in the service of the young gentleman himself, I hope you will tell him that if he fancies he was in my house, he is mistaken."

"Surely," said Ercòle.

"Besides," exclaimed Paoluccio, "how could he know where he was? Are not all inns on these roads alike? He was in another, that is all. And what had I to do with that?"

"Nothing," assented Ercole. "I thank you for your conversation. I will take a glass of the aniseed before I go, if you please."

"Are you going already?" asked Paoluccio, as he went to fetch the bottle and the little cast glass from which he himself had drunk.

"Yes," Ercole answered. "I go to Rome. I stopped to refresh myself."

"It will be hot on the road," said Paoluccio, setting the full glass down on the table. "Two sous," he added, as Ercole produced his old sheepskin purse. "Thank you."

"Thank you," Ercole answered, and tipped the spirits down his throat. "Yes, it will be hot, but what can one do? We are used to it, my dog and I. We are not of wax to melt in the sun."

"It is true that this dog does not look as if he were wax," Paoluccio remarked, for the qualities of Nino had not escaped him.

"No. He is not of wax. He is of sugar, all sugar! He has a very sweet nature."

"One would not say so," answered Paoluccio doubtfully. "If you go to the city you must muzzle him, or they will make you pay a fine. Otherwise they will kill him for you."

"Do you think any one would try to catch him if I let him run loose?" asked Ercole, as if in doubt. "He killed a full-grown wolf before he was two years old, and not long ago he worried a sheepdog of the Campagna as if it had been nothing but a lamb. Do you think any one would try to catch him?"

"If it fell to me, I should go to confession first," said Paoluccio.

So Ercole left the inn and trudged along the road to Rome with Nino at his heels, without once looking behind him; past the Baldinotti houses and into the Via Appia Nuova, and on into the city through the gate of San Giovanni, where the octroi men stopped him and made him show them what he had in his canvas bag. When they saw that there was no cheese left and but little bread, they let him go by without paying anything.

He went up to the left and sat down on the ground under the trees that are there, and he filled his little clay pipe and smoked a while, without even speaking to his dog. It was quiet, for it was long past the hour when the carts come in, and the small boys were all gone to school, and the great paved slope between the steps of the basilica and the gate was quite deserted, and very white and hot.

Ercole was not very tired, though he had walked all night and a good part of the morning. He could have gone on walking till sunset if he had chosen, all the way to his little stone house near Ardea, stopping by the way to get a meal; and then he would not have slept much longer than usual. A Roman peasant in his native Campagna, with enough to eat and a little wine, is hard to beat at walking. Ercole had not stopped to rest, but to think.

When he had thought some time, he looked about to

see if any one were looking at him, and he saw that the only people in sight were a long way off. He took his big clasp-knife out of his pocket and opened it. As the clasp clicked at the back of the blade Nino woke and sat up, for the noise generally meant food.

The blade was straight and clean, and tolerably sharp. Ercole looked at it critically, drew the edge over his coarse thumb-nail to find if there were any nick in the steel, and then scratched the same thumb-nail with it, as one erases ink with a knife, to see how sharp it was. The point was like a needle, but he considered that the edge was dull, and he drew it up and down one of the brown barrels of his gun, as carefully as he would have sharpened a razor on a whetstone. After that he stropped it on the tough leathern strap by which he slung the gun over his shoulder when he walked; when he was quite satisfied, he shut the knife again and put it back into his pocket, and fell to thinking once more.

Nino watched the whole operation with bloodshot eyes, his tongue hanging out and quivering rhythmically as he panted in the heat to cool himself. When the knife disappeared, and the chance of a crust with it, the dog got up, deliberately turned his back to his master, and sat down again to look at the view.

"You see," said Ercole to himself and Nino, "this is an affair which needs thought. One must be just. It is one thing to kill a person's body, but it is quite another thing to kill a person's soul. That would be a great sin, and besides, it is not necessary. Do I wish harm to any one? No. It is justice. Perhaps I shall go to the galleys. Well, I shall always have the satisfaction, and it will be greater if I can say that this person is in Paradise. For I do not wish harm to any one."

Having said this in a tone which Nino could hear, Ercole sat thinking for some time longer, and then he rose and slung his gun over his shoulder, and went out from under the trees into the glaring heat, as if he were going into the city. But instead of turning to the left, up the hill, he went on by the broad road that follows the walls, till he came to the ancient church of Santa Croce. He went up the low steps to the deep porch and on to the entrance at the left. Nino followed him very quietly.

Ercole dipped his finger into the holy water and crossed himself, and then went up the nave, making as little noise as he could with his hob-nailed boots. An old monk in white was kneeling at a broad praying-stool before an altar on the left. Ercole stood still near him, waiting for him to rise, and slowly turning his soft hat in his hands, as if it were a rosary. He kept his eyes on the monk's face, studying the aged features. Presently the old man had finished his prayer and got upon his feet slowly, and looked at Ercole and then at Nino. Ercole moved forward a step, and stood still in an attitude of respect.

"What do you desire, my son?" asked the monk, very quietly. "Do you wish to confess?"

"No, father, not to-day," answered Ercole. "I

come to pray you to say three masses for the soul of a person who died suddenly. I have also brought the money. Only tell me how much it will be, and I will pay."

"You shall give what you will, my son," the monk said, "and I will say the masses myself."

Ercole got out his sheepskin purse, untied the strings, and looked into it, weighing it in his hand. Then he seemed to hesitate. The monk looked on quietly.

"It is of your own free will," he said. "What you choose to give is for the community, and for this church, and for the chapel of Saint Helen. It is better that you know."

Ercole drew the mouth of the purse together again and returned it to the inside of his waistcoat, from which he produced a large old leathern pocket-book.

"I will give five francs," he said, "for I know that if you say the masses yourself, they will be all good ones."

A very faint and gentle smile flitted over the aged face. Ercole held out the small note, and the monk took it.

"Thank you," he said. "Shall I say the masses for a man or a woman?"

"As it pleases you, father," Ercole answered.

"Eh?" The old monk looked surprised.

"It does not matter," Ercole explained. "Is not a mass for a man good for a woman also?"

"We say 'his' soul or 'her' soul, as the case may be, my son."

"Is that written in the book of the mass?" inquired Ercole distrustfully.

"Yes. Also, most people tell us the baptismal name of the dead person."

"Must I do that too?" Ercole asked, by no means pleased.

"Not unless you like," the monk answered, looking at him with some curiosity.

"But it is in the book of the mass that you must say 'his' or 'her' soul?"

"Yes."

"Then the masses will not be good unless you say the right word." Ercole paused a moment in deep thought, and looked down at his hat. "It will be better to say the masses for a female," he said at length, without meeting the monk's eyes.

"Very well," the latter answered. "I will say the first mass to-morrow."

"Thank you," said Ercole. "My respects!"

He made a sort of bow and hurried away, followed by Nino. The old monk watched him thoughtfully, and shook his head once or twice, for he guessed something of the truth, though by no means all.

CHAPTER XVI

"One might almost think that you wished to marry Aurora yourself," said Corbario, with a sneer.

He was standing with his back to the fire in the great library of the villa, for it was late autumn again; it was raining hard and the air was raw and chilly.

"You may think what you please," Marcello answered, leaning back in his deep leathern chair and taking up a book. "I am not going to argue with you."

"Insufferable puppy," growled Folco, almost under his teeth; but Marcello heard.

He rose instantly and faced the elder man without the slightest fear or hesitation.

"If this were not my house, and you my guest, I would have you put out of doors by the servants," he said, in a tone Corbario had never heard before. "As it is, I only advise you to go before I lose my temper altogether."

Corbario backed till his heels were against the fender, and tried to smile.

"My dear Marcello!" he protested. "What nonsense is this? You know I am not in earnest!"

"I am," said Marcello quietly enough, but not moving.

The half-invalid boy was not a boy any longer, nor

an invalid either, and he had found his hold on things, since the days when Folco had been used to lead him as easily as if he had no will of his own. No one would have judged him to be a weak man now, physically or mentally. His frame was spare and graceful still, but there was energy and directness in his movements, his shoulders were square and he held his head high; yet it was his face that had changed most, though in a way very hard to define. A strong manhood sometimes follows a weak boyhood, very much to the surprise of those who have long been used to find feebleness where strength has suddenly developed. Marcello Consalvi had never been cowardly, or even timid; he had only been weak in will as in body, an easy prey to the man who had tried to ruin him, body and soul, in the hope of sending him to his grave.

"I really cannot understand you, my dear boy," Corbario said very sweetly. "You used to be so gentle! But now you fly into a passion for the merest thing."

"I told you that I would not argue with you," Marcello said, keeping his temper. "This is my house, and I choose that you should leave it at once. Go your way, and leave me to go mine. You are amply provided for, as long as you live, and you do not need my hospitality any longer, since you are no longer my guardian. Live where you please. You shall not stay here."

"I certainly don't care to stay here if you don't want me," Folco answered. "But this is really too absurd! You must be going mad, to take such a tone with me!"

"It is the only one which any honourable man who knows you would be inclined to take."

"Take care! You are going too far."

"Because you are under my roof? Yes, perhaps. As my guest, if I have been hasty, I apologise for expressing my opinion of you. I am going out now. I hope you will find it convenient to have left before I come in."

Thereupon Marcello turned his back on Corbario, crossed the great library deliberately, and went out without looking round.

Folco was left alone, and his still face did not even express surprise or annoyance. He had indeed foreseen the coming break, ever since he had returned to the villa three weeks earlier, when Marcello had received him with evident coldness, not even explaining where he had been since they had last parted. But Folco had not expected that the rupture would come so suddenly, still less that he was literally to be turned out of the house which he still regarded as his own, and in which he had spent so many prosperous years. There had, indeed, been some coldly angry words between the two men. Marcello had told Folco quite plainly that he meant to be the master, and that he was of age, and should regulate his own life as he pleased, and he had expressed considerable disgust at the existence Folco had been leading in Paris and elsewhere; and Folco had always tried to laugh it off, calling Marcello prudish and hypersensitive in matters of morality, which he certainly was not. Once he had attempted an appeal to Marcello's former affection, recalling his mother's love for them both, but a look had come into the young man's eyes just then which even Corbario did not care to face again, and the relations between the two had become more strained from that time on.

It might seem almost incredible that a man capable of the crimes Corbario had committed in cold blood, for a settled purpose, should show so little power of following the purpose to its accomplishment after clearing the way to it by a murder; but every one who has had to do with criminals is aware that after any great exertion of destructive energy they are peculiarly subject to a long reaction of weakness which very often leads to their own destruction. If this were not a natural law, if criminals could exert continually the same energy and command the same superhuman cunning which momentarily helped them to perpetrate a crime, the world would be in danger of being possessed and ruled by them, instead of being mercifully, and perhaps too much, inclined to treat them as degenerates and madmen. Their conduct after committing a murder, for instance, seems to depend much more on their nerves than on their intelligence, and the time almost invariably comes when their nerves break down. It is upon the moment when this collapse of the will sets in that the really experienced detective counts, knowing that it may be hastened or retarded by circumstances quite beyond the murderer's control. The life of a murderer, after the deed, is one long fight with such circumstances, and if he once loses his coolness he is himself almost as surely lost as a man who is carried away by his temper in a duel with swords.

After Folco had killed his wife and had just failed to kill Marcello, he had behaved with wonderful calm and propriety for a little while; but before long the old wild longing for excitement and dissipation, so long kept down during his married life, had come upon him with irresistible force, and he had yielded to it. Then, in hours of reaction, in the awful depression that comes with the grey dawn after a night of wine and pleasure and play, terrible little incidents had come back to his memory. He had recalled Kalmon's face and quiet words, and his own weakness when he had first come to see Marcello in the hospital — that abject terror which both Regina and the doctor must have noticed — and his first impression that Marcello no longer trusted him as formerly, and many other things; and each time he had been thus disturbed, he had plunged deeper into the dissipation which alone could cloud such memories and keep them out of sight for a time; till at last he had come to live in a continual transition from recklessness to fear and from fear to recklessness, and he had grown to detest the very sight of Marcello so heartily that an open quarrel was almost a relief.

If he had been his former self, he would undoubtedly have returned to his original purpose of killing Marcello outright, since he had not succeeded in killing him by dissipation. But his nerve was not what it had been, and the circumstances were not in his favour.

Moreover, Marcello was now of age, and had probably made a will, unknown to Corbario, in which case the fortune would no longer revert to the latter. The risk was too great, since it would no longer be undertaken for a certainty amounting to millions. It was better to be satisfied with the life-interest in one-third of the property, which he already enjoyed, and which supplied him with abundant means for amusing himself.

It was humiliating to be turned out of the house by a mere boy, as he still called Marcello, but he was not excessively sensitive to humiliation, and he promised himself some sort of satisfactory vengeance before long. What surprised him most was that the first quarrel should have been about Aurora. He had more than once said in conversation that he meant to marry the girl, and Marcello had chosen to say nothing in answer to the statement; but when Folco had gone so far as to hint that Aurora was in love with him and was about to accept him, Marcello had as good as given him the lie direct, and a few more words had led to the outbreak recorded at the beginning of this chapter.

As a matter of fact Corbario understood what had led to it better than Marcello himself, who had no very positive reason for entirely disbelieving his stepfather's words. The Contessa and her daughter had returned to Rome, and Corbario often went to see them, whereas Marcello had not been even once. When Marcello had last seen Folco in the Engadine, he had left him sitting in their little room at the hotel. Folco was not at all too old to marry Aurora; he was rich, at least for life, and Aurora was poor; he was good-looking, accomplished, and ready with his tongue. It was by no means impossible that he might make an impression on the girl and ultimately win her. Besides, Marcello felt that odd little resentment against Aurora which very young men sometimes feel against young girls, whom they have thought they loved, or are really about to love, or are afraid of loving, which makes them rude, or unjust, or both, towards those perhaps quite unconscious maidens, and which no woman can ever understand.

" My dear Harry, why will you be so disagreeable to Mary ? " asks the wondering mother. " She is such a charming girl, and only the other day she was saying that you are such a nice boy ! "

" Humph ! " snorts Harry rudely, and forthwith lights his pipe and goes off to the stables to growl in peace, or across country, or to his boat, or to any other heavenly place not infested by women.

There had been moments when, in his heart, Marcello had almost said that it would serve Aurora right to be married to Corbario; yet at the first hint from the latter that she was at all in danger of such a fate, Marcello had broken out as if the girl's good name had been attacked, and had turned his stepfather out of the house in a very summary fashion.

Having done so, he left the villa on foot, though it was raining hard, and walked quickly past San Pietro in Montorio and down the hill towards Trastevere.

The southwest wind blew the rain under his umbrella; it was chilly as well as wet, and a few big leaves were beginning to fall from the plane-trees.

He was not going to the little house, where Regina sat by the window looking at the rain and wishing that he would come soon. When he was down in the streets he hailed the first cab he saw, gave the man an address in the Forum of Trajan, and climbed in under the hood, behind the dripping leathern apron, taking his umbrella with him and getting thoroughly wet, as is inevitable when one takes a Roman cab in the rain.

The Contessa was out, in spite of the weather, but Marcello asked if Aurora would see him, and presently he was admitted to the drawing-room, where she was sitting beside a rather dreary little fire, cutting a new book. She threw it down and rose to meet him, as little outwardly disturbed as if they had seen each other constantly during the past two years. She gave him her hand quietly, and they sat down and looked at the fire.

"It won't burn," Aurora said, rather disconsolately. "It never did burn very well, but those horrid people who have had the apartment for two years have spoilt the fireplace altogether."

"I remember that it used to smoke," Marcello answered, going down on his knees and beginning to move the little logs into a better position.

"Thank you," Aurora said, watching him. "You won't succeed, but it's good of you to try."

Marcello said nothing, and presently he took the

queer little Roman bellows, and set to work to blow upon the smouldering spots where the logs touched each other. In a few seconds a small flame appeared, and soon the fire was burning tolerably.

"How clever you are!" Aurora laughed quietly.

Marcello rose and sat upon a low chair, instead of on the sofa beside her. For a while neither spoke, and he looked about him rather awkwardly, while Aurora watched the flames. It was long since he had been in the room, and it looked shabby after the rather excessive magnificence of the villa on the Janiculum, for which Corbario's taste had been largely responsible. It was just a little shabby, too, compared with the dainty simplicity of the small house in Trastevere. The furniture, the carpets, and the curtains were two years older than when he had seen them last, and had been unkindly used by the tenants to whom the Contessa had sub-let the apartment in order to save the rent. Marcello missed certain pretty things that he had been used to see formerly, some bits of old Saxe, a little panel by an early master, a chiselled silver cup in which there always used to be flowers. He wondered where these things were, and felt that the room looked rather bare without them.

"It burns very well now," said Aurora, still watching the fire.

"What has become of the old silver cup," Marcello asked, "and all the little things that used to be about?"

"We took them away with us when we let the apartment, and they are not unpacked yet, though we have been here two months."

"Two months?"

"Yes. I was wondering whether you were ever coming to see us again!"

"Were you? I fancied that you would not care very much to see me now."

Aurora said nothing to this, and they both looked at the fire for some time. The gentle sound of the little flames was cheerful, and gave them both the impression of a third person, talking quietly.

"I should not have come to-day," Marcello said at last, "except that something has happened."

"Nothing bad, I hope!" Aurora looked up with a sudden anxiety that surprised him.

"Bad? No. At least, I think not. Why are you startled?"

"I have had a headache," Aurora explained. "I am a little nervous, I fancy. What is it that has happened?"

Marcello glanced at her doubtfully before he answered. Her quick interest in whatever chanced to him took him back to the old times in an instant. The place was familiar and quiet; her voice was like forgotten music, once delightful, and now suddenly recalled; her face had only changed to grow more womanly.

"You never thought of marrying Folco, did you?" he asked, all at once, and a little surprised at the sound of his own words.

"I?" Aurora started again, but not with anxiety. "How can you think such a thing?"

"I don't think it; but an hour ago, at the villa, he told me in almost so many words that you loved him and meant to accept him."

A blush of honest anger rose in the girl's fair face, and subsided instantly.

"And what did you say?" she asked, with a scarcely perceptible tremor in her tone.

"I turned him out of the house," Marcello answered quietly.

"Turned him out?" Aurora seemed amazed. "You turned him out because he told you that?"

"That and other things. But that was the beginning of it. I told him that he was lying, and he called me names, and then I told him to go. He will be gone when I reach home."

To Marcello's surprise, Aurora got up suddenly, crossed the room and went to one of the windows. Marcello rose, too, and stood still. She seemed to be looking out at the rain, but she had grasped one of the curtains tightly, and it looked as if she were pressing the other hand to her left side. For a second her head bent forward a little and her graceful shoulders moved nervously, as though she were trying to swallow something hard. Marcello watched her a moment, and then crossed the room and stood beside her.

"What is it?" he asked in a low voice, and laying his hand gently on hers that held the curtain.

She drew her own away quietly and turned her head. Her eyes were dry and bright, but there were deep bistre shadows under them that had not been there before, and the lower lids were swollen.

"It is nothing," she answered, and then laughed nervously. "I am glad you have made your stepfather go away. It was time! I was afraid you were as good friends as ever."

"We have not been on good terms since we parted in Pontresina. Do you remember when I left him in your sitting-room at the hotel? He had been trying to persuade me to go back to Paris with him at once. In fact — " he hesitated.

"You intended to go," Aurora said, completing the sentence. "And then you changed your mind."

"Yes. I could not do it. I cannot explain everything."

"I understand without any explanation. I think you did right."

She went back to the fireplace and sat down in the corner of the sofa, leaning far back and stretching out one foot to the fender in an unconscious attitude of perfect grace. In the grey afternoon the firelight began to play in her auburn hair. Now and then she glanced at Marcello with half-closed lids, and there was a suggestion of a smile on her lips. Marcello saw that in her way she was as beautiful as Regina, and he remembered how they had kissed, without a word, when the moon's rays quivered through the trees by the Roman shore, more than two years ago. They had been children then. All at once he felt a great longing to kneel down beside the sofa and throw his arms round her waist and kiss her once again; but at almost the same instant he thought of Regina, waiting for him by the window over there in Trastevere, and he felt the shame rising to his face; and he leaned back in his low chair, clasping his hands tightly over one knee, as if to keep himself from moving.

"Marcello," Aurora began presently, but she got no further.

"Yes?" Still he did not move.

"I have something on my conscience." She laughed low. "No, it is serious!" she went on, as if reproving herself. "I have always felt that everything that has happened to you since we parted that morning by the shore has been my fault."

"Why?" Marcello seemed surprised.

"Because I called you a baby," she said. "If you had not been angry at that, if you had not turned away and left me suddenly — you were quite right, you know — you would not have been knocked down, you would not have wandered away and lost yourself. You would not have lost your memory, or been ill in a strange place, or — or all the rest! So it is all my fault, you see, from beginning to end."

"How absurd!" Marcello looked at her and smiled.

"No. I think it is true. But you have changed very much, Marcello. You are not a boy any longer. You have a will of your own now; you are a man. Do you mind my telling you that?"

"Certainly not!" He smiled again.

"I remember very well what you answered. You

said that I should not laugh at you again. And that has come true. You said a good many other things. Do you remember?"

"No. I was angry. What did I say? Everything that happened before I was hurt seems very far off."

"It does not matter," Aurora answered softly. "I am glad you have forgotten, for though I was angry too, and did not care at the time, the things you said have hurt me since."

"I am sorry," Marcello said gently, "very, very sorry. Forgive me."

"It was all my fault, for I was teasing you for the mere fun of the thing. I was nothing but a silly school-girl then."

"Yes. You have changed, too."

"Am I at all what you expected I should be?" Aurora asked, after a moment's silence.

Marcello glanced at her, and clasped his hands over his knee more tightly than ever.

"I wish you were not," he answered in a low voice.

"Don't wish that." Her tone was even lower than his.

Neither spoke again for some time, and they did not look at each other. But the flames flickering in the small fireplace seemed to be talking, like a third person in the room. Aurora moved at last, and changed her position.

"I am glad that you have quarrelled with your stepfather," she said. "He meant to do you all the harm he could. He meant you to die of the life you were leading."

"You know that?" Marcello looked up quickly.

"Yes. I have heard my mother and Professor Kalmon talking about it when they thought I was not listening. I always pretend that I am not listening when anybody talks about you." She laughed a little. "It is so much simpler," she added, as if to explain. "The Professor said that your stepfather was killing you by inches. Those were his words."

"The Professor never liked him. But he was right. Have you seen him often?"

"Yes." Aurora laughed again. "He always turns up wherever we are, pretending that it is the most unexpected meeting in the world. He is just like a boy!"

"What do you mean? Is he in love with you?"

"With me? No! He is madly in love with my mother! Fancy such a thing! When he found that we were coming back to Rome he gave up his professorship in Milan, and he has come to live here so as to be able to see her. So I hear them talking a great deal, and he seems to have found out a great many things about your stepfather which nobody ever knew. He takes an extraordinary interest in him for some reason or other."

"What has he found out?" asked Marcello.

"Enough to hang him, if people could be hanged in Italy," Aurora answered.

"I should have thought Folco too clever to do anything really against the law," said Marcello, who did not seem much surprised at what she said.

"The Professor believes that it was he that tried to kill you."

"How is that possible?" Marcello asked, in great astonishment. "You would have seen him!"

"I did. You had not been gone three minutes when he came round to the gap in the bank where I was standing. He came from the side towards which I had seen you go. It was perfectly impossible that he should not have met you. The Professor says he must have known that you were there, looking at the storm, but that he did not know that I was with you, and that he was lying in wait for you to strike you from behind. If we had gone back together he would not have shown himself, that's all, and he would have waited for a better chance. If I had only followed you I should have seen what happened."

"That is the trouble," said Marcello thoughtfully. "No one ever saw what happened, and I remember nothing but that I fell forward, feeling that I had been struck on the back of the head. Did you not hear any sound?"

"How could I, in such a gale as was blowing? It all looks dreadfully likely and quite possible, and the Professor is convinced that your stepfather has done some worse things."

"Worse?"

"Yes, because he did not fail in doing them, as he did when he tried to kill you."

"But what must such a man be?" cried Marcello, suddenly breaking out in anger. "What must his life have been in all the years before my mother married him?"

"He was a kind of adventurer in South America. I don't quite know what he did there, but Professor Kalmon has found out a great deal about him from the Argentine Republic, where he lived until he killed somebody and had to escape to Europe. If I were you I would go and see the Professor, since he is in Rome. He lives at No. 16, Via Sicilia. He will tell you a great deal about that man when he knows that you have parted for good."

"I'll go and see him. Thank you. I cannot imagine that he could tell me anything worse than I have already heard."

"Perhaps he may," Aurora answered very gravely.

Then she was silent, and Marcello could not help looking at her as she leaned back in the corner of the sofa. Of all things, at that moment, he dreaded lest he should lose command of himself under the unexpected influence of her beauty, of old memories, of the failing light, of the tender shadows that still lingered under her eyes, of that exquisite small hand that lay idly on the sofa beside her, just within his reach. He rose abruptly, no longer trusting himself.

"I must be going," he said.

"Already? Why?" She looked up at him and their eyes met.

"Because I cannot be alone with you any longer. I do not trust myself."

"Yes, you do. You are a man now, and I trust you."

He had spoken roughly and harshly in his momentary self-contempt, but her words were clear and quiet, and rang true. He stood still in silence for a moment.

"And besides," she added softly, "she trusts you too."

There was a little emphasis on the word "she" and in her tone that was a reproach, and he looked at her in wonder.

"We cannot talk of her, you and I," she said, turning her eyes to the fire, "but you know what I mean, Marcello. It is not enough to be kind. We women do not think so much of that as you men fancy. You must be true as well."

"I know it," Marcello answered, bending his head a little. "Good-bye, Aurora."

"No. Not good-bye, for you will come again soon, and then again, and often."

"Shall I?"

"Yes, because we can trust each other, though we are fond of each other. We are not children any longer, as we used to be."

"Then I will come sometimes."

He took her hand, trying not to feel that it was in his, and he left her sitting by the rather dreary little fire, in the rather shabby room, in the grey twilight.

As he drove through the wet streets, he went over all she had said, went over it again and again, till he knew her words by heart. But he did not try, or dare to try, to examine what he felt, and was going to feel. The manliness that had at last come to its full growth in him clung to the word "true" as she had meant it.

But she, being left alone, leaned forward, resting her elbows on her knees and clasping her hands as she gazed at the smouldering remains of the fire. She had known well enough that she had loved him before he had come; she had known it too well when he had told her how he had driven Folco out of his house for having spoken of her too carelessly. Then the blood had rushed to her throat, beating hard, and if she had not gone quickly to the window she felt that she must have cried for joy. She was far too proud to let him guess that, but she was not too proud to love him, in spite of everything, though it meant that she compared herself with the peasant girl, and envied her, and in all maiden innocence would have changed places with her if she could.

CHAPTER XVII

It was late in the evening when Marcello reached the villa, and was told that his stepfather had left suddenly with his valet, before sunset, taking a good deal of luggage with him. The coachman had driven him to the station and had seen no more of him. He had not left any message or note for Marcello. This was as it should be, and Marcello did not care to know whither he had gone, since he was out of the house. He was glad, however, that he had left Rome at once instead of going to an hotel, which would have made an interesting topic of conversation for gossips.

Marcello vaguely wondered why Folco had told a perfectly gratuitous falsehood about Aurora, and whether he could possibly have lied merely for the sake of hurting him. If so, he had got his deserts. It mattered very little now, and it was a waste of thought to think of him at all.

The young man had a big fire built in the library, and sat down in his favourite leathern chair under the shaded light. He was tired, but not sleepy, and he was glad to be alone at last, for he had felt Corbario's evil presence in the house, though they had met little of late, and it was a great relief to know that he would never return.

He was glad to be alone, and yet he felt lonely, for the one condition did not make the other impossible. He was glad to be able to think in peace, but when he did think, he longed for some companionship in his thoughts, and he found that he was wishing himself back in the room that looked down upon the Forum of Trajan, with Aurora, and that she was telling him again that she could trust him; and yet the very thought seemed to mean that he was not to be trusted.

Psychological problems are only interesting when they concern other people than ourselves, for there can be no problem where there is not a difficulty, and where the inner self is concerned there can be no difficulty that does not demand immediate solution if we are to find peace. Some men of very strong and thoughtful character are conscious of a sort of second self within themselves, to which they appeal in trouble as Socrates to his Dæmon; but most men, in trouble and alone, would turn to a friend if there were one at hand.

Marcello had none, and he felt horribly lonely in his great house, as the faces of two women rose before him, on the right and left.

But he was a man now, and as he sat there he determined to face the problem bravely and to solve it once and for ever by doing what was right, wheresoever he could convince himself that right lay, and without any regard for his own inclinations.

He told himself that this must be possible, because where right and wrong were concerned it was never possible to hesitate long. A man is never so convinced that right is easy to distinguish and to do as when he has lately made up his mind to reform. Indeed, the weakness as well as the strength of all reformers lies in their blind conviction that whatever strikes them as right must be done immediately, with a haste that strongly resembles hurry, and with no regard for consequences. You might as well try, when an express train is running at full speed on the wrong track, to heave it over to the right one without stopping it and without killing the passengers. Yet most reformers of themselves and others, from the smallest to the greatest, seem to believe that this can be done, ought to be done, and must be done at once.

Marcello was just then a reformer of this sort. He had become aware in the course of that afternoon that something was seriously wrong, and as his own will and character had served him well of late, he trusted both beforehand and set to work to find out the right track, with the distinct intention of violently transferring the train of his existence to it as soon as it had been discovered. He was very sure of the result.

Besides, he had been brought up by a very religious woman, and a strong foundation of belief remained in him, and was really the basis of all his thinking about himself. He had been careless, thoughtless, reckless, since his mother had died, but he had never lost that something to which a man may best go back in trouble. Sometimes it hurt him, sometimes it comforted him vaguely, but he was always conscious that it was there, and had been there through all his wildest days. It was not a very reasoning belief, for he was not an intellectual man, but it was unchangeable and solid still in spite of all his past weakness. It bade him do right, blindly, and only because right was right; but it did not open his eyes to the terrible truth that whereas right is right, the Supreme Power, which is always in the right, does not take human life into consideration at all, and that a man is under all circumstances bound to consider the value of life to others, and sometimes its value to himself, when others depend upon him for their happiness, or safety, or welfare.

Animated by the most sincere wish to find the right direction and follow it — perhaps because Aurora had said that she trusted him — yet blind to the dangers that beset his path, there is no knowing how many lives Marcello might not have wrecked by acting on the resolutions he certainly would have made if he had been left to himself another hour.

He was deep in thought, his feet stretched out to the fire, his head leaning back against the leathern cushion of his chair, his eyes half closed, feeling that he was quite alone and beyond the reach of every one, if he chose to sit there until morning wrestling with his psychological problem.

He was roused by the sharp buzz of the telephone instrument which stood on the writing-table. It was very annoying, and he wished he had turned it off before he had sat down, but since some one was calling he got up reluctantly to learn who wanted him at that hour. He glanced at the clock, and saw that it was nearly half-past ten. The instrument buzzed again as he reached the table.

"I want to see Signor Consalvi at once; is it too late?" asked a man's voice anxiously.

"I am Consalvi. Who are you, please?" asked Marcello.

"Kalmon. Is it true that Corbario has left the villa?"

"Yes. He left this afternoon."

"Where is he now?"

"He drove to the railway station. I don't know where he is gone. He left no address."

"— railway station — no address —" Marcello heard the words as Kalmon spoke to some other person at his elbow, wherever he was.

"May I come at once?" Kalmon asked.

"Yes. I am alone. I'll have the lower gate opened."

"Thanks. I shall be at the gate in twenty minutes. Good-bye."

"Good-bye."

Marcello hung up the receiver, rang the bell, and gave the order for the gate, adding that the gentleman who came was to be shown in at once. Then he sat down and waited.

It was clear that Kalmon had learned of Corbario's departure from Aurora, perhaps through her mother. He had probably dined with them, for he was intimate at the house, and Aurora had spoken of Marcello's visit. There was no reason why she should not have done so, and yet Marcello wished that she had kept it to herself a little longer. It had meant so much to him, and it suddenly seemed as if it had meant nothing at all to her. She had perhaps repeated to her mother everything that had been said, or almost everything, for she was very fond of her.

Marcello told himself roughly that since he had no right to love her, and was determined not to, he had no claim upon such little delicacies of discretion and silence on her part; and his problem stuck up its head again out of the deep water in which it lived, and glared at him, and shot out all sorts of questions like the wriggling tentacles of an octopus, inviting him to wrestle with them, if only to see how useless all wrestling must be. He rose again impatiently, took a cigar from a big mahogany box on the table, lit it and smoked savagely, walking up and down.

It was half finished when the door opened and Kalmon was ushered in. He held out his hand as he came forward, with the air of a man who has no time to lose.

"I am glad to see you," Marcello said.

"And I am exceedingly glad that you were at home when I called you up," Kalmon answered. "Have you really no idea where Corbario is?"

"Not the slightest. I am only too glad to get rid of him. I suppose the Contessa told you—"

"Yes. I was dining there. But she only told me half an hour ago, just as I was coming away, and I rushed home to get at the telephone."

It occurred to Marcello that Kalmon need not have

driven all the way to Via Sicilia from the Forum of Trajan merely for the sake of telephoning.

"But what is the hurry?" asked Marcello. "Do sit down and explain! I heard this afternoon that you had strong suspicions as to Folco's part in what happened to me."

"Something more than suspicions now," Kalmon answered, settling his big frame in a deep chair before the fire; "but I am afraid he has escaped."

"Escaped? He has not the slightest idea that he is suspected!"

"How do you know? Don't you see that as he is guilty, he must have soon begun to think that the change in your manner toward him was due to the fact that you suspected him, and that you turned him out because you guessed the truth, though you could not prove it?"

"Perhaps," Marcello admitted, in a rather preoccupied tone. "The young lady seems to have repeated to her mother everything I said this afternoon," he added with evident annoyance. "Did the Contessa tell you why I quarrelled with Folco to-day?"

"No. She merely said that there had been angry words and that you had asked him to leave the house. She herself was surprised, she said, and wondered what could have brought matters to a crisis at last."

Marcello's face cleared instantly. Aurora had not told any one that he had quarrelled with his stepfather about her; that was quite evident, for there were not two more truthful people in the world than the

Contessa and Kalmon, whose bright brown eyes were at that moment quietly studying his face.

"Not that the fact matters in the least," said the Professor, resting his feet on the fender and exposing the broad soles of his wet walking-boots to the flame. "The important fact is that the man has escaped, and we must catch him."

"But how are you so sure that it was he that attacked me? You cannot arrest a man on suspicion, without going through a great many formalities. You cannot possibly have got an eye-witness to the fact, and so it must be a matter of suspicion after all, founded on a certain amount of rather weak circumstantial evidence. Now, if it was he that tried to kill me, he failed, for I am alive, and perfectly well. Why not let him alone, since I have got rid of him?"

"For a very good reason, which I think I had better not tell you."

"Why not?"

"I am not sure what you would do if you were told it suddenly. Are your nerves pretty good? You used to be a delicate boy, though I confess that you look much stronger now."

"You need not fear for my nerves," Marcello answered with a short laugh. "If they are sound after what I have been through in the last two years they will stand anything!"

"Yes. Perhaps you had better know, though I warn you that what I am going to say will be a shock to you, of which you do not dream."

"You must be exaggerating!" Marcello smiled incredulously. "You had better tell me at once, or I shall imagine it is much worse than it is."

"It could not be," Kalmon answered. "It is hard even to tell, and not only because what happened was in a distant way my fault."

"Your fault? For heaven's sake tell me what the matter is, and let us be done with it!"

"Corbario wanted to get possession of your whole fortune. That is why he tried to kill you."

"Yes. Is that all? You have made me understand that already."

"He had conceived the plan before your mother's death," said Kalmon.

"That would not surprise me either. But how do you know it?"

"Do you remember that discovery of mine, that I called 'the sleeping death'?"

"Yes. What has that to do with it?" Marcello's expression changed.

"Corbario stole one of the tablets from the tube in my pocket, while I was asleep that night."

"What?" Marcello began to grow pale.

"Your mother died asleep," said Kalmon in a very low voice.

Marcello was transfixed with horror, and grasped the arms of his chair. His face was livid. Kalmon watched him, and continued.

"Yes. Corbario did it. Your mother used to take phenacetine tablets when she had headaches. They were very like the tablets of my poison in size and shape. Corbario stole into my room when I was sound asleep, took one of mine, and dropped in one of hers. Then he put mine amongst the phenacetine ones. She took it, slept, and died."

Marcello gasped for breath, his eyes starting from his head.

"You see," Kalmon went on, "it was long before I found that my tablets had been tampered with. There had been seven in the tube. I knew that, and when I glanced at the tube next day there were seven still. The tube was of rather thick blue glass, if you remember, so that the very small difference between the one tablet and the rest could not be seen through it. I went to Milan almost immediately, and when I got home I locked up the tube in a strong-box. It was not until long afterwards, when I wanted to make an experiment, that I opened the tube and emptied the contents into a glass dish. Then I saw that one tablet was unlike the rest. I saw that it had been made by a chemist and not by myself. I analysed it and found five grains of phenacetine."

Marcello leaned back, listening intently, and still deadly pale.

"You did not know that I was trying to find out how you had been hurt, that I was in communication with the police from the first, that I came to Rome and visited you in the hospital before you recovered your memory. The Contessa was very anxious to know the truth about her old friend's son, and I did what I could. That was natural. Something told me that Corbario had tried to kill you, and I suspected him, but it is only lately that I have got all the evidence we need. There is not a link lacking. Well, when I came to Rome that time, it chanced that I met Corbario at the station. He had come by the same train, and was looking dreadfully ill. That increased my suspicion, for I knew that his anxiety must be frightful, since you might have seen him when he struck you, and might recognise him, and accuse him. Yet he could not possibly avoid meeting you. Imagine what that man must have felt. He tried to smile when he saw me, and said he wished he had one of those sleeping tablets of mine. You understand. He thought I had already missed the one he had taken, though I had not, and that he had better disarm any possible suspicion by speaking of the poison carelessly. Then his face turned almost yellow, and he nearly fainted. He said it was the heat, and I helped him to his carriage. He looked like a man terrified out of his senses, and I remembered the fact afterwards, when I found that one tablet had been stolen; but at the time I attributed it all to his fear of facing you. Now we know the truth. He tried to murder you, and on the same day he poisoned your mother."

Kalmon sat quite still when he had finished, and for a long time Marcello did not move, and made no sound. At last he spoke in a dull voice.

"I want to kill him myself."

The Professor glanced at him and nodded slowly, as

if he understood the simple instinct of justice that moved him.

"If I see him, I shall kill him," Marcello said slowly. "I am sure I shall."

"I am afraid that he has escaped," Kalmon answered. "Of course there is a possibility that he may have had some object in deceiving your coachman by driving to the railway station, but it is not at all likely. He probably took the first train to the north."

"But he can be stopped at the frontier!"

"Do you think Corbario is the man to let himself be trapped easily if he knows that he is pursued?" asked Kalmon incredulously. "I do not."

He rose from his chair and began to walk up and down, his hands behind him and his head bent.

Marcello paid no attention to him and was silent for a long time, sitting quite motionless and scarcely seeming to breathe. What he felt he never could have told afterwards; he only knew that he suffered in every fibre of his brain and body, with every nerve of his heart and in every secret recess of his soul. His mother seemed to have been dead so long, beyond the break in his memory. The dreadful truth he had just heard made her die again before his eyes, by the hand of the man whom he and she had trusted.

"Kalmon," he said at last, and the Professor stopped short in his walk. "Kalmon, do you think she knows?"

It was like the cry of a child, but it came from a man who was already strong. Kalmon could only shake his head gravely; he could find nothing to say in answer to such a question, and yet he was too human and kind and simple-hearted not to understand the words that rose to Marcello's lips.

"Then she was happy to the end — then she still believes in him."

Kalmon turned his clear eyes thoughtfully towards Marcello's face.

"She is gone," he answered. "She knows the great secret now. The rest is nothing to the dead. But we are living and it is much to us. The man must be brought to justice, and you must help me to bring him down, if we have to hunt him round the world."

"By God, I will!" said Marcello, in the tone of one who takes a solemn obligation.

He rose and stood upright, as if he were ready, and though he was still pale there was no look of weak horror left in his face, nor any weakness at all.

"Good!" exclaimed Kalmon. "I would rather see you so. Now listen to me, and collect your thoughts, Marcello. Ercole is in Rome. You remember Ercole, your keeper at the cottage by the shore? Yes. I got the last link in the evidence about Corbario's attack on you from him to-day. He is a strange fellow. He has known it since last summer and has kept it to himself. But he is one of those diabolically clever peasants that one meets in the Campagna, and he must have his reasons. I told him to sleep at my house to-night, and when I went home he was sitting up in the entry with his dog. I have sent him to the station to find out whether Corbario really left or not. You don't think he will succeed? I tell you there are few detectives to be compared with one of those fellows when they are on the track of a man they hate. I told him to come here, no matter how late it might be, since he is your man. I suppose he can get in?"

"Of course. There is a night-bell for the porter. Ercole knows that. Besides, the porter will not go to bed as long as you are here. While we are waiting for him, tell me what Ercole has found out."

They sat down again, and Kalmon told Marcello the sailor's story of what his captain had seen from the deck of the brigantine. Marcello listened gravely.

"I remember that there was a small vessel very far in," he said. "Aurora will remember it, too, for she watched it and spoke of it. We thought it must run aground on the bar, it was so very near."

"Yes. She remembers it, too. The evidence is complete."

There was silence again. Marcello threw another log upon the fire, and they waited. Kalmon smoked thoughtfully, but Marcello leaned back in his chair, covering his eyes with one hand. The pain had not begun to be dulled yet, and he could only sit still and bear it.

At last the door opened, and a servant said that Ercole was waiting, and had been ordered to come, no matter how late it was. A moment later he appeared, and for once without his dog.

He stood before the door as it closed behind him.

waiting to be told to come forward. Marcello spoke kindly to him.

"Come here," he said. "It is a long time since we saw each other, and now we are in a hurry."

Ercole's heavy boots rang on the polished floor as he obeyed and came up to the table. He looked gloomily and suspiciously at both men.

"Well?" said Kalmon, encouraging him to speak.

"He is still in Rome," Ercole answered. "How do I know it? I began to ask the porters and the under station-masters who wear red caps, and the woman who sells newspapers and cigars at the stand, and the man who clips the tickets at the doors of the waiting-rooms. 'Did you see a gentleman, so and so, with a servant, so and so, and much luggage, going away by the train? For I am his keeper from the Roman shore, and he told me to be here when he went away, to give him a certain answer.' So I said, going from one to another, and weeping to show that it was a very urgent matter. And many shook their heads and laughed at me. But at last a porter heard, and asked if the gentleman were so and so. And I said yes, that he was so and so, and his servant was so and so, and that the gentleman was a rich gentleman. And the porter said, 'See what a combination! That is the gentleman who had all his luggage brought in this afternoon, to be weighed; but it was not weighed, for he came back after a quarter of an hour, and took some small things and had them put upon a cab, but the other boxes were left in deposit.' Then I took out four sous and showed them to the porter, and he led me to a certain hall, and showed me the luggage, which is that of the man we seek, and it is marked 'F. C.' So when I had seen, I made a show of being joyful, and gave the porter five sous instead of four. And he was very contented. This is the truth. So I say, he is still in Rome."

"I told you so," said Kalmon, looking at Marcello.

"Excuse me, but what did you tell the young gentleman?" asked Ercole suspiciously.

"That you would surely find out," Kalmon answered.

"I have found out many things," said Ercole gloomily.

His voice was very harsh just then, as if speaking so much had made him hoarse.

"He took some of his things away because he meant to spend the night in Rome," Kalmon said thoughtfully. "He means to leave to-morrow, perhaps by an early train. If we do not find him to-night, we shall not catch him in Rome at all."

"Surely," said Ercole, "but Rome is very big, and it is late."

CHAPTER XVIII

IT was still raining when the three men left the villa, and the night was very dark, for the young moon had already set. The wind howled round San Pietro in Montorio and the Spanish Academy, and whistled through the branches of the plane-trees along the winding descent, and furiously tore the withering leaves. They struck Ercole's weather-beaten face as he sat beside the coachman with bent head, with his soft hat pulled down over his eyes, and the rain dripped from his coarse moustache. Kalmon and Marcello leaned as far back as they could, under the deep hood and behind the high leathern apron.

"There is some animal following us," the cabman said to Ercole as they turned a corner.

"It is my dog," Ercole answered.

"It sounds like a calf," said the cabman, turning his head to listen through the storm.

"It is not a calf," answered Ercole gruffly. "It is my dog. Or if you wish it to be the were-wolf, it will be the were-wolf."

The cabman glanced uneasily at his companion on the box, for the were-wolf is a thing of terror to Romans. But he could not see the countryman's features in the gloom, and he hastened his horse's pace down the hill, for he did not like the sound of those galloping feet behind his cab, in that lonely road, in the dark and the rain.

"Where am I to go?" he asked, as he came near the place where a turn to the right leads out of the Via Garibaldi down to the Via Luciano Manara.

But Kalmon knew where they were, even better than Marcello, to whom the road was familiar by day and night, in all weathers.

"We must leave that message first," said the Professor to Marcello. "We are coming to the turning."

"To Santa Cecilia," Marcello called out to the cabman, thrusting his head forward into the rain, "then I will tell you where to go."

"Santa Cecilia," echoed the cabman.

Ercole growled something quite unintelligible, to which his companion paid no attention, and the cab rattled on through the rain down the long paved street. It made such a noise that the dog's feet could not be heard any more. There were more lamps, too, and it seemed less gloomy than up there under the plane-trees, though there were no lights in the windows at that late hour.

"Now to the right," said Ercole, as they reached the back of Saint Cecilia's at the Via Anicia.

"To the right!" Marcello called out a second later from under the hood.

"You seem to know the way," said the cabman to Ercole. "Why don't you give me the address of the house at once and be done with it?"

"I know the house, but not the street, nor the number."

"I understand. Does your dog also know the house?"

To this question Ercole made no answer, for he considered that it was none of the cabman's business, and, moreover, he regretted having shown that he knew where his master was going. Marcello now gave the final direction to the cabman, who drew up before a door in a wall, in a narrow lane, where the walls were high and the doors were few. It was the garden entrance to the little house in Trastevere.

Marcello got out, opened the door with the key he carried, and went in. It was raining hard, and he disappeared into the darkness, shutting the door behind him. It had a small modern lock with a spring latch that clicked sharply as it shut. The cab had stopped with the door on the left, and therefore on the side on which Ercole was sitting. Nino, the dog, came up from behind, with his tongue hanging out, blood-red in the feeble light of the cab's lamp; he put his head up above the low front wheel to have a look at Ercole. Being satisfied, he at once lay down on the wet stones, with his muzzle towards the door.

Two or three minutes passed thus, in total silence. The cab-horse hung his head patiently under the driving rain, but neither stamped on the paving stones nor shook himself, nor panted audibly, for he was a pretty good horse, as cab-horses go, and was not tired.

Suddenly Nino growled without moving, the ominous low growl of a dog that can kill, and Ercole growled at him in turn, making a sound intended to impose silence. There was no reason why Nino should growl at Marcello. But Nino rose slowly upon his quarters, as if he were about to spring at the door, and his rough coat bristled along his back. Then Ercole distinctly heard the latch click as it had done when Marcello went in, and Nino put his muzzle to the crack of the closed door and sniffed up and down it, and then along the stone step. To Ercole it was clear that some person within had opened the door noiselessly a little way and had shut it again rather hurriedly, on hearing the dog and seeing the cab. Whoever it was had wished to see if there were any one outside, without being seen, or perhaps had meant to slip out without being heard by any one in the house.

Kalmon, leaning back inside, had not heard the sound of the latch, and paid no attention to Nino's growl. It was natural that such an animal should growl and snarl for nothing, he thought, especially on a rainy night, when the lamps of a cab throw strange patches of light on the glistening pavement.

There was some reason why Ercole, who had heard, did not get down and tell the Professor, who had noticed nothing. One reason, and a good enough one, was that whoever it was that had opened the door so cautiously, it certainly was not the man they were all hunting that night. Yet since Ercole knew the little house, and probably knew who lived there, and that it belonged to Marcello, it might have been supposed that he would have told the latter, whose footsteps were heard on the gravel a few moments afterwards. But though Marcello stood a moment by the wheel close to Ercole, and spoke across him to the cabman, Ercole said nothing. Nino had not growled at Marcello, even before the latter had appeared, for Nino had a good memory, for a dog, and doubtless remembered long days spent by the Roman shore, and copious leavings thrown to him from luxurious luncheons. Before they had left the villa he had sniffed at Marcello's clothes and hands in a manner that was meant to be uncommonly friendly, though it might not have seemed reassuring to a stranger; and Marcello had patted his huge head, and called him by name.

The young man had given the cabman the address of the office of the Chief of Police, and when he had got in and hooked up the leathern apron, the cab rolled away over the stones through the dark streets, towards the bridge of Saint Bartholomew.

Within the house Regina sat alone, as Marcello had found her, her chin resting on the back of her closed hand, her elbow on her knee, her eyes gazing at the bright little fire that blazed on the polished hearth. Her hair was knotted for the night, low down on her neck, and the loose dressing-gown of dove-coloured silk plush was unfastened at the neck, where a little lace fell about her strong white throat.

She had sprung to her feet in happy surprise when Marcello had entered the room, though it was not two hours since he had left her, and she could still smell the smoke of his last cigarette. She had felt a sudden chill when she had seen his face, for she never saw him look grave and preoccupied without believing that he had grown suddenly tired of her, and that the end had come. But then she had seen his eyes lighten for her, and she had known that he was not tired of her, but only very much in earnest and very much in a hurry.

He had bidden her find out from Settimia where Corbario was, if the woman knew it; he had told her to find out at any cost, and had put a great deal of emphasis on the last words. In answer to the one question she asked, he told her that Corbario was a murderer, and was trying to escape. He had not time to explain more fully, but he knew that he could count on her. She did not love Folco Corbario, and she came of a race that could hate, for it was the race of the Roman hill peasants. So he left her quickly and went on.

But when he was gone, Regina sat quite still for some time, looking at the fire. Settimia was safe in her own room, and was probably asleep. It would be soon enough to wake her when Regina had considered what she should say in order to get the information Marcello wanted. Settimia would deny having had any communication with Corbario, or that she knew anything of his whereabouts. The next step would probably be to tempt her with money or other presents. If this failed, what was to be done? Somehow Regina guessed that a bribe would not have much effect on the woman.

Marcello had wished to send her away long ago, but Regina had persuaded him to let her stay. It was part of her hatred of Corbario to accumulate proofs against him, and they were not lacking in the letters he wrote to Settimia. Regina could not understand the relation in which they stood to each other, but now and then she had found passages in the letters which referred neither to herself nor Marcello, but to things that had happened a good many years ago in another country. She was convinced that the two had once been companions in some nefarious business, of which they had escaped the consequences. It was her intention to find out exactly what the deed had been, and then to bring Corbario to ruin by exposing it. It was a simple scheme, but it seemed a sure one, and Regina was very patient. Corbario had tried to separate her from Marcello, and she had sworn that he should pay her for that; and besides, he had wished to kill Marcello in order to get his money. That was bad, undoubtedly — very bad; but to her peasant mind it was not unnatural. She had heard all her life of crimes committed for the sake of an inheritance; and so have most of us, and in countries that fondly believe themselves much more civilised than Italy. That was extremely wicked, but the attempt had failed, and it sank into insignificance in comparison with the heinous crime of trying to separate two lovers by treachery. That was what Regina would not forgive Corbario.

Nor would she pardon Settimia, who had been Corbario's instrument and helper; and as she meant to include the woman in her vengeance, she would not let her go, but kept her, and treated her so generously and unsuspiciously that Settimia was glad to stay, since Corbario still wished it.

Regina looked at the little travelling-clock that stood on the low table at her elbow, and saw that it was half-past eleven. Behind the drawn curtains she could hear the rain beating furiously against the shutters, but all was quiet within the house. Regina listened, for Settimia's room was overhead, and when she moved about her footsteps could be heard in the sitting-room. Regina had heard her just before Marcello had come in, but there was no sound now; she had probably gone to bed. Regina lit a candle and went into her own room.

On a shelf near the little toilet-table there was a box, covered with old velvet, in which she kept the few simple pins and almost necessary bits of jewellery which she had been willing to accept from Marcello. She took it down, set it upon the toilet-table and opened it. A small silver-mounted revolver lay amongst the other things, for Marcello had insisted that she should have a weapon of some kind, because the house seemed lonely to him. He had shown her how to use it, but she had forgotten. She took it out, and turned it over and over in her hands, with a puzzled look. She did not even know whether it was loaded or not, and did not remember how to open the chamber. She wondered how the thing worked, and felt rather afraid of it. Besides, if she had to use it, it would make a dreadful noise; so she put it back carefully amongst the things.

There were the cheap little earrings she had worn ever since she had been a child, till Marcello had made her take them out and wear none at all. There was a miserable little brooch of tarnished silver which she had bought with her own money at a country fair, and which had once seemed very fine to her. She had not the slightest sentiment about such trifles, for Italian peasants are altogether the least sentimental people in the world; the things were not even good enough to give to Settimia, and yet it seemed wrong to throw them away, so she had always kept them, with a vague idea of giving them to some poor little girl, to whom they would represent happiness. With them lay the long pin she used to stick through her hair on Sundays when she went to church.

It had been her mother's, and it was the only thing she possessed which had belonged to the murdered woman who had given her birth. It was rather a fine specimen of the pins worn by the hill peasant women, and was made like a little cross-hilted sword, with a blade of fire-gilt steel about eight inches long. A little gilt ball was screwed upon the point, intended to keep the pin from coming out after it was thrust through the hair. Regina took the ball off and felt the point, which was as sharp as that of a pen-knife; and she tried the blade with her hands and found that it did not bend easily. It was strong enough for what she wanted of it. She stuck it through the heavy knot of her hair, rather low down at the back of her neck, where she could easily reach it with her right hand; but she did not screw on the ball. It was not likely that the pin would fall out. She was very deliberate in all she did; she even put up her hand two or three times, without looking at herself in the mirror, to be quite sure where to find the hilt of the pin if she should need it. Marcello had told her to get the information he wanted "at any cost."

Then she went back, with her candle, through the cheerful sitting-room, and out through a small vestibule that was now dark, and up the narrow staircase to find Settimia.

She knocked, and the woman opened, and Regina was a little surprised to see that she was still dressed. She was pale, and looked very anxious as she faced her mistress in the doorway.

"What is the matter?" she asked, rather nervously.

"Nothing," Regina answered in a reassuring tone. "I had forgotten to tell you about a little change I want in the trimming of that hat, and as I heard you moving about, I came up before going to bed."

Settimia had taken off her shoes more than half an hour earlier in order to make no noise, and her suspicions and her fears were instantly aroused. She drew her lids together a little and looked over Regina's shoulder through the open door towards the dark staircase. She was not a tall woman, and was slightly made, but she was energetic and could be quick when she chose, as Regina knew. Regina quietly shut the door behind her and came forward into the room, carrying her candlestick, which she set down upon the table near the lamp.

"Where is that hat?" she asked, so naturally that the woman began to think nothing was wrong after all.

Settimia turned to cross the room, in order to get the hat in question from a pasteboard bandbox that stood on the floor. Regina followed her, and stood beside her as she bent down.

Then without the slightest warning Regina caught her arms from behind and threw her to her knees, so that she was forced to crouch down, her head almost touching the floor. She was no more than a child in the peasant woman's hands as soon as she was fairly caught. But she did not scream, and she seemed to be keeping her senses about her.

"What do you want of me?" she asked, speaking with difficulty.

Policemen know that ninety-nine out of a hundred criminals ask that question when they are taken.

"I want to know several things," Regina answered.

"Let me go, and I will tell you what I can."

"No, you won't," Regina replied, looking about her for something with which to tie the woman's hands, for she had forgotten that this might be necessary. "I shall not let you go until I know everything."

She felt that Settimia's thin hands were cautiously trying the strength of her own and turning a very little in her grasp. She threw her weight upon the woman's shoulders to keep her down, grasped both wrists in one hand, and with the other tore off the long silk cord that tied her own dressing-gown at the waist. It was new and strong.

"You had better not struggle," she said, as she got the first turn round Settimia's wrists and began to pull it tight. "You are in my power now. It is of no use to scream either, for nobody will hear you."

"I know it," the woman replied. "What are you going to do with me?"

"I shall ask questions. If you answer them, I shall not hurt you. If you do not, I shall hurt you until you do, or until you die. Now I am going to tie your wrists to your heels, so that you cannot move. Then I will put a pillow under your head, so that you can be pretty comfortable while we talk a little."

She spoke in a matter-of-fact tone, which terrified Settimia much more than any dramatic display of anger or hatred could have done. In a few moments the woman was bound hand and foot. Regina turned her upon her side, and arranged a pillow under her head as she had promised to do. Then she sat down upon the floor beside the pillow and looked at her calmly.

"In this way we can talk," she said.

Settimia's rather stony eyes were wide with fear now, as she lay on her side, watching Regina's face.

"I have always served you faithfully," she said. "I cannot understand why you treat me so cruelly."

"Yes," Regina answered, unmoved, "you have been an excellent maid, and I am sorry that I am obliged to tie you up like the calves that are taken to the city on carts. Now tell me, where is Signor Corbario?"

"How should I know?" whined Settimia, evidently more frightened. "I know nothing about Signor Corbario. I swear that I have hardly ever seen him. How can I possibly know where he is? He is probably at his house, at this hour."

"No. You know very well that he has left the villa. It will not serve to tell lies, nor to say that you know nothing about him, for I am sure you do. Now listen. I wish to persuade you with good words. You and Signor Corbario were in South America together."

Settimia's face expressed abject terror.

"Never!" she cried, rocking her bound body sideways in an instinctive attempt to emphasise her words by a gesture. "I swear before heaven, and the saints, and the holy —"

"It is useless," Regina interrupted. "You have not forgotten what you and he did in Salta ten years ago. You remember how suddenly Padilla died, when 'Doctor' Corbario was attending him, and you were his nurse, don't you?"

She fixed her eyes sternly on Settimia's, and the woman turned livid, and ground her teeth.

"You are the devil!" she said hoarsely. "But it is all a lie!" she cried, suddenly trying denial again. "I was never in South America, never, never, never!"

"This is a lie," observed Regina, with perfect calm. "If you do not tell me where Signor Corbario is to-night, I shall go to the police to-morrow and tell all I know about you."

"You know nothing. What is all this that you are inventing? You are a wicked woman!"

"Take care! Perhaps I am a wicked woman. Who knows! I am not a saint, but you are not my confessor. It is the contrary, perhaps; and perhaps you will have to confess to me this night, before going to the other world, if you confess at all. Where is Signor Corbario?"

As she asked the question, she quietly took the long pin from her hair and began to play with the point.

"Are you going to murder me?" groaned the wretched woman, watching the terrible little weapon.

"I should not call it murder to kill you. This point is sharp. Should you like to feel it? You shall. In this way you will perhaps be persuaded to speak."

She gently pressed the point against Settimia's cheek.

"Don't move, or you will scratch yourself," she said, as the woman tried to draw back her face. "Now, will you tell me where Signor Corbario is? I want to know."

Settimia must have feared Corbario more than she feared Regina and the sharp pin at that moment, for she shook her head and set her teeth. Perhaps she believed that Regina was only threatening her, and did not mean to do her any real bodily hurt; but in this she was misled by Regina's very quiet manner.

"I shall wait a little while," said Regina, almost

indifferently, "and then, if you do not tell me, I shall begin to kill you. It may take a long time, and you will scream a good deal, but nobody will hear you. Now think a little, and decide what you will do."

Regina laid the pin upon the floor beside her, drew up her knees, and clasped her hands together over them, as the hill women often sit for hours when they are waiting for anything.

Her face hardened slowly until it had an expression which Marcello had never seen. It was not a look of cruelty, nor of fierce anticipated satisfaction in what she meant to do; it was simply cold and relentless, and Settimia gazed with terror on the splendid marble profile, so fearfully distinct against the dark wall in the bright light of the lamp. The strength of the woman, quietly waiting to kill, seemed to fill the room; her figure seemed to grow gigantic in the terrified eyes of her prisoner; the slow, regular heave of her bosom as she breathed was telling the seconds and minutes of fate, that would never reach an hour.

It is bad to see death very near when one is tied hand and foot and cannot fight for life. Most people cannot bear the sight quietly for a quarter of an hour; they break down altogether, or struggle furiously, like animals, though they know it is perfectly useless and that they have no chance. Anything is easier than to lie still, watching the knife and wondering when and where it is going to enter into the flesh.

Regina sat thinking and ready. She wished that she had Corbario himself in her power, but it was something to have the woman who had helped him. She was very glad that she had insisted on keeping Settimia in spite of Marcello's remonstrances. It had made it possible to obtain the information he wanted, and which, she felt sure, was to lead to Corbario's destruction. She was to find out "at any cost"; those had been Marcello's words, and she supposed he knew that she would obey him to the letter. For she said to herself that he was the master, and that if she did not obey him in such a matter, when he seemed so much in earnest, he would be disappointed, and angry, and would then grow quickly tired of her, and so the end would come. "At any cost," as he had said it in his haste, meant to Regina at the cost of blood, and life, and limb, if need were. Corbario was the enemy of the man she loved; it was her lover's pleasure to find out his enemy and to be revenged at last; what sort of woman must she be if she did not help him? what was her love worth if she did not obey him? He had been always kind to her, and more than kind; but it would have been quite the same if he had treated her worse than a dog, provided he did not send her away from him. She belonged to him, and he was the master, to do as he pleased. If he sent her away, she would go; but if not, he might have beaten her and she would never have complained. Now that he had given a simple command, she was not going to disobey him. She had pride, but it was not for him, and in her veins the blood of sixty generations of slaves and serfs had come down to her through two thousand years, the blood of men who had killed when they were bidden to kill by their masters, whose masters had killed them like sheep in war and often in peace, of women who had been reckoned as goods and as chattels with the land on which their mothers had borne them — of men and women too often familiar with murder and sudden death from their cradles to their graves.

The minutes passed and Settimia's terror grew till the room swam with her, and she lost hold upon herself, and did not know whether she screamed or was silent, as her parched lips opened wide upon her parted teeth. But she had made no sound, and Regina did not even look at her. Death had not come yet; there was a respite of seconds, perhaps of minutes.

At last Regina unclasped her hands and took up the pin again. The miserable woman fancied that she already felt the little blade creeping through her flesh and blood on its way to her heart. For Regina had said she would take a long time to kill her. It must have been a strong reason that could keep her silent still, if she knew the answer to the question.

Regina turned her head very slowly and looked coldly down at the agonised face.

"I am tired," she said. "I cannot wait any longer."

Settimia's eyes seemed to be starting from her head, and her dry lips were stretched till they cracked, and she thought she had screamed again; but she had not, for her throat was paralysed with fear. Regina rose upon her knees beside the pillow, with the pin in her right hand.

"Where is Corbario?" she asked, looking down. "If you will not tell I shall hurt you."

Settimia's lips moved, as if she were trying to speak, but no words came from them. Regina got up from the floor, went to the washstand and poured some water into the glass, for she thought it possible that the woman was really unable to utter a sound because her throat was parched with fear. But she could speak a little as soon as Regina left her side, and the last peril seemed a few seconds less near.

"For the love of God, don't kill me yet," she moaned. "Let me speak first!"

Regina came back, knelt down, and set the glass on the floor, beside the pin.

"That is all I want," she said quietly, "that you should speak."

"Water," moaned Settimia, turning her eyes to the glass.

Regina held up her head a little and set the tumbler to her lips, and she drank eagerly. The fear of death is more parching than wound-fever or passion.

"Now you can surely talk a little," Regina said.

"Why do you wish to know where he is?" Settimia asked in a weak voice. "Are the police looking for him? What has he done? Why do you want me to betray him?"

"These are too many questions," Regina answered. "I have been told to make you tell where he is, and I will. That is enough."

"I do not know where he is."

In an instant the point of the sharp little blade was pressing against the woman's throat, harder and harder; one second more and it would pierce the skin and draw blood.

"Stop," she screamed, with a convulsion of her whole body. "He is in the house!"

CHAPTER XIX

WITH a single movement Regina was on her feet, for she had been taken by surprise, and her first instinct was to be ready for some new and unsuspected danger. In a flash it seemed to her that since Corbario was in the house, he might very possibly enter suddenly and take Settimia's defence. Regina was not afraid of him, but she was only a woman after all, and Corbario was not a man to stop at trifles. He was very likely armed, and would perhaps shoot her, in order to make good his escape with Settimia, unless, as was quite probable, he killed his old accomplice too, before leaving the room.

Regina stood still a moment, reflecting on the dangerous situation. It certainly would not be safe to release Settimia yet; for if Corbario were really in the house, the two together could easily overpower one woman, though she was strong.

"I am sorry that I cannot untie you yet," Regina said, and with a glance at the prostrate figure she took up her candle-stick, stuck her pin through her hair before the mirror, and went to the door.

She took the key from the lock, put it back on the outside, and turned it, and put it into her pocket when she had shut the door after her. Then she slowly descended the stairs, stopping now and then to listen, and shading her candle with her hand so that she could see over it, for she expected to be attacked at any moment. At the slightest sound she would have snatched her pin from her hair again, but she heard nothing, and went cautiously down till she reached the vestibule outside the sitting-room. She entered the latter and sat down to think.

Should she boldly search the house? Settimia could hardly have had any object in lying. If she had meant to frighten Regina, she would have spoken very differently. She would have made out that Corbario was almost within hearing, waiting in a dark corner with a loaded revolver. But her words had been the cry of truth, uttered to save her life at the moment when death was actually upon her. She would have screamed out the truth just as certainly if Corbario had already left Rome, or if he were in some hotel for the night — or even if she had really known nothing. In the last case Regina would have believed her, and would have let her go. There is no mistaking the accent of mortal terror, whether one has ever heard it or not.

Corbario was somewhere in the house, Marcello's enemy, and the man she herself had long hated. A wild longing came over her to have him in her power, bound hand and foot like Settimia, and then to torment him at her pleasure until he died. She felt the strength of half a dozen men in her, and the courage of an army, as she rose to her feet once more. She had seen him. He was not a big man. If she could catch him from behind, as she had caught the woman, she might perhaps overpower him. With the thought of near revenge the last ray of caution disappeared, and from being fearless Regina became suddenly reckless.

But as she rose, she heard a sound overhead, and it was the unmistakable sound of footsteps. She started in surprise. It was simply impossible that Settimia should have loosed the cord that bound her. Regina had been brought up in the low hill country and in the Campagna, and she could tie some of the knots used by Roman muleteers and carters, which hold as well as those men learn at sea. She had tied Settimia very firmly, and short of a miracle the woman could not have freed herself. Yet the footsteps had been distinctly audible for a moment. Since Settimia was not walking about, Corbario must have got into the room. Yet Regina had locked the door, and had the key in her pocket. It was perfectly incomprehensible. She left the sitting-room again, carrying her candle as before; but at the door she turned back, and set the candle-stick upon the table. She would be safer in the dark, and would have a better chance of taking Corbario by surprise.

Poor Regina had not grown up amongst people who had a high standard of honour, and her own ideas about right and wrong were primitive, to speak charitably. But if she had dreamt of the deed that was being done upstairs, her heart would have stood still, and she would have felt sick at the mere thought of such villainy.

She had left the room and locked the door, and while

her footsteps had been audible on the stairs no other sound had broken the stillness. But a few seconds later a whispered question came from some person out of sight.

"Is she gone?" the whisper asked.

"Yes," answered Settimia in a very low voice, which she knew Regina could not hear.

Corbario's pale face cautiously emerged from the closet in which he had been hidden, and he looked round the room before he stepped out. Settimia could not turn over to see him, but she heard him coming towards her.

"Cut this cord," she said in an undertone. "Make haste! We can be out of the house in less than half a minute."

Corbario knelt beside her, and took out a handsome English clasp-knife. But he did not cut the cord. He looked down into Settimia's face, and she understood.

"I could not help it," she answered. "She would have killed me!"

Corbario laid his left hand upon her throat.

"If you try to scream I shall strangle you," he said in a whisper. "You have betrayed me, and I cannot afford to trust you again. Do you know what I am going to do?"

She tried to turn her head, but his hand was heavy on her throat. She strained frightfully to move, and her stony eyes lit up with a dying glare of terror.

"Do it quickly!" she gasped.

"Hush!" His hand tightened on her throat. "If

you were in Salta, you should die by tenths of inches, if it took all night! That would be too good for you."

He spat in her face as she writhed under his grasp. He looked into her living eyes once more with all the cowardly hate that possessed him, he struck deep and sure, he saw the light break in the pupils, and heard the awful rattle of her last breath.

In an instant he was at the window, and had thrown it wide open. He got out quickly, let himself down with his hands, and pushed himself away from the wall with his feet as he jumped down backwards, well knowing that there was grass below him, and that the earth was as soft as sponge with the long rain. He was sure that he could not hurt himself. Yet before his feet touched the ground he had uttered a low cry of fear.

He was on his legs now and trying to run, but it was too late. There was the flash of a lantern in the wet garden, and between him and the light, and just below it, he saw two points of greenish fire coming at him; for he saw everything then; and he heard the rush of a heavy beast's feet, tearing up the earth with iron claws, and the savage breath, and the loud hiss of a man setting the creature on; for he heard every sound then; and he knew that the thing of terror would leap up with resistless strength and hurl its weight upon him, and bury its jagged fangs in his throat and tear him, in an instant that would seem like an hour of agony, and that the pain and the fear would be as if he were hung up by all the nerves of his body, drawn out and twisted; for he knew everything then; and in that immeasurable time which is nothing, and yet is infinite, he remembered his evil life, his robberies, his murders, and his betrayals, one by one, but he remembered with most frightful clearness how he had tried to kill Marcello, how he had corrupted him from his childhood, with bad counsels very cunningly, and prepared him to go astray, how he had thrust evil in his path and laughed away the good, and had led him on, and poisoned him, and would have brought him to his death and damnation surely, but for one sinning devoted woman that loved him; for he remembered everything then; and from very far away, out of memories of his youth, there came a voice that had once been gentle and kind, but that rang in his ears now, like the blast of the trumpet of the last judgment.

"Whosoever shall offend one of these little ones which believe in Me, it were better for him that a millstone were hanged about his neck, and that he were drowned in the depth of the sea."

Far better, indeed, for it all came, when the immeasurable second's length was past, and he was thrown down against the wall, and torn, and shaken like a rat; it all came just as he had felt that it was coming, and it lasted long, a long, long time, while he tried to howl, and the blood only gurgled in his throat. And then, just as many strong hands dragged away the thing of terror, and the light of a lantern and of a lamp flashed in his eyes, he fell asleep in the wet grass.

For they had caught him fairly and brought him

down. Kalmon had watched him long, and had told some of his suspicions to the Chief of Police, and the latter, unknown to Kalmon, had caused him to be watched from time to time. But he, who had been watched before and had once already escaped for his life, had sometimes seen faces near him that he did not trust, and when he had turned back from the station that afternoon he had seen one of those faces; so he had driven away quickly in a cab, by winding ways, so as not to be followed. Yet Kalmon and Marcello, talking as they drove, grew more and more sure that he would wish to see Settimia before he left Rome, the more certainly if he believed himself pursued, as seemed likely from his changing his mind at the station. So they had stopped their cab before they had reached their destination, and had sent Ercole back to Trastevere with the key of the garden gate, bidding him watch, as it was most probable that Corbario would try to get out through the garden; and before long they had come back to the door of the house that opened upon the street, and had let themselves in quietly, just in time to hear the noise of the struggle as the dog threw Corbario to the ground. For the other entrance to the little vestibule opened upon the garden within, at the very spot where Corbario alighted when he jumped from the window.

And now they stood there in the rain round the wounded man, while Marcello held the lantern to his face, and Regina thrust a lamp out of the lower window which she had thrown open.

"Is he dead?" she asked, in the silence that followed when Ercole had got control of the dog again.

At the sound of her voice Ercole started strangely and looked up to her face that was not far above his own, and his eyes fixed themselves upon her so intently that she looked down at him, while she still held out her lamp. She could not remember that she had ever seen him; but he had seen her many times since he had made his visit to the inn on the Frascati road.

"Is he dead?" she repeated, putting the question directly to him as he was nearest.

Still he looked at her in silence, with his deep-set, unwinking eyes. Marcello and Kalmon were bending over Corbario, Marcello holding the lantern, while the Professor listened for the beating of the heart and felt the pulse. They paid no attention to Regina for the moment.

"Why don't you speak?" she asked, surprised by Ercole's silent stare.

"You don't know me," he said slowly, "but I know you."

The rain was beating upon her lamp, and at that moment the shade cracked under the cold drops and fell to pieces, and the wind instantly extinguished the flame of the flaring wick. Regina withdrew into the room to get another light, and Ercole stared after her into the gloom.

"He is alive," said Kalmon, looking up to see why the light had gone out. "We must get him inside at once, or he will die here. Come, Ercole! Make that dog lie down and keep quiet."

Between them they carried Corbario into the house. Nino watched on the step in the rain, but when the door was shut behind him, he crawled down to the wet grass and lapped the blood and water in the dark. They carried Corbario upstairs to an empty room there was, and as they went Regina tried to tell Marcello what she had done. They opened Settimia's door, which was still locked, and they found her quite dead, and the window was wide open; then Regina understood that Corbario had been hidden within hearing, and had killed the woman because she had confessed.

The men who had been sent from the central police station at Kalmon's request arrived a few minutes later. One was at once sent for a surgeon and for more men; the other remained. Soon the little house was full of officials, in uniform and in plain clothes. They examined everything, they wrote rapidly on big sheets of stamped paper; their chief took the first deposition of Regina, and of the three men, and of the surgeon. At dawn a man came with a rough pine coffin. Officials came and went, and were gravely busy. One man spoke of coffee when it was day, and went and made some in the little kitchen, for the two young women who cooked and did the work of the house did not sleep there, and would not come till past seven o'clock.

During the long hours, when Regina and Marcello were not wanted, they were together in the sitting-room downstairs. Regina told Marcello in detail everything she knew about the events of the night, and much which she had found out earlier about Settimia but had never told him. Kalmon came in from time to time and told them what was going on, and that Corbario was still alive; but they saw no more of Ercole. He had made his first deposition, to the effect that he had been set to watch the house, that the murderer had jumped from an upper window, and that the dog had pulled him down. The officials looked nervously at the dog, produced by Ercole in evidence, and were glad when the beast was out of their sight. There were dark stains about the bristles on his jaws, and his eyes were bloodshot; but Ercole laid one hand on his uncouth head, and he was very quiet, and did not even snarl at the policemen.

Regina and Marcello sat side by side, talking in a low voice, and looking at each other now and then. The little house in which they had been happy was turned to a place of death and horror, and both knew that some change was coming to themselves.

"You cannot live here any more," Marcello said at dawn, "not even till to-night."

"Where could I go?" Regina asked. "Why should I not stay here? Do you think I am afraid of the dead woman?"

"No," Marcello answered, "but you cannot stay here."

He guessed what talking and gossiping there would be when the newspapers told what had happened in the little house, how the reporters would hang about the street for a week to come, and how fashionable people would go out of their way to see the place where a murder had been committed by such a well-known person as Corbario, and where he had been taken almost in the very act, and himself nearly killed. Besides all that, there would be the public curiosity about Regina, who had been so intimately concerned in a part of the tragedy, and whose name was everywhere associated with his own.

He would have taken her away from Rome at once, if he could have done so. But he knew that they would both be called upon during the next few days to repeat in court the evidence they had already given in their first deposition. There was sure to be the most frightful publicity about the whole affair, of which reports would be published not only in Rome but throughout Italy, and all over the world. In real life the consequences of events generally have the importance which fiction is obliged to give the events themselves; which is the reason why the things that happen to real people rarely come to any precise conclusion, like those reached by a play or a novel. The "conclusion" lies in the lives of the people, after the tragedy, or the drama, or the comedy has violently upset their existences.

"You cannot stay here," Marcello repeated with conviction.

"You will go on living at your villa," Regina answered. "Why should I not go on living in this house? For a few days I will not go out, that is all. Is it the end of the world because a person has been killed who ought to have died in the galleys? Or because the man who tried to kill you was caught in a place that belongs to you? Tell me that."

"You cannot stay here," Marcello repeated a third time.

For a while Regina was silent. They were both very white and heavy-eyed in the cold daylight, though they could not have slept. At last she looked at him thoughtfully.

"If we were married, we should go on living in our own house," she said. "Is it true, or not? It is because there will be talking that you are ashamed to let me stay where I am, and would like to get me away. This is the truth. I know it."

Marcello knew it too and did not answer at once, for it was not easy to decide what he ought to do. The problem that had seemed so hard to solve a few hours earlier was fast getting altogether beyond solution. There was only one thing to be done in the first present difficulty; he must take Regina to some other place at once. No doubt this was easy enough. He would take an apartment for her elsewhere, as far as possible from the scene of the tragedy, and in a few hours she could be installed there out of the way of annoyance. He could buy a house for her if he chose, for he was very rich. Possibly some house already belonging to him was vacant; his lawyer would know.

But after that, what was to come? If Corbario lived,

there would be a sensational trial in which he and Regina would be witnesses together, and Kalmon too, and very surely Aurora and her mother. For Aurora would be called upon to tell what she knew of Marcello's movements on the morning when he had been knocked down near the gap.

Every moment of his past life would be publicly examined, to prove Corbario's guilt. Worse than that, there would be a long inquiry to show that Corbario had murdered his mother. Skilled surgeons were tending the man's wounds and reviving him by every means that science could suggest. Kalmon said that he might live. He was being kept alive in order to be condemned to the expiation of his crimes in penal servitude, since Italian law could not make him pay for them with his life. The man would be watched by day and night, lest he should try to commit suicide, for he was to suffer, if he lived. He was to suffer horribly, without doubt, and it was right and just that he should. But Marcello would suffer too. That was not just. The name of his saintly mother would be in the mouths of all kinds of witnesses, in the columns of all sorts of newspapers. Lawyers would make speeches about her to excite the pity of the jury and to turn the whole tide of feeling against Corbario. Marcello would himself be held up to public commiseration, as one of Corbario's victims. There would be allusions covert and open to Regina and to the position in which she stood to Marcello. There would be talk about Aurora. People would suddenly remember her mother's sad story and gossip about her; people would certainly say that there had been talk about marrying Aurora to Marcello, and that Regina had come between them. Yes, there would be much talk about Aurora; that was certain.

All this was coming, and was not far off, if Corbario lived; and even if he died there would be a vast amount said and written about all the people concerned.

And Regina was there, beside him, telling him that if they were married they could go on living in the little house, just as if nothing had happened. It was not true, but he could not find heart to tell her so. It was the first time that any suggestion of marriage had come from her, who had always told him that marriage was impossible. If she wished it now, could he refuse?

Suddenly he knew that he had reached one of the great cross-roads in his life, and that fate had dragged him violently to it within the last few hours, to make him choose his way. The full-grown character of the man rebelled against being forced to a decision in spite of himself, but revolted at the thought of fearing to do what was right and honourable. He was not hesitating as he sat still in silence after Regina had spoken. He was thinking, with the firm determination to act as soon as he had reached a decision. When a man can do that, his weakness is past.

Regina did not interrupt the current of his thoughts, and as she watched him she forgot all about the present; and they were just together, where they had so often been happy, and she loved him with all her heart. That was her strength. It had nothing to do with right or wrong, honour or dishonour, credit or discredit, or any choice of ways. She had no choice. She loved. It was a very simple thing.

He looked up at last. She was still wearing the loose dressing-gown she had worn all night.

" Could you sleep now? " he asked.

" No."

" Then you must dress," he said. " While you are dressing I will walk up to the villa and give some orders. Then I will come and get you in a closed carriage. Put together what you may need for the day, and I will have all your things moved before night."

" Are you really going to take me away from here? " Regina asked, regretfully.

" Yes. I must. It will be easy to find a place that will please you better. Will you do as I have said? "

" Why do you ask? I go."

She rose and stood beside him a moment while he sat still, and her hand caressed his short fair hair. She bent down and kissed the close waves of it, near his forehead.

" We have been very happy here," she said quietly.

She slipped away as he rose to his feet, with the sudden conviction that something had happened.

" What is it? " he asked quickly, and making a step after her.

" I am going to dress," she answered.

She turned her head and smiled, but there was a touch of sadness in the look, as if she was saying good-bye. He partly understood, and her expression was reflected in his own face. They had been so happy in the little house in Trastevere.

When the door had closed Marcello went to find Kalmon. He met him at the foot of the stairs.

"The fellow is alive, and will probably recover," said the Professor, in answer to the unasked question in Marcello's eyes.

"It would simplify matters if he died," said Marcello. "Will you walk up to the villa with me and have coffee? We cannot get a cab at this hour on this side of the Tiber."

"Thank you," Kalmon answered, "but I must go home. The house is in charge of the police, and there is nothing more to be done here. They have already taken the woman's body to San Spirito, and they will move Corbario in a few hours. He is badly mauled, but no big arteries are torn. I must go home and write a letter. The Contessa must not hear what has happened through the newspapers."

"No. Certainly not. As for me, I am going to take Regina away at once. I shall bring my own carriage down from the villa."

"By the bye," Kalmon said, "I had thought of that. The house in which I live is divided into many small apartments. There is a very good one to let, decently furnished. I thought of taking it myself, and I looked at it yesterday. You might put the young lady there until you can find what you may prefer. She can move in at once."

"Nothing could be better. If you are going home,

will you say that I take the place and will be there in an hour? No. 16, Via Sicilia, is it not?"

"Yes. I'll see to it. Shall I take the lease in your name?"

"No. Any name will do better. The reporters would find her at once under mine."

"I'll use my own," said the Professor. "I'll say that she is a lady who has arrived to consult me — I daresay she will — and that I'm responsible for her."

"Thank you," answered Marcello gratefully. "And thank you for all that you have done to help me."

"My dear Marcello," Kalmon said, smiling cheerfully, "in the first place, I have done nothing to help you, and secondly, through excess of zeal, I have got you into a very unpleasant situation, by indirectly causing a woman to be murdered in your house, and the murderer almost mauled to death by that very singular wild beast which your man calls a dog, and which I had often noticed in old times at the cottage. So there is nothing at all to thank me for, though I am most heartily at your service."

The Professor was positively in high spirits just then, and Marcello envied him as they parted and took opposite directions.

Though the Via Sicilia was a long way from the Janiculum, Marcello had been only too glad to accept Kalmon's suggestion at such a moment. Regina would feel that she was protected by Marcello's friend, and though she might rarely see him, it would be better for her than to be lodged in a house where she knew no one. Kalmon was a bachelor and a man of assured position, and it had cost him nothing to undertake to give Regina his protection ; but Marcello was deeply grateful. He had already made up his mind as to what he would do next.

It had stopped raining at last, and the wind had fallen to a soft breeze that bore the morning mist gently away towards the sea, and hardly stirred the wet leaves that strewed the road all the way up to San Pietro in Montorio. Marcello found the gate of the villa already open, for it was nearly eight o'clock by the time he got there.

He summoned the servants to the library, told them briefly what had happened, and warned them that they might be summoned as witnesses at the coming trial, as most of them had been in his mother's service. In the days before Corbario had lost his head, and when he had controlled the household, it had been a part of his policy to have really respectable servants about him, and though some of them had never quite trusted him, they had all been devoted to the Signora and to Marcello. They listened in respectful silence now, and waited till he was out of the house before meeting to discuss the tragedy and to decide that Corbario had got his deserts at last.

In a few hours Regina was installed in her new lodging with such belongings as she needed immediately. Kalmon, having finished writing his letter to the Contessa, left nothing undone which could contribute to the comfort of the "lady who had arrived to consult him."

He had a respectable old woman servant, who had been with him for years, and who came from his native town. He took her into his confidence to some extent, and placed her in charge of Regina. As she thought that everything he did must be right, she accepted his statement that the young gentleman who would often come to see the young lady was deeply interested in the latter's welfare, and that, as the poor young lady had no relations, he, the Professor, had taken her under his protection while she remained in Rome.

The old servant's name was Teresa, and she belonged to a certain type of elderly old maids who take a very kindly interest in the love affairs of the young. She smiled, shook her head in a very mild disapprobation, and did much more than Kalmon had asked of her; for she took the very first opportunity of informing Regina that the Professor was the greatest, wisest, best, and kindest of mankind; and Regina recognised in her a loyal soul, and forthwith liked her very much.

It was late in the November afternoon when Marcello ascended the stairs and stopped before the door of the little apartment. He realised that he had no key to it, and that he must ring the bell as if he were a mere visitor. It was strange that such a little thing should affect him at all, but he was conscious of a sort of chill, as he pulled the metal handle and heard the tinkling of one of those cheap little bells that feebly imitate their electric betters by means of a rachet and a small weighted wheel. It was all so different from the little house in Trastevere with its bright varnished doors, its patent locks, its smart windows, and its lovely old garden. He wished he had not brought Regina to Via Sicilia, though Kalmon's advice had seemed so good. To Kalmon, who was used to no great luxury in his own life, the place doubtless seemed very well suited for a young person like Regina, who had been brought up a poor child in the hills. But the mere anticipation of the dark and narrow entry, and the sordid little sitting-room beyond, awoke in Marcello a sense of shame, whether for himself or for the woman who loved him he hardly knew.

Old Teresa had gone out for something, and Regina opened the door herself.

CHAPTER XX

"I have come to see if you need anything," Marcello said, when they were in the sitting-room. "I am sorry to have been obliged to bring you to such a wretched place, but it seemed a good thing that you should be so near Kalmon."

"It is not a wretched place," Regina answered. "It is clean, and the things are new, and the curtains have been washed. It is not wretched. We have been in worse lodgings when we have travelled and stopped in small towns. Professor Kalmon has been very kind. It was wise to bring me here."

He wished she had seemed discontented.

"Have you rested a little?" he asked.

"I have slept two or three hours. And you? You look tired."

"I have had no time to sleep. I shall sleep to-night."

He leaned back in the small green arm-chair and rested his head against a coarse netted antimacassar. His eyes caught Regina's, but she was looking down thoughtfully at her hands, which lay in her lap together but not clasped. Peasant women often do that; their hands are resting then, after hard work, and they are thinking of nothing.

"Look at me," Marcello said after a long time.

Her glance was sad and almost dull, and there was no light in her face. She had made up her mind that something dreadful was going to happen to her, and that the end was coming soon. She could not have told why she felt it, and that made it worse. Her eyes had the indescribable look that one sees in those of a beautiful sick animal, the painful expression of an unintelligent suffering which the creature cannot understand. Regina, roused to act and face to face with danger, was brave, clever, and quick, but under the mysterious oppression of her forebodings she was the Roman hill woman, apathetic, hopeless, unconsciously fatalistic and sleepily miserable.

"What is the matter?" Marcello asked. "What has happened?"

"I shall know when you have told me," Regina answered, slowly shaking her head; and again she looked down at her hands.

"What I have come to tell you will not make you sad," Marcello replied.

"Speak, heart of my heart. I listen."

Marcello leaned forward and laid his hand upon hers. She looked up quietly, for it was a familiar action of his.

"I am going to marry you," he said, watching her, and speaking earnestly.

She kept her eyes on his, but she shook her head again, slowly, from side to side, and her lips were pressed together.

"Yes, I am," said Marcello, with a little pressure of his hand to emphasise the words.

But she withdrew hers, and leaned far back from him.

"Never," she said. "I have told you so, many times."

"Not if I tell you that nothing else will make me happy?" he asked.

"If I still made you happy, you would not talk of marriage," Regina answered.

For the first time since she had loved him he heard a ring of bitterness in her voice. They had reached that first node of misunderstanding in the love relations of men and women, which lies where the one begins to think and act upon a principle while the other still feels and acts from the heart.

"That is not reasonable," Marcello said.

"It is truth," she answered.

"But how?"

"How! I feel it, here!"

Her hands sprang to life and pressed her bosom, her voice rang deep and her eyes flashed, as if she were impatient of his misunderstanding.

He tried to laugh gently.

"But if I want to marry you, it is because I mean never to part from you," he said.

"No!" she cried. "It is because you are afraid that you will leave me, unless you are bound to me."

"Regina!" Marcello protested, by his tone.

"It is as I say. It is because you are honourable. It is because you wish to be faithful. It is because you want to be true. But what do I care for honour, or faith, or truth, if I can only have them of you because you are tied to me? I only want love. That is everything. I want it, but I have never asked it of you, and never shall. Is love money, that you can take it out of your purse and give it? Is love a string, that the priest and the mayor can tie the ends so that they can never come undone? I do not know what it is, but it is not that!"

She laughed scornfully, as if she were angry at the thought. But Marcello had made up his mind, and was obstinate.

"We must be married at once," he said quietly, and fully believing that he could impose his will upon hers. "If I had not been weak and foolish, we should have been married long ago. But for a long time after my illness I had no will of my own. I am sorry. It was my fault."

"It was not your fault, it was the illness, and it was my will. If I had said, any day in those first two years, 'Make me your wife, for I wish to be a real signora,' would you not have done it?"

"You know I would."

"But I would not, and I will not now. I am not a real signora. I am beautiful — yes, I see that. Am I blind when I look into my glass? I am very beautiful. We have not often met any woman in our travels as beautiful as I am. Am I blind? I have black hair, like the common people, but my hair is not coarse, like a mule's tail. It is as fine as silk. My eyes are black, and that is common too; but my eyes are not like those of the buffaloes in the Campagna, as the other women's are where I was born. And I am not dark-skinned; I am as white as the snow on Monte Cavo, as white as the milk in the pan. Also I have been told that I have beautiful feet, though I cannot tell why. They are small, this is the truth, and my hands are like those of a signora. But I am not a real signora, though I have all this. How can you marry me? None of your friends would speak to me, because I have not even been an honest girl. That was for you, but they do not count love. Your servants at the villa would laugh at you behind your back, and say, 'The master has married one of us!' Do you think I could bear that? Tell me what you think! Am I of stone, to bear that people should laugh at you?"

She took breath at last and leaned back again, folding her arms and fixing her splendid eyes on his face, and challenging him to answer her.

"We will go and live in Calabria, at San Domenico, for a while," he said. "We need not live in Rome at all, unless we please, for we have the whole world before us."

"We saw the world together without being married," Regina answered obstinately. "What difference would there be, if we were husband and wife? Do you wish to know what difference there would be? I will tell you. There would be this difference. One day I should see no light in your eyes, and your lips would be like stone. Then I should say, 'Heart of my heart, you are tired of me, and I go.' But you would answer, 'You cannot go, for you are my wife.' What would that be? That would be the difference. Do you understand, or do you not understand? If you do not understand, I can do nothing. But I will not marry you. Have you ever seen a mule go down to the ford in spring, too heavily laden, when there is freshet? He drowns, if he is driven in, because the burden is too heavy. I will not be the burden; but I should be, if I were your wife, because I am not a real signora. Now you know what I think."

"Yes," Marcello answered, "but I do not think in the same way."

He was not sure how to answer her arguments, and he lit a cigarette to gain time. He was quietly determined to have his own way, but in order to succeed he knew that he must persuade her till she agreed with him. He could not drag her to the altar against her will.

Before he had thrown away the match, Regina had risen from her chair. She leaned against the little marble mantelpiece, looking down at him.

"There are things that you do not know," she said. "If you knew them you would not want to marry me. In all the time we have been together, you have hardly ever spoken to me of your mother."

Marcello started a little and looked up, unconsciously showing that he was displeased.

"No," he answered. "Why should I?"

"You were right. Your mother is now one of the

saints in Paradise. How do I know it? Even Settimia knew it. I am not going to talk of her now. I am not fit to speak her name in your hearing. Very well. Do you know what my mother was?"

"She is dead," Marcello replied, meaning that Regina should let her memory alone.

"Or my father?" she asked, going on. "They were bad people. I come of a bad race. Perhaps that is why I do wrong easily, for you. My father killed a man and left us, though he was allowed to go free, and I never saw him again. He had reason to kill the man. I was a little girl, but I remember. My mother took other men. They came and went; sometimes they were drunk and they beat us. When I was twelve years old one of them looked upon me with bad eyes. Then my mother cursed him, and he took up a stone and struck her on the head, and she died. They sent him to the galleys, and me to work at the inn, because I had no friends. This is the family of Regina. It is a race of assassins and wicked women. If I were your wife, that would be the family of your wife. If God sent children, that would be the blood they would have of me, to mix with that of your mother, who is one of the saints in heaven. This is the truth. If you think I am telling you one thing for another, let us go to the inn on the Frascati road. Paoluccio and Nanna know. They would laugh if they could see me dressed like a real signora, and they would say, 'This girl is her mother's daughter!' And so I am."

She ceased speaking, and again waited for his answer, but he had none ready, and there was silence. She had put the ugly truth too plainly before him, and he could not shut up his understanding against it; he could not deny what she said, he could never teach himself to believe that it did not matter. And yet, he did not mean to draw back, or give up his purpose, even then. Men of good birth had married peasant women before now. They had given up the society of their old friends, they had lived in remote places, they had become half peasants themselves, their sons had grown up to be rough farmers, and had done obligatory military service in the ranks for years, because they could not pass an easy examination. But was all that so very terrible after all, in the light of the duty that faced him?

The woman had saved his life, had carried him in her arms, had tended him like a child, had stolen food to keep him alive, had faced starvation for him when she had got him to the hospital, had nursed him — had loved him, had given him all she had, and she would have died for him, if there had been need. Now, she was giving him something more, for she was refusing to be his wife because she was sure that sooner or later she must be a burden to him, and that her birth would be a reproach to his children. No woman could do more for a man than she had done. She had been his salvation and his good angel; when she had found out that the life in Paris that amused her was killing him, she had brought him back to himself, she had made him at last fit and able to face those who would have destroyed him. She had loved him like a woman, she had obeyed him and served him like a devoted servant, she had watched over him like a faithful dog; and he had given her nothing in return for all that, not one thing that deserved to be counted. Perhaps he had not even really loved her; most surely his love had been far less large and true and devoted than hers, and he felt that it was so. The reparation he was determined to make was not really for her honesty's sake; it was to be an attempt at repaying a debt that was weighing upon his conscience like a debt of honour.

That was it. He felt that unless he could in some way repay her for what she had done, his man's honour would not be satisfied. That was very well, in its way, but it was not love. It was as if he had said to himself, "I cannot love her as she loves me, but I can at least marry her; and that is better than nothing, and has the merit of being morally right."

She had told him that if she still made him happy he would not talk of marriage. The brutal truth shamed him, now that he knew it from her own lips. It was not the whole truth, but it was a great part of it. If he was happy with her now, when there was nothing to disturb them, it was by force of habit, it was because her beauty appealed to him, it was because her touch was dearer to him than her heart's devotion. Now that he was a grown man, he knew well enough that he craved something else which poor Regina could never give him.

For he felt the want of companionship. Those who have lost what is most worth having, whether by death or by their own fault, or by the other's, miss the companionship of love more than anything else, when the pain of the first wrench is dulled and the heart's blood is staunched, and the dreadful bodily loneliness comes only in dreams. Then the longing for the old sweet intercourse of thought and word makes itself felt and is very hard to bear, though it is not sharp like the first wound ; and it comes again and again for years, and perhaps for ever.

But where there is no true companionship while love lasts, there is something lacking, and such love cannot live long. Men seem to want it more than women do ; and women, seeing that men want something, often fancy they want flattery, and flatter the men they love till they disgust them ; and then the end comes suddenly, much to the astonishment of those women.

Regina was too womanly not to feel that Marcello was in real need of something which she had not, and could never have. She had known it from the first, and had almost told him so. She gave what was hers to give, as long as he wanted it ; when he wanted it no more, she meant to leave him, and it would make no difference what became of her afterwards.

When she had finished speaking, Marcello was very miserable, because he could find no answer to what she had said, and he felt that she had no right to say it at all. His head ached now, from excitement and want of sleep, and he almost wished that he had put off speaking to Regina about her marriage. He rested his head in his hand as he sat thinking, and she came and stood beside him as she had done in the morning in the little house in Trastevere. But it was not the same now. She hoped that he would put up his other hand to find hers, without looking at her, as he often did, but it gripped his knee as if he did not mean to move it, and he did not raise his head.

She looked up from his bent figure to the window and saw that the light was reddening with the first tinge of sunset. It would soon be night, Marcello would go away, and she would be dreadfully lonely. It was not like being in the little house, knowing that he was near her, in the great villa on top of the hill, hidden from her only by trees. She was in a strange place now, and he would be far away, across the Tiber, and the great dark city would be between her and him.

For an instant her lip quivered, and she thought she was going to cry, though she had never cried in her life, except for rage and when she had been a little girl. She shook her handsome head impatiently at the mere sensation, and held it higher than ever. Then Marcello looked up at last.

As their eyes met they heard the tinkle of the little bell. Regina at once left his side to go and open the door. It was not till she had left the room that Marcello rose, asking himself suddenly why it had not occurred to him to go himself. He realised that he had always allowed her to wait on him without question. Yet if she were his wife, he would not think of letting her do what she was doing now. He would even open the door of the room for her to go out.

He knew why he had never treated her in that way. She was a peasant girl, she had been a servant in an inn; it was natural that she should serve him too. She often brought him his shoes when he was going out, and she would have put them on for him and laced them if he would have let her do it. It seemed natural that she should answer the bell and open the door, as it seemed unnatural that she should ever be his wife. The thought stung him, and again he was ashamed.

While these things were passing in his mind, he heard a familiar voice in the dark entry.

"Signora, you will excuse me," Ercole was saying. "I asked the Professor and he told me. I beg the favour of a few words."

"Come in," Regina answered, and a moment later they both entered the sitting-room.

Ercole stood still when he saw Marcello, and began to turn his hat in his hands, as if it were a rosary, which he generally did when he was embarrassed. Marcello wondered what the man wanted.

"Were you looking for me?" he asked. "Come in! What is it? Has anything happened?"

"No, sir, nothing new has happened," answered Ercole.

"What is it, then? Why did you come here?"

Ercole had dressed himself for the occasion in his

best clothes. He had on a snowy shirt and a new keeper's jacket, and his boots were blacked. Furthermore, he had just been shaved, and his shaggy hair had been cut rather close. He did not carry his gun about with him in the streets of Rome, though he felt that it was slightly derogatory to his dignity to be seen without it, and Nino was not with him, having been temporarily chained to the wall in the court of the stables at the villa.

He stood still, and looked from Marcello to Regina, and back to Marcello again.

"It cannot be done," he said suddenly. "It is useless. It cannot be done."

Without another word he turned abruptly and was going to leave the room, when Marcello stopped him authoritatively.

"Come here, Ercole!" he cried, as the man was disappearing into the entry.

"Did you speak to me, sir?" Ercole inquired, stopping in the doorway.

"Yes. Shut the door and come here." Ercole obeyed with evident reluctance. "Now, then," Marcello continued, "come here and tell me what you want, and what it is that cannot be done."

"I desire a few words with this lady, and I did not know that you were here, sir. Therefore I said, it cannot be done. I mean that while you are here, sir, I cannot speak alone with this lady."

"That is clear," Marcello answered. "You cannot be alone with this lady while I am in the room. That certainly cannot be done. Why do you wish to be alone with her? You can speak before me."

"It will not be so easy, sir. I will come at another time."

"No," Marcello answered, not liking his manner. "You will say what you have to say now, or you will say nothing, for you will not come at another time. The lady will not let you in, if you come again. Now speak."

"It will be a little difficult, sir. I would rather speak to the lady alone."

Regina had stood listening in silence, and looking intently at Ercole's face.

"Let me speak to him," she said to Marcello. "What is your full name?" she asked, turning to Ercole again.

"Spalletta Ercole, to serve you," was the prompt answer.

"Spalletta?" Marcello asked in surprise, for strange as it may seem to any but Italians, it was quite natural that he should never have known Ercole's family name. "Spalletta? That is your own name, Regina! What a strange coincidence!"

"Yes," Ercole said. "I know that the young lady's name is Spalletta. It is for this reason that I desire the favour of a few words with her alone."

"There is no need," Regina answered. "Since we have the same name, there is no doubt. I remember your face now, though until last night I had not seen you since I was a little child. Yes. I know what you have come to say, and it is quite true."

"What?" asked Marcello with some anxiety.

"This man is my father," Regina said, very quietly.

"Your father!" Marcello made half a step backwards in his surprise.

"Yes. I have told you what he did." She turned to Ercole. "What do you want of me? Is it money that you want, perhaps?"

Ercole stiffened himself and seemed to grow taller. His black eyes flashed dangerously, and his heavy eyebrows were suddenly stern and level, as Regina's were.

"You are your mother's daughter," he said slowly. "Did I take money from her? I took blood, and when I was tried for it, I was set free. I was told that it was my right under our law. I do not want money. I have brought you money. There it is. It will buy you some bread when your lover turns you into the street!"

He took out his old sheepskin purse with a quick movement, and laughed harshly as he tossed it at her. Marcello sprang forward and caught him by the collar, to thrust him out of the room; but Ercole was tough and wiry, and resisted.

"Will you hinder me from giving money to my daughter?" he asked fiercely. "It was yours, for you paid it to me; but when I knew, I saved my wages to give them back, for I will not take your money, sir! Take your hands from me, sir! I have a right to be here and to speak. Let me go, I tell you! I am not in your service any longer. I do not eat your cursed bread. I am this woman's father, and I shall say what I will."

Marcello withdrew his hands and pointed to the door.

"Go!" he said, in a voice of command.

Ercole backed away a little, and then stood still again.

"I have to tell you that I have spent five francs of that money," he said, speaking to Regina. "But it was spent for you. I found a good monk, and I gave him the five francs to say three masses for your soul. The masses were said in August, and now it is November, and you are still alive!"

"Go!" cried Marcello, understanding, and advancing upon him once more.

"I go," answered Ercole hoarsely. "Let her live, till you are tired of her, and she dies in a ditch! I told the monk to say the masses for a female. They will do for the woman who was killed last night. One female is worth another, and evil befall them all, as many as they are! Why did the Eternal Father ever create them?"

He had turned before he spoke the last words, and he went out deliberately, shutting the door behind him. They heard him go out upon the landing, and they were alone again. Regina leaned back against the mantelpiece, but Marcello began to walk up and down the room.

"You have seen," she said, in a rather unsteady voice. "Now you know of what blood I am, and that what I said was true. The son of your mother cannot marry the daughter of that man."

"What have you to do with him?" Marcello asked sharply, stopping in his walk.

But Regina only shook her head, and turned away. She knew that she was right, and that he knew it too, or would know it soon.

"You will never see him again," he said. "Forget that you have seen him at all!"

Again she shook her head, not looking at him.

"You will not forget," she answered, "and I shall always remember. He should have killed me, as he meant to do. It would have been the end. It would have been better, and quicker."

"God forbid!"

"Why? Would it not have been better?"

She came close to him and laid one hand upon his shoulder and gazed into his eyes. They were full of trouble and pain, and they did not lighten for her; his brow did not relax and his lips did not part. After a little while she turned again and went back to the fireplace.

"It would have been better," she said in a low voice. "I knew it this morning."

There was silence in the room for a while. Marcello stood beside her, holding her hand in his, and trying to see her face. He was very tender with her, but there was no thrill in his touch. Something was gone that would never come back.

"When all this trouble is over," he said at last, "you shall go back to the little house in Trastevere, and it will be just as it was before."

She raised her head rather proudly, as she answered.

"If that could be, it would be now. You would have taken me in your arms when he was gone, and you would have kissed my eyes and my hair, and we should have been happy, just as it was before. But instead, you want to comfort me, you want to be kind to me, you want to be just to me, instead of loving me!"

"Regina! I do love you! I do indeed!"

He would have put his arms round her to draw her closer to him, in the sudden longing to make her think that there was no change in his love, but she quietly resisted him.

"You have been very good to me, dear," she said, "and I know you will always be that, whatever comes. And I am always yours, dear, and you are the master, whenever you choose to come and see me. For I care for nothing that God has made, except you. But it will never be just as it used to be."

"It shall!" Marcello tried to put conviction into the words. "It shall! It shall!"

"It cannot, my heart," she answered. "I used to say that when this came, I would go away. But I will not do that, unless you bid me to, for I think you would be sorry, and I should be giving you more pain, and you have enough. Only leave me a little while alone, dear, for I am very tired, and it is growing late."

He took her hands and kissed them one after the other, and looked into her face. His own was very weary.

"Promise me that I shall find you here to-morrow," he said.

"You shall find me," she answered softly.

They parted so, and he left her alone, in the dark, for the glow of the sunset had faded and the early November evening was closing in.

Old Teresa came and brought a lamp, and drew the curtains, and gave her a message from Kalmon. If she needed anything she was to send for him, and he would come at once. She thanked Teresa. It was very kind of the Professor, but she needed nothing. Not even a fire; no, she hardly ever felt cold. Teresa brought something to eat, and set the little table for her. She was not hungry, and she was glad when the good soul was gone.

She could open the windows when she was alone, and look out into the silent street. There was moonlight now, and it fell across the walls and trees of the Villa Aurora upon her face. It was a young moon, that would set before midnight, but it was very clear and bright, and the sky was infinitely deep and very clear behind it. Regina fancied that if there were really angels in heaven, she should be able to see them on such a night.

If she had been in Trastevere she would have gone out to walk up and down the old paved paths of the little garden, for she could not sleep, though she was so tired. The lamp disturbed her and she put it out, and sat down by the window again.

It was very quiet now, for it was past nine o'clock.

She heard a step, and it almost surprised her. A man with a big dog was walking in the shadow on the other side of the street, and when he was opposite the house he stood still and looked up at her window. He did not move for some time, but the dog came out into the moonlight in a leisurely way, and lay down on the paving stones. All dogs think it is warmer in the light than in the shadow.

Regina rose, got a long black cloak and a dark veil without lighting a candle, and put them on. Then she went out.

CHAPTER XXI

ERCOLE walked on when he saw some one come out of No. 16, for he did not recognise Regina. She followed him at a distance. Even if he should pass where there might be many people, she would not lose sight of him easily because he had his dog with him. She noticed that his canvas bag was hung over one shoulder and that it seemed to be full, and his gun was slung over the other. He meant to leave Rome that night on foot. He walked fast through the new streets in the upper quarter, turned to the right when he reached the Via Venti Settembre, and went straight on, past the top of the hill, and along the Quirinal Palace; then down and on, down and on, through moonlight and shadow, winding streets and straight, till the Colosseum was in sight. He was going towards the Porta San Sebastiano to take the road to Ardea.

The air was very clear, and the moonlight made the broad space as bright as if there were daylight. Regina walked fast, and began to overtake her father, and the dog turned his head and growled at the tall woman in black. She came up with Ercole by the ruin of the ancient fountain, and the dog snarled at her. Ercole stopped and looked at her sharply, and she raised her veil.

"I have followed you," she said. "We are alone here. We can talk in peace."

"And what am I to say to you?" Ercole asked, in a low and surly voice.

"What you will, little or much, as you please. You shall speak, and I will listen. But we can walk on under the trees there. Then nobody can see us."

Ercole began to go on, and Regina walked on his left side. The dog sniffed at the hem of her long black cloak. They came under the shade of the trees, and Ercole stopped again, and turned, facing the reflection of the moonlight on the vast curve of the Colosseum.

"What do you want of me?" he asked. "Why do you follow me in the night?"

"When you saw that the Signore was with me to-day, you said, 'It cannot be done.' He is not here now."

She stood quite still, looking at him.

"I understand nothing," he said, in the same surly tone as before.

"You wished to kill me to-day," she answered. "I am here. This is a good place."

Ercole looked about him instinctively, peering into the shadows under the trees.

"There is no one," Regina said. "This is a good place."

She had not lifted her veil, but she threw back the collar of her cloak, and with quick fingers undid the fastenings of her dress, opening it wide. Rays of moonlight fell through the trees upon her bosom, and it gleamed like fine ivory newly cut.

"I wait," she said.

She stood motionless before him, expecting the knife, but her father's hands did not move. His eyes were fixed on hers, though he could not see them through the veil.

"So he has left you?" he said slowly.

"No. I am waiting."

Not a fold of her cloak stirred as she stood there to die. It seemed a long time, but his hands did not move. Then he heard the sound of her voice, very low and sweet, repeating a little prayer, but he only heard the last words distinctly.

"— now, and in the hour of our death!"

His right hand moved slowly and found something in his pocket, and then there was the sharp click of a strong spring, and a ray of moonlight fell upon steel, and her voice was heard again.

"— in the hour of our death. Amen!"

An unearthly sound rent the stillness. The huge dog sat upright on his haunches, his head thrown up and back, his terrible lower jaw trembling as he howled, and howled again, waking great echoes where the roar of wild lions had rung long ago.

Regina started, though she did not move a step; but an unreasoning fear fell upon Ercole. He could not see her face, as the dark veil hung down. She was so motionless and fearless; only the dead could be as fearless of death and as still as she. Her breast was so white; her hands were like marble hands, parting a black shroud upon it. She was something risen from the grave to haunt him in that lonely place and drive him mad; and the appalling howl of the great dog rose deafeningly on the silence and trembled and died away, and began again.

Ercole's hand relaxed, and the knife fell gleaming at his feet. One instant more and he turned and fled through the trees, towards San Gregorio, his dog galloping heavily after him.

Regina's hands fell by her sides, and the folds of her cloak closed together and hung straight down. She stared into the shadowy distance a moment after her father, and saw his figure twice in the light where the trees were wider apart, before he disappeared altogether. She looked down and saw the knife at her feet, and she picked it up and felt the point. It was as sharp as a needle, for Ercole had whetted it often since he had sat by the gate in the early morning last August. It was wet, for the grass under the trees had not dried since the rain.

She felt the point and edge with her hand, and sighed. It would have been better to have felt it in her breast, but she would not take her own life. She was not afraid to do it, and her young hand would have been strong enough and sure enough to do it quickly. It was not the thought of the pain that made her close the knife; it was the fear of hell. Nothing she had done in her life seemed very bad to her, because it had all been for Marcello. If Ercole had killed her, she thought that God would have forgiven her after a time. But if she killed herself she would instantly be seized by devils and thrust into real flames, to burn for ever, without the slightest chance of forgiveness. She had been taught that, and she believed it, and the thought of the fire made her shut the clasp-knife and slip it into her dress with a sigh. It would be a pity to throw it away, for it seemed to be a good knife, and her father could not have had it very long.

She fastened her frock under her mantle and went a few steps down the little slope towards the Colosseum. To go on meant to go home, and she stopped again. The place was very lonely and peaceful, and the light on the great walls was quiet and good to see. Though she had stood so still, waiting to die, and had said her little prayer so calmly, her brave heart had been beating slow and hard as if it were counting the seconds before it was to stop; and now it beat fast and softly, and fluttered a little, so that she felt faint, as even brave people do after a great danger is past. I have seen hundreds of men together, just escaped from destruction by earthquake, moving about listlessly with veiled eyes, yawning as if they were dropping with sleep, and saying childish things when they spoke at all. Man's body is the part of himself which he least understands, unless he has spent half his life in studying its ways. Its many portions can only telegraph to the brain two words, 'pain' and 'pleasure,' with different degrees of energy; but that is all. The rest of their language belongs to science.

Regina felt faint and sat down, because there was no

reason for making any effort to go home. Perhaps a cab would pass, returning from some outlying part of the city, and she would take it. From the place where she sat she could see one far off, if any came.

She sank down on the wet ground, and drew up her knees and pulled her cloak round her; and gradually her head bent forward and rested upon her hands, till she sat there like a figure of grief outlined in black against the moonlight on the great wall. She had forgotten where she was, and that there was any time in the world.

Half an hour passed, and the moon sank low, and an hour, and the deadly white mist began to rise in the shadow round the base of the Colosseum, and crept up under the trees; and if any one had come upon her then, he would have seen its dull whiteness crawling round her feet and body, a hand-breadth above the wet ground. But she did not know; she had forgotten everything.

Nothing was real any more. She could have believed that her father had killed her and left her corpse there, strangely sitting, though quite dead.

Then she knew that the light had gone out; and suddenly she felt her teeth chatter, and a chill ran through her bones that was bad to feel. She raised her head and saw that the great walls were dark against the starry sky, and she rose with an effort, as if her limbs had suddenly become lead. But she could walk, though it was like walking in sleep.

She did not afterwards remember how she got home,

but she had a vague recollection of having lost her way, and of finding a cab at last, and then of letting herself into the little apartment in the dark.

When she was next aware of anything it was broad daylight, and she was lying on her bed, still dressed and wearing her cloak; and Kalmon was bending over her, his eyes on hers and his fingers on her pulse, while old Teresa watched her anxiously from the foot of the bed.

"I'm afraid it is a 'perniciosa,'" he said. "Put her to bed while I call a regular doctor."

Regina looked up at him.

"I have fever, have I not?" she asked quite quietly.

"Yes. You have a little fever," he answered, but his big brown eyes were very grave.

When Marcello came, an hour later, she did not know him. She stared at him with wide, unwinking eyes, and there were bright patches of colour in her cheeks. Already there were hollows in them, too, and at her temples, for the perniciosa fever is frightfully quick to waste the body. In the Campagna, where it is worst, men have died of it in less than four hours after first feeling it upon them. Great men have discovered wonderful remedies for it, but still it kills.

Kalmon got one of the great men, who was his friend, and they did what they could. A nursing sister came and was installed. Marcello was summoned away soon after noon by an official person, who brought a carriage and said that Corbario was now conscious and able to speak, and that it was absolutely necessary that Marcello should be confronted with him, as he might not live another day. It was easier to go than it would have been if Regina had been conscious, but even so it was very hard. The nun and Teresa stayed with her.

She said little in her delirium, and nothing that had any meaning for either of the women. Twice she tried to tear away the linen and lace from her throat.

"I wait!" she cried each time, and her eyes fixed themselves on the ceiling, while she held her breath.

The women could not tell what she was waiting for, and they soothed her as best they could. She seemed to doze after that, and when Marcello came back she knew him, and took his hand. He sent away the nurses and sat by the bedside, and she spoke to him in short sentences, faintly. He bent forward, near the pillow, to catch the words.

She was telling him what she had done last night.

"But you promised that I should find you here to-day!" Marcello said, with gentle reproach.

"Yes. I did not mean to break my word. But I thought he would do it. It seemed so easy."

Her voice was weak with the fever, and sank almost to a whisper. He stroked her hand affectionately, hoping that she would go to sleep; and so a long time passed. Then Kalmon came in with his friend the great doctor. They saw that she was not yet any better; the doctor ordered several things to be done and went away. Kalmon drew Marcello out of the room.

"You can do nothing," he said. "She has good

care, and she is very strong. Go home and come back in the morning."

"I must stay here," Marcello answered.

"That is out of the question, on account of the Sister of Charity. But you can send for your things and camp in my rooms downstairs. There is a good sofa. You can telephone to the villa for what you want."

"Thank you." Marcello's voice dropped and shook. "Will she live?" he asked.

"I hope so. She is very strong, and it may be only fever."

"What else could it be?"

"Pneumonia."

Marcello bit his lip and closed his eyes as if he were in bodily pain, and a moment later he turned away and went down to Kalmon's apartment.

The Professor went back to Regina's side, and stood quietly watching her, with a very sad look in his eyes. She opened hers and saw him, and she brought one hand to her chest.

"It burns," she said, almost in a whisper, but with a strange sort of eagerness, as if she were glad.

"I wish I could bear it for you, my poor child," Kalmon answered.

She shook her head, and turned uneasily on the pillow. He did not understand.

"What is it?" he asked gently. "What can I do for you? Tell me."

"I want to see some one very much. How long shall I live?"

"You will get quite well," said Kalmon, in a reassuring tone. "But you must be very quiet." Again she moved her burning cheek on the pillow.

"Do you want to see a priest?" asked the Professor, thinking he had guessed. "Is that it?"

"Yes — there is time for that — some one else — could you? Will you?"

"Yes." Kalmon bent down quickly, for he thought the delirium was coming again. "Who is it?" he asked.

"Aurora — I mean, the Signorina — can you? Oh, do you think you could?"

"I'll try," Kalmon answered in great surprise.

But now the hoarseness was suddenly gone, and her sweet voice was softly humming an old song of the hills, forgotten many years, and the Professor saw that she did not know him any more. He nodded to Teresa, who was in the room, and went out.

He wondered much at the request, but he remembered that it had been made in the full belief that he would say nothing of it to Marcello. If she had been willing that Marcello should know, she would have spoken to him, rather than to Kalmon. He had seen little enough of Regina, but he was sure that she could have no bad motive in wishing to see the young girl. Yet, from a social point of view, it was not exactly an easy thing to propose, and the Contessa would have a right to be offended at the mere suggestion that her daughter should speak to "Consalvi's Regina"; and there could not be anything clandestine in the meeting, if Aurora consented to it. Kalmon was too deeply attached to the Contessa herself to be willing to risk her displeasure, or, indeed, to do anything of which she would not approve.

He went to her house by the Forum of Trajan, and he found her at home. It was late in the afternoon, and the lamp was lighted in the little drawing-room, which did not seem at all shabby to Kalmon's accustomed eyes and not very exigent taste. The Contessa was reading an evening paper before the fire. She put out her hand to the Professor.

"It is a bad business," she said, glancing at the newspaper, which had a long account of Corbario's arrest and of the murder of his old accomplice. "Poor Marcello!"

"Poor Marcello! Yes, indeed! I'm sorry for him. There is something more than is in the papers, and more than I have written to you and told you. Regina has the perniciosa fever, complicated with pneumonia, and is not likely to live."

"I am sorry," the Contessa answered. "I am very sorry for her. But after all, compared with what Marcello has learned about his mother's death — and other things Corbario did — "

She stopped, implying by her tone that even if Regina died, that would not be the greatest of Marcello's misfortunes. Besides, she had long foreseen that the relations of the two could not last, and the simplest solution, and the happiest one for the poor devoted girl, was that she should die before her heart was broken. Maddalena dell' Armi had often wished that her own fate had been as merciful.

"Yes," Kalmon answered. "You are right in that. But Regina has made a rather strange request. It was very unexpected, and perhaps I did wrong to tell her that I would do my best to satisfy her. I don't think she will live, and I felt sorry for her. That is why I came to you. It concerns Aurora."

"Aurora?" The Contessa was surprised.

"Yes. The girl knows she is dying, and wishes very much to see Aurora for a moment. I suppose it was weak of me to give her any hope."

The Contessa dropped her newspaper and looked into the fire thoughtfully before she answered.

"You and I are very good friends," she said. "You would not ask me to do anything you would not do yourself, would you? If you had a daughter of Aurora's age, should you let her go and see this poor woman, unless it were an act of real charity?"

"No," Kalmon answered reluctantly. "I don't think I should."

"Thank you for being so honest," Maddalena answered, and looked at the fire again.

Some time passed before she spoke again, still watching the flames. Kalmon sighed, for he was very sorry for Regina.

"On the other hand," the Contessa said at last, "it may be a real charity. Have you any idea why she wishes to see Aurora?"

"No. I cannot guess."

"I can. At least, I think I can." She paused again. "You know everything about me," she continued presently. "In the course of years I have told you all my story. Do you think I am a better woman than Regina?"

"My dear friend!" cried Kalmon, almost angrily. "How can you suggest — "

She turned her clear, sad eyes to him, and her look cut short his speech.

"What has her sin been?" she asked gently. "She has loved Marcello. What was mine? That I loved one man too well. Which is the better woman? She, the peasant, who knew no better, who found her first love dying, and saved him, and loved him — knowing no better, and braving the world? Or I, well born, carefully brought up, a woman of the world, and married — no matter how — not braving the world at all, but miserably trying to deceive it, and my husband, and my child? Do you think I was so much better than poor Regina? Would my own daughter think so if she could know and understand?"

"If you were not a very good woman now," Kalmon said earnestly, "you could not say what you are saying."

"Never mind what I am now. I am not as good as you choose to think. If I were, there would not be a bitter thought left. I should have forgiven all. Leave out of the question what I am now. Compare me as I was with Regina as she is. That is how I put it, and I am right."

"Even if you were," Kalmon answered doubtfully,

"the situation would be the same, so far as Aurora is concerned."

"But suppose that this poor woman cannot die in peace unless she has asked Aurora's pardon and obtained her forgiveness, what then?"

"Her forgiveness? For what?"

"For coming between her and Marcello. Say that, so far as Regina knows, my daughter is the only human being she has ever injured, what then?"

"Does Aurora love Marcello?" asked Kalmon, instead of answering the question.

"I think she does. I am almost sure of it."

Kalmon was silent for a while.

"But Marcello," he said at last, "what of him?"

"He has always loved Aurora," the Contessa answered. "Do you blame him so much for what he has done? Why do you blame some people so easily, my dear friend, and others not at all? Do you realise what happened to him? He was virtually taken out of the life he was leading, by a blow that practically destroyed his memory, and of which the consequences altogether destroyed his will for some time. He found himself saved and at the same time loved — no, worshipped — by one of the most beautiful women in the world. Never mind her birth! She has never looked at any other man, before or since, and from what I have heard, she never will. Ah, if all women were like her! Marcello, weak from illness, allowed himself to be worshipped, and Corbario did the rest. I understand it all. Do you blame him very much? I don't. With all your strength of character, you would have done the same at his age! And having taken what she offered, what could he do, when he grew up and came to himself, and felt his will again? Could he cast her off, after all she had done for him?"

"He could marry her," observed Kalmon. "I don't see why he should not, after all."

"Marriage!" There was a little scornful sadness in Maddalena's voice. "Marriage is always the solution! No, no, he is right not to marry her, if he has ever thought of it. They would only make each other miserable for the rest of their lives. Miserable, and perhaps faithless too. That is what happens when men and women are not saints. Look at me!"

"You were never in that position. Others were to blame, who made you marry when you were too young to have any will of your own."

"Blame no one," said the Contessa gravely. "I shall give Aurora Regina's message, and if she is willing to go and see her, I shall bring her to-morrow morning — to-night, if there is no time to be lost. The world need never know. Go and tell Regina what I have said. It may comfort her a little, poor thing."

"Indeed it will!"

Kalmon's brown eyes beamed with pleasure at the thought of taking the kindly message to the dying girl. He rose to his feet at once.

"There is no one like you," he said, as he took her hand.

"It is nothing. It is what Marcello's mother would

have done, and she was my best friend. All I do is to take the responsibility upon myself, however Aurora may choose to act. I will send you word, in either case. If Aurora will not go, I will come myself, if I can be of any use, if it would make Regina feel happier. I will come, and I will tell her what I have told you. Goodnight, dear friend."

Kalmon was not an emotional man, but as he went out he felt a little lump in his throat, as if he could not swallow.

He had not doubted his friend's kindness, but he had doubted whether she would feel that she had a right to "expose her daughter," as the world would say, to meeting such a "person," as the world called Regina — "Consalvi's Regina."

CHAPTER XXII

ALL that night and the following day Regina recognised no one; and it was night again, and her strength began to fail, but her understanding returned. Marcello saw the change, and made a sign to the nurse, who went out to tell Kalmon.

It was about nine o'clock when he entered the room, and Regina knew him and looked at him anxiously. He, in turn, glanced at Marcello, and she understood. She begged Marcello to go and get some rest. Her voice was very weak, as if she were suffocating, and she coughed painfully. He did not like to go away, but Kalmon promised to call him at midnight; he had been in the room six hours, scarcely moving from his seat. He lingered at the door, looked back, and at last went out.

"Will she come?" asked Regina, when he was gone.

"In half an hour. I have sent a messenger, for they have no telephone."

A bright smile lighted up the wasted face.

"Heaven will reward you," she said, as the poor say in Rome when they receive a charity.

Then she seemed to be resting, for her hands lay still, and she closed her eyes. But presently she opened them, looking up gratefully into the big man's kind face.

"Shall I be alone with her a little?" she asked.

"Yes, my dear. You shall be alone with her."

Again she smiled, and he left the nurse with her and went and waited downstairs at the street door, till the Contessa and Aurora should come, in order to take them up to the little apartment. He knew that Marcello must have fallen asleep at once, for he had not rested at all for twenty-four hours, and very little during several days past. Kalmon was beginning to fear that he would break down, though he was so much stronger than formerly.

Marcello had always been grateful to Regina, even when he had convinced himself that he loved her. Love is not very compatible with gratitude. Two people who love each other very much expect everything because they are always ready to give everything, not in return or by way of any exchange, but as if the two were one in giving and taking. A man cannot be grateful to himself. But Marcello had never felt that dear illusion with Regina, because there had been no real companionship; and so he had always been grateful to her, and now that she was perhaps dying, he was possessed by the horribly painful certainty that he could never repay her what he owed, and that this debt of honour must remain unpaid for ever, if she died. There was much more than that in what he felt, of course, for there was his very real affection, tormented by the foreboding of the coming wrench, and there was the profound sympathy of a very kind man for a suffering woman. But all that together was not love like hers for him; it was not love at all.

Kalmon waited, and smoked a little, reflecting on these things, which he understood tolerably well. The quiet man of science had watched Marcello thoughtfully, and could not help asking himself what look there would be in his own eyes, if Maddalena dell' Armi were dying and he were standing by her bedside. It would not be Marcello's look.

A closed cab stopped before the entrance, and almost before he could throw away his cigarette, the Contessa and Aurora were standing beside him on the pavement.

"She is very weak," he said, "but she will not be delirious again for some time — if at all."

Neither of the ladies spoke, and they followed him in silence up the ill-lighted staircase.

"That is where I live," he said, as he passed his own door on the second landing. "Marcello is camping there. He is probably asleep now."

"Asleep!" It was Aurora that uttered the single word, in a puzzled tone.

"He did not go to bed last night," Kalmon explained, going on.

"Oh!" Again the Professor was struck by the young girl's tone.

They reached the third landing, and Kalmon pushed the door, which he had left ajar; he shut it when they had all entered, and he ushered the mother and daughter into the small sitting-room. There they waited a moment while he went to tell Regina that Aurora had come.

The young girl dropped her cloak upon a chair and

stood waiting, her eyes fixed on the door. She was a little pale, not knowing what was to come, yet feeling somehow that it was to make a great difference to her ever afterwards. She glanced at her mother, and the Contessa smiled gently, as much as to say that she was doing right, but neither spoke.

Presently Kalmon came out with the Sister of Charity, who bent her head gravely to the two ladies.

"She wishes to see you alone," Kalmon said, in explanation, while he held the door open for Aurora to pass in.

He closed it after her, and the two were together.

When Aurora entered, Regina's eyes were fixed upon her face as if they had already found her and seen her while she had been in the other room. She came straight to the bedside and took the hand that was stretched out to meet hers. It was thin and hot now, and the arm was already wasted. Aurora remembered how strongly it had lifted her to the edge of the rock, far away by Pontresina.

"You are very kind, Signorina," said the faint voice. "You see how I am."

Aurora saw indeed, and kept the hand in hers as she sat down in the chair that stood where Marcello had left it.

"I am very, very sorry," she said, leaning forward a little and looking into the worn face, colourless now that the fever had subsided for a while.

The same bright smile that Kalmon had seen lighted up Regina's features.

"But I am glad!" she answered. "They do not understand that I am glad."

"No, no!" cried Aurora softly. "Don't say you are glad!"

The smile faded, and a very earnest look came into the hollow dark eyes.

"But I have not done it on purpose," Regina said. "I did not know there was fever in that place, or I would not have sat down there. You believe me, Signorina, don't you?"

"Yes, indeed!"

The smile returned very gradually, and the anxious pressure of the hand relaxed.

"You must not think that I was looking for the fever. But since it came, and I am going from here, I am glad. I shall not be in the way any more. That hindrance will be taken out of his life."

"He would not like to hear you speak like this," Aurora said, with great gentleness.

"There is no time for anything except the truth, now. And you are good, so good! No, there is no time. To-morrow, I shall be gone. Signorina, if I could kneel at your feet, I would kneel. But you see how I am. You must think I am kneeling at your feet."

"But why?" asked Aurora, with a little distress.

"To ask you to forgive me for being a hindrance. I want pardon before I go. But I found him half dead on the door-step. What could I do? When I had seen him, I loved him. I knew that he thought of you. That was all he remembered — just your name, and I hated it, because he had forgotten all other names, even his own, and his mother, and everything. He was like a little child that learns, to-day this, to-morrow that, one thing at a time. What could I do? I taught him. I also taught him to love Regina. But when the memory came back, I knew how it had been before."

Her voice broke and she coughed, and raised one hand to her chest. Aurora supported her tenderly until it was over, and when the weary head sank back at last it lay upon the young girl's willing arm.

"You are tiring yourself," Aurora said. "If it was to ask my forgiveness that you wished me to come, I forgave you long ago, if there was anything to forgive. I forgave you when we met, and I saw what you were, and that you loved him for himself, just as I do."

"Is it true? Really true?"

"So may God help me, it is quite true. But if I had thought it was not for himself—"

"Oh, yes, it was," Regina answered. "It was, and it is, to the end. Will you see? I will show you. For what the eyes see the heart believes more easily. Signorina, will you bring the little box covered with old velvet? It is there, on the table, and it is open."

Aurora rose, humouring her, and brought the thing she asked for, and sat down again, setting it on the edge of the bed. Regina turned her head to see it, and raised the lid with one hand.

"This is my little box," she said. "What he has given me is all in it. I have no other. Will you see?

Here is what I have taken from him. You shall look everywhere, if you do not believe."

"But I do believe you!" Aurora cried, feeling that tears were coming to her eyes.

"But you must see," Regina insisted. "Or perhaps when I am gone you will say to yourself, 'There may have been diamonds and pearls in the little box, after all!' You shall know that it was all for himself."

To please her Aurora took up some of the simple trinkets, simpler and cheaper even than what she had herself.

"There are dresses, yes, many more than I wanted. But I could not let him be ashamed of me when we went out together, and travelled. Do you forgive me the dresses, Signorina? I wore them to please him. Please forgive me that also!"

Aurora dropped the things into the open box and laid both her hands on Regina's, bending down her radiant head and looking very earnestly into the anxious eyes.

"Forgiveness is not all from me to you, Regina," she said. "I want yours too."

"Mine?" The eyes grew wide and wondering.

"Don't you see that but for me he would have married you, and that I have been the cause of a great wrong to you?"

For one instant Regina's face darkened, her brows straightened themselves, and her lip curled. She remembered how, only two days ago, in the very next room, Marcello had insisted that she should be his wife. But as she looked into Aurora's innocent eyes she understood, and the cloud passed from her own, and the bright smile came back. Aurora had spoken in the simplicity of her true heart, sure that it was only the memory of his love for her that had withheld Marcello from first to last; and Regina well knew that it had always been present with him, in spite of his brave struggle to put it away. That memory of another, which Regina had seen slowly reviving in him, had been for something in her refusal to marry him.

With the mysterious sure vision of those who are near death, she felt that it would hurt Aurora to know the truth, except from Marcello himself.

"If you have ever stood between us," she said, "you had the right. He loved you first. There is nothing to forgive in that. Afterwards he loved me a little. No one can take that from me, no one! It is mine, and it is all I have, and though I am going, and though I know that he is tired of me, it is still more than the world. To have it, as I have it, I would do again what I did, from the first."

The voice was weak and muffled, but the words were distinct, and they were the confession of poor Regina's life.

"If he were here," she said, after a moment, "I would lay your hand in his. Only let me take that memory with me!"

The young girl rose and bent over her as she answered.

"It is yours, to keep for ever."

She stooped a little lower and kissed the dying woman's forehead.

* * * * *

Under the May moon a little brigantine came sailing up to a low island just within sight of Italy; when she was within half a mile of the reefs Don Antonino Maresca put her about, for he was a prudent man, and he knew that there are just a few more rocks in the sea than are in the charts. It was a quiet night, and he was beating up against a gentle northerly breeze.

When the head yards were swung, and braced sharp up for the other tack, and the little vessel had gathered way again, the mate came aft and stood by the captain, watching the light on the island.

"Are there still convicts on this island, Don Antonino?" the young man asked.

"Yes, there are the convicts. And there is one among them whom I helped to put there. He is an assassin that killed many when he was at liberty. But now he sits for seven years in a little cell alone, and sees no Christian, and it will be thirty years before he is free."

"Madonna!" ejaculated the mate. "When he has been there thirty years he will perhaps understand."

"It is as I say," rejoined the captain. "The world is made so. There are the good and the bad. The Eternal Father has created things thus. Get a little more on the main sheet, and then flatten in those jibs."

Under the May moon, in the small shaft of white light that fell through the narrow grated window, a man sat on the edge of his pallet bed. His face was ghastly, and there were strange scars on his bare throat. His cell was seven feet by six, and the air was hard to breathe, because the wind was not from the south. But the moon was kinder than the sun. He heard the ripple of the cool sea, and he tried to dream that a great stone was hung to his neck, and that he had been thrown into a deep place. Perhaps, some day, the gaoler would forget to take away the coarse towel which was brought with the water in the morning. With a towel he could hang himself.

Under the May moon a small marble cross cast its shadow upon young roses and violets and growing myrtle. In the sweet earth below a very loyal heart was at rest for ever. But the flowers were planted and still tended by a woman with radiant hair; and sometimes, when she stooped to train the young roses, bright drops fell quietly upon their bloom. Also, on certain days, a man came there alone and knelt upon the marble border within which the flowers grew. But the man and the woman never came together; and he gave the gardener of that place money, praising him for the care of the flowers.

Under the May moon the man and the woman went down from the cottage by the Roman shore to the break in the high bank, and stood still a while, looking out at the peaceful sea and the moon's broad path. Presently they turned to each other, put out their hands, and then their arms, and clasped each other silently, and kissed.